Praise for the novels of

MICHAEL PAINE

"Impressive . . . Fast-moving, scary, and a lot of fun to read. A startlingly good writer. Read him."—Charles Grant

"Dark, creepy, and totally satisfying."
—Robert R. McCammon

"Terrific . . . really well-done."   —Chet Williamson

THE NIGHT SCHOOL

MICHAEL PAINE

BERKLEY BOOKS, NEW YORK

THE BERKLEY PUBLISHING GROUP
Published by the Penguin Group
Penguin Group (USA) Inc.
375 Hudson Street, New York, New York 10014, USA
Penguin Group (Canada), 90 Eglinton Avenue East, Suite 700, Toronto, Ontario M4P 2Y3, Canada
(a division of Pearson Penguin Canada Inc.)
Penguin Books Ltd., 80 Strand, London WC2R 0RL, England
Penguin Group Ireland, 25 St. Stephen's Green, Dublin 2, Ireland (a division of Penguin Books Ltd.)
Penguin Group (Australia), 250 Camberwell Road, Camberwell, Victoria 3124, Australia
(a division of Pearson Australia Group Pty. Ltd.)
Penguin Books India Pvt. Ltd., 11 Community Centre, Panchsheel Park, New Delhi—110 017, India
Penguin Group (NZ), Cnr. Airborne and Rosedale Roads, Albany, Auckland 1310, New Zealand
(a division of Pearson New Zealand Ltd.)
Penguin Books (South Africa) (Pty.) Ltd., 24 Sturdee Avenue, Rosebank, Johannesburg 2196, South
Africa

Penguin Books Ltd., Registered Offices: 80 Strand, London WC2R 0RL, England

This is a work of fiction. Names, characters, places, and incidents either are the product of the author's imagination or are used fictitiously, and any resemblance to actual persons, living or dead, business establishments, events, or locales is entirely coincidental. The publisher does not have any control over and does not assume any responsibility for author or third-party websites or their content.

THE NIGHT SCHOOL

A Berkley Book / published by arrangement with the author

PRINTING HISTORY
Berkley mass-market edition / April 2006

Copyright © 2006 by John M. Curlovich.
Cover design by Steven Ferlauto.
Interior text design by Kristin del Rosario.

ISBN: 0-425-20916-4

BERKLEY®
Berkley Books are published by The Berkley Publishing Group,
a division of Penguin Group (USA) Inc.,
375 Hudson Street, New York, New York 10014.
BERKLEY is a registered trademark of Penguin Group (USA) Inc.
The "B" design is a trademark belonging to Penguin Group (USA) Inc.

PRINTED IN THE UNITED STATES OF AMERICA

10 9 8 7 6 5 4 3 2 1

for
Randy Hecht

Death is nothing at all; it does not count.
I have only slipped away into the next room.

—HENRY SCOTT HOLLAND, 1810

PROLOGUE

MATTHEW MORGAN

"THERE'S a voicemail from Mom. Do you want to hear it?"

Tanner Morgan was lying on the living room couch, staring out at a grey suburban landscape and listlessly dialing his friends' phone numbers. A white Persian cat slept at the other end of the couch.

It was nearly seventy degrees outside; the holiday would be warm and rainy. Neighbors were out in shorts and T-shirts, decorating their houses; a few were even doing yardwork.

No one was answering, and he didn't bother to leave messages.

His sister Alexis was hanging ornaments on an artificial Christmas tree and looking bored. "Why? I can tell you what she says." She reached up and arranged the treetop to her satisfaction. " 'We miss you. Wish you were here. The weather here is lovely and the shopping is wonderful.' Or 'terrible,' if she hasn't been able to find anything she likes. Help me with these bubble lights."

"I'm opening the windows."

"Tanner, don't. You'll have to take off all the weather stripping, and as soon as it gets cold again we'll have to redo it all."

"It's stuffy in here."

"It's always stuffy in here. We're in Fox Chapel. Turn on the air."

"I don't think the filters were ever changed." He stood up and stretched.

"Just open the front door or something, then." She threw a handful of tinsel at him and missed. "Look at it out there. You can't spit without hitting a bank executive."

He ducked and woke up the cat, who jumped down and headed quickly for the kitchen. "Now, now, Miss Morgan, good little women mustn't say things like that. Our neighbors are fine people. They treat their servants well." He pushed the button to delete his mother's message without bothering to listen to it, hitting it rather forcefully. "And that's for the Bahamas."

"Will you come over here and help me with these lights?"

"Only little people decorate their own Christmas trees."

"Dammit, Tanner, I need a hand."

He sighed an exaggerated sigh, put down the phone and crossed the room to help her.

Alexis was seventeen and an attractive girl, blonde, blue-eyed, clear-skinned, the kind of young woman who, if she disappeared, would make the national news. Tanner, a year younger, was blond and blue-eyed too, but he was short and thin. Only his consistently downbeat attitude kept him from being a classic nerd. Weirdly for suburban siblings, they actually liked each other a bit. He got up and held the string of lights while Alexis arranged them carefully on the tree.

Their brother Matt came in suddenly. Even though he was Alexis's twin, he was tall, dark and muscular. It was a standing joke among the three of them that there had to be a way for a woman to have twins by two different fathers. He was in sweaty gym shorts, a tank top and sneakers, and he was carrying a basketball. "What are you two doing?"

Tanner didn't look at him. "We're dancing. What do you think?"

Matt threw the ball and hit Tanner's head with it. Tanner stumbled and fell into the tree, nearly knocking it over and wrecking half of what Alexis had done.

"Goddammit, Matt!"

"What's the matter, can't you take it?" He retrieved his ball.

"It's Christmas, for God's sake."

"I'm sick of shooting baskets. There's nobody around. They're all doing family stuff and holiday stuff and Christ knows what else."

Alexis struggled with a tangled light cord. "Poor Matt, he doesn't have anyone to play with."

Tanner laughed. "I thought he liked playing with himself."

Matt ignored them and pulled a small stack of envelopes out of his waistband. "Mail's here."

Alexis set about righting the tree. "More cards from people Dad does business with. That's what I like about Christmas—all the deep sentiment."

"There are letters for the three of us from Washington Academy."

"Swell."

"I opened mine. I've been accepted."

Tanner bent and picked up the fragments of a shattered ornament. "Mom's going to kill you. This was one of her grandmother's."

"We'll have the tree up again before they get back. She'll never know. Don't you want to read yours?"

"Why bother?" Alexis reached up to adjust the treetop star. "Uncle Peter's on the board. There's no way we haven't been accepted."

Matt sat down, opened theirs and scanned them. "You're right."

"Nothing's ever predictable for you, is it?" She and Tanner began to rearrange the lights on the tree. "Besides, I don't really want to go there. All my friends go to Fox Chapel."

"Let's drive down into Pittsburgh and see the place."

"They haven't started renovating it yet. There's nothing to see but a ruin. Will you get over here and help us?"

Matt ignored her and stretched out on the couch. "I can't wait. I'll be able to help shape some brand-new teams."

Tanner didn't bother looking at him. "Yeah, and nothing's more important than sports."

"Sports builds character."

"Then what happened to you?"

Matt kicked his sneakers off. "Uncle Peter says they'll have lacrosse and jai alai. Maybe even handball courts."

"What, no polo?"

"Only the poor associate with lower mammals, Tanner. I'm going to take a quick shower and drive down there. Who's coming?"

Neither of them said a thing.

"Fine, I'll go alone, then."

They kept quiet and went on fixing the tree.

Matt stood up and stretched. "You both sure?"

"We're sure." They said it in unison.

AN hour later he had showered and changed—polo shirt, linen slacks, loafers. From under his mattress he got a couple hits of X and swallowed them dry. Happily, he galloped downstairs to where Alexis and Tanner were still working on the tree. "I'm taking the Beamer."

"You know Dad doesn't want you driving it. Take the Explorer."

"What parents don't know won't hurt them."

As he was going out the door she called after him. "I'm cooking dinner, Matt. Baking a ham. Don't be late, okay?"

"And a merry Christmas to you."

"Just because our parents aren't here doesn't mean we can't be a family."

"You and Tanner be a family. I'll be back when I feel like it."

"I won't hold dinner for you."

"Good. Don't."

He walked quickly out to the driveway, got into the BMW convertible, lowered the top, lit a joint and drove off.

IT took him a while to find his way to the old, long-abandoned George Washington High School. Suburban kid, not familiar with the city, thought it was beneath him in a vague way. No malls.

Jumonville Street was only a block long, but it was a city block; it ran on a slight grade between Fifth and Forbes Avenues in the part of Pittsburgh called the Hill

District. It was a slum. Jesus Christ, it was a slum. He had
known it was in the center city, but this . . .

He was expecting to find the place under construction,
or at least being readied for it. Scaffolding, sheets of plastic. But it was just an old, boarded-up monstrosity, one of
a number in the neighborhood, the largest of them. He
pulled up in front of it, parked, gunned the engine for effect, then switched it off.

The building was covered with soot and grime. And
urban graffiti. The architecture was an uneasy mix of
Romanesque, Gothic Revival, Victorian gingerbread
and several other styles not immediately identifiable—a
lunatic mixture of styles. There were lancet windows,
ornate stonework, gargoyles, even a spire. It had been
empty for nearly forty years and looked it.

On the front was a large sign that read. PROPERTY FOR
SALE. Surely it had been bought. The school wouldn't be
accepting students if it didn't own the place. On the stone
lintel was carved GEORGE WASHINGTON HIGH SCHOOL.
Matt stood staring at it for a moment, then looked up and
down Jumonville Street.

An old African-American man wearing a sandwich
sign of some sort was standing on the corner watching
him. And laughing, or at least smiling broadly enough to
suggest it. The old guy waved at Matt, who quickly
turned his attention back to Washington High, or Washington Academy, as it was soon to become. There was
a chain-link fence across the front entrance, and every
window he could see was boarded. But there had to be a
way in.

A couple of little black girls came barreling toward
him on roller skates. He didn't see them till the last moment and tried to step aside, but one of them collided
with him. His linen slacks were soiled. Irritably, he

helped her to her feet, asked if she was okay and sent her on down the street. The old gent on the corner was laughing even harder.

"I don't see what's so funny."

The man grinned but didn't move or say anything. Crazy. Wino. One of those mentally ill homeless.

Matt walked to the school's front entrance and put his fingers through the chain-link. It was firm; he wouldn't be able to pry an opening for himself.

"That's trespassing, young man."

Startled, he turned to see the old black guy standing behind him. "No it isn't. I'm going to be a student here. And my uncle's on the board."

"My, my, your uncle's on the board." He seemed to find it awfully amusing.

"I'm . . . I'm . . ." What was the proper etiquette? He was dealing with someone from . . . someone who was . . . he wasn't even sure of the right way to think about it. But he was a stranger in the man's neighborhood. He decided to take charge of the situation. "My name is Matthew Morgan. I'm from Fox Chapel."

"You are." He was stifling laughter. Matt could tell.

"I'm probably going to be captain of at least one of the sports teams."

"You don't say." The man put on a wide grin. The teeth he still had were rotten. "I'm Hap."

"You're selling drugs, right?"

Hap laughed again. "This is just a guess, son, but you watch a lot of local news programs, don't you?"

For the first time, Matt took a good look at his sandwich sign. It was covered with lucky numbers, dream books, horoscopes and the like.

Hap noticed his interest. "You should buy one."

"No, thanks."

"You going to be hanging in this neighborhood, you ought to learn neighborhood ways."

"Uh . . ." He leaned down for a closer look. Dozens of little booklets with cheap, monochrome cardboard covers. All he could think was how corny it all was.

"I wouldn't sell you anything that wasn't true. You see that bar over there?" Hap nodded in the direction of a place across the street. A neon sign announced SAM'S. "Sam bought that place with the money he won in the lottery from a lucky number I sold him."

Matt was feeling uncomfortable. He looked around. A little girl in a pink plaid dress was watching them from the corner. "Thanks. I don't think so, though."

"You still going inside there?"

"Yeah, I want to see what the sports facilities look like."

"You need to buy a fortune, then."

"Thanks, but I said no." He started to move away from the man.

"Don't be a damn fool. There's a ghost in there."

Matt froze. "I am not," he said heavily, "a fool."

"You going in there, you are." Hap laughed, turned his back and walked off up the street. "Nice car, too. Too bad."

The board would have to do something about the locals, keep them away from the students. Matt pulled at the chain-link again; it wouldn't yield. He went around one side of the building, then to the back. One window there was patched over with tar paper instead of plywood. He gave a yank and pulled it down.

Matt suddenly realized there was another black kid watching him, a boy this time, maybe eight or ten years old. Matt made himself smile. "You want to make five bucks?"

The kid's face was blank. "No."

"Come here." He took the kid's hand and led him out to Jumonville Street. "You see that car?"

The kid nodded but didn't say anything.

"If anybody gets near that car, you come and get me, okay?" He got out his wallet and pressed a bill into the boy's hand.

"There's a ghost in there, mister."

"If you're afraid to come inside, just come and holler through the window, okay? I'll hear you."

The boy looked doubtful. Matt got out another five and gave it to him. "You keep an eye on my car. I won't be in there long." The kid looked at the bills in his hand as if they were the strangest things he'd ever seen.

Matt went back to that now-open window and hoisted himself up to the ledge, then jumped inside. He was in the gym.

The boy followed him curiously from a distance and watched him go in. Then he looked around, his eyes a bit wide. He ran quickly back out to Jumonville Street. Hap was back on his corner, and the boy rushed to him. "Why'd you let him go in there, Mr. Conklin?"

"Couldn't stop him."

"You could of told him."

"I tried to sell him a fortune. He wouldn't buy."

They talked for a while. Matt did not come out. It started to rain lightly. Hap left for home. The boy waited a while longer, but there was no sign of the white guy. When the downpour turned heavy, the boy ran home.

Matt was inside the school for hours. People passing the building heard low cries, almost moans, and there were even sharp, piercing screams. There were stretches of silence, then more cries. Bypassers heard them and walked more quickly, pretending to have heard nothing at all.

After dark the rain tapered off and Hap showed up again. The fancy convertible was still parked in front of Washington High, the roof still down. It must have gotten soaked. He wanted a drink. It was Christmas Eve. Sam's was closed. Under his breath he muttered, "Shit."

IT was well after eleven when Matt got home. Tanner and Alexis were in the kitchen, washing the dishes from a late dinner. The cat sat in a corner, busily washing its face. They heard the car drive up and could tell Matt was driving too quickly to be safe. Tanner made a gesture like someone holding a bottle to his lips and drinking. The car screeched to a halt and Matt gunned the engine loudly, then shut it off.

Matt burst into the kitchen violently. "Where's the good silver?"

He looked like hell. Skin pale like cigarette ash, eyes wide with circles around them. He hadn't just been drinking; something was wrong. Tanner watched him. Alexis put down the plate she was drying. "What?"

"The silver. The goddamned Georgian silver. Mom has fifty-thousand dollars' worth of Georgian silver around here. You know, the stuff we're not allowed to touch. Where is it?"

"Uh . . . in the breakfront. Matt, are you all right? There's ham in the refrigerator if you want some."

"Mind your own fucking business."

Neither Alexis nor Tanner had ever seen him quite like this. They glanced at each other, expressing their alarm wordlessly. Matt stormed into the dining room and tore open the doors of the breakfront, bellowing, "Where the fuck is it?"

Tanner followed him. "Matt, what's wrong?"

"I want the goddamned silver."

"It's on the bottom. Left-hand door. Matt, what's—"

"Leave me the fuck alone."

Tanner went back to the kitchen. "What do we do?"

"Hope it passes, I guess."

"We should call somebody."

"Who? He's our brother. We can't call the police."

Suddenly Matt burst in on them again. "Silver polish. I need silver polish." His manner was more and more manic, more and more furious. The cat ran out of the room and hid. "It's fucking Christmas. If I'm going to have Christmas ham, I want to do it with style."

"In the drawer there." Alexis pointed.

Matt ripped the drawer open, pulling it out of the cabinet and spilling half of what was in it. He got down on his knees and began rummaging through the things.

"Matt, calm down."

"Shut the fuck up."

He was examining each object frantically, then tossing them all around the room. Alexis crossed to him. "Matt, will you for God's sake stop this?"

He pushed her away. She fell on the floor, slamming her elbow against the refrigerator. Her scream was the first thing to drown out the sounds of Matt's rage.

Finally he found what he was looking for. From his pocket he pulled a pair of his mother's ornate silver forks and a carving knife. He opened the tin of polish and began to buff them as if it were the most important thing in the world. Tanner helped Alexis to her feet. Her arm was exploding with pain. "Call 911."

Matt ignored this and went on polishing. He rubbed the silverware again and again until it gleamed.

Tanner made the call and told the operator what was happening, keeping his voice as low as he could. "I think he's on something. Please, get here fast."

Finally Matt seemed satisfied with the state of the silver. It shone brilliantly. He got to his feet and stretched. Standing tall, looking like the young athlete he was, he smiled at his brother and sister. "Merry Christmas." He placed the knife carefully on the kitchen counter in front of him, then held up the two forks, one in each hand.

He plunged them into his eyes. Alexis and Tanner screamed. Before they could move he groped for the knife, picked it up and pushed it into his throat and tore it open. His head, half-severed, lolled forward horribly. Blood splattered everything in the room, including his brother and sister. Then his body collapsed.

Alexis and Tanner were quite numb by the time the police and the ambulance arrived. Medics covered the body with a sheet and took it away. Police officers got statements from both of them.

Then they were alone again. Alexis tried calling their parents, each in turn, but all she could do was leave voicemails for them. Neither she nor her brother could admit how shaken they were. They slept separately in their own rooms and tried to pretend everything would be all right.

Late that night an arctic cold front passed through and the temperature plunged below freezing. Toward morning it snowed. It was a white Christmas, just like the ones they used to know.

ONE

SAM

"DON'T look now, but there's something prowling around out there, and it's a lot whiter than the snow."

In Sam's bar on Jumonville Street, at the edge of the Pittsburgh neighborhood called the Hill District, Hap sat and watched the beginnings of a late afternoon snowstorm. Sam, the bartender and owner, left off cleaning glasses and joined his only customer at the front window. They both had drinks on the house; the place didn't make much profit anyway, so why worry? Sam switched on the TV. The four o'clock newscast was just starting; there were blizzard warnings.

The snow was still light, though it seemed to be getting steadily more heavy. A well-dressed white man—fur coat and hat, expensive shoes—had just parked his Lexus across the street. Now he was standing on the curb, in front of what used to be Washington High School, looking around as if he'd suddenly found himself on another planet, which in a way he had. Tall, grey hair, especially pale skin.

Sam opened a fresh bottle of Seagram's and refilled their glasses. "Here."

"You ought to save some of that for him, Sammy." Hap toasted him with his glass, then nodded at the scene outside. The white guy was sniffing around the old school, rubbing at all the spray-painted graffiti with a fingertip and trying to pry up a corner of the plywood on one of the windows to see inside. "It looks like he's gonna need it."

"Not now, he won't. I'm sure he's doing us a big favor just by being here."

"Don't they all?"

"Any idea who he is?"

"Hell, no. Somebody from city council?"

"No, he's too well dressed."

The man looked up and down the street as if he was expecting someone who was overdue. Then he pulled out his cell phone, dialed a number, waited, scowled unhappily, then snapped the phone shut and put it back in his pocket.

Hap walked back to the booth where he'd left his coat and other things. "I think I ought to go out and sell him a fortune. He looks like he doesn't know what he's in for."

"Not hanging around that old place, he doesn't. Why don't you bring him in here for a drink, Hap? What I charge him for a glass of brandy will pay for everything you and I have had already."

Hap went to the front window again for another look. The man was trying every piece of plywood he could reach. Then he went to the school's main entrance and shook the chain-link barrier. A couple of kids walked by, not dressed for the weather, carrying skateboards. The white man looked at them with mild alarm in his face, as if he was afraid they'd mug him. "Maybe he's a graduate and left his class ring inside."

A city salt truck rumbled down the street, rather pointedly not spreading any salt. Two black kids and a white one, not wearing coats, ran after it, shouting something Hap and Sam couldn't make out. The man disappeared around the side of the school building, only to reappear again a minute later. Then, suddenly noticing he was being watched from the bar, he crossed the street and headed for it.

"Here he comes, Sammy. Champagne for everyone!"

Sam ignored him and took his place behind the bar. An instant later the man came in. He stood at the door for a moment, seeming to be unsure whether he ought to stay; he brushed snow off his shoulders. Tentatively, he smiled and said, "Hello."

Hap smiled back at him. "Hello."

"It's snowing."

"Yeah, that would have been my guess."

The man ignored this and walked to the bar. "A Black Russian, please."

Hap stifled a laugh. Sam avoided making eye contact and pretended to wipe something off the bar. "I'm afraid this is more a shot-and-a-beer kind of place."

"Oh." He looked at Hap, daring him to laugh again. "I'll have a shot and a beer, then."

"Good choice." Sam filled a shot glass, then poured a draft.

The man smiled at him and drank. Hap sidled up beside him. "You ought to be careful. If you're not used to that stuff . . ."

"Are you going to keep goading me?"

"Goading? Oh, no sir! I was hoping we might do some business, that's all."

The man's face turned blank. "Business."

Hap grinned and nodded.

But the man turned back to the bartender. "I'm D. Michael Canning." He produced a pair of calling cards and gave one to each of them. They put them on the bar without reading them. "You'll be seeing a lot of me around the neighborhood."

Sam reached out, shook his hand and told him his name.

"Is this your place?"

"Yep. Thirty years now."

"What's it called?"

"Uh . . . Sam's."

Hap stifled another laugh. "You want to be careful, Mr. Canning." He leaned on the "Mr." just heavily enough for Canning to pick up on the irony in his voice. "Bad things happen to people in that old ruin across the street. People say it's haunted. I'd think twice before I went messing around in there."

Canning found a bit more snow on his coat and brushed it off. "Houses get haunted, not schools."

"You really ought to buy something off me. You're going to need it."

Canning ignored him and took a drink of his beer. It was worse than he had expected, and he wrinkled his nose.

Sam went back to cleaning the counter. "You thinking about buying that old place, then?"

"Not me, no. The Greater Pittsburgh Educational Enterprises Corporation, Inc. It's a good building, from the look of it, and it's been empty too long."

"It's the ugliest building in the neighborhood."

Hap climbed onto a stool. "Give me another drink, Sammy." Then he turned to Canning. "That's not the school board, is it?"

Not quite sure whether Hap was still making fun of him, Canning addressed his answer to Sam. "No, it's a private company. Corporation. For-profit."

"White folks looking to make a profit in the ghetto? Now there's a surprise." Hap laughed out loud this time. "Your company find a way to make money out of ghosts, then?"

Canning got up and moved away from him, quite pointedly. The expression on his face suggested he smelled something unpleasant on Hap. Sam, enjoying them both, smiled and waited for Canning to go on.

"The corporation's planning to open a private school here. To be called the Washington Academy. The sale just went through today. I've been hired as principal, and I wanted to take a look at the place as soon as—" He caught himself, wondering if he was telling them a bit too much. "I'm on the board, too. I wanted to get a good look at the place."

"You're going to put a bunch of rich white kids in there?!?" Hap was finding this funnier and funnier.

"Look, I'm not at all sure what you find so entertaining, sir."

"You can call me Hap."

"Hap, then. The board argued long and hard about whether to renovate that old building over there. A lot of them argued against it."

"I'll just bet they did."

"But EdEntCo is a company with a social conscience." He was in PR mode, and percolating. "We decided placing the school here would give our students a much richer educational experience. Expose them to the rich diversity of the inner city, and—"

"And save money by not having to put up something new. And probably get big tax breaks from the city and state, too." Hap took a long drink. "Why do people like you always think they're being so subtle?"

"Listen, Hap"—he said the name as if it left a bad taste in his mouth—"we're trying to do the right thing by the neighborhood. The students—and their families—will spend a lot of money here. Places like Sam's will boom."

But Hap was on a tear. "Sam can't afford the kind of liquor folks like you drink. I saw the look on your face when you downed that Seagram's just now." He put on a posh accent. "Oh, good heavens, Mavis, I simply can't force myself to imbibe such liquids. Let us patronize an establishment where we can get a Black Russian."

Sam finally decided to get between them. "Look, Hap, why don't you go and settle into your booth and stop needling Mr.—?"

"Canning. D. Michael Canning."

"Mr. Canning, here."

Hap laughed at Sam exactly as he'd been laughing at Canning. But he picked up his drink and walked back to his booth.

Sam turned back to Canning, a bit shamefaced. "A lot of people get crazy when they get to his age. I make a living selling them the stuff that makes them that way, so I just smile and listen. I'm surprised my own mind hasn't gone yet."

Canning took a sip of his beer. "There's no need to apologize."

"That wasn't an apology. Just an explanation."

"Oh."

From his booth Hap shouted, "Everyplace on Jumonville Street is cursed. This place is cursed. You know it, Sammy, and you'd admit it if it wasn't bad for business."

Canning asked Sam for a glass of water. "The real estate agents told us there was a fire in the school, way back. Do you happen to know when, exactly?"

"Well, it was sort of a fire, I guess."

He noticed the glass was dirty but drank anyway. "How do you *sort of* have a fire?"

"It wasn't just that, Mr. Canning. The place got bombed."

"Bombed?" Canning didn't try to hide his astonishment. "This is Pittsburgh, not Vietnam."

"Vietnam didn't have riots."

"Oh."

"You should have seen the neighborhood then, Mr. Canning. It looked like . . . well, it looked like hell. Houses gutted, businesses looted."

"And somebody bombed the school building? The Realtors didn't tell us that, either."

Sam poured himself another long whiskey. "Self-destructiveness knows no bounds." He saluted Canning and took a long swallow. It occurred to him Sam might not be talking about the old race riots back in the late 60s, but then . . . what else could he mean?

Hap laughed, and quite loudly. "There's been something wrong on Jumonville Street a long time before that, and you know it."

On the bar in front of Canning there were two empty tumblers and a shot glass. He gestured to Sam to refill them all. "One of the other board members was supposed to meet me here with the keys. I think the snow must have—"

"It wasn't the snow, mister." Hap howled with laughter. "He just came to his senses and decided to stay off Jumonville Street and out of Washington High School."

"Washington Academy." Canning looked at Sam. "Is

he always this annoying, or does bad weather bring out the worst in him?"

"When you're ninety-six, people will put up with *your* eccentricities, too."

"He's that old?" Canning looked at Hap as if he hadn't seen him before, then back at Sam. "He looks like he's in his fifties. I would never have imagined."

" 'I would never have imagined.' " Hap mimicked him.

Canning decided to pick up the thread of the conversation. "So, why didn't the city ever reopen the school?"

"Mr. Canning." Sam looked him square in the eye. "If you have to ask that, you really are in the wrong neighborhood."

"Oh."

Hap suddenly got up out of his booth and put on a threadbare overcoat. "I think I'll be heading home now, Sammy. She'll have dinner ready any time now."

"Your wife?" Canning tried to show polite interest.

"Wife? Hell, no. I live with my grandmother." He waited for Canning to realize he was being pricked again, then laughed at him even harder than before.

Canning's cell phone rang. "Canning. Oh, Peter. Yeah, I'm there now. In a neighborhood bar just across the street. You might have told me the building was such a monstrosity. And why the hell aren't you here with the keys?"

Sam busied himself cleaning the bar. Hap ignored them both. Canning stepped to the back of the room and lowered his voice.

"Look," he whispered. "I've been talking to some of the locals. They say the building was firebombed. Back during the race riots. Did the agents tell you that? What?! Then why the hell didn't you tell me?"

Outside, it was snowing much more heavily. What

little traffic there was moved slowly. Another salt truck rumbled by; this one wasn't spreading salt either.

Hap pulled his coat tightly around himself and wrapped a long red scarf around his neck. Then he picked up his sandwich sign, the one with the horoscopes and lucky numbers and such, which had been sitting in his booth.

"No, Peter, but I think you ought to have told me. If there should be any trouble about the structure . . . No, but . . . All right, fine. Oh, and there's a ghost. Did they tell you that?" Canning laughed. "No, just something I heard from a crazy old black guy here, that's all." He snapped the phone shut and put it away.

Hap picked up the sandwich board and hung it around his neck; it made him stoop a bit. Smiling, he approached Canning. "Why don't you buy a fortune from me?"

"Thank you, no."

"I know I've been sniping at you, mister, but it was only in fun. You really need a fortune, and I'm the guy who can sell you one."

"I'm afraid I'm not superstitious."

Sam spoke up. "He's not kidding you, Mr. Canning. Sam's fortunes are for real. I bought this place when I won the lottery on a lucky number he sold me."

"No, thank you." It was clear he didn't know whether they were making fun of him again. "I think I'll just trust my fortune to EdEntCo."

Hap planted himself directly in front of Canning. "Listen, mister. I'm trying to tell you something. That place is haunted. Ask anyone in the neighborhood, ask any kid playing in the street. There'll be blood. There'll be—" He stopped short and, improbably, grinned.

Out of his depth once again, Canning looked to Sam, who made his face neutral. "Everyone says so, Mr. Canning. He's right—everyone on the block says so."

They had to be kidding. Canning stepped way from Hap. "Even so."

"Well, you go ahead and take your chances, then." A slow grin spread across Hap's face. "I'm just trying to help you, that's all. Firebombs aren't the worst thing that ever happened over there. And worse will happen again." He shook Sam's hand and left without glancing at Canning.

Canning stood looking after him. "What an interesting neighborhood we're moving into."

"Interesting, Mr. Canning? Yeah, I guess that would be one word."

"Look, it's been nice meeting you, Sam." He put a twenty on the bar. "Will that cover it?"

"And then some."

"Keep the change. I really want to get over there and find a way inside before it starts getting dark." He buttoned up his coat and headed for the door.

"Are you sure you want to do that?"

"What do you mean?" He paused, his hand on the doorknob.

"Look at it out there, Mr. Canning. I wouldn't want to be in that school alone, period. On an evening like this, with the snow falling harder and harder . . . If you need help, it could take forever to get here. I'm telling you, that place is dangerous."

"I'm really not worried. Whatever happened there happened thirty, forty years ago." He looked confidently at the building across the street. "Even if somebody died in the riots, why would he be angry at me?"

"Nobody said he died in the riots."

This brought him up short. For an instant Canning seemed unsure of himself. "Oh. Well, even so."

Sam looked and sounded doubtful. "Well good luck."

He reached up and switched off the TV. "And welcome to Jumonville Street."

Canning smiled, waved a slight wave and stepped out onto the sidewalk. There had to be a way to get inside an abandoned building in a place like this. . . . Homeless people would be living in it. Or drug addicts. Or . . . who knew? But there had to be a way in.

As he was crossing the street, a kid on a bike nearly clipped him. The kid shouted something he couldn't make out and kept going. Canning was going to shout something after him, but what would be he point?

Every window in the place was sealed but one. It had been covered with tar paper, but someone had pulled it down. He made a quick stop at his car, to get a flashlight out of the trunk.

The two skateboarders he had seen earlier walked up behind him, carrying their boards. They stood and stared at him. It took him a moment to realize they were there. Every inch a principal, he scowled at them. "What do you want?"

The older of the two kids scowled back. "No, what are *you* doing here?"

He went back to searching his trunk. He found the flashlight under a stack of old newspapers.

The younger kid spoke up. "What are you going to do in that old school?"

Canning was not used to being cross-examined by people this age. "Why?"

" 'Cause nobody goes in there."

"I do. Why aren't you wearing coats?"

"My brother went in there once." This from the older kid. "Somebody cut him. On the neck. He said they tried to cut his head off."

"Well, there's no one in there now."

"That's what you think."

The younger one made to grab his flashlight. Canning pulled it back and away, forcefully.

"I just want to see it."

"Never mind." Voice dripping with irony he added, "Thank you for the warning."

They stared at him. He felt a bit of a heel, but he was there on business. "Look, we're reopening this place. As a private school. There'll be construction crews here within a couple of weeks." They didn't move. "Okay?"

"You're not from the city?"

"No." He started to tell them about EdEntCo but thought better of it.

"We won't have to go to school here, then?"

"No."

"Good."

This caught Canning a bit off guard, but he was determined not to let it show. "Thank you for your interest." The boys knew they had been dismissed. Canning slammed the trunk shut loudly, turned his back on them and headed back to the open window.

With a bit of strain, he hoisted himself up onto the windowsill and peered inside. It was darker and gloomier than he'd expected. There would be rats, there would be homeless people, there would be needles on the floor, perhaps AIDS-infected needles. He edged carefully across the sill, then dropped to the floor of what had been the gymnasium/auditorium.

His flashlight's beam shone out brightly, but it seemed small and insignificant in the massive darkness. There were random bits of debris littering what had been the basketball court—scraps of wood, some broken glass, even what looked like pieces of a shattered mirror. All the seats had been removed from the hall except, oddly, one.

He found his way slowly, cautiously into the main part of the school building and checked out the first classroom he came to.

The blackboards had faded to a pale grey. Bare wires that had once held light fixtures hung down from the ceiling. There were no desks or other schoolroom equipment. The city would have had it all hauled away when the place closed, he guessed; secondhand, it would have been worth at least something.

He stepped into the hall and walked from one room to the next. There were no doors on any of them. More rubbish. More wires hanging down. A student's desk sat outside a doorway, the only one in sight. Why had they left it?

Canning stood and listened. If there was anyone in the building, they were being exceptionally quiet. For a long moment he didn't move, but there was no sound. Not even the scratching of a rat or the scuttling of cockroaches. It didn't seem right.

Behind him, the faintest light came through the open window he had entered by. Farther down the hall, it was pitch-dark. The late afternoon light would be gone soon enough, and the storm would only make things worse. He ought to come back some better time.

And yet . . . it seemed to him there *were* sounds now, but they were so indistinct he couldn't be quite sure he was hearing them. He switched on his flashlight and headed down the hall.

Room after room was like the one he'd entered first. Empty, cluttered with litter; there was no sign anyone had been inside. Suddenly there came a faint howl, like someone in pain, from a distant part of the building. He froze, then relaxed. It must have been a siren or something from outside.

At the intersection of two halls was a large office with a sign reading PRINCIPAL. He went in and looked. More old furniture was piled up in a corner. What would be his own office seemed acres too small for his taste and his dignity; a wall would have to be knocked out. He'd have a word with the architect.

Then there were voices.

Or perhaps one voice.

Or perhaps none at all.

He couldn't be sure. Those kids, toying with him. They had followed him inside and were playing with his head. What else could it be?

There was wind, or rather a draft. It must be coming from outside, from the window he'd come in through.

No, the draft was coming from ahead of him. Had he missed another way in, an easier one?

"Hello? Who's there?"

Winos, junkies, vagrants—it had to be. Who else would be in a place like this . . . ? Part of him wanted to leave. But he had to see.

Downstairs. The voice, or voices, or perhaps no voice, was coming from the basement. He planted himself at the top of a stairwell, pointed the beam of his light downward and listened. Silence. A voice. Many voices. None at all.

"Hello!"

Silence. No—a voice.

"You need to get out of here." He called it loudly and clearly. "This building is the property of a private company now."

A scream; a cry in the darkness.

"Did you hear me?" He shouted it.

It suddenly occurred to him that they—whoever they were—might be dangerous. Drug addicts had knives and maybe guns. The homeless were mentally ill. Maybe there were gangs. But he decided there was no reason to be afraid. He was in the right. And he had gotten along well enough with those two men in the bar, hadn't he?

Slowly, carefully, he walked down the steps, listening for more. He hadn't been quite certain he had heard anything in the first place; now he was even less sure.

There was more debris littering the stairs; he stepped gingerly. Then he was in the basement, and it was pitch-black. Someone cried. It was in the room right behind him, but when he turned, he was alone. This was not possible. This was not right.

If they were there, they could get him. His mind began to spin B-movie fantasies about deranged, homeless cannibals. Consciously, he knew it was nonsense; the subconscious part of his mind, however, was beginning to be afraid. But this was his building, now, and he had to see.

The basement was vast. The beam of his flashlight seemed near useless. In a corner more desks were stashed; these were obviously broken. Books were scattered about on the floor. A metal cabinet stood against one wall; he pried open the rusted doors. It was full of old dissection kits from the biology lab—scalpels, scissors, pins, all rusted.

But there was no sign anyone had been there for years. No empty food containers, no needles, no . . . he wasn't even certain what else he expected. But there was none of it.

A scratching sound.

Canning spun around quickly, and faced . . . nothing.

But the sound persisted. It was coming from inside the wall. He moved closer and listened. Yes, there was something there. And there came another of those moans, those muffled howls. There. In the wall.

He examined it close-to, in the beam of his light.

Down near the base of the wall was a crack, just the tiniest chink. He kicked it with the toe of his shoe and the plaster fell away. His foot plunged into open air.

There was a room hidden behind the wall.

Expecting rats, or worse, he stepped quickly back. But there was nothing.

He got down on all fours and tried to see into the room. The darkness was total; his flashlight barely cut it. He looked around. No rats, no kids playing pranks; he was quite alone. He began gently prying loose the plaster. It came off in large chunks. Why would anyone have hidden a room like this?

It wasn't large, six feet by eight, and the ceiling was barely five-feet high; it hardly amounted to more than a crawlspace. It could never have been more than a pantry or a small storage room or . . . who knew what? He peered in. It was quite empty. No desks, no cabinets, no litter—nothing. Well, almost nothing: In one corner there was what appeared to be a bowling ball. That was all. Except . . .

There. Right in the center of the floor. It looked like . . .

It couldn't be.

He had to be seeing wrong.

He inched inside the room and stood over it.

Bones. A human hand and forearm. Sticking up out of the dirt floor. A body, buried here. Why? How?

He got down on his hands and knees.

No mistaking it: a skeleton.

He stood and stared at it for a long moment. Again, he tried to convince himself this was not possible. Some ousted drug lord or petty dealer, some crack whore who didn't pay up, buried here, in *his* school.

What to do?

He flipped open his cell phone and dialed.

"Peter, it's Michael again. We have a problem here."

THE afternoon light was nearly gone; it was almost night. The snow was still falling steadily. Across the street, Sam's place looked warm and inviting. Except for streetlights at the far intersections, it provided the only light. Canning took a moment to get a brush and clean the snow off his car. Then he headed for the bar again.

The place was empty except for Sam. He had the TV on again and was watching a PBS costume drama. When he heard the door, he looked up, and he didn't try to hide his surprise. "You're still here?"

Canning smiled. "Obviously. Set 'em up."

Sam poured a shot, then a draft. "If you don't mind my saying so, Mr.—?"

"Canning. Michael Canning." He seemed a bit annoyed at having to repeat it.

"If you don't mind my saying so, Mr. Canning, you have some mighty odd work habits. There's six inches of snow out there, and they're saying we'll get a foot and a half, maybe two."

Canning gestured at the TV. "I would have expected sports."

"No cable."

"Oh." He glanced around the bar. "The snow keeping all your regulars away?"

Sam nodded. "It's too bad, too. Start of President's Day, a long weekend. I hope the snow doesn't get too bad or the place'll be empty all weekend. I could put on some music, if you like."

"Sure. And I'd appreciate some conversation."

Sam turned off the television and switched on the

radio. To Canning's obvious surprise, it was tuned to a classical station. "Hope you don't mind classical."

Canning shrugged. "At least it isn't opera." It was organ music. He glanced across at the school building. "This neighborhood keeps surprising me."

"'Those houses that are haunted are most still'." Sam grinned. "'Till the devil be up'."

"Is that Shakespeare? I thought I knew all the—"

"Webster." Sam put on a self-satisfied grin. "*The White Devil.*"

Was he being made fun of yet again? Canning drank his whiskey.

Unasked, Sam told him, "I open at noon, but there's never much business till dinner time. Leaves a lot of time for books and music." He nodded in the direction of the radio. "Couperin. François. French baroque."

"Give me Sinatra."

Sam made a sour face. "Easy listening. Nothing should ever be easy."

"Nothing ever is. Somebody's going to be joining me here. Keep the drinks coming."

"In this storm?"

"Our head of security, Nick Brookhiser."

"Security? Good lord, Mr. Canning, there can't be anyone in that place. I mean, everyone knows . . ." He thought better of what he was going to say and let the sentence trail off, unfinished.

"Just a slight problem, that's all. But it has to be dealt with. What do you know about that building? I mean its history."

"Not much." He picked up a cloth and started polishing the bar. "What everybody knows, I guess."

"It's been closed since . . . ?"

"Nineteen sixty-eight. There was some talk about the school board selling it to some guy who wanted to turn it into luxury condos. Then he got a good look at the neighborhood."

"And before it was a school?"

"That's ancient history, Mr. Canning."

"Call me Michael, please. Somebody has to know. There are always people who know their local history, neighborhood lore, that kind of thing."

"Hap Conklin would be your man, then."

"That old guy who was here before?"

Sam smiled and nodded. "He knows everything about everything around here. You should let him give you a horoscope. I know most of that stuff is bull, Mr. Canning, but like I said before, Hap's really work."

"Call me Michael."

"No, sir. Mr. Canning suits me fine."

They went on chatting, making small talk, gossiping about sports. Outside, snow fell more and more quickly and heavily. It was an hour and a half before Nick Brookhiser's Hummer pulled up and parked behind Canning's Lexus, which was again covered. Canning watched him get out of the vehicle and stare directly up at the top of the school building. What could he be seeing there? When he lost interest in whatever it was, he walked purposefully across the street to Sam's.

At the doorway he slapped himself to get the snow off. It was falling fast enough now that the minute or two he was out in it was enough to coat his parka. He recognized Canning and strode the length of the bar to greet him. The radio was playing a Haydn quartet. Gesturing at it, Brookhiser said, "Evening, Michael. Is this a gay bar or something?"

Sam glared at him. "Can I get you something, sir?" He leaned heavily on the final word so Brookhiser wouldn't miss the irony. White men often did.

"No, thank you. I've got work to do, it seems."

Canning shook his hand. "Go on and have a drink. What we have to deal with isn't going anywhere." He signaled to Sam, who set up a shot glass and a beer glass.

"Weird thing. Just as I was parking, I thought I saw a gleam of light inside."

Canning looked out the front window. There was no sign of any light.

Sam rang up the sale. "I told you, Mr. Canning, people stay out of there. There's nothing that could start a fire."

Brookhiser drank up quickly. "Come on. My wife's pissed I had to come out on a night like this. So am I. This better be good."

Canning got into his coat and gloves. "Oh, it's good all right. Did Peter tell you to bring lights and plaster?"

"Yeah, they're in the Hummer."

A minute later they were at Brookhiser's car, getting out a battery of work lights, a small gas-powered generator, a sack of plaster, water and some tools. He jerked a thumb over his shoulder at Sam's. "You do know we're going to have to close that place, don't you?"

"That might not be a good idea. I think it's a bit of a neighborhood institution."

"Even so. Law says no saloons within five hundred feet of a school."

"I like him. I think he likes me. There has to be a way around it."

"None that I know of." He slammed the rear door. "Let's go."

They both carried portable flashlights. Brookhiser

unlocked the chain-link gate that blocked the front door and they went inside.

"Which way?"

"Downstairs. Over here."

Except for the two of them, the place was quite still and perfectly dark. Brookhiser looked around. "Where are the crackheads?"

"I was wondering the same thing. Sam says no one ever comes in here. No one. Some neighborhood superstition or something. I went through the building pretty thoroughly before, and there was no sign of anyone."

Down the stairs. Basement. Pitch-black but for their lights. "Over here." Canning pointed his beam at the hole he'd made in the wall.

"What the hell were you doing down here?"

Canning made himself smile. "I'm a hands-on principal."

"Hands on what?"

"You'll see."

Stooping, they entered the small room. Canning had done more digging after he called for assistance. A good bit of the skeleton was exposed. But it was headless. There were some scraps of blue cloth and a few miscellaneous objects scattered around it.

"Jesus." Brookhiser was tall for the low space, but he stood and prodded the bones with the toe of his boot.

"No, I doubt if it's him."

"Don't be blasphemous, Mr. Canning."

"Call me Michael. I don't mean to be. But I . . . I guess I don't know how else to react to a thing like this. I mean, who would have expected . . . ?"

"Why didn't you just call the police?"

"And have them track their gum boots all over my building?"

"You've got a corpse here."

"It's not just a corpse. Look." He got down on one knee and held up some of the things he'd found around the body. They were clearly Native-American artifacts—beads, an arrowhead, a shred of blanket. He looked up at Brookhiser. "You see the problem?"

"Frankly, no. The police have jurisdiction when Indians get killed, too."

"What makes you think this man was killed?"

He paused. "I think the fact that there's no head might indicate something like that. Or hadn't you noticed?"

"These things are old, Nick. If this is part of some kind of Indian burial ground or something . . ."

"Oh. I see what you mean." He stood up, stooping to avoid bumping his head.

"The construction crews are due here Tuesday to start the renovation. We can't let them find this. We'd have to call in archaeologists to excavate the whole damned site. And they'd probably notify the local Indian council. Red tape, maybe court battles, God knows what else. It could tie us up for months."

Brookhiser knelt down beside him. "Years, more likely."

"We're cutting things close as it stands. If there's much delay, we might not be able to open for the fall term. The board wouldn't be happy." He exhaled deeply. "I wouldn't be happy."

"Where's the head?" Brookhiser dug his fingers into the dirt just above the skeleton's shoulders.

"I couldn't find it."

"It's got to be here. From what I know, Indians wouldn't have buried him without it."

"Maybe it's off looking for a body of evidence."

"That isn't helpful." Brookhiser glared at him and

started crawling around the little room, probing the dirt with his fingers. He turned up some fragments of pots, more beads, more arrowheads, a large square of white cloth and what looked like a pipe, but no skull. Canning watched him, mildly amused.

After a few minutes of this, Brookhiser got up and dusted off his pants. "Come on. We can get it out to my car. Or yours. All we have to do is dump it someplace."

"That was my first thought. But no."

"What do you mean, no? We have to get rid of it."

"All we'd need is for the cops to stop us for some reason or other." Canning got down and began sifting the dirt with his fingers. "I keep imagining some Hitchcock scenario where the police stop me for some routine reason, a burned-out turn signal or something, and they do a search and find the damned thing."

"Don't do anything suspicious, then."

"Just being out on a night like this is suspicious. There's a blizzard raging. You did notice?"

"We're not common criminals. We're EdEntCo."

"Even so, Nick. Corporate executives have been arrested before this. Or hadn't you heard?"

"I'm claustrophobic. I want to get out of here. What do you think we should do?"

"Rebury it. Then seal up the wall."

"You think the workmen won't find it? You think they won't notice fresh plaster in a hundred-year-old building?"

Canning switched on his principal's manner. "I'll tell them to ignore it. They work for us, after all."

The generator was filling the small space with fumes. "We need to get out of here for a few minutes and get some air. And let this space air out."

"I want to get this done."

"Do you want to join our friend here?"

"We have to get this done, Nick."

Reluctantly, obviously unhappy, Brookhiser began to dig a hole that could serve as a proper grave. The only digging tool he had was a large spade, so it took some time. But after twenty minutes the skeleton was covered, along with every trace of the things that seemed to have been buried with it.

He shoved the spade into the earth, meaning to leave it there. But it struck something; there was a ringing sound. Metal.

Curious, he dug. In a moment he had turned up a sword, partly corroded but generally in good shape, at least to the extent he could tell. He held it out. "Michael, look at this."

Canning took it and held it up to one of the lights. "Nick, this is incredible. This is an antique—1800, maybe earlier. I'll have to get it appraised. It could be worth a lot."

Nick was in no mood for this. "Fine. Now can we get out of here, Michael?"

"We have to seal up the wall."

Canning had been squatting, watching the work. He straightened up without thinking and bumped his head. Brookhiser laughed at him. "It's not funny, Nick. Let's get this stuff out of here."

They moved their things out of the room. Brookhiser did a quick check to make sure he had everything. "Should we take that bowling ball?"

"Why? Do you want to get in a quick game before you head home?"

"Who would have left a thing like that here?"

He shrugged. "Maybe whoever killed the poor guy was a bowler. Maybe it was Rip Van Winkle."

Brookhiser moved the lights out of the room. Canning took one last look around. "Wait a minute. There's something beside it."

Canning reentered the little space. The air was thick with exhaust fumes from the generator. When he got to the back corner, the generator stopped and the lights went out. "Shit. Where's my flashlight?"

"Damned if I know." Brookhiser tried to restart the engine.

From the darkness there came the sound of Canning falling heavily to the floor.

"Nick! Something's got me."

"I'll have this started again in a minute."

"Something's got me, for Christ's sake!" He screamed.

Brookhiser finally managed to restart the generator. The work lights flickered and came back on. Canning was lying on the ground, holding his ankle. There was blood, a lot of it, and Brookhiser could see deep scratches. "You stumbled over something, that's all."

"No, something caught at my foot."

"What? There's nothing there."

"Hand me my flashlight." He pointed to it; it was what he had seen in the corner.

Brookhiser crawled back into the room, got the light, switched it on and handed it to Canning. There were four deep gashes in his ankle; blood was pouring out of them. Canning got out a handkerchief and wrapped it.

"Does it hurt?"

"What do you think?"

"Jesus, look."

The skeleton's hand was exposed, reaching out of the earth. For a moment they both gaped at it. It had been buried. Brookhiser had covered it; Canning had watched. It had been buried, and now it wasn't.

Brookhiser reached out and touched it with a fingertip. "You must have uncovered it when you fell. The toe of your shoe disturbed the soil, that's all."

"Yeah, that must be it." He didn't sound quite convinced. "Come on, let's patch up the wall and get out of here."

"Yeah."

It took another half-hour's work to get the opening plastered over. Canning found an old water faucet, badly corroded; to his surprise, when he turned the handle, water came out. "I wonder who's been paying the bills all these years."

Finally they were finished. As unpleasant as it had been, Canning seemed satisfied. "No one will ever know. If anyone asks, we'll simply tell them not to pry. The dead are dead, and there's no point digging them up."

"Not even by accident."

A few minutes later they stood on the sidewalk facing one another, not certain what else to say. It was completely dark now; the only light came faintly from streetlights at the far corners and from the front window of Sam's. The snow was coming down as thickly as either of them had ever seen. A foot had accumulated since they went into the school. Each got a brush and began cleaning off his car. Even though Brookhiser's car was bigger, he finished first and went to help Canning. "You going to make it home okay? I'll have a rough enough time in my Hummer."

"I'll be fine. It looks like they've been scraping the main roads." He pointed toward the corner. Fifth Avenue seemed to be reasonably clear. "I might need you to give me a push so I can get out of this space, though."

"Sure."

They both started their engines and let them warm up. Brookhiser got out of his car and stared at the school building, as he'd done when he first arrived. "A school with a corpse in the cellar."

"Hmm?" Canning got out of his car and stood beside him. A salt truck headed up Fifth. "See? We'll be fine."

"I was just thinking how weird it is to have a dead body in the basement of a school."

"Don't give it another thought, Nick. No one will ever know."

"You know how kids can be."

"No. It's buried. It'll stay buried. We have a school to run. We can't let things like that distract us."

Brookhiser seemed uncertain. They made idle talk for another few minutes. Another salt truck passed, this one on Forbes Avenue. Finally they got into their cars and headed away from the Hill and Jumonville Street. Canning switched on his radio, hoping for some cool jazz, but all the got were weather bulletins predicting a citywide emergency. It looked like they'd be getting three feet or more. If it took the city too long to clear it all, work might not even begin on Tuesday.

Home would be warm and dry, and he couldn't wait to get there.

TWO

MATT LARRIMER

WASHINGTON High School—or, to give it its now-proper due, Washington Academy—was surrounded by scaffolding and large sheets of thick plastic. Chutes ran down from the top of the building, pouring debris into dump trucks. Jumonville Street was lined with light construction vehicles. Generators roared, running the various machinery. The sound of sandblasting equipment was overpowering. Workers wore face masks.

Several buildings adjacent to the school had been demolished to make room for a pair of parking lots. The smaller of them had a large sign that read FACULTY. Part of it was filled with more construction equipment, mostly small trucks, but there was also a crane and a small bulldozer. The other part of the lot was filled with expensive cars—Caddies, Corvettes, Lincolns and a particularly shiny black Lexus. The second lot, much larger and presumably for students, was still being paved.

Matt Larrimer drove down Jumonville and tried to turn into the faculty lot. A young African-American man in a bright orange vest waved him to a stop. "Yes?"

Matt told him his name. "I'm on the faculty." He smiled.

"Hi, Mr. Larrimer. I'm Cal. You can't park here. Only administrators and board members today." He smiled back at Matt. A college kid working a summer job.

"Oh." He craned his neck. "There are a few open spaces."

"We have to keep them clear." He seemed to think this obvious, but Matt looked puzzled, so he added, "For emergency vehicles."

"Oh."

Cal smiled again. "You'd be amazed at the number of accidents we've had on this job. Just this morning a guy cut nearly through his leg with a power saw." He suddenly looked concerned and lowered his voice. "We're not supposed to tell anyone."

"Well, it looks like I'm no one around here, so you're safe." Matt gunned his engine and backed out of the driveway.

He glanced at his watch: 11:40. Orientation was supposed to begin at noon, sharp. He'd have to hope he found a place to park quickly.

He had to circle several blocks before he found a space for his Toyota. He got out, double-checked to make sure all the doors were locked, looked around and tried to convince himself the neighborhood was safe. His interviews had taken place in a downtown office building; this was a bit more "inner city" than they'd led him to expect. Just up Fifth and Forbes Avenues was Oakland and the city's major universities; a block or two in the opposite direction was the Hill. The ghetto. But then, hell, his car was twelve years old. Even in a bad neighborhood, who would bother to steal it?

From the corner of Fifth he could just see down to the Monongahela River and the Birmingham Bridge that crossed it from the main part of Pittsburgh to the South Side. It was a bright day, hot with haze (as the authorities now chose to call pollution), and he found himself wishing he was water skiing instead of starting a new job at a new school. But of course there was no way around it. It was bound to be better than Roland High.

As he neared the school again, the sound of the work seemed almost deafening. How on earth were they going to conduct an orientation? Just above Fifth Avenue, where it intersected with Jumonville Street, was a fairly steep hillside. A number of old wood-frame houses sat on it, all but one of them boarded up. And there was an ancient apartment building. Struggling down its steep steps was Hap Conklin, wearing his sandwich sign as always. He called to Matt. "Fortune, mister?"

"No, thanks." He kept walking, barely paying the man any notice.

Taped to the plastic at the school's main entrance was a hand-lettered sign: TEMPORARY FACULTY ENTRANCE. An arrow pointed to the side of the building that faced the parking lot. Matt leaned close to the plastic and shaded his eyes to see what he could of the main entrance. Not much. It was clean, freshly sandblasted and looking new, and what seemed to be an imposing metal-and-stained-glass lantern hung there. The building dated from the Belle Epoque, he knew. If the crews were restoring everything as well as they had the entrance, it would be a pleasure to work here. He hoped.

Something fell, evidently from the roof, not far from

him and just on the other side of the plastic sheet. Startled, he jumped back, stumbled at the edge of the curb and hit the ground.

He looked up to find an attractive thirty-something woman standing over him, grinning. "This is just a guess, but you're not the gymnastics coach, are you?"

"Good guess." He got to his feet and dusted himself off. "You think they'll be able to have a serious orientation with all this going on?"

"Let's hope not. I'm Diana Ketterer." She held out a hand.

"Matt Larrimer." They shook hands.

"Faculty?"

He nodded. "History."

"I teach English and film."

"There'll be a film course here?"

She nodded. "Film history and theory. But mostly I'm just a plain old English teacher."

"So we're both required."

She laughed. "And a good thing, too. Otherwise we'd be lecturing to empty classrooms."

"No, we'd simply get the smartest students. Have you been inside yet?"

"No. I stopped in that bar over there"—she gestured at Sam's—"for a quick pick-me-up. Vodka on the rocks can make any meeting easier to face. Then I saw you, needing to be picked up yourself."

"You sound like a streetwalker," Matt said, laughing.

"Well, I'm a teacher. Just one more corporate whore. Come on, let's see what's going on inside. We're just on time." She glanced at her watch, then headed off around the side of the school with Matt happily behind her. She was, as his father used to say, quite a looker. Tall, dark hair, blue eyes, and she obviously worked out. He'd have at least one congenial colleague. He tried to imagine her in a pair of spandex shorts and a sports bra.

She looked back over her shoulder. "Is this your first teaching job?"

"No, I've spent the last two years at Roland, over on the South Side." He gestured vaguely toward the bridge. "Do I look that young?"

"Don't flatter yourself. It's just that I saw a glimmer of life in your eyes. Not many experienced teachers have that."

He laughed. "What about you?"

"Believe it or not, I moved here from Detroit for this job. Is Roland inner city?"

"Yep. This will be heaven by comparison."

"Tell me about it."

Talking loudly to be heard over the machinery and the workers, they followed a series of arrowed signs through an alley, to what turned out to be a side entrance to the gym. Finally a sign with no arrow read FACULTY HERE. Diana paused and looked back at Matt. "Do we dare?"

"Why not? At least it doesn't say ABANDON ALL HOPE."

"I'm not sure I like the comparison to hell."

"Try visiting Roland High some day."

"Or Detroit Central. After five years there, I really *was* ready to abandon hope. If I hadn't gotten this job, I'd be selling hearing aids or something." She pulled the plastic aside and stepped lightly into the building. Matt hesitated for a moment, looked up at the scaffolding, then followed her. "I wonder if we ought to wear face masks, like the construction guys. This air's pretty foul." It reeked of paint, plaster, dust and various unidentifiable chemicals.

A low, wide flight of marble steps opened in front of

them. They were polished to a high sheen, and the brass light fixtures, which were either antiques or very new and expensive, gleamed too. There was plush furniture, also apparently pricey, arranged to make a small waiting area; it looked more like a business office than a school. And there was good art on the walls, mostly modern, mostly prints, but Diana said she thought some of them might be originals. "I'd swear this is an authentic Duchamp." She took it all in with a wry grin. "Very posh. I deserve to work in surroundings like these."

There was also a portrait of George Washington, a rather idealized one. Diana scowled at it. "Well, at least it isn't a copy of the hideous Gilbert Stuart thing you see everywhere."

Beside it, in a brightly-lit display case, was what seemed to be an antique sword. It was brightly polished, and it gleamed under the track lighting. A card beneath it read: BATTLE SABER, 18TH CENTURY, PROBABLY FRENCH. GIFT OF DR. D. MICHAEL CANNING.

Diana glanced at it and snickered. "Well, if one of the kids decides to go on a rampage, he'll know just where to find a lovely weapon, probably French."

"Diana, really."

At the top of the steps, a sign directed them to their right. Just around the corner, behind a large old desk, sat a hatchet-faced woman in a rather severe black business dress. Her makeup was at least two layers too thick. She glared at them. Matt and Diana both paused without thinking and glanced at each other.

"Yes?" The woman looked up, folded her hands and inspected the new arrivals.

Diana spoke up first. "We're here for faculty orientation." She looked around, a bit uncertain of herself. "This is the right day, isn't it?"

The woman ignored her question and picked up a clip-board. "You are . . . ?"

"Diana Ketterer. English lit. and film."

"Matthew Larrimer. American history. We're not late, are we?"

"You are exactly two minutes away from being late."

Diana grinned. "So we're early, then."

The woman found their names on her list and, for no evident reason, scowled. "I am Mrs. Newburg, Dr. Canning's secretary." Then she switched on the least sincere smile Matt had ever seen. "*Executive* secretary."

"Well, we should both be on your list, Mrs. Newburg." Diana opened her purse, got out a compact and pretended to check her makeup.

"That's Larrimer with two *r*s," Matt added.

"Yes, you are both here." There were a few name badges in plastic holders on her table. She found theirs and pushed the badges toward them. Apparently, there were a few more teachers still to come. "The faculty lounge is being painted. You may both proceed to the auditorium."

Without taking her eyes off the mirror, Diana asked, "And that is . . . ?"

"Down the hall to your right. You will find signage, of course."

"Will we, indeed?" Without saying another word, Diana walked off down the hall. Matt muttered a quick thank-you to Mrs. Newburg and followed her. "You shouldn't antagonize the school secretary. She'll probably end up running the place."

From behind them Mrs. Newburg said loudly, "*Executive* secretary."

"Uh, yes, Mrs. Newburg."

Diana giggled. Matt, not wanting to, did as well.

Under his breath he asked, "Are school secretaries such gorgons in Detroit?"

"Of course they are. I think it's a law of nature, like evolution."

"She looks like she could be trouble for you."

"Let her." She tucked her compact back into her purse. "I've tackled worse than her."

"Really? Where? Are you a lady wrestler or something?"

"Don't be flippant, Mr. Larrimer."

Ahead of them, a number of people were milling around in the hall. From the look of them, more faculty. They were huddled in small groups, having what must have been serious conversations, or at least quiet, proper ones. Diana leaned close to Matt and whispered, "Those would be our colleagues, I gather, or some of them." She scowled. "At my old school, that would be a riot of polyester."

"You should have seen the way the teachers at Roland dressed. Our faculty meetings looked like the last stages of a rummage sale."

"That place really got to you, didn't it?"

The hallway approaching the auditorium was lined with tables covered with snacks. The food was better than either of them had expected—good cheese and canapés, fresh fruit and, surprisingly, red and white wine, the white properly chilled. Matt bit into a thin wedge of aged Asiago. "This is delicious. EdEntCo really does plan to make this into a properly high-toned school for the children of the wealthy."

"With us their humble servants."

Unattractive thought. Matt put his cheese down on the table and reached for a wineglass. "You having some?"

"No, thanks, Matt. I'm still feeling the drink I had at Sam's."

Matt got out a cigarette and lit it. Properly armed with tobacco and alcohol, he took a step toward their colleagues. They were all wearing their name badges; the type was too small and too ornate to be read easily.

One of the male teachers, his hands and mouth full of food, noticed them and shouted, "Look, everyone, fresh troops!" His manner was too hearty by half.

The others looked. A woman in a grey dress took a few steps toward them and barked angrily, "We're not allowed to smoke in here." She looked to be the oldest one there.

Matt was thrown off balance by her apparent hostility.

"It's a city ordinance." The woman glared at him. "It's not our fault. Really."

"I didn't say it was."

Diana stepped between them and held out a hand to the woman. "No, you sure didn't. You've got us there." She introduced herself and Matt.

"I am Mrs. Eleanor Bettis. I am the drama instructor."

"And here you are, stirring some up already." Diana hadn't stopped smiling.

"There's hardly any call for sarcasm, Miss Ketter."

"Ms. Ketterer. What play are you planning to do first? *The Taming of the Shrew* might be good."

Matt was feeling uncomfortable, but there didn't seem to be any simple way to make peace between them.

Fortunately, another teacher approached them, a man this time. He was middle-aged and shapeless. "Bill Cullen. Like the game show host. Physics."

They shook his hand. Matt was a bit puzzled. "What game show host?"

Cullen looked at Mrs. Bettis. "They're younger than they look."

Diana's smile got even wider. "Or you're older."

Matt pulled her aside and whispered, rather desperately, "I wish you'd stop baiting them. We have to work with these people."

"Wait till the first day of class."

"Diana, please." He was grateful she'd passed on the wine.

The man who had called out the crack about fresh troops approached them and introduced himself as Jack Clemm, the basketball and track coach. He quickly took charge and introduced them to everyone else. Names flew by quickly: The badges were all but indecipherable; Matt knew he'd never remember them all. He made himself concentrate on the fact that this was an elite new academy, the kind of school he'd always dreamed of, a wonderful place to teach. First impressions notwithstanding.

Mrs. Newburg stepped out of the auditorium and clapped her hands loudly. Matt looked back down the hall, to where she'd been sitting. How had she gotten there? Her voice seemed even more shrill than it had before. "Everyone, please listen. If you have all had enough food, we're ready to begin the welcome. If you would all please step into the auditorium." It was an order, not a request.

They followed her in groups of twos and threes. Matt found himself keeping a few paces away from Diana. Her attitude wouldn't do, certainly not on the first day. But damn it, he found her so attractive. The way she moved, the way she carried herself, even the sarcastic tone she used—it was all so sexy to him.

The auditorium was gorgeous, more like a spanking new theater than a school hall. Matt took a seat, sipped his wine and gaped. The seats were plush, stadium-style theater seats, of the kind the students would know well from their local mall multiplexes. The walls were covered with art and tapestries; Matt recognized Picasso, Miró, Matisse, Diego Rivera. . . . Reproductions, he guessed; they had to be. But they had been chosen carefully; even though the art was modern and the building old, they somehow went together.

The middle-aged woman beside him said dryly, "You're gaping. Like a tourist."

"Am I?"

She introduced herself as the girls' gym coach, Mandy Pinello. "You've never worked with rich kids before, have you?"

"No, I haven't been that lucky."

"It's not easy to stay one-up on them. Let them see you gawking at a Picasso, you're dead."

"And I thought I had to stay on my toes in a public school."

"Compared to a place like this, the ghetto's a piece of cake."

Unhappy thought. "At least this is an academy, a real academy. With academic standards."

"You don't believe that, do you? I mean, there are dumb rich kids. And half the ones who aren't stupid will be drugged out." She smiled. "Just like their parents."

The faculty was larger than he had expected; there seemed to be nearly fifty people milling around, socializing, finding seats for themselves. At his interview he'd been told the student body would be limited to 750. The classes would be so much smaller than the ones at Roland. Then he caught a glimpse of Diana through the crush; she had gotten a glass of wine after all. He put his doubts aside, crossed to her with a wide smile and said, "I do believe I've died and gone to heaven."

"A few minutes ago it was hell. Are you schizo or something?"

"No, just optimistic."

"Sooner or later, that comes to the same thing. If I'd known the wine was going to be this strong, I'd have skipped Sam's vodka."

"It's not. I'm not feeling it."

"Look, Matt, I really don't want to deflate your balloon, but you have to go into this with your eyes open. The kids we'll be teaching are rich. Spoiled. Privileged. They'll have a sense of entitlement that'll scare you. And just wait till you meet the parents. Most of them are 'new money.'" She paused and grinned broadly, to show him she was perfectly serious. "If you know what I mean."

He did, or thought he did. It still had to be better than . . . Oh, shit, what was the point? All of a sudden, Diana was looking a lot less attractive to him. "You speak from experience?"

"My first teaching job, ten years ago and fresh out of school, was at a private school like this one. I was an idealistic dope. When I flunked the son of a bank president, all hell broke loose. I decided I wanted to 'help people,' so I left for a public school in the center city. Do I *look* that stupid?"

He was feeling the wine after all. "You look fantastic."

This seemed to catch her off guard. "I think you probably ought to slow down a bit."

Mrs. Newburg was on the stage. Seated in a semicircle behind her were a dozen men, all but one of them white, all plainly affluent. Tailored suits, impeccable grooming, that sense of obvious self-importance that comes with being a corporate executive or a politician. They were in plush leather chairs; each had a small table beside him, some with wineglasses, some with water or whatever drink might pass for it. It dawned on Matt that he had never seen alcohol on a school's premises before; he knew it wouldn't last, and he sipped his wine contentedly. Among the board members he recognized a member of the county council, the city solicitor, an Episcopal bishop and at least one CEO, Peter Morgan, owner of a local specialty-metals corporation.

In the center of them sat D. Michael Canning, looking pleased with himself, not drinking and not quite as conspicuously well dressed as the rest. There was not the slightest hint about him of nervousness or anticipation at the opening of his new school. Off to one side stood Nick Brookhiser in a not-very-good suit, standing with his hands clasped in front of him like a Secret Service agent, watching the crowd as if he knew they were potential terrorists.

WORK crews were scattered throughout the academy building. The last classrooms were being painted. In utility areas, drywall was still being installed, plastered and painted. A crew of women from the neighborhood dusted, polished floors and washed windows that would obviously have to be washed again when the construction finally stopped in a few days. Outside, sandblasting crews cleaned the surface of the century-old building.

Canning's office had been duly expanded. There was an outer waiting room, for students. Then an inner one, with much better furniture, for his private guests. His own sanctum was done in leather.

Work had just finished on the athletic complex, and crews were taking down their scaffolds and drop cloths. There was a pool; indoor tennis, handball and racquetball courts; a basketball court of course; spanking new locker rooms, as yet untainted by hazing incidents. It would have been the envy of a lot of small colleges.

Most of the construction workers were white; most of the clean-up people were not. Canning had had sense enough to know that providing jobs, even low-paying ones, would generate good will in the neighborhood. There had been some grumbling around the Hill that all the best-paying jobs had gone to people from *outside* the neighborhood, but nothing much came of it. One more source of pride for Canning. He was showing the board what an adept manager they had hired, all right.

There were two foremen, one for construction, one for the cleaning crew. They worked together, consulting often. It was their job to keep things moving; the school was to open the following week.

The air was filled with the sounds of construction. Hammering, sanding, drilling . . . The whine of the floor-polishing machines was deafening (fortunately, it was limited to the part of the building farthest from the auditorium).

Then, at noon, a whistle blew and everything abruptly came to a stop. Lunchtime. The workers put down their various tools and headed outside, some quickly, some at a more leisurely pace. A few of them strolled across the street to Sam's, hoping the foremen wouldn't notice.

Some of them filtered toward the parking lot. Cal, the young, orange-vested guy doing lot security, tried to shoo them away; it would certainly not do for anyone to spill his or her lunch on the car of a board member. Then somebody offered him a joint. He lit up, smoked contentedly and forgot about his duties; this was only a summer job, after all.

But a few minutes later, the construction foreman,

Tony Mandarino, saw them and ordered them out of the lot. The college kid was left to smoke alone, which was okay with him. He got out his cell phone and called a girl he knew. He hadn't had any for days.

There was something wrong. Tony couldn't put his finger on it, but there was something wrong. He finally realized two of his best men were missing. Not overly concerned, he began asking around, going from one group of workers to the next. "Anyone seen Jack Sharp and Leo Smolensky?" No one had.

Tony had lost track of where they'd been working. Had they been in the basement? He went to the construction trailer to find his assignment sheets.

Suddenly there was the sound of a power saw, then (he thought) a nail gun, mingled with an ear-piercing scream.

CANNING was on the stage, enjoying himself and introducing the board members one by one. For each he had a little joke prepared, or the kind of thing that passed for a joke at business meetings. The atmosphere was more corporate office than school. Matt decided he could safely ignore most of it.

Then came those horrible sounds—the power equipment, the pathetic cry. They were impossibly loud, almost deafening; they didn't subside for several seconds. Some of the faculty jumped, perfectly startled; others simply looked around in confusion. Canning paused, waited to see if there'd be more, made a little joke about construction noise, then went ahead. It was obvious he was a bit shaken; there were no more lame jokes after that, just business.

Next came Peter Morgan, who, as CEO of EdEntCo, made a welcoming speech that was almost point-for-point identical to what Canning had said: "a proud day . . . glad to welcome you all on board . . . a shining new beacon in Pittsburgh's education community . . . sure to set a new standard nationwide," and on and on. The only departure from the script was a joke about Canning wanting his title to be, not principal, but "headmaster." There wasn't much laughter, but Canning fidgeted uncomfortably in his seat just the same.

Nick Brookhiser made an awkward, halting little speech about how Washington Academy would have state-of-the-art security. There would be a dozen men on his team, and the board had given him strict instructions there were to be no security lapses "of any kind." It seemed excessive to Matt, and he wasn't even quite certain what it all meant. When Brookhiser had finished, Canning pointed out to the audience, with some pride, that the new security chief was an ex-Marine.

It was during Canning's remarks that Tony Mandarino showed up at the side of the stage, looking extremely uncomfortable. He waved his hands and got Mrs. Newburg's attention, and she discreetly made her way over to him. There was a quick, anxious, whispered conversation. She frowned; her expression was uncertain, quite uncharacteristically so. Matt watched this with interest and amusement. Something or someone was not on-message.

After a moment of plain uncertainty, Mrs. Newburg finally crossed the stage to Canning's chair. It was obvious she hoped no one would notice how off-script this was, so everyone did. She bent down and whispered something to Canning. He turned pale, then whispered back, and she pointed to Mandarino, who was still standing self-consciously at the far side of the stage.

As discreetly as he could, Canning got to his feet,

crossed to his foreman and took him by the arm, ushering him gently into the wings. Mrs. Newburg and Brookhiser followed them. Morgan had been thrown off balance for a moment, but he recovered quickly, got to his feet and began another speech. End of show. Matt's attention began to stray again.

When Morgan finished talking, he looked around for Canning, who rushed back onstage, obviously flustered. Even though he didn't seem to be sweating, he got out a handkerchief and mopped his forehead. "Thank you, Peter. I'm sure we all appreciate your comments. Now, the next item on today's agenda is for you all to tour the building, so you can get yourselves properly oriented. I'm afraid there will be a slight delay. There has been an unfortunate accident involving two of our construction workers."

Someone in the audience asked what kind of accident. Canning dodged the question, saying only it was a fluke, an isolated incident, the kind of thing that almost never happens. He requested that everyone take the next few minutes to have more refreshments and get to know one another. There was time for departmental meetings. A group of volunteer students was waiting to show them all around the facility; perhaps the faculty could take this opportunity to get to know their guides.

He rushed off the stage. Obviously a bit puzzled but not looking too concerned, Peter Morgan followed.

When the teachers filed back out of the auditorium, a group of a dozen or so young people was waiting for them. One of them, a very-well-dressed, very-well-groomed young man, announced that teachers whose names began with A–C were in the first group, D–F in the next and so on.

Just then Peter Morgan joined them. "Excuse me, Tanner, but there will be a slight delay." He had a quick, whispered exchange with the boy, then turned to the entire group and invited them to go ahead and have more food and drink. Matt watched as the man poured a large glass of wine for the kid.

Privileged white kids, sure. But underage drinking on school property? This was less and less like what Matt was used to. Neither the man nor the boy seemed to find anything unusual in it. Everyone else seemed not to notice, or else they were simply ignoring it.

A bit curious, a bit startled and a bit at sea, he crossed to where the boy was standing, sipping his wine, quite alone. "Hi. I'm Mr. Larrimer."

The boy had been absorbed in thought, or maybe he was only daydreaming. He quickly collected himself and held out a hand. "Tanner Morgan. Welcome to Washington Academy."

"Thanks. You sound like you've got pride of ownership or something."

"Well . . . my uncle's the CEO."

Matt connected their names. He smiled. "A useful kind of uncle to have."

"I guess so. You're teaching junior history, right?"

"Mm-hmm."

"I'm in one of your classes. Nice to meet you." He smiled at Matt. "Do you have any idea what's causing the delay?"

"They said something about a construction accident."

"Oh—that noise we heard a few minutes ago." Tanner looked down the hall as if he was expecting to see something there.

Matt found the boy a bit odd. "I don't know. That did kind of sound like something was wrong with the machinery, didn't it?"

Tanner's face lit up. "Let's go and see."

"We're supposed to wait here."

"Even better. Come on."

"But Dr. Canning and your uncle—"

"Won't say *boo* to me. Come on."

Matt glanced out the nearest window. Despite the blinding sunshine he could see the red spinning lights of emergency vehicles, reflecting off the neighboring buildings. It got his curiosity up, and against his better judgment he said, "Sure, let's go." He decided he had definitely had too much to drink.

Tanner strode confidently off down the hall; Matt followed, feeling slightly out of his depth. If they got into trouble, he could hardly blame the boy.

They stopped at the main entrance. Outside were police cars and EMS vans, all with red lights spinning. The crews seemed to be heading to the building's side entrance, the one opposite from where the faculty entered.

Tanner put his glass down on the floor and reached into his pocket. "You smoke?"

"Smoking's not permitted in the building."

"I mean weed. You're greener than you look."

"I hope that's supposed to be a compliment. Do me a favor and don't put me in a spot where you have to find out."

The boy put the joint back in his pocket and shrugged it off. "Come on."

Around the next corner they came on a pretty blonde girl making out with a rather good-looking boy who appeared to be two or three years younger. When the girl saw them she jumped away from her partner. "Tanner! What are you doing here?"

He ignored her question and introduced her to Matt. "This is my sister, Alexis."

She smiled and shook Matt's hand. "You teach juniors, right?"

He nodded.

"Well, I'm a senior." And that, apparently, was that.

The boy she'd been kissing made a show of brushing off his clothes. "I'm Charley Morgan." He extended a hand to Matt. "Charlton, actually."

In a stage whisper Tanner explained, "Uncle Peter's son. He's dangerous, Mr. Larrimer. He's the smartest of us, even smarter than his father. He reads things. He knows things. A lot of things. And not the kind of things teachers want their students to know."

It took a moment for the relationship to register with Matt. Cousins. He decided it was time to act like a teacher. "If the two of you are going to do that, you should at least find a more private place. I'd hate to have to report you."

"Report us for what?" Charley adjusted his necktie. "And to who?"

Point taken. But Matt decided he had to assert himself. "You ought to be more discreet. Sooner or later that kind of behavior—"

"There isn't a thing you can do to us."

Charley took Alexis's hand and they walked off together, ignoring Matt completely. For the first time he found himself wondering seriously what he'd gotten himself into. Oh well, not many more students could be related to board members.

Tanner walked off toward the building's side entrance as if none of this had taken place. Matt, feeling more than slightly disconcerted, followed.

Several police officers were standing outside the entrance, looking a bit bored. Inside, there was no one.

Then they heard voices coming up from below. Tanner looked at Matt conspiratorially. "Come on."

"I'm not sure we ought to."

"Don't be a damned pansy."

"Tanner, I—"

The boy headed purposefully down the stairs without waiting for him to finish what he was saying. The voices from below were louder now, and clearer, and they sounded agitated. Matt, curious, followed Tanner downstairs.

At the first landing there was still no one. The voices were coming from somewhere in the basement. Tanner went on, and Matt followed.

At the foot of the steps, a maze of rooms opened off a dimly lit central corridor. In the last of them, under a set of stark, brilliant work lights, they saw it: a corpse lying precisely at the center of an otherwise dark room. Its head had been cut off and set upright on its chest. And the head was studded with six-inch spikes. Blood and fragments of splintered bone covered the floor, the walls, even parts of the ceiling.

Tanner recoiled and pressed himself back against Matt; Matt put a hand on his shoulder.

At the far side of the room a construction worker stood, handcuffed and flanked by two policemen. Like the walls, he was soaked with blood. Not far from him, on the floor, sat a power saw and a nail gun, both red with the gore of the dead man. More cops, in plain clothes but unmistakable, seemed to be combing everything for evidence.

A few feet away stood Canning, Brookhiser, Mrs. Newburg and Peter Morgan, whispering among themselves. None of them seemed upset at the scene; they had the cool of corporate executives dealing with a PR problem. The two crew foremen stood behind them, looking shaken. Morgan noticed Tanner and Matt and crossed to them quickly. Voice hushed, he asked, "Tanner, what the hell are you doing here?"

"I heard voices and wanted to see, that's all."

"And you—aren't you faculty?"

"Yes, sir. Matt Larrimer." He didn't know whether to offer his hand.

"Exactly what are you doing here with my nephew?" His voice suggested it might be any number of things, none of them savory.

But Tanner spoke up. "Mr. Larrimer saw me heading this way and tried to stop me. Don't blame him."

Morgan glared at Matt. "Is that true?"

"Yes, sir." He kept his face a blank.

"Oh." Morgan seemed a bit doubtful. "You're not the first one Tanner's gotten in trouble."

"Am I in trouble, then, sir? I really didn't mean to start my tenure here this way."

"No, don't give it another thought. Just get my precocious nephew out of here and keep him out, will you?"

"Yes, sir."

Unexpectedly, Morgan smiled, and it was warm and ingratiating. "I appreciate it."

Matt got a firm grip on Tanner's shoulder and pushed him toward the stairs. Offering no resistance, Tanner went. When they reached the landing, he pulled free of Matt's grip, turned to face him and grinned. "Uncle Peter likes you. We'll be able to get away with murder here."

"Are you planning to commit any murders?"

The boy laughed. "You never know. It looks like we got here too late."

"I hear they've had a lot of accidents here."

"Yeah. Heads get lopped off all over the place."

Matt hesitated for a beat. "Thanks for covering for me down there."

"It's okay. You owe me now." The kid looked him up and down, paused for a second, then threw his arms around him. "You're mine now." He turned and ran up the stairs, leaving Matt alone on the landing. Peculiar boy. A moment later an EMS crew appeared, carrying a stretcher downstairs. They ignored Matt. When he reached the entrance he saw a news van pull up. There would doubtless be more. Not the kind of publicity the academy needed.

Matt rejoined the faculty gathering on the main floor. A tall, middle-aged blond man with an artificial tan approached him and introduced himself as Bill "Mort" Mortkowski, the History Department chair. (He was also the boys' wrestling and lacrosse coach.) They weren't going to have a formal department meeting. Mort had been in touch with his teachers for weeks by phone and e-mail, and everything was set. But he wanted them to get together and huddle, "to break the ice."

There were six of them. Mort introduced them all, and again the names went by too fast for Matt. He tried to convince himself they didn't look like a central-casting history faculty, but they did. You could smell the dust. But his mind wasn't really on them.

He was still wondering what to make of Tanner Morgan. Several more teachers introduced themselves; several others he had already met chatted briefly. But it had such an unreal air. That corpse in the basement. That odd boy—who Matt had to see and work with every day. He poured himself a large glass of chardonnay and sipped. It was too warm.

Diana saw him through the crowd and came up to him. "And where have you been, Mr. Larrimer?"

He forced a pleasant smile onto his lips. " 'A boy's will is the wind's will'."

" 'And the thoughts of youth are long, long thoughts.' I see you've made the acquaintance of young Master Morgan."

"Yes. You know him, Diana?"

"Slightly. Weird kid, huh?"

"Well, let's say *singular*."

"Let's be honest and say *weird*. His sister's even worse, Matt. But then they've been through a lot. Coming from a family like that . . ." She made a vague gesture as if to suggest Matt knew what she meant, which he didn't.

"His uncle seems nice."

"In some ways. Which way did you have in mind?"

Mrs. Newburg appeared, again seemingly out of nowhere. She announced there would be a bit more of a delay, just an accident, nothing to be concerned over. "We shall have the tours of the building now instead of later. The program will conclude after everyone has been properly oriented."

There was a bit of commotion as everyone sorted themselves into their groups. All of the student guides were well dressed, well groomed and seemingly friendly. Tanner took charge of his group in the most affable way, quite unlike his earlier demeanor.

There were four teachers in the group, including Matt. They introduced themselves and shook hands all around. Tanner worked them like a young politician, smiling, ingratiating himself, even to the ones who wouldn't actually be teaching him. Matt decided CEOness must be genetic.

The classrooms were beautifully designed and appointed, and marvelously equipped. Tanner used the term *state-of-the-art* more than once. The athletic wing gleamed, the labs sparkled, the latest-generation computers were everywhere, and Tanner assured them they'd be replaced as often as necessary to keep Washington, well, state-of-the-art.

Tanner showed them the saber, eighteenth century, probably French. "They told us to make a big deal out of it on our tours. The sports teams are all going to be nick-named the Sabers."

Everyone but Matt seemed duly impressed, and it was easy to feel a rising level of enthusiasm among them for this bright new school.

One member of the group was Jerry Robson, the head of the Biology Department. Late middle age, nondescript, hadn't said much till the tour was nearly over. Then, out of nowhere it seemed, he gushed about it all. He seemed to realize he was being a bit more enthusiastic than was quite comfortable, so he added, "But, you know, I keep hearing these rumors. People say this place is haunted."

The teachers all laughed.

"No, I'm serious. Something about this building hav-ing a sick history. People going mad, murders and mutila-tions. They say this place does awful things to people."

It was a joke, of course; coming from a scientist, it pretty much had to be.

But Tanner didn't crack a smile. Instead he said curtly, "Where there's smoke . . ." He waved vaguely with both hands and glanced at his watch. "It's probably time we re-joined the others."

They were the first group to get back to the reception area outside the auditorium. Matt decided he still needed more wine. As he was pouring it, he found Tanner stand-ing beside him again. For some reason he felt vaguely ashamed, and told the boy, "I don't usually drink this much."

Tanner smiled, a wide grin. "That's all right. You'll get used to it. We all do."

"Why do I get the feeling there's not a lot I can teach you?"

"There is." The boy turned suddenly serious. "There's one thing nobody ever teaches us."

"And what's that?"

"Don't you know, Mr. Larrimer?" He looked around, apparently to make sure no one was listening to them.

"No, Tanner, I don't. What do you want to learn?"

Very softly, almost whispering, Tanner said, "The truth."

It was the last thing Matt expected to hear. "Haven't your other schools taught you the truth?"

"Not about the things that matter, no."

"Maybe they don't know it. Maybe no one does."

"Somebody does. Uncle Peter, Mr. Canning, maybe even you. I want to be let in on it."

"Truth about what, Tanner?"

"About the dead guy in the basement. About how Uncle Peter could stay so calm down there. About . . . I don't know."

"You seemed fairly collected yourself."

"Yeah, well, I've seen a lot."

The other tour groups gradually filtered back. Teachers pressed around the table for more food and wine. Matt noticed some EMS people and police officers at the far end of the hall, in a hushed conference with Peter Morgan. They were nodding, like underlings who know their place and their duty.

Finally, Mrs. Newburg announced they were ready to continue with the orientation, and everyone filed back into the auditorium. Despite all the alcohol, or maybe because of it, Matt couldn't get the image of that dead construction worker out of his mind. He was more shaken by it than he realized at first.

Morgan, Canning and the rest took their places on the stage again. There were more speeches, most of them about corporate identity, "branding" and such rather than about education. Matt tuned them out. The day had seemed longer and was definitely stranger than he'd expected. Mrs. Newburg circulated among the faculty, passing out handbooks on EdEntCo personnel policies and school procedures.

The floor was opened up for questions. People asked routine first-day-of-a-new-job things, about leave policies, that kind of thing. Somebody asked about a union and was cut off. Then a voice in the back of the hall asked about the rumor that the building was haunted. "I keep hearing it all around the neighborhood."

Canning took the question, and he was not amused. "The residents of this neighborhood are not necessarily in tune with our mission. I wouldn't take anything they say or do too seriously."

Someone else called out, "I like the idea of having a school ghost. It's like being in a Harry Potter movie."

There was general laughter. Jerry Robson, the biologist, who was sitting just in front of Matt, added, "Maybe the first play the students do should be a tragedy."

It was all very light and entertaining, it seemed—for everyone but Matt. He decided he'd drunk too much. First time since college, what the hell.

Canning introduced Bishop Grover Hinkle, the board member who, he announced, was also to serve as school chaplain—"a very distinguished spiritual advisor for our student body." Hinkle was to end the orientation with a "nondenominational" prayer. Matt tuned out again. Looking around the hall, he saw that most of his colleagues had too. Why bother with the thing, then? But the meeting ended on that pious note.

Outside, in the hall again, some of the teachers left right away. Others lingered and chatted in small groups. Still others, not many, went back to the food tables yet again. Matt felt a strange compulsion to go back down to the basement. The corpse and the killer must be gone now, but for some reason he needed to see for himself.

He found Canning at his side. "I hope you'll keep what you saw downstairs to yourself, Matt."

"Yes, sir. It seemed like . . . I don't know, it seemed unreal."

"Reality often does. We mustn't let word about what happened spread, not through the faculty and certainly not among the students. Their parents would be concerned."

"You can count on me. I'd be more concerned about the Morgan boy."

"Peter will take care of him."

"Oh." He downed the last of his wine. "The secret's safe, then."

"No one must ever know." Canning's tone made it clear he was giving an order.

"Please, Dr. Canning, don't give it another thought."

For the first time, Canning smiled. "I think you may have a promising career ahead of you here, Matt."

"Thank you, sir. Do we have any idea what happened?"

"No." It didn't seem to be something he wanted to discuss. "The dead man was sleeping with the other one's wife. Or girlfriend. Or . . . who knows? It doesn't really make any difference."

Without another word, Canning left him and joined a group of men who were talking sports loudly. That was that. For the first time Matt noticed that his principal walked with a slight limp.

He decided it was time to go. There was no sign of Tanner, and he was grateful for it. But just as he was leaving he saw Diana with Peter Morgan. They were off in a cor-

ner, out of sight of most of the faculty, talking in a way
that seemed rather intimate. Their body language rein-
forced that impression. He guessed that Diana was sleeping with him. It would certainly explain why she felt
confident enough to make inappropriate wisecracks.

Outside, the sun was blinding and unbearably hot. He
took off his jacket, loosened his tie, took a deep breath of
heavy city air and headed for his car.

At the next corner stood Hap Conklin in his sandwich
sign. Matt walked past him, barely noticing there was
anyone there.

THREE

JONATHAN LAMPL

BY day, the work continued, and EdEntCo paid its nonunion workers overtime to get everything finished by the first day of school. There were more accidents, as there are on any work site, but none were as awful was what happened in the basement on orientation day.

By night, the people in the neighborhood, such of them as had not been driven away by the construction/renovation, avoided the place. There were unpleasant sounds, even disturbing ones, and they knew all too well what it meant. Because Sam's bar had gone out of business, there was not even a convenient place where they could go to forget, or to reach that kind of oblivion where the groans and cries didn't matter. Most of them made up their minds to move, not that they had much choice.

And then . . .

* * *

THE first day of school came, and Alexis was dreading it. It was cool and sunny, quite a lovely late summer day. Heavy storms and lightning would have suited her mood much better.

She drove around the block time after time, watching her soon-to-be classmates and marveling at how deeply ugly the building was. And how artificial most of the girls looked. At least the boys were cute. And at least most of the kids were dressed well.

Her Uncle Peter had given Charley a new car for the daily commute from the northern suburbs. Not to be outdone, her parents had bought cars for her and Tanner, a Mustang for her, a Corvette for him. They were used but looked new. Hers was red; she hated it. Charley only had a Volvo.

There were still a few work crews in evidence. The back of the school was still covered in those plastic sheets, though all the work seemed to have been finished. She wondered in a vague, detached way whether they'd had trouble keeping the construction workers on the job. Her brother had told her about the beheading in the basement. The board's clout had kept it off the news. And there had been other accidents, she knew. Uncle Peter liked to vent to her father. It all reminded her vaguely of Matt's suicide, but there were too many other things to think about for it to bother her much.

The entrance to the student lot was around the corner from the faculty one. Unhappily she pulled in. A young man, African American, twentyish and rather handsome, waved her on. She pulled up beside him, stopped and powered the window down. "Good morning."

"Morning, miss." He felt the rush of air-conditioning from the open window. "Lovely this morning, isn't it? Why the canned air?"

"I like it cool." Who did he think he was?

"There are a few spaces left at the back of the lot." He gestured to show her where. He had a nice smile.

"It's almost full, already? School doesn't start for half an hour."

"I think more students drove than they were expecting." He shrugged.

Damn—she'd have to get here early every day. "Are you going to work here full-time?"

"Part-time. I'm in school. West Penn."

"Can't you find anything better?"

"I wouldn't worry about that, miss."

Attitude. The nerve. "What's your name?"

"What's yours?"

"Never mind." She stepped on the gas and drove to the rear of the lot faster than she should have.

And nearly hit a young man who was walking from his car to the school. She swerved to avoid him and scratched a parked Mercedes.

"Shit." She pulled into the first space she saw. The boy she'd almost hit was clearly shaken. "Are you okay?"

Jumping away from her car, he had bruised his elbow on a parked one. He made a show of rubbing it as he crossed to her. "I think so. Where'd you get your driver's license?"

"Saks. Don't be a smart shit." He had bright red hair and pale white skin; she decided she didn't like the look of him.

"I think a guy who was nearly killed by a ditzy woman driver has the right to be a smart shit." He pointed to the car she'd scraped. "Whose is this?"

"How should I know?"

"Aren't you going to leave a note?"

"I'll tell them in the office. They'll take care of it."

Still rubbing his elbow, he glared at her. "There is such a thing as personal responsibility."

"Why do I get the feeling you're at the wrong school?"

A slow, sarcastic smile spread across his lips. "Tell them in the office. They'll take care of it." He turned his back on her and walked off.

All of Alexis's friends had told her she was lucky to be going to Washington Academy. It was looking less and less that way to her.

She saw Tanner swing his Corvette into the lot and drive—fast—to the back. Passing by, he nearly clipped her. "Dammit, Tanner!"

He pulled into one of three remaining spaces, again much too fast, jumped out of the car and waved to her. "You left early."

"It was the only way to avoid you."

"Good." He turned and ran into the school.

In the next lot, the faculty's, she saw Matt Larrimer; he was just parking. She resented the memory of their first encounter, the previous week. But at least he wouldn't make fun of her. As he got out of his car, she waved. It took Matt a moment to realize who she was. "Oh, Alexis," he shouted. "Good morning."

"Hello!" She sounded happy to see him; he had no idea why. But she walked quickly toward him, stepping over the low concrete barrier that separated the two lots.

He was just getting the last of his things out of his car when she reached him. "How are you, Mr. Larrimer?"

"Just fine." He was quite puzzled by her friendliness. "And you?"

"Okay, I guess. I really don't want to be coming here. I'm not happy about it."

"Tell me the truth—do you know anyone who's really happy?"

"Only morons. Tanner said you're an okay guy."

This was unexpected. "Uh, thanks."

"Thanks for not squealing on Charley and me."

"Don't give it another thought." He didn't want to be having this conversation. There was too much else to think about.

"They caught us anyway. Later on. We were in a broom closet." She laughed. "We were doing a lot more than just kissing."

"I don't want you to be telling me this."

"Oh." She shrugged. "I guess I don't blame you. Anyway, Charley's no prize, but he's there, if you know what I mean."

He did. But he said he didn't.

Eleanor Bettis pulled up in a Buick that looked like it was twenty-five years old. She parked, got out of the car and walked past them with a no-nonsense air. "Good morning, Mr. Larrimer."

"Good morning." He had no clear recollection who she was, and he was afraid he was letting it show. But she walked briskly on, no amenities, no small talk. Matt was grateful.

"You don't remember her, do you?" Alexis was smiling.

"Uh . . . no." He hoped he didn't look as sheepish as he felt.

"Mrs. Bettis. The drama teacher. They say she went to acting school with John Wilkes Booth."

"It doesn't do to talk about the faculty that way. At least not to other faculty."

"In the sunlight, she looks even older than she does indoors."

"Alexis, please."

"What's the matter, can't you take it?"

He wanted her to go away. "You and your brother are slightly bratty, aren't you?"

"Just wait till you get to know us."

He had no intention of getting to know her. With Tanner, he had no choice, but Alexis . . .

Suddenly, just outside the school door, Mrs. Bettis stopped, turned back and quickly rejoined them. "Mr. Larrimer, you teach history, don't you?"

"Yes, I do." He had no idea what to make of her, or of the situation.

"Are you by chance the faculty advisor to the history club?"

"No, Mrs. Bettis."

"Are you advising any other student groups?"

"No. Mrs. Bettis, I—"

"Excellent. I'll need you to help me with a project for the drama club, then."

Matt saw Alexis from the corner of his eye; she was suppressing laughter. "Drama? I'm afraid I'm not really qualified to—"

"We're having a playwriting competition. Students will be writing plays on historical subjects. You can provide valuable guidance for them."

"But Mrs. Bettis, I—"

"You know all extracurricular activities are supposed to be interdisciplinary, don't you?"

"Yes, but—"

"And faculty are expected to do everything possible to encourage that?"

"Yes, but—"

"Excellent. I'll tell the office you're helping. You'll receive an extra paycheck, of course." She made a faintly distasteful face. "And I'll expect you in the Drama Department Saturday at eleven A.M. sharp."

"But I—"

"Good morning." She turned and left, obviously pleased with her recruitment of a colleague.

Flustered, Matt looked at Alexis, who was laughing at him quite openly now.

He didn't want to talk to her any more than he already had. "Look, I have to get inside and open my homeroom. I'll see you around."

"She thinks you're cute."

"She does not."

"And she's right. You are."

"Good-bye, Alexis." He started to walk off before she could say anything more.

To his back, she called, "You're going to like working with us."

Matt felt his heart sink. He stopped walking and looked back at her. "You're in the drama club?"

"I am now."

Splendid. There was nothing to do but avoid her. "Good morning, Alexis." He quickly went inside.

The student lot was quite full now. Alexis wondered where the kids who came late would leave their cars. Were the streets safe? She glanced at her watch. Still twenty-five minutes till classes started. There was no way she was going in until she had to. She glanced back at the spot where she'd left her car. That parking-lot attendant was watching her, grinning. Something else to tell them about in the office.

Slowly she walked around the school building, taking it in, in all its architectural ugliness, and alternately checking out what she could see of the neighborhood. Nothing she saw struck her as the least bit appealing, or even interesting. All the school building needed was gargoyles and it would have been a complete horror.

Jumonville Street was lined with cars. Here and there small groups of students collected and chatted. On appearance, none of them seemed as unhappy as she felt. An old black man wearing some kind of sandwich board was going from one group to another, and they were doing their best to ignore him.

Across the street, on the corner, was a convenience store. The sign said it was called Sam's. Maybe a candy bar . . .

There were a dozen or so other students in the store, most of them talking together in a group. But the store was virtually empty of stock; there were lots of racks for merchandise—signs indicated MAGAZINES, COSMETICS, FIRST AID and so on—but most of them held nothing. Fortunately, there were candy bars. She got a Baby Ruth and walked to the register.

"Morning, miss." The cashier was a middle-aged black guy. "This be all?"

"Yes. Are you going out of business or something?"

"I already have."

She looked around. "What are you talking about?"

"This was my bar, till your school moved into the neighborhood. There's a law says no saloons near schools. I had to close last week. And most of my stock's late, so I'm losing money."

"That's too bad. Between the unhappy students and the miserable faculty, you would have cleaned up." She put a dollar on the counter.

He rang up the sale and gave her her change. "They keep telling us we should be happy the school's here. Lots of history here, miss. All being swept away. The building that used to be where your school sits was part of the Underground Railroad. *You* don't sound too happy."

" 'They' keep telling you? Who are they?"

"EdEntCo. Their lawyers haven't exactly made a good impression here. Putting people out of business. All those fine old buildings they leveled so you all would have a place to park. They actually told me I should be glad to be losing my bar."

"Well, I guess this is a bit more respectable."

"I liked being a saloon owner. I always liked it."

"Oh." She decided she didn't want a candy bar after all. But she took her change and put it and the Baby Ruth in her pocket. "I'm sorry, I guess. I thought we'd be more welcome here."

"You always do."

This wasn't exactly the kind of encounter Alexis wanted on her first morning. Her mood was unpleasant enough already. She left the store without saying anything else. Outside, the sun was beginning to warm the morning air. She stood at the edge of the sidewalk, fingered the candy bar in her pocket and decided to eat it after all. What the hell.

"That's not exactly a healthy breakfast, miss." It was the old guy with the sandwich sign. He had spotted her standing alone at the curb and was making straight for her. She didn't quite know whether to be alarmed. But she waited for him to reach her. "Morning, miss."

"Good morning." She tried to make her voice cold; but he was the first one all morning to show her the least shred of friendliness. She bit forcefully into her candy bar. It was fairly obvious he was selling something, but she didn't care.

"Like to buy a fortune?"

"A what?"

"A fortune. You know."

"I'm afraid I don't believe in that kind of thing."

"Nobody does. Till it comes true."

She looked him up and down. Deep black skin, bright grey hair, piercing eyes. For an old man, his posture was bolt upright. He smiled, and she saw there were teeth missing. "Your principal had the chance to buy one, and I'll bet now he wishes he had."

"Dr. Canning?"

"Dr. D. Michael Canning." He laughed; she wasn't sure what was funny. "He'll regret it, sure as anything."

She scanned his board. It was covered with little pamphlets called "dream books" and "mystical guides." "Where are your fortunes, then?"

He held out a punchboard. "Right here. You pick a number and I punch it out for you. It's on a little slip of paper, you know? My fortunes are always true."

"Sure they are." She looked around self-consciously. What would the other students think if they saw her talking to him? "How much?"

"One dollar, miss."

"A dollar? That's pretty steep for a slip of paper."

"It's not steep for the truth, though, is it?"

For the most fleeting instant she saw her brother Matt and felt his blood all over her. Without quite realizing it, she wrapped her arms around herself.

"My name's Hap." Still grinning, he held out a hand to her.

"I'm Alexis." Uncertainly, she shook it.

Hap watched her. "Alexis, then. Pleased to meet you. You need the truth, miss. More than anybody I've seen here today."

"What I need is a hit of something."

"Try my fortunes. They're strong stuff."

Again she found herself looking around. The other students were paying her no attention. "I don't want to be coming here. Can your fortune tell me when I'll get to go back to Fox Chapel High?"

"Fox Chapel, is it? Nice school, I hear. Very ritzy."

"All my friends are there. People there are friendly."

"Miss, this neighborhood is the friendliest place I know. You just have to make the effort."

That college boy from the parking lot was still watching her. Or rather, watching the two of them, now. "Look at him." She pointed. "Look at how rude he's being."

"He just thinks you're pretty, that's all."

"I think I'm a bit afraid of him. I'll have to tell them how he's watching me."

"Cal's a good boy. No need to be afraid of him."

"Cal? You know him?"

"He's my great-grandnephew. First one to go to college, you know. Whole family's proud of him. He's going to be an actor someday. He lives with me. Up there." He pointed to the apartment building up on the hillside above Fifth Avenue.

"Well, I wish he'd stop staring."

"Buy a fortune. Maybe he's in it."

She looked at Cal again. He was watching her and smiling. Then she turned back to Hap. "Oh, all right." She fished a bill out of her pocket and handed it to him. "It better be good, though."

"This is a five, miss."

"I don't care, keep it. Give me my fortune."

He held up his punchboard. "Pick a number."

She pointed to one. Hap used the tip of a ballpoint to push it through, and the fortune slipped out the back. Alexis took it quickly, unrolled it and read it out loud. "'Your past is your future. Everyone's past is everyone's future. There is no way to escape it.'" She gaped at Hap.

He whistled softly. "That one's serious. Usually they're little rhymes."

"What the hell's it supposed to mean?"

"Just what it says, I imagine."

"Well, I don't like the sound of it." She crumpled it and tossed it into the gutter.

"I'm sorry, miss."

"I told you, my name's Alexis."

"Then I'm sorry, Alexis."

Uncomfortable with what they were talking about, she paused and looked around. "There's nobody on the street but us schoolkids. Where's everyone from the neighborhood?"

"Most have moved away. Only a few of us left." Slowly, making each syllable a harsh word, he added, "Ed. Ent. Co. I can't tell you how we all miss Sam's bar. Best place this neighborhood ever had. He kept the dealers out."

"Are there dealers around here?" She couldn't hide her interest.

"EdEntCo wouldn't like me telling you about that, miss."

"Why didn't Sam just move his bar to another block?"

Unexpectedly, Hap laughed at her. "You think this big rich company was going to pay for him to do that? Buy him another building? Hell, he only has this one 'cause he won the lottery." Pointedly, he added, "With a lucky number he bought from me."

"Well, it doesn't look like it turned out so lucky after all, does it?"

He smiled and shrugged. "Take your next fortune."

Uncertainly, she pointed to another number, and Hap punched it out and handed her the slip.

"You're right, Hap. This one's a poem. Not that it makes any more sense than the first one."

"What's it say?"

She read:

> *Burn faces.*
> *Faces burn.*
> *Dark places.*
> *Never learn.*

Just as she had the first one, she crumpled it. "Gibberish."

"Hold onto it," Hap said. "Besides, we'd appreciate it if you wouldn't litter in our neighborhood." He added, with emphasis, "On top of everything else."

Self-consciously, she put the crumpled fortune into her pocket.

It was nearly time for classes to begin. The rest of the students came out of Sam's in a group and crossed quickly to the school. Alexis, sounding more than a bit uncertain about it, told Hap it was nice meeting him and followed them.

"You have three more fortunes coming, Alexis," Hap called after her. "Don't you want them?"

"Another time. Let's say you owe me three, okay?"

She wished he'd been selling weed. Or something, anything to help her make it through the day. Why hadn't she brought something?

MATT checked in at the office, where he got the usual icy reception from Mrs. Newburg. Several dozen students were there, pressing against the counter, trying to get various problems solved; and there was a gaggle of teachers, all of them turning in their employee handbook vouchers. Newburg and her staff looked properly put-upon. How dare these ordinary people expect attention from the ones whose job was running the school?

Turning in his own handbook, he bumped into another teacher, a dark-haired woman in a plain white blouse and black skirt.

"Excuse me."

"That's okay." She smiled; she was ten years older than him. "You're Matt . . . Matt . . . ?"

"Larrimer."

"And you teach social studies, right?"

"History."

"Oh." She laughed. "I'm Carolyn Lisniecki. Chemistry."

"Nice to meet you. I remember seeing you at orientation last week."

"From the attention you were paying to that wine, I'm surprised you remember much of anything."

He felt himself blushing, and she laughed again.

Diana was there, chatting with Canning in a corner. When Canning saw Matt, he smiled, waved and then headed quickly into his inner office. Matt noticed that his limp was worse than it had been during orientation.

Diana looked like hell, as if she hadn't slept for days. Matt waved a big cheery hello, and she walked over to him and Carolyn. She glared at Matt. "You're not by any chance a morning person, are you?"

"Nope. It's just because it's the first day. Have you two met?"

Diana nodded. "It's Carolyn, isn't it?"

Carolyn nodded and glanced at her watch. "Listen, I have to get moving. I'll be orienting all the chem classes in the lab all week. Drilling them in the procedures—you know the kind of thing.

Matt didn't, but he nodded as if he did. Carolyn left them, and he turned back to Diana. "How was your week?"

"Lousy." She lowered her voice to a confidential whisper. "I spent most of it with Pete Morgan."

"I won't spread it around."

"Neither did he. That's the problem."

"Oh."

At the counter, among the dozen or so students, there was a young man with bright red hair; he looked pale and shaken and was rubbing his right elbow. When he finally managed to get Mrs. Newburg's attention, he explained loudly and angrily that he had nearly been hit by another student's car in the parking lot.

"Do you know who he was?" Mrs. Newburg turned even more unfriendly than usual. This was clearly not something she wanted to deal with.

"*She.* I don't know her name. But I got her license number." He handed Newburg a slip of paper.

She glanced at it, scowled and said nothing.

"You can find out who she is, right? We did all have to register our numbers with you."

"Yes, of course."

The boy was in pain; it was more and more obvious. Matt decided to step between them. "Shouldn't you be down at the nurse's office?"

"I wanted to report that girl first."

"It looks like that's really hurting you. Go and get it looked at. What's your name?"

"Michael Monticelli."

The name registered. He was one of a handful of students invited to Washington on a sports scholarship. "I'm Mr. Larrimer. You're in my third period."

Diana put a hand on Matt's shoulder. "If you're going to play nurse, I'm heading off to my homeroom. See you later."

But he was focused on the boy. "Go down to the

nurse's office now. I'm sure Mrs. Newburg will see that everything's taken care of. And she'll let your homeroom teacher know you'll be late." He turned to her and added pointedly, "Won't you, Mrs. Newburg?"

She stiffened. "Yes. Of course."

Michael left. Mrs. Newburg turned her back on Matt; he crossed the office to check his mailbox and then headed to his homeroom, again wondering how long it would take the students to start calling her by the obvious nickname. There was just time to get a cup of coffee in the faculty lounge. Then work.

His room was on the second floor, at the east end of the building, facing the parking lot. He unlocked the door, switched on the lights and sat at his desk. Plastic sheeting hung outside the windows; nevertheless, brilliant sunlight came in. When he started to review his class lists, he found it was blinding him. He crossed the room and adjusted the miniblinds, which were encased between two panels of glass.

There were fifteen students in his homeroom class; none of them had shown up yet. The only one on the list whose name he recognized was Tanner Morgan.

Just then Mort Mortkowski stuck his head in the door. "Morning, Matt."

"Mort. Hi."

"Getting settled in?"

"I guess. I'm sure I've forgotten something. I always do, first day."

"Everybody does. I just thought I'd check with you and make sure you have everything you need here."

"I think so, sure."

"Classroom all equipped? Plenty of chalk?"

"Yep."

"All the forms and other paperwork?"

"I'm fine, Mort. Thanks for checking."

That seemed to be that. But Mort lingered in the doorway, a bit awkwardly. "I got here early and spent some time checking around the neighborhood."

Matt got his lesson plans out of his briefcase and arranged them on the desk. "Does the neighborhood need checking too?"

"You know. *Checking*" He seemed to think the word explained something more than the obvious, which it didn't.

"I haven't really had time to. Is there anything interesting?"

"Not a thing. It's worse than I expected. Bums, con artists, drug dealers. And they're not even dealing any useful drugs. I don't suppose . . . you don't have any contacts around here, do you?"

Odd question. "Contacts?"

"You know."

"No, Mort." He laughed and said pointedly, "I don't."

"I'm one of the coaches."

Matt was lost. "Yes? And?"

"Don't be dense, Matt."

Matt shrugged. "I can't help it. I was born like this. Would you mind telling me what the devil you're talking about?"

"West Penn University's just a half mile up the avenue." Mort lowered his voice to a confidential whisper. "We can probably get what we need there. Their athletic department . . . somebody there's bound to . . ." He looked around. "But we—the coaches, I mean—we were kind of hoping we could get stuff cheaper around here."

"Um . . . stuff?"

"Stop playing dumb. We have to do what we have to

do. After all, sports is an important part of any scholastic program. Sports builds character."

"Oh, sure."

Just at that moment a pair of students showed up, excused themselves as they passed Mort, and took seats at the rear of the classroom. Matt couldn't have been more grateful to see them.

But Mort walked over to his desk and asked in a low voice, "I don't suppose you have a source, do you?"

Oh. Steroids. Matt shook his head and smiled. "I'm just a humble history teacher."

"Even so, you might—"

"No, Mort, I'm afraid I really can't help you there." He shuffled a few of the papers on his desk to indicate that Mort was keeping him away from them. "I've never been the athletic type, so I've never needed anything like that."

"You should be. Sports really does build character." Mort waved at him cheerily and headed for the door. "We'll make do, somehow."

The room was getting a bit stuffy and warm. Matt realized he couldn't open the windows; they were all locked. And only the maintenance staff and the administrators had keys. He'd have to wait for the ventilation system to clean the air. He hoped it would.

More students filtered in by ones and twos. He picked out types: nerds, jocks, smart kids, dumb kids. Some of them smiled, said good morning, introduced themselves. Others sat quietly, even sullenly. One or two of them closed their eyes and dozed, which was okay with Matt. Tanner Morgan was the last one to arrive. He smiled, saluted Matt with a fingertip and sat in the last available chair. And promptly closed his eyes. Matt was reasonably sure he was stoned.

A minute later the morning bell rang, or rather, what

passed for a bell at Washington—it was the first four notes of Beethoven's Fifth, repeated half a dozen times over the PA system. Canning's voice came on, announcing there would be a student assembly promptly at eight forty-five; everyone was required to attend this orientation. Further announcements would be made there. Homeroom teachers should be certain to complete roll call before their students left for the auditorium.

Inevitably, inescapably, school had begun. Matt felt his previous enthusiasm disappearing, and he wasn't at all certain why. New school, new students, new career. He should have felt . . . well, he should have felt better about it all than he did. Why did the damned windows have to be locked?

THERE wasn't much reason to expect anyone to pay any attention to the assembly, and not many people did. Bishop Hinkle opened with what he called an invocation, a prayer for the school's success both academically and at sports. Sports, he reminded everyone in the hall, builds character. Matt wondered how many times he was going to hear that corny nonsense repeated.

Canning read a list of rules and regulations. Mrs. Newburg, who was careful to explain to the students that she was an *executive* secretary, detailed policies for absence and tardiness. Nick Brookhiser explained security regulations. The students all knew the rules would be bent for some of them, like the jocks, and not others. Why listen?

Matt paced up and down a side aisle during all this, watching the kids, trying to get their range. He saw boys groping girls, girls groping boys, girls groping girls, boys groping boys. He saw pills changing hands and wondered if Mort Mortkowski had tried buying his drugs from any of the kids.

A member of the board made a speech that was mostly corporate cheerleading; it made the students sound like employees, expected to be dutiful to EdEntCo.

Then Bishop Hinkle led the students in still another prayer, the Lord's Prayer this time, which seemed to bewilder a lot of them. Classes would be abbreviated today, to accommodate the time taken up by the assembly. Canning made one last comment, telling the student body that Beethoven's Fifth had been chosen because it signaled victory. Matt knew that Beethoven himself had said it signaled fate, inexorable fate. But there didn't seem much point in saying so.

THE first day of class went reasonably well, it seemed to Matt. His students were, as he put it to himself, "independent-minded," which meant it was hard to impose and maintain order. These were young people used to having things their way. It was an interesting challenge.

There was also the fact that a lot of them seemed to be stoned. Or drunk. Or . . . whatever. Packets of this and that changed hands; no one made much of an attempt to hide it, at least not from Matt. He wasn't quite certain what to do about it. Reporting the offenders hardly seemed to have any point; there were too many of them. One day after class he mentioned it to Tanner Morgan. Tanner's response was to laugh at him. "Why worry about it? Nobody else does."

"Nobody?"

"Nobody. What did you do about all the drugs in the public school where you taught?"

"Point taken." Matt sighed. "But you're all bright kids—well, most of you are—from good families. Wealthy, powerful families. Shouldn't I expect better of you?"

"Be serious."

"I am serious, Tanner. I—"

"What do you think 'good families' with money do? You think the Kennedys deny themselves anything they want? You think the Bushes deny themselves anything when they need to feel better? So why should we?" A smile spread across his face. "I've got some Maui. You want a hit?"

"No, thanks." So much for chemical warfare.

But there were also a lot of eager, attentive students. And to his surprise, that included a lot of the ones who were altering themselves chemically. He got the impression pretty quickly that that was not so much because they cared about world history or even American history, but because they understood it might be useful to them in their careers. Tanner said that his father wanted him to have a career in politics. "You know how it impresses voters when you can say something about the Founding Fathers?"

Not a bad motive. So Matt imagined. Or tried to imagine.

Chatter in the faculty lounge during his free periods left him thinking everyone else seemed to see the school and the student body the way he did, or the way Tanner thought he should. He even saw a few teachers pop pills themselves.

NOW and then there were howls. Ear-piercing, blood-curdling cries that echoed through the corridors and classrooms.

The first few times, everyone and everything stopped.

Teachers walked out into the halls and looked up and down, baffled, disturbed, trying to sense where the awful sounds were coming from. A few kids, mostly girls, became more and more visibly agitated each time it happened. Students lost their cool, superior airs and looked to their teachers for explanation, but there were none forthcoming.

The first time it happened was at the end of Matt's third-period American history class. They heard desperate, agonized wailing, the sound of a man dying or being tortured. It seemed to penetrate everything and everyone, cutting into people's guts and shattering their composure. It took Matt a moment to shake off its effect, and just then the tones of Beethoven's Fifth came through the room's loudspeaker, and class ended.

The kids filed out, silently for once, many of them clearly shaken. Matt sat down at his desk and closed his eyes. There were five minutes till fourth period began.

When he opened his eyes again, Tanner was standing beside his desk, his palm outstretched. There were two pills in it. He smiled. "Here, Mr. Larrimer. It looks like you need them."

"What are they?"

"Ecstasy."

"No, thanks."

He pushed them toward Matt. "Go ahead. You'll feel better."

"I don't do drugs, Tanner, and neither should you."

"You'll like it. You'll love everyone. Even that poor guy who's screaming, whoever he is. I do. I figure it must be one of the janitors or something, huh?"

Matt stood up. "Thank you for the thought, Tanner, but no."

"Go on."

"Do you want me to report this?"

"To my Uncle Peter? Go ahead. You ought to see all the stuff he has at his place. He lets me take my dates there, so my parents won't know, and I can use anything—"

"Tanner, will you go?"

"Okay, okay." Partly annoyed, partly genuinely puzzled, Tanner headed off to his next class.

Matt was left wondering to himself, "I can handle the students. Why am I afraid I can't handle the school?"

HE was not the only one so completely unsettled by those sounds. D. Michael Canning kept a bottle of aged bourbon in his desk. The second time the cries reverberated through the halls, he found himself reaching for it. They could not be coming from the basement, he told himself; they could not, they could not, they could not. They were not human sounds, those anguished cries; they couldn't be. The sounds were structural. Or there was some underground construction someplace nearby, and the sounds were carrying. Or . . . or . . . he told himself a dozen things and believed none of them.

But the headless corpse in the basement . . . the cries from the lowest part of the building . . . No, they couldn't be connected. He had buried it. He had hidden it behind a wall. It was at rest. It had to be. How could it be crying? There is no such thing as a ghost. The dead can not affect the living. There is no such thing as a ghost, damn it. There is no such thing. . . .

But each time the ghastly keening echoed through the school, he filled his glass just a bit higher.

* * *

AND the first week drew to a close. Friday afternoon, another beautiful day, and no one—not the students, not the faculty—had any interest in schoolwork. Summer would be gone soon enough.

The boys in gym class were swimming, all but one kid who couldn't. He was being teased and bullied. The coach pretended not to see.

Bill Cullen's general science class was on the school roof, where a small observatory had been built. The image of the sun was being projected onto a bright white screen. Despite the careful warnings the students had been given, one girl reached out and passed a finger through the beam of light from the telescope. She cried out as the concentrated heat and light seared her flesh. For a moment everyone stood staring as her finger smoked. She cried hysterically. Cullen sent her immediately to the school nurse's office, with another student accompanying her to make sure she got there okay. No one else got near the beam. At least they learned that much, the teacher told himself.

Matt was teaching his last American history class of the week—the Massachusetts Bay Company, hiring the Puritans to staff its new colony. He was as restless as his students, but he did his best to make the lesson lively and interesting. Just down the hall, Diana was reading a Shakespearean sonnet to a class of bored students; their attention picked up when she pointed out it was addressed to another man. Jerry Robson was finishing his last introductory lecture to an advanced biology class.

And in the Chemistry Lab, Carolyn Lisniecki was orienting the last of her new classes in laboratory procedures and safety. Inevitably, some of the students were paying attention and others were doing anything but. The day was so beautiful, some of them had their full attention on the windows and the sunny world outside. Tanner Morgan, who was convinced he would never need to know chemistry for anything in his life, was doodling in his notebook. His doodles were caricatures of D. Michael Canning, his Uncle Peter, Mrs. Newburg and a number of faculty members; no one but Tanner would have recognized them, and he knew it and didn't care.

Mike Monticelli was in the class too, trying glumly to concentrate. His elbow had a hairline fracture and was heavily bandaged; he had been told not to play sports for at least two months. His father, unhappy, had beaten him, and his face was badly bruised. He was attending Washington on a sports scholarship—he wrestled and was a teenage judo champ. What would happen to his scholarship if his elbow didn't heal right? Chemistry seemed beside the point.

A wail began. It did not get terribly loud, and it did not last very long, not like the earlier ones. But everyone in the lab tensed. Carolyn fell silent for a moment. Students looked from her to one another: Why was this happening in their school?

And it passed. Carolyn went on with the lesson. Slowly, everyone relaxed.

No, not quite everyone relaxed. In the back of the lab, alone in the last row of benches, sat a boy named Jonathan Lampl. He was tall, thin, pale; he had collar-length black hair, very thick. He wanted to go out for the baseball team next spring and he had signed up for the school chorus. Beside him on the table sat a well-thumbed copy of the *Communist Manifesto* and a DVD of *The Passion of the Christ*. His father was a lawyer, a cousin of Bishop Hinkle, and his mother an eye surgeon. He never said or did much. No one, including Carolyn, had paid him much attention.

Unlike the others, he did not respond to the horrible sound. But a few minutes after it had passed, he got a wild look in his eye and stared frantically around the lab at his classmates and teacher. He took a ballpoint out of his pocket and began chewing on the end of it. Then a moment later he got slowly to his feet, took a step backward and pressed his body against the wall, like a caged animal.

Everyone else was watching Carolyn, or looking out the windows at the sunny afternoon, or simply daydreaming. She was struggling with an epidiascope that wouldn't work properly. Jonathan walked, quite unobtrusively, to a shelf where chemicals were stored. Hydrochloric acid, sulfuric acid, nitric acid . . . He got two large beakers and filled each one halfway with hydrochloric, then topped them off with nitric. This mixture, he knew, was called aqua regia, the mystical acid that could dissolve even gold.

Slowly, calmly, carrying the beakers behind his back, he walked to the front of the room. Quite casually, almost offhandedly, he threw one beaker into Carolyn Lisniecki's face. Her flesh began to steam almost at once. She cried out in pain, and it was almost as horrible a sound as the wail that had filled the building earlier. The students screamed and ran for the door. One of them knocked over a shelf holding more chemicals. A jar containing potassium, carefully suspended in liquid, shattered on the floor, and ignited a small fire.

Mike Monticelli scrambled to get the fire extinguisher off the wall. He stumbled and fell, hurting his elbow again. Jonathan Lampl turned, stood over him and poured the acid from the second beaker straight down toward his face. Mike ducked to one side, and Lampl kicked him viciously in the head. The acid splashed, burning Mike. He managed to trip Lampl with his legs. The boy fell on top of him, crying out, and Mike began punching him violently with his good arm.

In a moment the panic spread. Teachers from the surrounding science labs quickly imposed order on the horrified students. One put an arm around Carolyn. A student pulled the fire alarm. Jerry Robson ran from the Biology Lab straight into Carolyn's lab and got a headlock on the acid-thrower. Mike struggled to his feet. His arm was exploding with pain; he was swaying unsteadily on his feet, and he had to fight back tears. A student, a tall, athletic boy named Peter Dominic, got the extinguisher and put out the fire; it had not spread much.

Since it was still the first week of school, there had not been a fire drill yet. Some students poured out of their classrooms into the hall and made for the exits. Others remained calmly at their desks while their teachers tried to find out what was happening. Several students from the Chemistry Lab ran to the office and told Mrs. Newburg what was happening. "Call an ambulance Mrs. Newburg!" By the time she told D. Michael Canning and he got to the science wing to see for himself, Carolyn Lisniecki's face was gone.

IN no time, the whole school knew something was wrong. Mrs. Newburg called Nick Brookhiser's office at once, and his men went into action. Three of them headed to the chem lab, where they took charge of Jonathan Lampl. The rest locked down the school.

Canning made an announcement on the PA system that there had been an accident in the chem lab; everything was under control and there was no more danger. Classes were suspended as of that moment, but students and teachers were told to stay in their rooms till it was certain the emergency had passed. No one was permitted to leave, not for any reason at all.

Ambulances were called for Carolyn Lisniecki and Mike Monticelli. Carolyn had not stopped screaming and, not surprisingly, no one had been able to calm her down. And no one from the school had been able to reach her husband. Mike had felt more and more dizzy; he finally passed out.

A news crew arrived before the police and the first ambulance. One of the students—or one of the teachers?—must have called them on a cell phone. Brookhiser's men kept them away from the building and the student body, and Canning saw to it that the faculty was instructed not to cooperate with them. The reporters shot footage from the opposite sidewalk as the emergency vehicles finally arrived. And more reporters came, newspaper people and another TV crew.

Still screaming and crying, Carolyn was loaded into the ambulance. Canning wished she'd pass into unconsciousness, but for some reason she stayed quite awake. A man from one of Brookhiser's security teams was assigned to ride to the hospital with her. "And stay with her," Nick instructed him. "Don't let her tell them anything that might hurt EdEntCo."

Finally the student body was permitted to leave. Most of them lingered, talking among themselves. Gossip about what had happened spread; Canning's story about an accident had fooled no one. The reporters across the street eyed them; they had to get at least one student on record for their stories. In the meantime they interviewed

Hap Conklin, who was on the nearest corner, watching it all. He kept telling them he didn't know what happened; they pressed as if they didn't believe him.

After a time the students began heading for their cars or, in a few cases, the nearest bus stops. The reporters and photographers following them were approached by Brookhiser's men who handed out copies of an official statement EdEntCo's PR department had hastily prepared: unfortunate accident in one of the labs; nothing more to it than that. They'd have time to come up with something more convincing later.

In the middle of all the confusion, or perhaps because of it, no one noticed that Canning's antique sword had been removed from its case. The glass was shattered, and the sword lay on the floor. And the portrait of George Washington had been slashed to ribbons. None of this was found till the next morning.

AN hour later, there were no students left in the building but Alexis and Tanner. When they had seen each other in the hall just before dismissal, Tanner had whispered, "I saw it."

"What happened?"

"I'll tell you later." He looked around conspiratorially. "In the library. Nobody goes there after school."

They met half an hour later, huddled in the library stacks, and compared notes about what they had heard and seen. Tanner described Lampl's actions. "I don't think anyone really knew him."

"I've never even heard of him." Alexis was offhand. "He can't have been anybody. Who got him?"

"Some kid I don't know. A jock."

She shrugged. "Nobodies. This wouldn't have happened at Fox Chapel."

"You mean it would have been a well-known student there?"

"You know what I mean." Even though they were alone, she looked around and lowered her voice. "There's something wrong here. Those screams we hear."

"Canning says they're just something normal, like the building settling after all the renovation."

"Buildings don't cry when they settle."

"This one does, Lex." He ran his eye down a row of books. History. Why would anyone read them?

"That old black guy outside told me this used to be part of the Underground Railroad. I'll bet there must be lots of hidden places underneath the building." Mentioning Hap reminded her of something else. She wasn't sure she should mention it, but . . . "Tanner, look." Alexis found the second fortune Hap had sold her in her pocket and showed it to Tanner.

He read it. "This doesn't make sense."

"It's about what happened today. That old black guy knew. *Knows*. He knows there's something wrong here."

"No." He couldn't process the idea. "This is crazy."

"Tanner, read it. It's about what happened today. That old guy—he says his name's Hap—he knows there's something wrong here."

"Don't be silly." He hesitated and then reread the slip of paper in his hand. "You bought this from him?"

"Yeah." She looked a bit embarrassed. "And I have three more coming."

"What?"

She explained about the five dollars she'd given Hap. "I think . . . I think I'm afraid to get them, now."

"Don't be silly. What else does he sell?"

"Lucky numbers and horoscopes and stuff like that."

"And what else?"

She knew what he was asking. "No. He doesn't deal. I asked him."

"Too bad. I saw him selling stuff to some other kids and I thought . . . you know, when things get bad. When my usual suppliers tap out."

She shook her head. "He doesn't. I asked."

"Well, somebody around here must. We're in the god-damned ghetto. Let's get out of here."

Their cars were the last ones left in the student lot. There was no attendant. Alexis was grateful she didn't have to deal with Cal again, but there should have been someone watching their cars.

Tanner shaded his eyes against the sun and looked out to Jumonville Street. "No sign of him. I'll bet Brookhiser's guys chased him away."

"He said he goes to West Penn. I guess he just works mornings."

"I meant the old guy. I wouldn't mind buying a fortune from him myself."

"Tanner, don't. I think I'm a bit scared of all this."

He smirked. " 'Tanner, I'm scared.' He'd probably just laugh at you and tell you you're being silly."

"He says his fortunes always come true."

"Baloney."

"And you said you'd seem him selling them to other kids?"

Tanner nodded and got his keys out of his pocket. "And I'm going to buy one too."

"I wish you wouldn't. I don't even want my other three."

"You're such a girl."

She made a playful swipe at him but he ducked and

laughed. "All I want him to sell me is the address of a good pusher."

They got into their cars. Tanner gunned his engine and sped out of the lot. Alexis waited a few minutes, then circled the block slowly a few times, hoping she'd see Hap. She didn't.

FOUR

MIKE MONTICELLI

SATURDAY morning. Early; still dark. The air was thick and humid, and a dense fog had settled over Pittsburgh. Streetlights were still on, and the fog diffused their sickly yellow glow.

D. Michael Canning drove up to Washington Academy, yawning and wishing he could be home in bed. But he hadn't slept all night. The previous day's events . . .

Inevitably, the media had gotten hold of the story. NEW PRESTIGE SCHOOL OPENS TO HORROR, read the headline. TEACHER MUTILATED BY STUDENT. The broadcast news was even worse. The PR Department had drafted a second press release, and he had dutifully handed it out: "disturbed student . . . isolated incident . . . steps being taken to ensure this will never happen again." In a week they'd have forgotten all about it. But in the meantime . . .

There were concerned or angry parents to deal with.

And of course there was the board. But he'd tell them the same thing: There's a bad apple in every barrel. This was strictly an isolated incident; it could have happened anywhere. No parents had requested their children be taken out of Washington; the bottom line was safe, the students would get past it quickly and the story would blow over soon enough.

There was a chain across the entrance to the faculty parking lot. He got out of his car to open the lock, then realized he didn't have a key for it. He honked his horn loudly and repeatedly, hoping it would attract one of the maintenance people. No one came. He'd have to park on the street.

The day was just beginning to lighten; the fog was going from dark to light grey. There were no other cars on Jumonville. He parked directly in front of the school's main entrance, got out, looked around and yawned again.

Coffee would be wonderful; he should have had a cup before he left home. It was Mrs. Newburg's job to brew it for him; she wasn't due in yet. But there were lights on at Sam's.

The store's door was locked. Canning took the handle and rattled it. Inside he could see Sam, on his knees, stocking shelves. He knocked. Sam looked up and recognized him. A few seconds later he was at the door. "Dr. Manning."

"Canning." He was too sleepy to be annoyed. "Good morning, Sam."

"What are you doing here?"

The question was unexpected. "I'm going to work. What did you think?"

"It's Saturday."

"EdEntCo never sleeps."

"That's what some of us were afraid of." He smiled to show it wasn't a joke.

But Canning seemed not to realize what Sam had said. "There's no school on Saturday, but the building will be open for the sports teams and extracurricular activities."

"Oh." Sam looked over his shoulder at the spot where he'd been working, plainly wanting to get back to it. "Well, what can I do for you?"

"I was hoping some coffee . . ."

"The coffee maker's not on. I didn't think I'd be doing any business this morning."

"People will be getting here soon." He checked his watch. It was six thirty. The coaches and athletes would be arriving soon enough. He wasn't sure what other groups might be scheduled. And Mrs. Newburg would be coming in to oversee it all.

"So I might earn a bit of money on Saturdays, too?"

"A bit." Canning smiled. Sam wasn't sure why.

"Lucky me."

He walked farther into the store and looked around. "You've done a nice job here, Sam. This is going to be a nice little store when you get it all fixed up."

"Thanks."

"So there's no coffee, then?"

"'Fraid not. Look, I've got to get my shelves stocked, okay?"

"You've got the whole weekend."

"Church tomorrow. Aren't you a Christian?"

Canning frowned. Asking about someone's religion. "Yes, of course I am. My wife and I are High Church Anglican."

"Good for you. Look, do you mind if I get back to work?"

"Oh. Of course. So there's no chance you might . . . I mean, just one cup, for me?"

"Sorry."

It was clear Canning wasn't used to being treated like this. "Well. I'll just wait till my secretary gets in, then."

"She that mean-looking old bat?"

"Mrs. Newburg is invaluable. She keeps the school running."

"So she's the one I complain to when your rich students rip off candy bars?"

It was more and more clear to Canning that this was not the friendly reception he had expected. "Listen, Sam, there's really no reason for that attitude. Our students—"

"Your students have already stolen nearly twenty dollars' worth of stuff."

"Oh."

"I had my bar for twenty years and never had this kind of thing happen. I'm not likely to make much money on this place as it is. I don't suppose EdEntCo would pay to install security cameras?"

"Our students are not criminals."

"Oh?" Sam walked to the counter. He held up a newspaper, pointed to the headline and smiled sardonically.

Canning was not amused. "What happened yesterday was an isolated incident."

Sam laughed, loud and hard. "Look, do you want to buy anything?"

"If there's no coffee, no, I don't."

"I've got to get back to work, then."

Canning, more than mildly annoyed at Sam's attitude, said good morning and turned to go. He stopped at the door, wanting to make one more attempt to get what he wanted. "Warm morning, Sam."

"I guess."

"This used to be such a nice neighborhood. Rundown, but nice. People walking, kids playing on the sidewalks. Remember the first time I came here, last winter?

There were even kids out playing in that heavy snow. I wonder what happened."

Sam got down on his knees and went back to filling his shelves with merchandise. Without looking up he said, "Now, that's something for you to think about, isn't it?"

Canning said a diffident good morning and left.

A few minutes later, Hap appeared at the door. For once he wasn't wearing his sandwich sign. Sam was in no mood for more company. He unlatched the door and snapped, "What do you want?"

Like Canning, Hap was put off by his reception. "I was going to buy a cup of coffee."

"It's Saturday. I'm closed."

"You shouldn't be. Looks like it's going to be a busy day around here." He pointed over his shoulder. Cars were pulling up and parking along Jumonville. Cal was at the far end of the parking lot, unlocking and lowering the chain.

Sam was tired. Running a store, even a small one, was more work than he'd expected. He got slowly to his feet. "I'll make coffee, then. They sure as hell better not be here on Sundays."

"The Lord's day." Hap laughed.

"My day of rest," Sam corrected him. "If they're here, I'll have to be open. I can't afford not to be."

"No rest for the wicked, Sammy."

"My store isn't what draws the wicked here." He picked up the newspaper and pointed to the headline. "It's starting already, Hap."

Hap glanced at the paper and shrugged. "I know. We tried to warn them. They wouldn't listen." He put on a "darkie" accent. "Dem po' white folks sho' don't know nothin' 'bout nothin'."

"EdEntCo wouldn't like your attitude, Hap."

He laughed again. "Fuck 'em. Let 'em all go to hell. But meantime, I'll keep selling them fortunes and you keep selling them coffee and candy bars. Maybe they'll either learn something or wake up."

"I wouldn't count on it. They never do. They never have. The ghost has been here all this time and nothing like this ever happened. We know enough to respect it. They don't. And they won't."

"That's the difference between you and me, Sam. I have hope."

"Hope for what?" He swatted at a fly.

"Hope they'll get out of our neighborhood and leave us to live in peace again. Hope you can have your saloon back and that all the folks who had to move can get their homes back—the ones that weren't torn down. Hope not too many of those pretty rich children will die before it all happens."

"While you're at it, why don't you just hope for the ghost to leave?"

Hap did a razor-sharp imitation of D. Michael Canning. "Ghost? What ghost? Don't be foolish, my good man. There's no such thing."

"You're an evil man, Hap Conklin."

Hap cackled with laughter.

AT nine o'clock Matt Larrimer pulled into the parking lot at Mother of Mercy Hospital. The attendant took his five dollars and waved him to a space. The fog had lifted and the sun had come out. But now the sky was beginning to cloud up; the forecasters said there would be rain later.

The hospital building was old—red brick, vaguely Gothic. There were spires and low arches, and it all seemed oddly shadowy on such a sunny morning. A building out of

The Addams Family. The kind of forbidding hospital they built to house lunatics in the nineteenth century. He looked up at the top of the tallest spire and wondered what was holding the place up. Faith in the Mother of Mercy, maybe?

Inside, the reception area was dark and musty; there were lamps everywhere, but they didn't seem bright enough to cut the gloom. There was that distinct, unpleasant hospital smell everywhere, too. Staff and visitors came and went busily. There were nuns. Matt wished he was someplace else. The woman at the reception desk seemed bored; she looked up from her computer screen, and it was obvious she was surfing the Web. "Yes?"

"I'm here to see Michael Monticelli."

"Are you his father?"

"Teacher. I'm his teacher."

"Oh." She pulled up a database and told him Mike was in room 619. "There's a note on his file. Are you with EdEntCo?"

"I work for them, yes." White lie.

"Six-nineteen. That's the adolescent ward." Then she went back to browsing Harrison Ford memorabilia on eBay.

The elevator was crowded and slow. No one at the sixth floor nurse's station paid him any attention. He stuck his head in the door of 619. There were six beds, all but one of them empty. A heavyset boy slept soundly. No sign of Mike. Back to the nurse's station. A young man in scrubs smiled at him and said, "Help you?" Did he know where Michael Monticelli might be? "Try the rec room." The young man pointed vaguely toward the end of the hall, then turned away and started chatting with another nurse.

The large room was crowded, mostly with young people

but there were a few adults. There were computers, televisions, books and magazines, several dozen tables. A boy with a cut face and dozens of stitches. A girl with a missing right arm. Kids, all of them sick or mutilated. Not how the world was supposed to look.

Matt saw Mike at the far side of the room, reading. He was in hospital pajamas; his head was bandaged and his right arm was in a cast. Matt made his way through the crowd and smiled what he hoped looked like a sincere smile. "Mike. Good morning."

It seemed to take Mike a moment to recognize him. "Oh . . . Mr. . . . Mr. . . . Larrimer."

"That's right."

"What are you doing here?"

He spread his hands as if to ask, Isn't it obvious? "I came to visit you."

Mike shifted uncomfortably in his chair. "Why?"

"I'm your teacher. You're my student."

"Yeah? Nobody else from that school has come. Not to visit."

This wasn't quite what he had been expecting. "It seemed like the right thing to do, that's all. I'm sorry if I'm not welcome." Mike didn't respond. "Should I leave, then?"

"No, I guess not. It's just . . . you're the only one. That's all."

"Really? I'm sorry."

"It's not your fault. The only other one was that Mr. Brookhiser. Last night. And he wasn't visiting. He just wanted my parents to sign some kind of release form or something." He pulled it out of his pocket as if to prove what he was saying was true.

Matt looked at it. It seemed to be a standard release. "They didn't sign?"

"They haven't been here."

"Oh." Again, not what he had expected.

"My mom drinks. My dad . . . we don't get along."

"I'm sorry. If there's anything I can do, Mike . . ."

"I don't know what." He looked away from Matt. "I keep getting headaches, and my elbow aches like hell. I'm fucked, that's all." Then he looked at him again, self-consciously. "I shouldn't say that in front of a teacher, should I?"

"Don't worry about it."

"My arm hurts like hell. They won't give me anything for the pain."

"What do the doctors say?"

"It'll heal, but it's bad. They don't know if I'll be able to compete again. It might be too weak. And my head—I have a concussion. There are times when I can't even see straight. They're doing some kind of brain-scan thing on Monday. An EKG."

"Mike, I'm sorry. I'm sure the coaches will—"

"They won't. I'm the poor kid, remember? The one on a sports scholarship. Not a 'natural leader.' If they'd had any rich kids with balls enough to wrestle, ones who weren't fags, they wouldn't even have let me into that school."

"Now, don't talk like that. They want to win, that's all."

"You have a problem with the truth? First that bitch nearly hit me in the parking lot. Then nobody wants to talk to me. I don't dress right. I don't talk right. I'm some sort of untouchable freak. Now this. Some upper class. Some elite. I fucking hate them all."

Matt groped for something to say. "Do you mind if I sit down?" Mike didn't answer; Matt pulled up a chair and sat down next to him. "What part of town do you live in?"

"Why?"

Matt took a long, deep breath. "I grew up on the lower North Side. It was run-down, dirty; the city didn't seem to give a damn about it. Now I'm on the faculty at the most prestigious new academy in the region."

"Big deal."

"You're smart. I can hear it when you talk. A lot smarter than a lot of the other kids at Washington."

"What's that get me?"

"You keep your grades up, you'll have your pick of colleges. Scholarships. You want Yale? Princeton?"

"Yeah, like I'd fit in there any more than I do at Washington."

"Make them fit you."

This was all too close to home for Matt, too close to what he used to feel himself. He thought he saw tears beginning at the corners of Mike's eyes; but Mike fought them back.

Mike shifted his weight uncomfortably and, without seeming to realize it, began rubbing the cast on his bad right arm with his left hand. "What happened to the one that did it?"

"Jonathan Lampl? He's in custody."

"I can hear his lawyers telling the jury he's insane. His family's rich, right?"

"I don't know."

"He'll get off. If I could have gotten a headlock on him, if I could have gotten a good grip, even with my left hand—I'd have twisted his goddamn head off." He looked directly at Matt for the first time. "I still want to rip his fucking head off."

Matt was feeling more and more awkward. Talking to a boy this bitter, though his bitterness was justified, wasn't something he was prepared for. He kept silent for a moment, then tried to switch to a more neutral subject. "Do they let you go outside at all? It's a gorgeous morning. Cool. I think it might rain later, but . . . They say we'll have an early autumn."

Mike glared at him without saying anything.

"There's even a chance of frost tomorrow night. They say it's never happened this early in September."

"Look, did you really come here to talk about the weather?"

It was a hard blow, knowing the kid could see though him. "No. No, I guess I didn't. I just thought we might take a little walk, that's all, if you're allowed."

"I'm sorry, Mr. Larrimer. It's not like I don't appreciate you coming, or anything. Like I said, you're the only one. Though I bet they'll send some lawyer or something."

"Don't let your parents sign anything till you get a lawyer of your own."

"My parents don't care. They'll sign just to get Brookhiser off their backs."

"Try and talk them out of it."

Mike looked at him with something like contempt. "If I sue the school, I'll lose my scholarship for sure. I can't do that."

Matt shifted again in his chair. "Look, I'm willing to work with you to help keep your grades up. I can stop after school each day till you're back."

"What about my scholarship?"

"I'll do what I can to make sure it stays in place."

"I don't want to go back to Roland."

"You were at Roland?"

"Yeah, I thought you knew."

"No. You . . . you weren't in any of my classes, were you?"

Unexpectedly, Mike laughed. "No. No teacher could be that dumb."

"You'd be surprised."

The laughter eased the tension between them a bit. Mike actually smiled. "I do appreciate you coming to see me."

"Can I come again?"

"I guess so, sure."

They shook hands—left hands.

"Oh, and Mike?"

"Yeah?"

"Don't tell anyone from Washington I told you not to sign, okay?"

Mike laughed at their little conspiracy. "Sure."

"I know a few lawyers. I'll see if I can't get one of them to help you."

"Thanks, Mr. Larrimer. I'm sorry if I sounded disrespectful before, but I—"

"Don't give it another thought."

Matt left. He hoped his visit did Mike some good. Hell, he hoped *anything* he was doing might accomplish something good. His new career at Washington Academy was turning into more of a challenge than he'd expected. Those older teachers who'd warned him back on orientation day—they didn't know the half of it.

BY midmorning the school was full of activity. Athletes worked out in groups in the gym, the weight room, and the student parking lot. There was no actual athletic field, so there were no football or baseball teams, but no one seemed to mind. The students at Washington Academy preferred other sports. This pleased D. Michael Canning, and it pleased his board even more.

There was a pool. Boys and girls in Speedos raced, splashed, dove from the springboard and platform. The handball and jai alai courts were filled with frantic action. Wrestlers grappled on brand-new mats; karate and judo teams worked out. Canning walked among them all, beaming with pride. And the morning was just beginning. At ten o'clock some of the school clubs and extracurricular groups were to meet. What had happened in the chem lab was already in the past.

A pair of workmen appeared and began replacing the glass in the display case. Canning replaced the sword personally, being careful to polish it first.

There was thunder, or the sound of it. Quite sudden, quite deafening. The building shook. Everyone in the school stopped what they were doing. Mort Mortkowski told the boys on his team it sounded like the roar of cannons as he remembered it from the Gulf War. It was a cloudy morning, and rain was forecast; but thunder was not. Slowly it died away.

There was a wail, an extraordinarily loud cry, louder than anyone had heard before. Like the thunder, it faded and died.

Slowly, quite gradually, the students and their coaches began to play again. The silence that followed those terrible noises was almost as unbearable as the noises themselves had been, and everyone seemed to feel an instinctive need to cover up what they were feeling. Within moments jocks were shouting and slapping one another playfully again; water splashed; balls caromed off court walls.

Canning suddenly found himself ignoring them all and focusing on what he—and they—had heard. Somewhere in his school was . . . what?

Some inkling, some faint intuition, told him to check

in the basement. Hoping no one would notice him going there, he climbed deliberately down the main staircase. On the basement door was posted a prominent sign in large, red block letters: No Admission. He got out his keys, then realized the door wasn't locked as it should have been. It was open an inch or so.

More annoyed than angry, he pushed it open. There was a smell in the air; it took him a moment to realize it was marijuana. Firmly, he called out, "Who's there?"

There was no response. Not surprising. He stepped into the corridor. Since the renovation, the basement was divided into a labyrinth of rooms, each guarded by a heavy steel door. One by one he opened them; none were locked, which they should have been. The first few were quite empty. Faint smoke came from under the final one. He pushed it open. The room was dark, but in the light from the corridor he could see two shapes. He reached out quickly and switched on the light.

Tanner Morgan and his cousin Charley were there. Tanner palmed the joint. They both put on bland smiles, and Tanner said, "Dr. Canning."

"What are you two doing here?"

Tanner looked at Charley, who said, "Uh . . . we're . . . uh . . . we're here for our club meetings."

"Clubs don't meet in the basement, and you know it."

Tanner giggled; neither boy said anything.

"This basement is clearly posted as off-limits. If I catch you down here again, you'll go on report."

Tanner giggled again. Charley said, "My father doesn't care what we do."

"Your father isn't the principal here."

"No, but just try doing anything to us."

"Get out of here, both of you."

They walked slowly past him, their demeanor more

than a bit arrogant. Tanner had not stopped snickering. Just as they reached the bottom of the staircase, Canning called out, "Which clubs are you in?"

"I'm in the Gay-Straight Alliance." Tanner was laughing out loud now. "After that, I'm thinking about going to the first meeting of the Robotics Club."

Charley laughed and elbowed his cousin. "I'm in the Robotics Club too."

"Are you saying you're gay, Tanner?"

"No. I'm saying I'm in the Gay-Straight Alliance—the GSA. You're not allowed to ask me more than that. I know my rights." He started climbing the steps.

Charley lingered for a few seconds. "Have a nice day, Dr. Canning." Then he followed his cousin.

They had been in the room where the beheading had taken place. At the rear, freshly plastered, was the wall that hid the corpse Canning had found.

Once the boys were gone, the air became quite still. Canning cocked his head and listened. There was the faintest cry, much like the earlier, loud one—unmistakably so—but much softer.

It was coming from behind the wall.

He crossed the room and pressed his ear against the plaster. It was warm. The wall was warm, as warm as a living man's body. He pressed the flat of his hand against it. Warmth . . . and something more. It was pulsing—throbbing, ever so slightly, like living flesh.

At the bottom of his breath he whispered, "No." There was no way to account for this. After carefully locking all the doors, he climbed to the main floor and went quickly into his private office. He started to page Nick Brookhiser, then remembered his security chief didn't work on weekends.

His bottled-in-bond was nearly gone; he'd have to go

to a liquor store later to stock up. But he drank what there was, then turned his attention to composing a memo advising everyone—administrators, faculty, support staff and students—that the basement was absolutely off-limits. No one was to go there without his express permission. The maintenance people would have to, now and then, to tend the boiler and so on; he would make quite certain they only did so under his strict supervision.

Whatever was there must be kept hidden and buried.

For anyone to know would disrupt the school, his school, in ways he could not permit.

AT exactly eleven o'clock, Matt pulled into the faculty lot. The same young guy was on duty who was there weekdays. He smiled and waved Matt on. Then he followed him and smiled again as Matt got out of his car. "Good morning. Mr. Larrimer, isn't it?"

Matt smiled back. "How did you know?"

"I'm trying to learn all the teachers' names. You can't have too many friends on the job, after all."

"And what's your name?"

"Cal Conklin. Nice to meet you."

"Conklin. There's somebody . . . isn't there somebody else by that name?"

"Have you met Hap?"

"I don't think so, no."

"Old guy with the sandwich board and the fortunes?"

"Oh. I've seen him around, but I haven't really talked to him, no."

"My great-great-great-something uncle. He's ninety-six years old and still going."

"Sounds as though you like him."

"He's the head of our family. He keeps things stable."

"At ninety-six." Matt glanced at his watch. "Listen, I'm late. I'll see you around."

"Sure thing."

Just inside the door he ran into Canning, who was off on another little tour of the school. "Dr. Canning, good morning."

"Hello, Matt."

Canning was slightly unsteady on his feet, and he seemed to be limping heavily. Matt wondered why he didn't use a cane. Male vanity? There was the faintest smell of liquor about him. Matt made himself smile. "Er . . . can you remind me where the Drama Department is?"

"Drama? You're a history teacher."

"I know, but I've been asked to help with the Drama Club. Don't ask me why."

"It *is* EdEntCo policy that extracurricular activities, where possible, are to be interdisciplinary. You know that." Canning looked him up and down as he recited this boilerplate. "Most groups have more than one faculty advisor, from more than one department." He paused and managed to look disapproving and concerned at once. "Do you know anything about the stage?"

"I saw *Gypsy* once."

"Isn't it bad enough that so many of the students here are such smartasses?"

"Sorry. Mrs. Bettis said the club is planning to do plays based on history. I think she called them historical pageants or something of the like." He didn't add that it sounded ghastly to him.

"Something of the like."

"Yes, sir."

"There will be a faculty meeting on Monday after school to discuss yesterday's . . . unfortunate incident and EdEntCo's response to it."

"Is that what you call it when someone has her face peeled off? An unfortunate incident?"

"I'm warning you, Mr. Larrimer. You need to adjust your attitude." Without another word Canning walked off down the hall, heading for the sports wing. It was fairly obvious Matt had used up whatever good will he had earned on orientation day.

Matt went to the main office; Mrs. Newburg, talking to him as if he was a slow child, gave him explicit directions to the Drama Department. "There are two rehearsal rooms with small stages. The club is meeting in room B."

"Thank you, Mrs. Newburg."

"It seems to me you should know where you're going."

He decided to ignore it. "Thank you, Mrs. Newburg."

Diana was also in the office, checking her mailbox. She smiled and waved. "Matt! How's it going?"

He might have been kidding himself, but she sounded genuinely happy to see him. "Pretty well, I think."

"Good." She crossed the office to join him. Mrs. Newburg was standing close by, obviously planning to eavesdrop on them. Diana put on a big grin for her and said breezily, "Don't you have to go outside and run up the flag or something, Mrs. Newburg?"

The executive secretary, obviously unused to being talked to like that, sniffed and moved to another part of the office, her dignity wounded.

As he did every time he saw her, Matt found Diana gorgeous. He hoped he wasn't letting his schoolboy crush show. "How was your week?"

"Oh, just wall-to-wall grins. One darling little illiterate after another to deal with. One genius actually asked me, 'What's a poem, anyway?' The only good thing is knowing I won't have to deal with Jonathan Lampl anymore. Disagreeable kid. He was in my fourth period." She paused and looked back at Mrs. Newburg, who was clearly eavesdropping. "How's history?"

"About the same. Just as a little exercise, I had my American history class list as many presidents as they could think of. Some of them couldn't even come up with five. Two of them couldn't even name the current one."

"Well, he hardly counts."

"One girl listed Paul Revere, Charlton Heston and Elvis."

She laughed. "Oh, we've got the elite here, all right. Whoever thought money equals brains?"

Mrs. Newburg was still listening, and not liking what she heard. She rattled a stack of papers loudly to show it. Diana grinned at her again and said, "Could I perhaps get you a damp paper towel, Mrs. Newburg?"

"A paper towel? Whatever for?"

"So you can wipe that disapproving scowl off your face."

Mrs. Newburg slammed the stack of papers onto the countertop and stomped away.

Matt couldn't suppress a laugh. "You're going to get in trouble if you keep riding her like that."

"I can't help it. She looks like something out of a Universal horror movie, circa 1930. Besides, I'm a natural-born smartass."

He lowered his voice. "Canning just called *me* one too. We're made for each other."

"Why, Mr. Larrimer, are you asking me for a date?"

He felt himself blushing and wanted to crawl under the nearest table. "If you weren't spoken for, I would be."

"I am not," she said with emphasis, " 'spoken for.' Peter's fun. And useful."

"And rich."

"Well, yes, there is that. He has better liquor at his place than most of the bars in Pittsburgh."

"That wouldn't be hard. Uh . . ." He felt another blush coming on and wished there was some way to stop it. "So, do you maybe want to meet for a drink later?"

"No. I do not maybe want to meet for a drink later." She was beginning to understand what her smile did to him, so she smiled again. "I *definitely* want to meet for a drink later."

"Thanks." Blush. He felt like a kid. And hated it. "One o'clock?"

"I should be finished with the Poetry Club by then, sure." She looked around to make sure no one was watching them. Then she kissed him quickly on the cheek. "See you in the faculty lounge at one." And she was gone. She walked with that striking lightness. Matt knew that falling in love with a coworker was not a good idea. He wondered if he'd have any choice.

He had forgotten the directions to the Drama Department. There was no way he could face Mrs. Newburg, not after Diana had toyed with her. He stopped a girl in a cheerleader's outfit, and she told him the way.

The school was busier than he'd expected. Students and jocks seemed to be coming and going nearly everywhere. A boy with a film can under his arm smiled and said, "good morning"; Matt had no idea who he was. A trio of girls in gym outfits jogged down the hall. Two more, cheerleaders, strolled behind them. A kid carrying a large perforated crate marked Live Frogs made tracks for the Biology Lab.

The Drama Department door was closed and locked. Like all the doors, it had a small window set into it. He looked in. There were, maybe, two dozen students, being lectured by Mrs. Bettis. Alexis Morgan was at the back of the room, dressed in jeans, a dirty T-shirt and sandals, rather obviously daydreaming. He knocked. Mrs. Bettis glanced at the door, then went on with her talk. Second knock. Impatiently, she crossed to the door and opened it. "Yes?"

He smiled a professional smile. "Sorry I'm late."

"You should be. Come in."

He followed her into the room and she announced, "This is Mr. Larrimer, of the History Department. Some of you must know him." She said this in a tone suggesting that that was their hard luck. "He will be acting as advisor on this project."

He knew next to nothing about the project. Not wanting to admit it, he asked her if she might "recap" what they'd talked about. She saw through his ploy but backtracked to explain.

Rather than do a conventional school play, the Drama Club would research, write and stage a series of historical vignettes. The focus would be local history, the history of the region immediately surrounding the spot where the school stood. Matt was going to comment that doing research that focused and specific was a bit beyond the usual scope of high school studies, but he guessed there would be no point in arguing it. Mrs. Bettis would already have gotten approval for the idea. And this was Washington Academy, after all; the students were expected to excel, even the dumb ones.

"My own preference," Mrs. Bettis concluded grandly, "would be that we focus on George Washington himself. The school bears his name, and it seems fitting that we honor him with our first dramatic presentation."

An African-American student raised his hand. "I thought all the stuff about George Washington sleeping everywhere around Pittsburgh was just a lot of mythology."

Mrs. Bettis smiled a tight smile: dissension in the ranks. "Perhaps Mr. Larrimer would say a word about that." She shot a dark glance at him, as if to warn him not to sabotage her pet scheme.

Matt walked to the front of the room and planted himself, pointedly, between Mrs. Bettis and the students. He knew at least enough about theater to know how to upstage someone. He asked the boy his name.

"Ronald Lindsey."

"Well, Ron, you're right. There's a lot of mythology surrounding Washington in western Pennsylvania. Things are named after him that he can't have gotten anywhere near. Mount Washington, for instance—that huge bluff that overlooks downtown Pittsburgh—it's unlikely he was ever actually up there."

Ron's father was the managing editor of the Pittsburgh *Sun-Telegraph.* He was ambitious and he thought it would be good for his son to mix with the children of the upper class. To nearly everyone's surprise, Ron wasn't a jock. "But didn't Washington—"

Matt was on-message. "But it's also true that he and his men were here. I have to admit I don't know too many of the details myself. And I'm sure Mrs. Bettis doesn't." This got a bigger laugh than he was expecting. "Trying to get to the bottom of what really happened should be an interesting challenge. For all of us."

He looked over his shoulder at Mrs. Bettis, and she couldn't have looked unhappier. Her little pet project for historical plays was no longer quite her own. Matt was pleased.

There were a few more questions. It became rather apparent that the kids were glad he was there, if only as a buffer between them and Mrs. Bettis. Then Alexis

Morgan raised her hand. "So we're to write and perform plays about what's happened in the past, right?"

Mrs. Bettis beamed; at least one of her students was with the program. "That is quite correct, Alexis."

"Well, what about the recent past?"

Mrs. Bettis must have been the only one in the room who couldn't see where this was heading. "The recent past? Well, I suppose we might . . . er, what do you think, Mr. Larrimer?"

Like nearly everyone else, he had an uneasy idea where Alexis was going. "I'm not sure that would be a good idea, no."

Alexis pushed. "But the past is the past, Mr. Larrimer. Just because it's the recent past doesn't mean it's not history, right?"

Before he could answer, Mrs. Bettis piped up. "That is an excellent point. Perhaps we should broaden our scope a bit. What do you all think of the idea?"

There was an anxious silence. Finally, sensing she had won the little tug-of-war, Alexis said loudly, "Then I want to do a play about what Jon Lampl did yesterday."

Shock registered on Mrs. Bettis's face.

"And maybe we can get you to play Mrs. Lisniecki— okay, Mrs. Bettis?"

Students fidgeted in their seats. There were a few pockets of nervous giggling, but no one seemed quite sure how to react to this.

Matt got his wits about him and took charge. "That will be quite enough of that. We all know what happened yesterday, and we all know how awful it was. It's nothing to joke about."

Alexis said sweetly, "I wasn't joking, Mr. Larrimer."

"In that case, I think we'll have to make an appointment

for you with the school psychiatrist." The other kids laughed. Alexis fell silent but glared at the two teachers. Putting a student down that way was not what Matt would have preferred, but on the spur of the moment it was the first thing that came to him.

Another boy raised his hand. "I'm Claude Hinkle, Mr. Larrimer. Bishop Hinkle's nephew?" He seemed to think this was a big deal. "I'm wondering if we should confine ourselves to American history. I'd like to do biblical history for my play. That would be all right, wouldn't it?"

Claude looked pretty much like what Matt would expect a bishop's nephew to look like, which wasn't much. Thin, pale, thick eyeglasses . . . Matt restrained himself from saying that "biblical history" was a contradiction in terms. He smiled and said it would be fine.

After another moment's uncomfortable silence, Mrs. Bettis took over again. "Well, now that we've settled that . . . There's something else I wanted to tell you about. Even Mr. Larrimer doesn't know about this."

He wanted to say, Since I didn't know about anything else, why make a point of it? But he smiled a polite smile and nodded in her direction.

She went on. "The school's trustees have decided to sponsor a series of contests, with scholarships as the prizes. One of them will be a playwriting contest."

She was right; Matt hadn't heard a thing about this.

She went on. "By coincidence, the topic for the competition will be historical drama. Any historical subject will do. And I will be one of the judges. The contests will be announced next week at a school assembly. But I wanted to give you all a bit of advance notice, so you may begin to think about what you'd like to write. It would give me great pleasure to see a member of this club win the scholarship."

Matt liked the idea, despite a few misgivings. So he

added, "Mrs. Bettis is right. If I can be of any help to any of you in your research, just let me know."

Ron Lindsey raised his hand. "So, basically, the contest is for the same thing as our own club project?"

Mrs. Bettis nodded and smiled. At least one of them had gotten it. "Exactly."

Ron and several of the other students broke into wide smiles. "Thanks—that's great!"

There were a few more questions, and there was a bit of discussion about what subjects they might like to explore for the club project. The kids were enthusiastic, and Matt felt himself getting caught up in it. At last there was some semblance of the atmosphere he'd been hoping for when he came to Washington Academy.

"SO how do you like the Morgan children?"

Diana's apartment was large, larger than Matt's. Big rooms, huge windows—it was roomy and airy and he envied it. He tried to convince himself she must be paying her own rent and had simply lucked onto a great place that happened to be affordable. But he knew better.

They had met as planned and gone out for cocktails. Diana drank martinis. Matt commented that she was the only one he knew who drank them. "You're either a few decades behind the rest of us or a few years ahead."

She was wry. "Sophistication never dates."

There was a spark between them. As he'd hoped. As she'd known. From the bar they went to an Indian restaurant and had lunch. Then, before Matt quite knew what was happening, they were at her apartment in Shadyside, the next city neighborhood beyond Oakland. Convenient to the academy. Quite livable. He was aching to ask her if Peter Morgan was keeping her.

But she was the one who brought up the Morgans. Alexis was in one of her senior composition classes. She had met Tanner and Charley though Peter. "Little horrors, aren't they?"

"Alexis certainly is. I'm not so sure about Tanner. I can't quite figure him out."

"Have you considered the possibility there's nothing there *to* figure out?"

"He seems kind of lost."

She fixed more drinks for them. "I keep telling myself it's because of what they went through last winter. But I think it's more than that. Or less."

"Last winter?" She handed him a martini. Not his favorite drink, but he smiled and sipped it as she sat down beside him on the sofa.

"Their brother killed himself in front of them."

He remembered vaguely. It had been a minor news item, and it had slipped his mind altogether. Back then, the Morgans were nothing more to him than names in the *Sun-Telegraph*'s society column. "You can kind of see how that would have shaken them up a bit."

"Do you know Charley? Er, Charlton?"

His martini was too heavy on the vermouth. "Only to see."

"He's fucking them both."

Without realizing it, Matt whistled. "Jesus, I thought there was something going on. But that . . . !"

"A precocious brood."

"Does Peter know?"

She gave a slight shrug. "I don't get the impression he cares. Little Charlton could be screwing the family pets and Peter wouldn't care. Not unless it began to hurt the bottom line. The kid's dealing, too—I think heroin."

Matt took a long drink of his cocktail. "I spent two

years at Roland High. I saw drug deals, rapes, knifings. But these kids make the students there look like little porcelain choirboys."

She lifted her glass in a toast. "Here's to America's upper classes."

Feeling odd, he touched her glass with his and downed the rest of his drink. "Alexis has even come on to me."

"I don't blame her. You're a lot cuter than you seem to think. Charley's hit on me, too. I laughed at him and told him to come back when he's his father's age. And has his father's bankroll."

"You mean he offered to pay you?"

She laughed. "You're dealing with the corporate elite. They can't help treating everyone else like whores. It's genetic or something."

Quite impulsively, he kissed her. She kissed back, and she put her hand on his leg and rubbed. "Come on, let's go to bed."

"It's early yet."

"Even so."

"A bit more foreplay . . ."

"Peter's picking me up at six."

"Oh."

She stood up and began to undress. Her body was perfect to his eye, every bit as sweet as he'd wanted it to be.

When she was naked, she pulled him to his feet and led him by his hands to the bedroom. "Come on, Matt. There are things I want to lick."

So Peter was coming at six. Matt pushed the knowledge out of his mind. He had to see what she tasted like, every part of her.

* * *

"YOU wanted to see me?"

Alexis had been called back to the Drama Department by Mrs. Bettis. The morning had been a long one—first Drama Club, then Poetry. She didn't much like Ms. Ketterer and kept needling her by calling her "Aunt Diana," a joke the other students didn't get. Dealing with Mrs. Bettis again was just a bit too much.

Mrs. Bettis was sitting at her desk, reading Carl Sandburg's biography of Lincoln for some reason. Research? "Yes, Alexis. I need to advise you to adjust your attitude."

"Adjust?"

"You seem to have no respect for either your teachers or your classmates. Everyone says so, not just me."

"By everyone, you mean the faculty, right?"

"There have been complaints from students, too." Mrs. Bettis smiled a wide smile.

"From who?"

"That is hardly the issue."

"It is. Tell me who they are and I'll cut their damned heads off. You think I have to behave a certain way just because it's what you want. Well, you can forget that."

Mrs. Bettis stood up, hoping it would give her a bit more authority. "I must tell you, Alexis, that if you don't adopt a more respectful attitude, you will be expelled from the Drama Club."

Alexis walked slowly across the space between them and got directly in Mrs. Bettis's face. Slowly she said, "That's what you think. My uncle loves me."

The time for diplomacy was past. "I love my dog. But I keep her on a leash."

Alexis fumed. Her face turned red and she started shaking. For the help—the help!—to be talking to her like this! Not knowing how to react or what to say, she turned on her heel and stomped out of the room.

Mrs. Bettis was left alone to wonder whether the talk would have any effect. She doubted it.

Expecting to find Tanner and Charley waiting for her, as they'd arranged, Alexis headed for the student lot. There was no sign of them. The lot was nearly empty. They could be anywhere, doing anything, and she didn't much want to wait.

Sam's store was open. She decided she wanted something sweet. Like three or four candy bars.

The place was empty except for Sam and Cal. Sam had the radio tuned to the classical station; she hated it. All those shrill violins. Cal was browsing the magazines on the rack. He didn't notice her come in, or he pretended he didn't. It annoyed her.

Three Milky Ways. No, four. Hell, *five*. She could go to the gym later.

She went to the counter and spread them out, then reached into her pocket, fishing for change. "How much?"

Sam smiled. "Sixty cents each. Or five for five dollars."

His joke was lost on her. She got a five out of her pocket, threw it on the counter and stepped out onto the sidewalk. He called after her—"Miss!"—but she didn't hear or didn't choose to respond.

Cal and Sam looked at each other. Cal got her change and followed her outside.

She glared at him, but he kept smiling. She tore the wrapper off the first candy bar quite aggressively. "What do you want?"

"I just wanted to make sure you're all right, that's all." He gave her his most ingratiating smile and held out her two dollars.

She took it. "It's none of your business."

"My boss is Nick Brookhiser. Technically, I'm security."

"So what?"

"So, I have to make sure everything's okay around Washington Academy."

"Well, it's still none of your business."

"Oh." He was more amused than put off. "Well, if you're all right, how about sharing one of those candy bars?"

"You can buy one just inside that door."

Another smile. He moved closer. "I want one of yours."

It slowly began to dawn on her what was happening. His interest was not in her security; she was certain of it. She looked him up and down. "You're kind of . . ." Should she say it? "I mean, for a parking lot attendant."

"Yeah, that's what they tell me. You are too."

This was strange. This was worse than anything else that had happened. Or better. She could just hear her late brother Matt's voice in her head: *Be serious, Lex. I mean, you can't. He's a . . .*

But who knew? It might be fun. She took a step toward him. "I'm Alexis."

"I know it. I'm Cal."

"I know."

For a moment they stood watching each other, neither quite knowing what to say next. Finally she said, "I could have you fired, you know."

"Do it. Then I won't have to restrain myself."

Unexpectedly, Hap came around the corner. Cal quickly stepped away from Alexis. Hap saw them and put on an enormous grin. "Well, well, well, what do we have here?"

"We have," Alexis said grandly and irritably, "a presumptuous parking lot guard."

Hap looked from her to Cal, then back again. "I knew you were here, Miss Alexis Morgan. I came to give you your next fortune. But it looks to me like you might already have found it."

"Don't be foolish, uncle." Cal shifted his weight uncomfortably and stepped back away from them both. Then he threw his arms around Hap in a big bear hug and said, "I really ought to be going."

"Behave yourself, Calvin."

"Yes, sir." Looking uncertainly from Hap to Alexis, Cal turned and headed around the corner.

Hap cackled with delight. "Cal's a fine-looking young man, isn't he? Handsomer than Sidney Poitier. He'll make a fine actor."

"I'm afraid I don't notice people like that." She sniffed. "And I'm afraid I don't wish to."

"You sound like the snotty rich kid in one of those Little Rascals movies."

"And what does that make you?"

His smile disappeared. "You think you demonstrate your superiority by being rude to people. That's backward."

"Let me get this straight. You just insulted me, and you're trying to claim I'm the one who's out of line here?"

There didn't seem much point going on. "Miss Alexis, I—"

"I keep telling you, just call me Alexis. Or Lex."

"Miss Alexis, I am ninety-six years old, my back hurts, my teeth hurt—the few I have left—and I have arthritis in every joint in my body. But I could still take you over my knee and give you the thrashing you deserve. And nobody would blame me. Not anyone who knows you."

She couldn't believe she'd heard it. Was he joking? "You just try it, Hap." She said his name with obvious distaste. "See how long it takes me to cry rape. Look at us. Which one do you think the police will believe?"

Slowly, without saying another word, Hap reached down and took the fortune punchboard off his sandwich sign. Even more slowly, he held it out to her. "Here," he whispered. "Time for your next one. Take a fortune."

Without quite understanding why, Alexis was frightened. She stared at the punchboard. "N-no."

"Are you afraid?"

"No."

"Then do it."

"No, I said."

"You might find out what's wrong at Washington High—er, I mean Washington Academy. You might even find out what's wrong with your life."

She stayed silent, staring at the punchboard as if it was the most horrible thing in the world.

"Go ahead, Miss Alexis Morgan. Take a fortune."

Not wanting to, not knowing why she was doing it, Alexis took a ballpoint and punched one out. She took the little slip of paper and shoved it into her jeans pocket.

"Aren't you going to read it?"

"No."

"You're a coward, Miss Alexis. Your kind always are."

Finally she got control of herself. "Fuck off."

"My fortunes are always true. Face it."

"I said fuck off!" She screamed it. Her voice echoed through the street.

A group of students on the other side of Jumonville heard her. Ron Lindsey was one of them. Looking mildly concerned, he shouted, "Are you all right, Alexis?"

She forced herself to smile. "Thanks, Ron, I'm fine."

"Are you sure?"

"Yeah. No prob."

She turned to look at Hap again, but he was on his way into Sam's.

She fingered the fortune in her pocket. Should she read it? She knew there was no way she could force herself to do that.

Instead she went to the student lot, got into her car, sat behind the steering wheel, started the engine, turned on the air conditioning and began to cry.

No one noticed.

But a few moments later Tanner and Charley came out of the building. They headed for Tanner's car, talking and laughing. Just as they were about to get in, Charley noticed Alexis. They crossed quickly to her car. Charley tapped on the driver's-side window. "Lex?"

She looked up at them and tried to make herself smile. It wasn't convincing.

Charley gestured for her to roll the window down. "What's the matter?"

"Nothing."

"Yeah, I can tell."

She sniffled. "Where are the two of you going?"

"Out to get some lunch. Middle Eastern." He paused uncertainly. "You want to come?"

"No."

Tanner moved to the side of the car, reached in and took her hand. "What's wrong, Lex?"

She stared into his face as if it was the oddest question she could imagine. "Mrs. Bettis. She threatened to throw me out of the Drama Club." There was no reason to tell them any more than that.

"Is that all? Hell, Lex, we practically own this place. You know that. Uncle Peter can—"

"I don't want him covering for me all the time. That's okay for you two, but I—"

"My father," Charley said loudly, "does not cover for me. If anything, it's the other way around."

Alexis smirked at him. "Sure. Where are you going to lunch?"

"We don't know. We were thinking maybe Ali Khassan's." Tanner let go of her hand and stepped away from the car. "You sure that's all that's bothering you?"

"I want to be in the Drama Club. That's all."

"Then you should learn a lesson from Hamlet. Don't let what you feel exceed the fact of what's happening to you."

She smirked again. "Tanner Morgan, literary critic."

"I mean it, Lex. One school club just isn't that big a deal."

"It is to me. I want to major in theater in college. Having the club on my résumé . . ."

Charley offered to have his father talk to Mrs. Bettis.

"No. Don't do that."

It seemed to puzzle him. "You've got pull, Lex. Use it."

"No."

Still trying to be helpful, Tanner said, "Come and join the Robotics Club, then. With us."

"Robots?"

He nodded, obviously thinking it would be fun.

"Robots, Tanner? Can you see me tinkering with wires and gizmos?"

"And computers," Charley added.

"No, thanks."

But Charley was warming up to it. "We've hit on the coolest project. We're going to build a head. A fully functioning robot head."

Alexis stared at him and didn't say anything.

But he prodded. "Isn't that too fucking cool?"

Suddenly she was back in possession of herself. She wiped the last tears from her face, arranged herself in the seat and turned the ignition. "My advice to you, then, Charley, is to quit while you're ahead."

Tanner groaned, then growled softly. "See what we get for trying to comfort my sister? Her emotions don't exactly run deep."

Charley tried to play peacemaker. "She was crying, Tan."

Loudly, emphatically, Alexis said, "And she's not anymore." She laughed at them. "A head. An electronic head for Washington Academy. You guys are too much." Reaching into her pocket, she got her latest fortune, still unread, and pressed it into Charley's hand. "Here. Maybe this will do you some good."

He looked at the slip of paper. "What is it?"

"The future."

"Don't be crazy," Tanner hesitated. "If you don't care about robotics, how about coming to the Gay-Straight Alliance? We're having a dance."

"No, thanks. I don't think I'm ready for the sight of the two of you dancing cheek to cheek." She gunned her engine, backed out of her space and drove off.

Tanner and Charley were left gaping at one another. Finally Tanner said, "She's been getting crazier and crazier since Matt killed himself."

Charley started to unroll the slip. "You're okay, though, huh?"

"Don't be a prick, Charley."

He read it, then handed it to Tanner. "What the hell is this?"

Tanner read it aloud. "Baphomet prophesies. Baphomet speaks only the truth."

"Who's Baphomet?"

"I don't know. Muhammad with dyslexia?" He let the slip drop onto the ground, then they got into Charley's car and left.

FIVE

CHARLEY MORGAN

LATE September. The scientists all said an El Niño was forming in the Pacific, which meant a mild winter. There were skeptics: How could something that distant possibly affect Pittsburgh? Nonetheless, leaves were turning already; autumn would arrive early. Everyone was hoping it meant the coming winter wouldn't be long or harsh.

Things at Washington Academy had settled down. The horror that ended the first week of classes had faded into the background, into that nebulous realm known as "history." No one gave it much thought. Carolyn Lisniecki was still hospitalized. Her husband, Martin, talked to a lawyer; there was the threat of a lawsuit, which would of course be followed by a quick, quiet monetary settlement. It was not enough to impact EdEntCo's bottom line negatively; at their quarterly meeting, the board was satisfied that the business plan was on track.

D. Michael Canning spent days in his office, consulting

with the board, consulting with Peter Morgan, consulting with Nick Brookhiser, and largely avoiding the faculty and students. He was not a hands-on manager, more a hands-off worrier. Mrs. Newburg oversaw day-to-day operations quite efficiently, thank you, so that he could tend to the politics—dealing with unhappy parents, answering board members' questions, and on and on. The board seemed happy with both of them, and that was all that mattered.

The flow of bourbon in Canning's office was never that heavy, but it never seemed to stop. Teachers—the ones he liked and trusted—often stopped in after classes for a quick drink; sometimes they even stopped between classes. The students never noticed, or, if they did, never cared. They had their own sources of chemical euphoria. At the school's first pep rally, for the judo team, everyone was full of pep.

All of the sports teams were looking good. Canning happily reported this to the board, which received the news with obvious pleasure. Bishop Hinkle offered to attend all the school's sporting events and begin them with an invocation. But Canning and Morgan were cautious; there was the First Amendment to consider.

Hinkle was sanguine. "We're a corporation. Surely the Bill of Rights applies to the government, not to us."

"But Grover," Morgan explained patiently, "we'll be competing against public schools. There could be conflicts. It's best to let our athletes compete free of any kind of tension or controversy. We've had enough of that already. Don't you agree?"

It was obvious he didn't, but he went along for the sake of board unity. The other directors were relieved.

And so the sports programs went on as before. Teams drilled, individual jocks worked out. Athletes injected themselves with steroids or, more erotically, injected each other, and coaches pretended not to know it was happening. Sports builds character, and character precludes any such thing.

Matt and Diana were carrying on a quite active affair, when she wasn't with Peter Morgan—mostly weekend afternoons, with an occasional weeknight for good measure. Matt found her irresistible; the mere sight of her at the other end of the hall was enough to set his juices flowing. He kept telling himself he wasn't in love with her and shouldn't be. To help keep his mind occupied he became more actively involved in helping the students research their history/drama projects.

As for Diana, she carried on her affair with a Matt with a good bit of amusement and even more detachment. He was young, still in good shape, still full of hope, promise and ideas. But he was so naïve. How could so many of the students be so much more worldly? She thought he must be a bit crazy, but she liked him and she liked his body; the question of love never entered her mind.

The drama/history projects had excited the school in ways no one had quite anticipated, certainly not Matt or Mrs. Bettis. Clubs of every kind, from foreign language honor societies to the chess team to the Junior ROTC brigade, seemed engaged and enthusiastic. There was a sense of lively competition among them: Who would define history for the school? D. Michael Canning and his board knew the answer; it seemed no one else did.

Charley Morgan had been caught dealing heroin on school grounds and was punished appropriately: He was suspended for three days. There was, of course, no reason to tell the police about it, much less the parents of

Washington's students. When, in his absence, a few of his customers went into withdrawal, the school nurse sent them home with notes about a virus in the student population; it would pass in a few days. None of them was so seriously hooked that their parents found any reason to question the nurse's word or to be alarmed.

With no cousin to distract them, for three days Tanner and Alexis paid attention to their classes. They were bored. Alexis spent more and more time before classes talking with Cal Conklin; on days when he was still on duty in the afternoon, she hung with him then, too. Tanner saw what was developing between them. He watched with pleasure, actually; he found Cal attractive himself.

Mike Monticelli was back at school. He wasn't allowed to play sports for the rest of the semester, but he would be back on the teams come January. At the pep rally for the judo team he sat on the stage with the other athletes, but no one paid him much attention. Matt, as promised, had helped him keep current with his class work. His sports scholarship, at least for the time being, was secure.

A bond developed between them. Matt found Mike turning to him for advice, even just for company. "No one else seems to want to talk to me."

"That's your imagination, Mike." Matt wanted to be as upbeat as he could.

"No. I told you before: I'm different. They all know it and so do I. There's no use pretending I'm not."

"You're a great guy, Mike. No one's that different."

"For God's sake, Mr. Larrimer, look around. There are kids whose clothes cost more than my dad earned last week." He was trying, not very successfully, not to sound too bitter. "Or ever will."

"It's not that bad. You're a jock. Wait till you win a trophy for the school." Sports was the great leveler.

"The judo team won their first match without me."

There wasn't much Matt could say to that. But he and Mike kept talking. It seemed a bit strange to Matt. None of his students had ever seemed to regard him as a friend before, not at Roland and certainly not at Washington.

One of the board members was Dr. Millard Seaton, the CFO of the region's largest psychiatric hospital, where Jonathan Lampl was under careful observation and supervision. He saw to it that his staff certified Lampl insane. Everything that had happened was an isolated incident, quite impossible to predict or prevent; but steps were being taken to ensure it could never happen again. He and Morgan issued a joint press release to say so.

So all in all, things were going as well as could be expected at Washington. There were fights among the students, routine sports injuries (all of them isolated), nothing in the least out of the ordinary. A few kids overdosed on this or that. All run-of-the-mill stuff. The cries and groans that filled the air now and then had become familiar; no one paid much attention to them.

The opening bars of Beethoven's Fifth sounded so often and so regularly that even Matt eventually stopped remembering, every time he heard it, that those notes were meant to signify the implacable knock of fate.

THEN Carolyn Lisniecki died. She had been recovering from the effects of the acid reasonably well. But when the bandages came off and she saw her face, she waited patiently till none of the hospital staff was watching her, got hold of a pair of surgical scissors and slit her wrists and throat.

Canning told the faculty about it, then made the announcement to the entire school. Martin Lisniecki threatened legal action once again, and again there was a monetary settlement. The story got revived briefly in the press, but it didn't have legs.

As part of the settlement the board renamed the science wing the Lisniecki Science Wing in her honor. For once, the press was invited—to the dedication ceremony. It was a wise move. Her widower came to the ceremony and smiled for the cameras, and as far as anyone knew, all was well with Washington Academy. There was champagne to lubricate him and the reporters, just to make sure. The school's image, and EdEntCo's, couldn't have been rosier.

THE entire student body attended the dedication, of course. Bishop Hinkle led an invocation. Peter Morgan made a speech, and so did Canning. Nick Brookhiser, who seemed to know her better than anyone else—which was not very well—talked about what a wonderful, dedicated teacher she was. Martin Lisniecki spoke about what a great honor it was, and how touched Carolyn would have been by it.

Diana, standing next to Matt at one side of the hall, whispered, "A lot of good it does her."

He shushed her.

In the middle of the ceremony there was also a tribute to the school's sports teams; even a few individual athletes were singled out for recognition. Peter Morgan reminded everyone of the important role sports programs play in building character. Then the focus went back to Carolyn Lisniecki, where it belonged.

And so the dedication went on, at great, pompous

length. Jonathan Lampl's name was not mentioned once, quite properly so. His name had not been mentioned at all in a public context; it was as if he didn't exist.

Near the back of the auditorium, on the left aisle, sat Darren and Dima van der Maats. They were twin brothers, freshmen. They took all their classes together and, except for rest room visits, one was never seen without the other. Darren was fourteen minutes older. They were thin, pale, blue-eyed and quite startlingly blond.

They passed notes. "This sucks." "Let's cut." Neither had the least interest in the dead chemistry teacher, her husband or the school officials and their speeches. In class they could sleep. Here, teachers walked up and down the aisles to make sure everyone was behaving and listening attentively. There were cameras, after all. Everyone pretended.

Sometimes, among their classmates, they talked in unison. Sometimes they wouldn't talk at all. The other students found them odd, even by Washington standards, and tended to avoid them. There was a lot of speculation they were queer and lovers. But they were not, at least not consciously. Tanner Morgan had taken the step of inviting them to the Gay-Straight Alliance. They stared at him and didn't answer.

Their father was the owner and general manager of a radio station. Their mother had left when they were infants. Dima passed another note to his brother. "I hate this."

Darren responded with "Let's do it tonight."

Once the assembly ended, the school day was routine. Darren and Dima went from class to class, sometimes pretending interest, sometimes not bothering to. They whispered to each other a lot. On a trip to the men's room, Darren saw two boys come out of the same booth. When he rejoined his brother, he pointed at them, then mimed injecting something into his arm with a hypodermic. Dima laughed.

After Mr. Robson's biology class they sneaked into the lab and stole some dissecting scalpels. Then they made a mutual decision to cut gym, their last class of the day. Instead they crossed the street to Sam's and bought handfuls of Almond Joy bars, Darren's favorite. Dima preferred Mounds, but he let his older brother pick.

Their house was in Mount Lebanon, an upscale, affluent suburb. Fourteen rooms, four baths and an impressively large estate covered with ornamental trees. When they got home it was empty except for the live-in housekeeper, a plump, middle-aged woman named Rita. They never knew her last name; they didn't care. Dima took a pre-Columbian sculpture, a terra-cotta goddess, and beat her over the head with it till she passed out. Blood flowed from the wounds in entertaining little spurts until her heart finally stopped beating.

They undressed her, fucked her and then went to work cutting her into pieces with their scalpels. Parts of her body smelled; Darren didn't like it. Dima ate her eyes; he thought the way the stuff inside squirted into his mouth when he bit down was gross in a really funny way.

The carpeting in the house was white, and Rita had always kept it immaculate. Now it was stained with her blood. It was bright red at first, but by the time their father got home that evening it was drying to a duller, brownish shade of red.

He came in, saw it, called the twins' names. He was a large man. The terra-cotta goddess was too small to use on him. A crystal lamp base did the job. Fucking his corpse never occurred to them. His body parts smelled even worse than Rita's. Dima persuaded Darren to try one of the eyes, and they laughed together.

Their father had left the keys in his Mercedes convertible; he always did. They took the family bible and his credit cards, and hit the road. They took both eyeless heads with them.

Three days later, in Indiana, the police finally ran them to ground. It made the national news. The fact that they were students at Washington Academy in Pittsburgh seemed irrelevant. Only the local news people mentioned it. What did it matter, really? No one had known how sick they were, and no one could have seen the murders coming.

There was a brief discussion among Canning, Brookhiser and the science faculty about locking up any instruments that might be dangerous. But this had been an isolated incident; any such action seemed excessive.

TUESDAY, September 29. A sunny afternoon.

Matt was called to Canning's office during his afternoon free period. He wasn't at all certain why.

Canning offered him a drink, which he politely refused.

"You sure?"

"Yes, thanks. I can't handle it this early in the day."

Canning smirked. "Tell me about these history projects, these plays of yours."

Oh. So that was it. "Actually, they were Mrs. Bettis's idea. I came on board later, just to help the students with their research."

"She says it was you."

Bitch. "Absolutely not. She drafted me to help after things were already rolling. I really didn't have much choice but to go along."

"I see. And what do you think of the whole thing?"

Matt shrugged. "It's not a bad idea, I guess. The kids seem to be caught up in it."

"Will they be any good?"

"I don't know." Again he shrugged. "They're all still looking for ideas to use."

"But will they be any good?" Canning repeated it with enough emphasis for Matt to understand it wasn't an idle question.

"Well . . ." He looked out the window and saw Charley Morgan passing something to another student in the parking lot. Whatever it was, he wished he had some. "That'll depend on how well the students can write. And how well they stage them. Neither of those is my department."

"What do you expect?" Canning's face was neutral. Impossible to read. What could he be after?

Matt laughed. "I don't know. I have to say, I've never been much of a fan of historical dramas. I always find myself thinking of Cecil B. DeMille movies. Bad acting, laughable writing . . ." He smiled to show how seriously he meant this.

Canning let out a sigh, then paused for effect. "I'll be honest with you, Matt. EdEntCo is concerned about this. Whatever you think about DeMille, his movies are good. They shore up morale, they make people more cohesive. We don't want our students presenting any unpleasant truths in their plays."

None of this made much sense to Matt, but he said that he saw. "I see."

"We don't want them thinking about anything that might prove an embarrassment to the school and the company."

"Of course."

"I want you to oversee all this carefully. You will have

final approval of which plays actually get produced. Nothing touchy, nothing controversial. Understand?"

"Mrs. Bettis might not—"

"Leave Mrs. Bettis to me."

"Yes, sir."

"You're a good, solid man, Matt. I knew it back at orientation. EdEntCo won't forget."

"Thank you, Dr. Canning."

"Oh, and Matt?"

"Yes?"

"I know it sounds unlikely, but if anything they write has any actual commercial potential, you're to bring it to my attention at once."

"I doubt if there's much chance of it."

"Believe me, I know it." He scowled, for some reason. "Just don't forget that, okay?"

As he was leaving Canning's office he found a young girl waiting for him at the door. "Mr. Larrimer?"

"Yes." He smiled.

"George Washington was a lard-ass."

"I beg your pardon?"

"I said George Washington was a lard-ass." She had brown hair and green eyes; she was dressed in denim.

The day was getting odder and odder. "I think you've skipped ahead a few squares."

"Oh." She blushed. "I'm sorry. I'm Nell McCouver. From the Drama Club?"

He thought he remembered her but wasn't sure. "Nell. Now, why this interest in the father of our country's backside?"

"I found it in a book in the library. His butt was really huge. They used to make fun of him for it. A lot of them."

Be encouraging, like a good teacher. "Well, I'm glad you're reading history."

"I want to do my play about that. I think it could be really funny."

Oh. Dear.

"We could stuff some actor's pants with paper or something, and . . ."

"I'm not sure that's quite the kind of history we want to focus on, Nell."

"It could be hilarious. Like *Saturday Night Live* or something."

He paused. "I don't think you could get a project like that approved. The founding fathers . . ." He made a vague gesture and hoped she'd read enough into it.

"But—"

"No, I really don't think so."

"But—"

"Nell, you'll come up with something better, Something more interesting. And something with a lot more dramatic potential than a skit about somebody's backside." He smiled, trying to soften it. "You can do it."

Disappointed, she left.

Matt was pleased with himself. This was the kind of thing Canning wanted to prevent, and he had handled it perfectly. Matt Larrimer: organization man. Later in the day he wondered if that was quite what he had set out to become. But Canning was pleased. That meant EdEntCo would be too. And that was what mattered. Diana would like it, when he told her.

JERRY Robson loved his biology students and they loved him, or seemed to. He had a knack for making his subject lively and interesting, and he peppered his lectures with a lot of humor. He had even cracked wise about the occasional howls and thunder that shook the school.

One day when the howls were especially fierce, he made a joke about Dr. Canning's discipline methods being out of control.

It was another lab day. The table where the van der Maats twins had sat was empty. Jerry and his student assistant, Alex Marston, passed out dissecting trays and kits. Worms had come first, the previous week; everything had gone smoothly. Today, frogs.

Carroll Wilson was Tanner Morgan's lab partner. All the students had partners, even though there was more than enough money to provide each of them with materials. Teamwork, like sports, builds character.

The dissecting tray Jerry placed in front of them was metal, rectangular, fourteen inches by twelve. There was a thick layer of unattractive brown wax in it; here and there it was stained with something else, something left over from the worms. After the tray came a packet of three-inch-long black pins. Tanner picked it up and undid the strip of paper binding the pins together. Clumsily, he dropped them, and they scattered all over the tabletop.

Carroll was the son of the CEO of a local phone company. He had an alarmingly artificial tan. He shot Tanner a dirty glance, then started picking up the pins on his side of the table. Taking one, he plunged it into Tanner's thigh.

Tanner cried out, then punched Carroll defensively. Jerry saw the commotion and got between them at once. "What's going on?"

A trickle of blood ran from Tanner's leg, leaving a stain on his khakis. He pointed to it. "He stuck me."

"Those pins aren't sterile. Get down to the nurse's office and have her put some antiseptic on it."

Tanner left quickly. The puncture stung.

"As for you, Carroll, you'll work alone today."

Carroll snickered. "That's okay."

"And I expect to see you here after school. Unless you want me to report this."

"Okay. Whatever. It was just a pin."

"After school. Promptly. Understand?"

"Yeah."

Things then went smoothly for a while. Jerry and Alex placed the living frogs in a huge bell jar filled with ether. When they were quite unconscious, they distributed them to the pairs of students. Jerry demonstrated the proper way to place the frog on its back, spread its limbs and fix them to the wax with the pins. Before Carroll pinned his, he poked it several times with his index finger to make sure it really was out.

Then came the dissection, step by step. Jerry showed them how to make a long incision down the frog's stomach, followed by two more, at the top and bottom of the first cut and perpendicular to it; then how to peel back the flesh like two flaps, fixing them to the wax with more pins. A few students were squeamish and reluctant; most were enthusiastic or else simply didn't care.

The females had egg masses in their abdomens. Jerry demonstrated the proper technique for lifting them out. One by one, the students did so. Carroll decided, since the damn thing was going to end up dead anyway, why be picky about this stuff? He scraped the eggs out of his frog with his finger and shot them at a boy a few feet away. He missed. The eggs hit the floor without making a noticeable noise; neither his intended target nor anyone else seemed to have noticed.

The frogs, of course, were still alive, and their hearts were still beating. As the students realized this, one by one—realized that they were seeing a living, functioning heart—they let out various expressions of surprise. "Cool!" "Wow!" And so on.

Carroll poked his frog's heart with the tip of his finger. It was cold; not what he expected; it felt colder than the air in the room. Gross. He touched it again. When no one was looking, he leaned down and touched it with the tip of his tongue.

Tanner came back into the room. There was a large red stain on his trousers. Jerry gestured him to the front of the lab and whispered, "Work up here with Alex. He'll show you what you've missed."

Shooting Carroll a dirty look, Tanner took a seat beside Alex. Carroll made a face at him.

Jerry began describing the frogs' internal organs, one by one, and having the students remove and examine them as he went. A few students were obviously grossed out by it; most were fine. When it came time to remove the hearts, they were fascinated, even shocked, to see that the tiny red organs continued beating even after they were cut out.

Carroll shot his at that same boy; this time he hit his target. The beating heart hit the boy in the cheek, stuck, then slid slowly downward till it fell off and landed in his lap.

"Carroll!" Jerry bellowed it. "Go to the office! Now!"

Carroll ignored him. He picked up his dissecting scalpel and started hacking at the frog's head, and laughing as he did so. The animal writhed. Jerry started walking toward Carroll's lab table. Carroll held up a hand as if to tell him, Fine, okay, I'll go. He got to his feet.

At the front of the lab, where Tanner was working with Alex, all the extra, unused dissecting kits were sitting in a stack. Nonchalantly, as if he were making for the door to go to the office, Carroll sauntered forward. Then he lunged at Tanner, caught him by his hair, pulled his head back and shoved the scalpel into his throat and left it there. Laughing, he punched Tanner viciously on the side of his head, took a step backward and said, "Nobody gets me in trouble, faggot."

Jerry rushed to tackle him. Carroll grabbed another dissecting kit, ripped out the scalpel and slashed wildly. Jerry's hands and face were torn open. Students screamed. Jerry finally got hold of Carroll and caught him in a head-lock. But Carroll managed to reach back and push a scalpel into his eye.

Jerry let him go, reaching up to put a hand over his eye, and Carroll slashed viciously at his throat. Then he went after the hysterical girl who was sitting closest to him. He caught her by the hair, as he'd done with Tanner, and sliced her cheek open, then her throat.

Finally, two girls from the softball team tackled Carroll and pinned him to the floor. One of them got across his chest and punched him repeatedly, till he passed out.

It took a moment for everyone to realize the crisis was at an end. Tanner had fallen unconscious on the floor at the front of the lab. Blood was cascading from his throat. The girl Carroll had attacked had passed out too; her wounds weren't as serious as Tanner's. Jerry was standing against a blackboard with his head back, one hand over his eyes, the other holding his throat.

Alex took charge. He told someone to get to the office quickly and tell them what had happened. Then he knelt over Tanner and began applying pressure to his throat, to try and slow the bleeding. Everyone else in the room was either crying or numb, except for a few male jocks who gathered in one corner and made jokes about how the two girls who had stopped Carroll were probably dykes.

Within moments the school was in lockdown again. Brookhiser rushed to the lab to take command. By the time he got there, Jerry Robson was dead.

There were howls echoing through the halls of Washington Academy, the same wailing voice the students and faculty had become more or less used to. Clearly the same voice; no one could have mistaken it. But this time the voice was laughing wildly, not crying. The laughter was even more disturbing than the cries of pain had been.

THERE had been media, inevitably. Canning ordered the school kept under lockdown till the last of the reporters got tired, missed their deadlines and went away. All that aired on the evening news was some footage of the ambulances as they drove away and a few exterior shots of the Lisniecki Research Wing.

Diana had had a date with Peter Morgan that night, but he had to attend a hastily organized meeting, to plan damage control. She called Matt, he was free. They fucked. Neither of them talked much. Each seemed to want to become lost in that one instant, that one surge of intense pleasure that blocked out everything else in the world, at least for a moment.

School was canceled the following day. The board used their connections to keep the story out of the news spotlight; it would be dead in another day or two. Some students told their families; some seemed not to want to talk about it or anything else. Tanner and the girl were recovering. Tanner would miss a few weeks of school; the girl's wounds were much less serious, but her face would be scarred.

Then, when Washington reopened, everything and everyone was much quieter than usual. Diana described it as "subdued." Matt stared at her. " 'Numb' would be more the word, don't you think?"

"I warned you about the kind of kids we'd get here back when we first met. Remember?"

When the first notes of Beethoven's Fifth sounded, they seemed impossibly shrill; nearly everyone in the building wished Canning would find something else. Diana commented on it. Matt was wry. "How about Chopin's 'Funeral March'?"

There was an assembly. Bishop Hinkle led a big, long prayer; most of the students mumbled along with him, pretending it would do some good. But the assembly's primary goal was to warn the students not to talk to the media. Peter Morgan "advised" them to be discreet, on pain of expulsion. He was not happy; this venture was taking up more of his time that he had anticipated. Damned crazy kids.

Classes went well and quietly. Matt was still teaching precolonial history. It mattered. He believed that. His lectures were focused and intense, and even a few of his students came away with the conviction that, yes, old things and long-dead people mattered. If anyone had pressed them, they could never have explained why.

After his last class, Matt decided to avoid the faculty lounge. He put everything in order, closed his briefcase, put on his jacket and headed for the classroom door. Just as he reached it, Charley Morgan came in.

"Charley."

The boy smiled. "Mr. Larrimer."

"Who are you looking for?"

"You."

This was unexpected. He didn't want to talk to the boy. "Oh. Well, come in, then."

Charley sauntered into the room as if it was his, which in a way it was, and looked around. "Part of me loves this old building. Part of me wishes Dad had put up something new."

"Something that doesn't groan and wail and make awful noises?"

Charley shrugged. "Old buildings settle." He smiled again. "I'm going to be an architect."

"Not an easy way to make a living." Matt leaned against his desk.

"I'm not doing it to 'make a living.' I don't have to worry about that. But wait till you see what I build."

"I'd have pegged you for a future lawyer."

"I've thought about that, too. That's what Dad wants for me. Then politics. He says with my looks, I'd be a cinch."

Matt had never paid much attention to Charley's looks. He was short, a good four inches shorter than his cousins, maybe a bit more. His eyes were pale blue, his hair dark blond. And he had a bad complexion; Matt was pleased to see there are some things money can't buy. But overall, yes, the boy was rather handsome, in a clean-cut way. He had to force himself not to think of the Hitler Youth.

There was an awkward gap in the conversation. Matt felt himself fidgeting; he wanted to get out. "Have you been to see Tanner?"

"Yeah. He was passed out when I was there. He looks pretty when he's asleep."

"You'd know."

Smug smile. "I'd know. Tanner says you're clueless."

"Tanner would know about cluelessness."

Charley abruptly switched gears. "There's something wrong in this school, isn't there?"

Matt kept his voice neutral. "Is there?"

"Everyone in the student body knows it. Most of us don't care. As long as we don't get it next, that is."

"Look, horrible things have happened here, sure. We all know it. But they were freak occurrences, Charley."

"Dad and Canning have you housebroken. But I thought the phrase of choice was 'isolated incidents.' "

"If you prefer."

"Every time I hear that, I find myself wondering, Isolated from what, exactly?"

Matt was starting to feel uncomfortable. He had never really talked to Charley before. The boy was brighter than he'd expected. And much more direct. There was something unsettling about him.

Charley went on. "Do you really think whatever was wrong with Jon Lampl and Carroll Wilson and the van der Maats twins developed in them 'isolated' from everything else in society?"

Matt groped for words but couldn't find any.

"Relax, Mr. Larrimer. Nobody really cares about any of that, not as long as we're getting what we want. And that's not what I want to talk to you about, anyway."

Matt found himself looking out the windows at the parking lot. Alexis was there, talking to Cal Conklin. He forced himself to turn back to Charley. "What can I do for you, then?"

"I have an idea for a project—you know, one of those history plays. Mrs. Bettis said I have to get your approval before I can go ahead with it."

Matt relaxed a bit. "Shoot."

"That's not a verb you should use with a student in this school."

"Charley, please."

"Joke—it was just a joke."

"A bad one. What's your idea?"

"Well . . ." He suddenly sat down at one of the desks and put on what Matt was beginning to think of as the Morgan grin. "I've been reading about Franklin Roosevelt."

"Good subject." For whatever reason, the students really were starting to pay attention to history. "What, specifically?"

"I want to do a play about how he married his cousin."

It was the last thing Matt had expected to hear. And the last thing he wanted to. "I'm not sure that would be a good idea. You know why."

"You mean because of me and Alexis?"

"You know exactly what I mean."

"I only fuck her because it ticks Tanner off. And I only fuck him to annoy her. We're a big, happy family." He laughed, long and hard.

"I don't want to hear any more about it, Charley. I didn't even hear that. Do you understand?"

"Don't worry, my play wouldn't be like that. This would be all about how his wife turned out to be a dyke and he started screwing his secretary."

"Charley, stop it."

"From his wheelchair."

"Charley."

"It would be really dramatic, don't you think? This palsied old bastard, limping around on crutches, his queer wife, his secretary sucking his—"

"Charley! That's enough!"

Again the boy laughed. He was plainly on something. "If you say so. Can I go ahead with it?"

"You really are something, Charlton." He laid ironic emphasis on the boy's name.

"I knew you'd notice."

"You cannot do that play. Period. Understand?"

"How about a play based on Alexander Hamilton's love letters to John Laurens, then?"

Matt glared at him.

"Or Abe Lincoln's syphilis?"

Matt reached his limit. Tanner had said, way back when, that Charley was the brightest of their family. Matt would have given anything, just then, to have it otherwise. "All right, now look. You can go ahead and torment Tanner and Alexis all you want. There's nothing I can do about that. But don't play these games with me. You hear? Not again."

"Do you think I don't read? Do you think I don't know any history? You can't keep it hidden. It's dangerous to let it out, Mr. Larrimer, but it's even more dangerous to try and hide it. You know what William Blake said: " 'Expect poison from the standing water.' "

Matt kept his voice carefully neutral. "You read Blake."

"Doesn't everyone?" Charley shrugged.

"No. I never have."

"You should. Read *The Marriage of Heaven and Hell*. No book I've ever read has explained the world so clearly."

"A little learning is a dangerous thing, Charley."

"That's from Alexander Pope. From "An Essay on Man." Or is it his "Essay on Criticism"? I can never remember which, can you?"

The boy was one up on him yet again. Matt wished he'd gotten out of the building sooner.

Just at that moment Matt saw someone passing in the hall outside the classroom. A boy stuck his head in. "Charley. I've been looking all over for you."

Charley got up, and his manner turned formal. "Do you two know each other?" They both said no, and he made a show of introducing them. "Mr. Larrimer, Alex Marston."

"You're the student who—who—"

Charley laughed. "Yes, he's 'the student who,' all right."

Alex ignored all of this. "We just got our first ship-
ment of stuff for the head. Mr. Cullen's connecting it
right now."

"The head, Alex?" Matt was grateful for the interruption.

"The Robotics Club. We've decided to try and build a
fully functioning robotic head. One that can do everything a real human head can do."

Matt was a bit put off; science wasn't at all his thing.
"You must be the only club in the school that isn't doing
a history project."

Charley laughed again, even harder than before.
"That's what you think."

Before Matt could ask him to explain, the two boys
said good-bye and left, heading for the Lisniecki wing.

Matt made ready to leave again. And again he caught
sight of Alexis and Cal outside. They were kissing. Making a show of it. He wondered if they thought anyone
would care. Then it dawned on him that, yes, there were
people who would.

SUNSET.

The first Saturday in October. No school—happily for
nearly everyone—and the world was bathed in the deep
orange-red light of the dying sun. And all over the city,
the staff and students of Washington Academy were
bathed in it too.

D. Michael Canning was alone in the school building
except for the maintenance crew in the basement. No, not
in that warm, living place; he had made certain that was
off-limits to everyone. They were in the boiler room, getting drunk on cheap wine.

It was the students, Canning told himself. They were the
problem. The school was fine, the institution was fine,

everything about it was a sound idea. No, not merely sound: *good.* Washington Academy was good. Once he weeded out the bad students, everything would be . . .

But who were they? *Why* were they? What had made them into the creatures they were? He had talked to Nick Brookhiser about trying to screen out the bad ones, to test them all for evil propensities, but Nick said there was no reliable way. And there would be civil rights issues, inconvenient matters like presumption of innocence. The ACLU would be on their corporate ass in a heartbeat. Some of these kids came from liberal families.

Innocence. The presumption of innocence. What a joke. He poured himself a tall glass of bourbon and drank and laughed. An hour later he was drunk enough to pass out. . . .

Peter Morgan stripped naked and got on his knees in front of Diana Ketterer. She slapped him. He liked it. It gave him an erection. It made him shiver with pleasure. She slapped him again, much harder. It left a large red mark on his cheek, and he stiffened even more. And a third time, harder still. His breathing was heavy. She strapped a dog collar around his throat and yanked it till he had trouble getting his breath. "Now, little Peter," she whispered caressingly, "open your mouth." Between them, there was no presumption of innocence. . . .

In a dingy room in the Hill District, with the sounds of family members coming from the next room, Alexis Morgan undressed herself, then undressed Cal Conklin. His body was leaner and more beautiful than anything she'd ever touched before. They kissed, they made love, they fucked wildly. She knew better than to tell him she was falling in love with him, though, even though it was true. . . .

Mike Monticelli shot baskets in his family's driveway.

His arm ached, and he knew he shouldn't force it, but he couldn't resist. The pain, at least, was something he could feel. . . .

Matt Larrimer drove into the parking lot of Mount of Moses Hospital, the wealthiest private hospital in the region. Suburban; there were ornamental trees all around, a fantastic luxury. Were they there to screen patients from the world, or to keep the world from seeing the blood and the pain?

Tanner Morgan was asleep in a private room in the ICU. Matt stepped into the room, quite quietly, and watched him for a few moments. The boy's head and throat were bandaged. IV tubes fed him. Machines with lighted dials monitored him. The rise and fall of his chest was barely discernible.

A nurse stepped up behind Matt. "Can I help you?" She was short and a bit plump; her uniform was too tight.

Matt gestured at Tanner. "I'm one of his teachers."

"Oh. From—from—"

"Washington Academy."

"Washington Academy, yes."

There was a long beat; each waited for the other to go on. The nurse fidgeted. "You shouldn't be here."

"I had to see how he's doing."

"Critical condition. But stable and getting slowly better. You should leave."

"Has anyone else been here to . . . ?"

"His sister. And there's a cousin. Attractive boy."

He wasn't certain whether she meant Charley or Tanner. "What about the parents?"

"They're in Europe. On some kind of business trip, I think."

"Oh."

Another long pause. She looked him up and down. "My teachers were never so good-looking."

Matt felt himself blushing. "Thanks."

"Have you . . . have you seen the facility? Has anyone shown you around?"

"No, this is the first time I've been here." Again he gestured at Tanner's bed. "I thought I should . . . I thought someone should . . . Hell, I don't know what I thought. I guess I should be going."

"No." She smiled at him. "Let me show you around. I really shouldn't. I'm the only one on the floor right now. But . . ." Her smile got wider.

She looked cute in her tight uniform; it made her tits stand out. She showed him around her floor, one dark, secluded place after another. A few minutes later they were in a storage room, fucking like rats.

IT was nearly dark outside. Tanner woke and looked groggily around the room. The monitors he was connected to hummed and beeped. Just as he looked at it, the liquid-filled plastic bag connected to his IV bubbled.

Fuck this. Fuck just lying here. One by one, he pulled off the sensors. Then, quite violently, he pulled the IV needle out of his arm. It hurt; Tanner smiled. There was a flow of blood, and he licked it clean.

He got unsteadily to his feet; he had to hold the edge of the bed for a moment. The floor was cold, even though it was carpeted. He walked to the door.

There was no one at the nurse's station. He went to it, opened drawers, rummaged through the contents of shelves. Finally he found a bottle of OxyContin. *Yes.*

Two pills—no, four—no, eight.

He went back to his bed. He took the IV needle and plunged it back into his arm; it hurt even more than it had coming out, and he smiled a broad smile. He had no idea if it was in right, and he didn't care. One by one he reconnected the sensors to where he thought he remembered they'd been.

Charley kept telling him he loved him. So did his parents. So did Uncle Peter. So did Alexis. Here he was, alone.

He fell asleep. Deep asleep. There were dreams. He saw a headless figure, a huge ghost, twelve feet tall, stalking through the halls of Washington Academy. It carried a sword, and was cutting off the head of one student after another and slitting their bodies open.

On a table in a room filled with computers there was a bronze head, or brass—some yellow metal. The ghost took it and cradled it in the crook of its free arm. Then it placed the head on its shoulders, where its own head should have been.

Tanner was at the end of the hall, watching as one classmate after another was beheaded and disemboweled. Then he was the only one left. The ghost turned and walked slowly in his direction. He was trapped. The bronze head opened its mouth and spoke: "All this you will see come to pass. All this and more."

The ghost swung its sword, and Tanner felt it slice through his neck. The world spun, and he realized that his severed head was spinning through the air. With a wet thud, it hit the floor and lay on its right side.

The air was filled with what seemed to be black sparks. He tried to whisper to the ghost, "I am not dead." But even though his lips moved, there was no sound, no voice. The ghost walked slowly away, bronze head still balanced carefully on its shoulders. There were more and more black sparks, and Tanner realized that his disconnected brain and nerves were dying. This was what death looked like, then: more and more flecks of black nothing, floating, swirling, swarming, until finally they blocked out everything else.

SIX

TANNER

"MR. Larrimer!"

Matt was walking down a hallway, looking for Bill Cullen's office; they were on a faculty committee together. He heard a familiar voice calling him. Checking the nearest doorways, he finally saw Charley Morgan, Alex Marston and two other boys in the Physics Lab. His spirits dropped a bit; he was never quite comfortable around Charley. The kid was definitely on the odd side, and Matt knew a bit too much about his personal life for comfort.

"Mr. Larrimer! You've got to see this."

He stepped inside. "Yes?"

"Alex has got the first bit of our head up and working."

Matt stepped in and looked around. The lab was huge, certainly larger than any space the History Department had access to, and it was cluttered with all kinds of equipment and tools. The boys were clustered around a table with three computers, each with its own monitor, and a pair of large speakers; and there was what looked like a telescope on a stick. He smiled, said hi and crossed to them. "There isn't much I've 'got' to see in a place like this."

Alex piped up. "You'll want to see this. We just got everything connected. You're the first teacher—even Mr. Cullen hasn't seen it yet."

"Fine." He tried to hide his disinterest and smiled as he went to join them. Physics. If there was one subject he had hated in school . . .

As he approached, the telescope rotated on its "stick." It seemed to follow him; he actually had the feeling it was staring at him, which he knew was silly, but . . . It whirred. The movement startled him mildly, and he stared at the thing. It was a foot long; the front lens was two inches across, maybe a bit more. "So the Physics Department is designing security cameras for mall shops?"

"Better than that." Alex was pleased with himself; he let it show. "Look closer."

Matt was four feet from the thing. He took one more step forward and bent down to examine it. A distorted reflection of his eye peered back at him. A voice came from the speakers, but for an astonished moment Matt thought it had come out of midair, out of nowhere. Haltingly, it spoke. "T-t-t-t-addimet." The voice was disconcertingly human, even if it didn't seem to be saying anything intelligible.

Even more startled, he straightened up and backed away.

"Our voice synthesizer isn't working quite right yet." Alex was the soul of pride. "But we'll get it where it needs to be."

"And what, exactly, is 'Taddimet'?"

"It was trying to say your name. Like I said, we've still got work to do."

"It recognized me?"

Alex nodded. "Let me introduce you to everyone here. This is Claude Hinkle. Bishop Hinkle's nephew. The one who's writing that play. And this is Peter Dominic. Pete won that big wrestling match a couple weeks ago, remember? We're the core of the Robotics Club." He was simply beaming. Peter, a large, dark-haired boy with muscles showing through his clothes, didn't look especially happy or pleased the way the others did.

The mention of a play caught Matt's ear. "You've written a play, Claude?"

He nodded; Matt got the impression he was a bit shy. "About the beheading of John the Baptist."

"I thought all the plays were supposed to be about American history."

"This one isn't for the competition. It's just something I wrote. Mrs. Bettis says it's good. I based it part on the bible and part on Oscar Wilde."

"Oh." He was tempted to make a comment about Charley being part Oscar Wilde too, but he held his tongue.

"We're already in rehearsal. We open in two weeks."

So much for Matt's role in the Drama Department. He wondered if it would be any good; none of the other scripts students had shown him had had much merit.

Charley added, "Alexis is playing Salome. She was born for it."

Matt turned to Claude. "You cast her in the part?"

"Yeah, she wanted it. She fought for it, even."

Charley added, "I didn't think she would, not after . . . not after what happened last Christmas. But she really wants to play the part."

"What happened last Christmas?"

"Her brother . . . my cousin Matt . . ."

He remembered. And he thought it was nice that there were some topics that were too touchy even for Charley. But . . . more of the Morgans. Matt wished he'd never become involved with any of them, even at a distance. He had to censor himself from making a wisecrack about Alexis doing the "Dance of the Seven Veils" privately for Charley.

Alex was getting restless. The attention had been off him and his little gizmo too long. He stepped between Matt and Claude. "This focuses automatically. Of course, we've only just started. We're getting a second optical sensor. Once they're properly aligned, our head will have binocular vision."

And of course Charley had to speak up. "And that's just the beginning. There will be auditory sensors, heat sensors, all kinds of things. And we'll be getting a lot more computers, at least a dozen and maybe more than that, so it'll be able to do some really sophisticated things."

"It already can, I guess. How did it know me?"

"We've scanned in visual images of all the faculty. Multiple ones—images taken from multiple angles." Matt had noticed them taking pictures around the school; he had thought vaguely that it must be for the yearbook. "When we get enough memory, it'll even focus on parameters like eye color, maybe even retinal patterns. These lenses are large enough for it to see a lot—a lot more than we do. It would recognize you anywhere."

For some reason Matt didn't find this reassuring. "And the school's paying for all this?" It was more than slightly annoying. His own request for a set of maps had just been turned down, $180, and here was the school spending a fortune on toys.

"Some of it." Peter Dominic seemed less and less happy; Matt sensed it was something personal. Did the boy not want teachers to be in on their hotshot project?

"Alex is a wizard." Charley had obviously decided he'd better do the group's PR. "He's got connections out at CMU. There's a guy in their robotics program named Sean Kelly who works with Alex one-on-one. He's giving us stuff their program's done with. But it's still good."

Alex added, "Sean's a bit of a genius."

The speaker announced, "T-t-t-t-addimet. Keddy."

Alex cooed into its microphone. "That's right, this is Mr. Larrimer, and we're talking about Sean Kelly."

"Good," said the speaker. "Matt-yew Taddimet." Now that Matt was getting used to it, the voice sounded more and more artificial to him. But at first it had seemed quite human, and unsettling.

Peter grinned. "Why don't you say hello to it, Mr. Larrimer?"

He wanted to get out. "I don't know its name. Should I call it Hal? Or Colossus? Or what?"

"We haven't given it a name yet." Charley seemed dismayed at the realization.

"Cullen!" Peter beamed. "Let's name it after Mr. Cullen. He was the one who suggested it."

"*I'm* the one who suggested it." Alex sniffed. "Remember?"

Charley did. "It was my idea."

The boys had a quick conference and agreed they liked the name. Matt laughed. "Just don't go naming anything after me, okay?"

"Don't worry, we only do high tech."

It was a mild insult, but he didn't care. "Well, thanks for the demonstration. I'll see you all later, okay?" Pointedly, he added, "Good-bye, Cullen."

The computer didn't respond.

"We have to teach it its name," Claude said condescendingly.

Just then Bill Cullen stuck his head in the door. "How's it going, guys?" He saw Matt. "Oh, Mr. Larrimer, I was just going to come over to your wing and look for you."

"I've been here, holding a conversation with this gadget of yours. Or trying to."

"Come on, let's talk." Once they were out of earshot of the boys, Cullen lowered his voice and added, "If you think *that* was a one-way conversation, you should try talking to Canning. He's in his office, drunk again."

"I'm surprised the dragon lady let you in. She usually protects him."

"I'm a scientist, remember? I made myself invisible."

"Do you know they've named their little computer-telescope thing in there after you?"

"Really?"

"Yeah, just now."

"I guess I should be flattered."

"They said it was your idea, so . . ." He made a gesture, spreading his hands apart, rather than finishing the sentence.

"It wasn't my idea at all. It wasn't. Charley Morgan came up with it."

"Weird. I wouldn't have thought our little Charley was the type to share the credit with anyone else."

"He's not. But never mind him. With Canning drinking all the time, the faculty's got more and more to do in running the school."

"I'm starting to think this school's a mistake, Bill. There's something wrong here. We all know it." He found himself yawning. "Maybe we should just let everything unravel."

"So you don't need this job?"

"Point taken." Matt yawned a second time. "'Scuse me. Well, we have to do a better job than our august leader." He glanced back toward the lab. "I hope."

"What's that supposed to mean? How could we not?" Cullen looked around and lowered his voice. "At least we're sober."

From the lab behind them came a loud, staticky electronic squawk, followed even more loudly by the voice of the head. "Taddimet. Coo-lawn. Coo-lawn. Coo-lawn. Larrimet. Larrimer."

Matt found it annoying. "Should you be encouraging students to build a thing like that?"

"Robotics is a coming field, Matt. Cutting-edge. We owe it to our kids to put them on that track."

"Sure."

A low howl echoed through the halls. Neither of them paid it much mind.

In the lab, Alex played with some settings. "Cullen," he said patiently to his computer. "Cullen."

"Coo-lawn. Coo-lawn."

"Cullen."

"Coo-lawn."

Peter Dominic watched, still unhappy for no apparent reason. Under his breath he muttered, "Shit."

In the hall Matt and Bill finished their little confab. Nothing overt could be done about Canning, not without involving the board. But the faculty had to begin to take over some of the administration or the school would fold and they'd all be out of jobs. Matt hated the thought, but he promised Bill he'd talk privately with the teachers he knew he could trust.

As he was heading back to the Liberal Arts wing, just as he was passing the Physics Lab, he heard his name called. "Matthew Larrimer." It took him a moment to realize it was the computer talking, getting its pronunciation right now. Against his better judgment, he looked in.

There was another howl, louder and more agonized than the one before. The four boys looked at one another, not certain what to make of it. It was coming from their speakers.

LATE October was rainy and cool. The leaves on the few trees in the neighborhood turned early and were falling by the second week of the month. Canning asked for student volunteers to rake them from the school's sidewalks and parking lots; none came forward. More janitorial staff had to be hired, and EdEntCo was unhappy about it. The bottom line was slipping more and more. It would be worse in winter, when snow had to be cleared, but at least they had budgeted for that. Canning prayed for a warm, dry season.

He remembered his first visit to the school all too well. The echoing howls that everyone else had gotten used to still unsettled him. Bourbon helped.

The only one he could talk to—the only one who knew what he knew about the thing hidden in the school's basement—was Nick Brookhiser. But Nick seemed unconcerned. They talked often in Canning's private office.

"These wails we keep hearing, Nick. They're so awful."

"It's just the building settling, that's all."

"Buildings don't settle a hundred years after they're built, Nick. There's something else. There has to be."

"Listen to me, Michael, you're drinking too much, and it's getting the best of you. You can't let your imagination run away like this."

"My wife's been telling me for years I don't have any

imagination." Canning got the bottle and a pair of glasses out of his desk drawer. "You want one?"

Brookhiser shook his head.

"So . . . these horrible sounds we keep hearing. You're telling me they're imaginary?"

"No, Michael, I'm telling you you're imagining that they're something more than they really are."

"What are they?" He filled his glass and gestured to the second one. Brookhiser shook his head again. "What do *you* think they are?"

Brookhiser shrugged. "Does it make any difference?"

"And all these terrible things that keep happening here?"

"Coincidence. Isolated incidents. Michael, you're the principal here. You have to act more responsibly. If someone from the board drops by and sees you like this . . . It's eleven in the morning, for Christ's sake."

Long drink. "Screw the board. Nick, I don't think I'm going to get out of this alive. I'm not sure any of us will."

Brookhiser sat back in his chair. This was worse than he'd thought. Paranoia. Alcohol-induced? Should he tell Peter Morgan or someone else on the board? Should he be "loyal" to Canning? "Listen, Michael, if you're so worried about this place, call in a structural engineer and have him give it a thorough inspection. That's the only way you'll know for sure."

Canning held his empty glass in front of his eyes and stared into it. He seemed to be wondering whether to drink more or not. Finally he put it down on his desk. "You know we can't do that. A thorough inspection would turn up our friend downstairs."

"Let it get turned up, then."

"People are already starting to pull their kids out of Washington. More publicity would—"

"Who says we'd get publicity? This kind of thing can be done off the record. We're EdEntCo, remember?"

He poured himself another drink after all. "We're spending too much money. And losing revenue. Every time a student leaves . . ." He spread his hands in a helpless gesture. "And applications for the next school year are way below what we projected. The board's unhappy. They haven't said it, but I know they are."

"Well, all I know, Michael, is that having you drink around here isn't going to help anything."

"It helps *me*."

Brookhiser got to his feet. "You're useless when you're like this. Everyone's covering for you—the faculty, that witch who guards your door out there. A lot of us are getting tired of it."

"You can always go back to doing corporate security."

"You're right, I can. That's what this was supposed to be."

"Are you going to?"

"Sober up, Michael. We'll talk when you're sober." He turned and left, slamming the door rather pointedly.

Canning picked up his glass and toasted the empty air behind Brookhiser, then took a long drink. "If ever."

Almost at once there came a knock at the door. It opened, and Bishop Hinkle put his head in. "Hello, Michael. Are you busy?"

"Bishop." Canning quickly opened a desk drawer and put his drink and the bottle into it, hoping Hinkle hadn't noticed. "What a surprise."

Hinkle walked in and sat down, not bothering to shake Canning's hand. He sniffed the air: bourbon. Then he put on a big, artificial smile. "I stopped in to see how Claude's doing, and I thought I should pay my respects."

"It's always nice to see you." Polite lie. "Please, make

yourself comfortable. But you should have had Mrs. Newburg announce you."

"She wanted to, but I outrank her." Hinkle shifted uncomfortably. "So, how are things going, Michael?"

"Officially, things are marvelous." Was Hinkle checking him out on the board's behalf, then?

"And unofficially?"

"Things are marvelous."

"Hiding good bourbon in desk drawers isn't exactly a healthy sign, you know."

Canning felt himself blushing.

"The Lord gave us those grains so they could be used. Wasting them is sinful." He broke into a broad grin. "Besides, it's most rude not to offer a guest a drink."

"Bishop! I'm . . . I . . . I'm . . ."

"Did you think I was teetotal? Not with *my* wife." His smile disappeared. "Make it a tall one."

Canning got two glasses, then reached into the case under his desk, got a fresh bottle and opened it. In a moment they were both drinking deeply. And Canning was still registering surprise.

Hinkle, between swallows, put that smile back on. "If you could see what I have to deal with. Women ministers. Have you ever had to deal with a woman minister?"

"I haven't, no. Are they . . . ?"

"Bitches, every last one of them. And flaky bitches at that. And now we've got all these homosexuals wanting into the ministry." He drained his glass and held it out for a refill. "But that's not what I wanted to talk about.

"Good. I can't do much about that." He poured another drink for the bishop, filling his glass to the rim and letting some slosh over onto Hinkle's sleeve. Let him explain the smell to his wife.

"No, I wanted to talk to you about all these . . . unfortunate occurrences here."

Canning waved a dismissive hand. "Isolated incidents."

"Of course. Of course they are. But I've been thinking, Michael."

"Hmm?"

"There are all these rumors around the neighborhood. About this place being haunted. They've been making their way into the press."

"Don't I know it." He poured another drink for himself, too. "Every time somebody's car gets scratched in the parking lot, people start crying about the 'Washington Academy Curse' and the 'Washington Academy Ghost.'" He drank. Then he said, with strong emphasis, "There is no ghost."

"Exactly. As I said, I've been thinking."

"Yes?"

"Well, I mean, Michael . . . we'd have to run this past the rest of the board, of course. But I can't imagine they'd have any objections."

"For a plain-speaking bishop, you beat around the bush a lot." The drink was having its effect, and then some.

Hinkle took a deep breath. "I want to do an exorcism."

"A what?!"

"An exorcism. I propose we exorcise the school."

"I'm afraid I'm not religious enough to take that seriously, Bishop Hinkle."

"Oh, no, not a real one." He lowered his voice to a confidential whisper. "Between us, no one I know really believes in that sort of thing." He sat back in his chair and crossed, then uncrossed, his legs. "Well, maybe a few Catholics."

Canning had the impression he was pausing for dramatic effect.

"But as a public relations move, Michael, it could do enormous good. We'd do press releases, of course. It would be there in the papers, in black-and-white. 'Superstition says the school is haunted. Episcopal bishop Grover Hinkle, head of the largest Protestant denomination in Pittsburgh, proves it's not.'"

"No one would take it seriously. It would make us look ridiculous."

"You're wrong, Michael. Everyone would. When have you ever heard anyone in the public forum question any pronouncement by an established church?"

Canning's eyes narrowed. "You're a fraud. Do you know that?"

"How?" Hinkle's face was blank. "If we can use the Lord's work to protect this school . . ." He left the sentence unfinished and sat back in his chair, looking smug.

"Not to mention protecting your stock in EdEntCo."

"An incidental concern, I assure you."

"Let me think about this. I can't honestly say I like the idea. I think it would make us a laughingstock. Not to mention drawing more attention to everything that's happened."

"An unexamined life is not worth living, Michael." He became a stern bishop, sermonizing. "Can you say with any real authority that there absolutely isn't such thing as a ghost?"

"Of course not, but—"

"There you are, then." Again his tone turned confidential. "You'd be amazed what people will believe, if you only present it properly." Hinkle stood to go, quickly draining his glass. "I'd think about it fast and hard, if I were you, Michael. It may be the only way to spin things here in a positive way. This school is an important asset to the region. The church will be only too happy to help it continue. We would be derelict in our duty otherwise."

"Of course."

The drink had hit Hinkle harder than Canning had realized. Or had he been drinking before he got here? Either way, he staggered a bit as he was leaving. Canning watched him go, relieved to be alone. An exorcism. Damnfool nonsense. The board would quash it. It would turn Washington Academy into a circus, complete with clowns and monkeys.

Canning knew he had drunk more than enough. He wanted more, but . . . As he put the bottle back in the drawer, he found himself thinking, again and again, *There is no ghost, there is no ghost, there is none.*

Bishop Hinkle walked through the school to the back door, the one nearest the parking lot. A few students said respectful hellos to him, but he was too lost in thought, or simply too tipsy, to notice them. And he forgot about checking on his nephew, even when he reeled past the Physics Lab.

The four members of the Robotics Club had gone off to their various classes. But the robotic optical sensor rotated and watched him pass the door. "Hinkle," it said to itself. "Hinkle. Bishop. Fool. Dead soon."

A howl echoed through the halls.

AFTER the initial excited flurry of activity, the idea of plays about American history got old and other things captured the students' attention. Matt didn't seem to realize it, but he was part of what dampened everyone's enthusiasm. He had rejected too many ideas about problematic or embarrassing bits of the national past—slavery, rebellion, sexual scandals. It actually seemed to him that some of the students were going out of their way to dig up subjects that would make him uncomfortable: Jefferson's affair with Sally Hemmings; Franklin Pierce's love affair with Nathaniel Hawthorne. Using his own field of study against him. He didn't know whether he should feel paranoid.

Word spread about the play about John the Baptist and Salome; it was to be the Drama Club's first presentation, a few days before Halloween. It generated a surprising amount of comment; everyone wondered how far Alexis Morgan would strip. Mrs. Bettis, concerned about the rumors, had a long talk with her. "No surprises, Alexis, do you hear?"

"I believe in realism, Mrs. Bettis." Alexis goaded her. "Don't you?"

"Alexis, this is serious."

She let out an exasperated sigh. "You really don't have to worry. I may be a slut, but I'm not a dumb one."

"I never said you were a—"

"Don't give it another thought, okay, Mrs. Bettis?"

Mildly curious, Matt asked Mrs. Bettis if he might see the script. "Just to check for historical accuracy." He put on a sheepish grin. "I mean, I know it's based on the bible, but even so . . ."

"This is more of a fantasia on a historical incident. There's no need for you to review it."

"Oh." But he had to ask. "Can Claude write?"

"I've been getting complaints from students about you, Mr. Larrimer."

This caught him off guard. "What kind of complaints?"

"About you rejecting every idea they come to you with."

"Orders from above, I'm afraid."

She scowled. "Above? What 'above'?"

" 'D. Michael Canning' above. We're not to present anything that might make an audience uncomfortable."

"Oh."

"The trustees and their wives may well attend some of these plays. And a lot of them have kids here. We have to make certain what's presented is sound." This seemed to be a new idea to her, so he added helpfully, "Historically."

"I've seen a lot more history than you have, Mr. Larrimer. Very little of it is 'sound'."

"Even so. Our principal has spoken. What can I do? Besides," he decided to play with her head, "I hear this John the Baptist play is going to feature a cooch dance."

"Mr. Larrimer!"

He grinned at her. "I was only asking."

"Really!"

"You might do us both a favor and try to discourage the kids from any history that might be too touchy for the higher-ups, okay?"

"Several of them want to write about slavery."

"That's fine, as long as they understand that everyone hated it, even the slave owners, and the slaves' lives weren't really all that hard."

Mrs. Bettis narrowed her eyes. Matt had the feeling she could see inside of him. "I knew the day we met you were a company man. That's not what teaching is about."

"We won't be able to teach at all if we lose our jobs, right?" She was old; she had a pension from the school district where she'd taught most of her life. Which was to say she didn't need this job, not the way Matt did. It hardly seemed politic to say so. He was tempted to bring up the subject of Canning's drinking and of the faculty quietly assuming some of his responsibilities. But it was obvious she wouldn't be very receptive, at least not now.

She lowered her voice. "The entire idea behind this project—which, may I remind you, originated with the board—was to let our students explore history and voice their attitudes toward it."

"Look, Mrs. Bettis. Things are bad around here. Things are coming unstuck, in all kinds of ways." He hoped she'd realize he meant Canning. "Don't make them even worse, all right? There are some things our students are better off not knowing."

"Spoken like a true teacher." Her voice oozed sarcasm.

He had had enough of her. He said a curt "Good afternoon" and left.

THE school wrestling team, led by Peter Dominic and coached by Mort Mortkowski, won six consecutive meets. There had been complaints from other teams about illegal tactics and even viciousness on the part of Washington's athletes, but there was never anything concrete; it all happened in the heat of the moment—it wasn't *intentional*. So nothing was done.

Mike Monticelli was back in school, still recuperating, still not able to compete. But he was well enough to do a light workout with his teammates. The first few days, Mortkowski kept an eye on him, to make sure he didn't push himself too hard or too far; after that, Mike more or less faded. The other wrestlers ignored him, as they had before, once the novelty of having him back wore off. The scholarship kid.

Matt was happy to see him back. "You're looking great."

"Am I?" The fact that he was no more accepted now than he had been before sank in quickly.

"And you're back earlier than anyone expected."

"You helped, Mr. Larrimer. I hope you know how much I appreciate all the time you spent on me."

"It's my job." Matt smiled.

"But I can't tell you how I wish I was back at Roland. I had forgotten how much I hate this place."

"Oh." The best-laid plans . . . "I'm sorry, Mike."

"It's not your fault. You're the only one here who's ever been decent to me."

"That can't be true."

"Don't be a fool, Mr. Larrimer." He turned and started to go, then paused and looked back over his shoulder. "Thanks again."

Matt watched him go. Wishing he was back at Roland . . . It seemed such an alien thought. This was Washington Academy. Then, so abruptly it jarred him, Matt had the same thought.

In the third week of October there was a meet against a high school from the far eastern suburbs, Canon-Salem High. Mike was on the bench, in his unitard but not quite ready to compete yet. But he was making a show of supporting Peter and the others. "Kill him, Pete! Kill him!"

There was a complaint from the opposing coach: illegal holding. Peter's opponent was holding his crotch, claiming he'd been hurt there.

The match was halted while the coaches and officials discussed it. This sort of behavior was not to be encouraged; it was unsportsmanlike. The Washington fans booed. When the match resumed, Peter grabbed his opponent's crotch and twisted the protective cup as hard as he could. It took a bit of effort on Peter's part, but the boy finally cried out in pain. Peter laughed. No one had noticed.

The boy complained to the officials again, but this time not even his coach had seen what happened. The judge and referee warned him that he'd be penalized if he kept making frivolous complaints to slow down the match.

Action resumed. Again Peter waited for the moment when no one could see. He had his opponent in a tight hold. He kissed him on the cheek, licked it and left it wet, then whispered, "You're going to be my girl, bitch."

The Canon-Salem wrestler became so angry at what Peter was getting away with, he lost control of himself and attacked him, kicking him in the stomach. Peter fought back with a vengeance. He knocked the other wrestler down and began kicking him repeatedly. Then he jumped on his chest and began punching his face and head.

Mike Monticelli leapt to his feet, cheering Peter on. "Kill him, Pete! Tear his head off! Kill him!"

The Washington fans took their cue from Mike and began shouting for more violence. "Kill him! Kill him! Rip his fucking head off!"

The boy went into a seizure, then lost consciousness. The game was halted. When the medics arrived, his unconscious body was still twitching occasionally; they took him away quickly. But no one faulted Peter; the other athlete had started it. By week's end, even though the boy was still comatose in a suburban hospital, no one at Washington remembered his name. Peter was given the win by default. Canon-Salem protested the decision, but there was nothing to be done.

A few days after Mike came back to school, Tanner Morgan did too . It was grey and windy, the day Claude

Hinkle's *Salome* was to be performed for the student body, with Alexis in the lead.

It was Matt's morning free period. He was on his way to Bill Cullen's office for another meeting when he saw Tanner in what had been an unused storage room. He was tinkering with a row of computers.

As Matt walked into the room, twin optical sensors followed him. A low, synthesized masculine voice said, "Larrimer. Matthew Larrimer." He ignored it. Tanner switched off the speakers.

"Tanner. Hi. Good to have you back." He didn't mean it and hoped it wasn't obvious.

The boy was obviously weak, and a bit pale. "Hello, Mr. Larrimer."

"You're looking good."

"I look like bloody shit and you know it." There were scars; they showed.

Oh. "You don't look that bad. How are you feeling?"

"How do you think?"

"I'd guess you're something like your old self." He kept a straight face; it took Tanner a moment to realize Matt was kidding him. "I didn't know you were a computer nerd."

"This is the new Robotics Lab. Charley talked me into joining the group. He says I need to keep busy."

"Do you?"

"I think so, yeah. I've been having nightmares about what—" He backed off from what was plainly a tender subject. "Mr. Cullen says the 'head' project is taking over the Physics Lab. So we're moving everything in here."

"So I see." Matt crossed the room and leaned against a table. The computer's "eyes" followed him; he found it a bit unsettling. There were now seven PCs linked together, each with its own CRT display. Assorted cyber-gimmicks, none of them recognizable, lay scattered on tables around the room. "I can't say I really relate to this kind of thing."

"Neither can I. But Charley says—" He stopped in midsentence again. "They said you came to see me in the hospital. While I was still . . ."

"Yes. I did."

Suddenly there was a slight sense of urgency in Tanner's voice. "Why didn't you come again, after I was better?"

"I'm sorry I didn't. We had midterms. Things got busy." He didn't want to tell the boy he'd been assuming some of Canning's administrative duties. Or that he was avoiding that nurse he'd fucked.

"Charley never came to see me. Not even once. Lex came a lot, and even my parents now and then."

"Were you expecting him to?"

"He always said he—" He stopped still again; it was obvious he wasn't certain how open he wanted to be with his teacher. Suddenly, the old, accustomed Tanner resurfaced. "Are you still sleeping with my uncle's mistress?"

"Never mind me, Tanner. Tell me how you are."

The boy stood silent for a moment. Matt thought he saw tears forming in the corners of his eyes. For a brief second or two, Tanner actually started to shake. "I'm fucked, that's how I am. We all are."

Matt let the words hang in the air for a moment. Then, quietly, he asked, " 'We'? Who are 'we'?"

"Lex and me. And Charley—he's the worst. We're totally fucked in our heads. I don't know why. I keep having these nightmares. They won't stop. I think Lex is pregnant."

The computers howled. The sound was deafening. It echoed through the school PA system, filling corridors, penetrating classrooms. Matt and Tanner covered their ears. Matt shouted, "For God's sake, turn it off!"

"I did!"

"Then unplug the speakers!"

"They're wireless!"

The sound faded into nothingness. Matt was more rattled by it than he wanted to admit. "God, it keeps getting worse. I'll never get used to that."

"You think God has something to do with anything?"

"It was bad enough when those sounds came from the basement. Now this thing. It ought to be dismantled."

"The computer array or the building?"

Pause. He wanted to say, "Both." But he only shrugged. "It's too late." Tanner was smiling, quite broadly.

Another long pause. Then, "Is there anything I can do for you, Tanner?"

"Why didn't you come back to see me again?"

"I'm sorry. If I had known you were feeling like this . . ." Matt couldn't make himself finish the thought. He wasn't at all certain he wanted to become involved in this boy's life or problems, much less his sister's.

"How did you think I was feeling?" Once again, Tanner began to shake. Suddenly, impulsively, almost ferociously, he threw his arms around Matt. Then, with equal suddenness, he backed away. "I'm sorry, Mr. Larrimer."

"It's okay." He wasn't at all sure that it was. Groping for something to say, he looked at his watch. "The assembly will be starting. Your sister's play. We should go."

"Can I sit with you?"

"You'll have to stay with your class. You know that."

"Fuck them. I'm going backstage, then. I want to be there for Lex."

They loved each other, Tanner and Lex did. Or Matt thought they did. He envied them; at least they had that.

The two of them walked toward the door. Tanner switched off the lights. The computers whirred and beeped. Their monitors glowed.

"Can we talk again sometime?"

"I'm not sure how much we've actually said, Tanner."

"Please. You came to see me in the hospital."

"Well, sure, Tanner. Any time you need to. Now we ought to get going."

"Can I walk to the auditorium with you?"

"I have to stop at Mr. Cullen's office for a minute, You go on ahead."

Tanner wanted his company. It was clear. "Mr. Larrimer?"

"Go on. I'll see you after the show."

Tanner walked on ahead. He must have lost a lot of weight; he looked smaller.

A moment later, still a bit puzzled by the encounter, Matt knocked on the door of Bill Cullen's office and stuck his head in. "Are you busy?"

"Yeah, but come in anyway. I need to see a human face."

"I was just in the Robotics Lab, what there is of it. That howl . . ."

"Yes?"

"It came from the computers."

"Don't be silly."

"It did. Tanner Morgan and I were there. We both heard it."

Bill reached for his coffee mug. "That's nonsense, Matt. It must have been some freaky acoustical thing. Those sounds come from somewhere down below, that's all." He sipped, made a sour face and put the mug down. "My own guess is that this neighborhood sits on top of an old coal mine. Something's making those noises deep down there, some geological process, and somehow they're echoing." He shrugged. "It can't be anything more than that."

"We should find out."

"How do you mean?"

"We should go downstairs and dig. Or have some engineers do it for us. If there's something wrong with the building structurally . . ."

"They built solid, a hundred years ago. They built to last."

"Nothing lasts, Bill."

"Agnostic."

"I've been wanting to bring it up anyway. Now, with those sounds getting worse and worse . . . You're the science maven. You can get it to happen."

"You're right—I'm the science man. That's all I am. I don't have that kind of clout. But—"

"Yes?"

"Well, some of us have been talking, informally, to some of the board members. Peter Morgan's here all the time, you know, and Bishop Hinkle."

"Yes?"

"Well, we've suggested they add a dean of students to the administration. To help take some of the burden off Michael."

"Yes?"

"Stop saying 'yes.' We've recommended you for the job."

"No."

"Everyone likes you. And, more to the point, trusts you. You're sound. And young. And competent."

"Does it mean I'll be able to get that set of maps I've been asking for?"

"This is no time to be a smartass. Everyone on the

staff who knows about this thinks you're right for the job."

Matt sat in the chair beside Bill's desk, like a student being counseled. "This is so sudden."

"You sound like a girl who's just been proposed to."

"That's pretty much the way I feel. Bill, you should have talked to me about this before you took my name to the board. I feel like I'm having trouble coping with my teaching duties. Taking on more . . ." He smiled a sheepish smile. "And there's other stuff. I don't know if I can do it."

"Personal problems?"

Diana was seeing more and more of Peter and less and less of Matt. Every time he thought about her, he felt empty, useless. "No."

"Then . . . ?"

"I just don't think I'm the right one for the job, that's all."

"Well, it's not quite official yet." Bill glanced at his watch. "Promise me you'll think about it. It's time for the play—we should go. Think about it, all right?"

The conversation was over. Matt was relieved. "I'll think about that if you'll think about bringing in someone to give this place a good, thorough going-over, okay?"

Bill frowned. "All right, I guess. But I'm telling you it's nothing."

"So is being dean of students, as far as I'm concerned."

AND then it was time for the season's first student play to be presented, Claude Hinkle's *Salome*. There was an assembly. The board wanted the entire student body exposed to the arts as often as possible, as a matter of corporate policy.

The stage curtain was open. There was a rudimentary set, a vague suggestion of ruined palaces and temples; it had been designed by one of the Drama Club members, Nell McCouver. One of the spotlights was flickering. A student stagehand brought a ladder out onstage and climbed up to change the bulb.

Like the grey, dead day, the students were subdued. The kind of rowdiness that usually preceded an assembly of any kind, for any purpose, was simply not there.

Matt and Bill walked into the auditorium side by side, paused and gaped at each other. Matt let out a little laugh. "Are we in the right place?"

In a mock-confidential whisper Bill said, "I've been slipping Valium into the drinking water."

Matt whispered back, not at all jokingly, "You think these kids would even notice?"

Diana was standing at the back of the hall, looking as subdued as everyone else in the place. Matt walked back to join her.

She was in a dark mood. "There's something wrong here today."

"Isn't there always?"

"Tanner's back in school. Did you know? I just saw him heading backstage."

"He's worried about his sister." He didn't want to spill too many beans.

"Why? She's the star."

"Of a student play by a bishop's nephew. Not exactly the pinnacle of the actor's art."

"Even so. Have you ever seen so many students in one place be so quiet?"

"It's the weather." He paused for a beat. "How's Peter?"

She stiffened. "I've told you before how unattractive your jealousy is, Matt."

"I'm not jealous."

"No, and God didn't make little apples."

"Diana, will you stop it?" He was beginning to raise his voice. A few students turned and stared at them, and he lowered it to a whisper. "We'll talk about his later."

"We've talked about it already." She whispered even lower. "I've told you half a dozen times: I'm not in love with you. Can't we just have fun and leave it at that?"

"But you're in love with Peter, right?"

"Stop it."

"That isn't 'just fun'."

"Matt."

A girl, a freshman from the looks of her, approached and asked Diana for permission to go to the rest room. Grateful for the interruption, Diana walked the girl to the auditorium door, watching Matt over her shoulder.

From out of nowhere, Mrs. Bettis descended on Matt, stern as usual. "Where's Dr. Canning?"

The question startled him. "Am I my principal's keeper?"

"No one can find him."

"Let's count our blessings."

She pointed a finger at his chest. "Really, Mr. Larrimer, you have to do something to adjust that attitude."

"I'm taking it into the shop first thing tomorrow."

Irritably, she walked away.

Bishop Hinkle walked onto the stage, and what little noise there was subsided. A stagehand lowered the house lights. A single spotlight was trained on the bishop; he adjusted himself in the beam as if it was an old habit. "Dr. Canning was supposed to be here to preside over the opening of our first student play. But he has been unavoidably detained."

Matt wondered why. A date with Jack Daniels or Jim Beam, most likely. The thought of D. Michael Canning gay, even by proxy, brought an involuntary smile to his lips.

Hinkle said an invocation and made a little speech about how, even though Washington was not a religious school, there were a great many valuable lessons to be learned from the Bible. And he couldn't resist adding a comment about how proud he was of Claude. When he was finished, his spot faded, and he exited in darkness. There was the sound of him stumbling over some prop or piece of scenery. Again Matt found himself smiling. There was some soft murmuring in the audience, but the students remained remarkably well-behaved.

The play began unassumingly enough. There was the court of King Herod Antipas, as played by Charley Morgan in gold-edged robes, heavy makeup and a false beard. The familiar story was played out: Herod's court; John the Baptist preaching against Herod's marriage to his brother's widow, Herodias (Claude had been wise enough to avoid using the word "incestuous"); his lust (*desire*) for Herodias's daughter, Salome. One side of Charley's beard kept coming loose.

Diana, once her annoyance passed, rejoined Matt, and they watched from the rear of the auditorium with some amusement. Matt whispered, "You ever see the old Rita Hayworth movie about this?"

She was bored. "No, I missed that. I'll bet it's a real cinematic milestone, though."

"It's a laugh riot. Salome dances to *save* John the Baptist." He made a sour little face. "Hollywood history."

"Everyone else edits history to suit themselves, Matt. Politicians, teachers. Why shouldn't Hollywood?"

"Teachers do not 'edit history.' We tell the truth, or try to."

"Right."

Then came the scene in which Herod propositioned his stepdaughter Salome. Charley sat, quite convincingly superior, on a throne. Alexis stood trembling before him. Matt found himself admiring the way Claude conveyed what was happening without using any explicit language. Yet the subject matter was . . . unexpected for a high school play. He asked Diana if she'd ever read the Oscar Wilde version of the story.

"No. No one ever does. It's nothing but a curiosity."

"I'm just wondering how much of Wilde's language Claude plagiarized."

"He's a bishop's nephew. So the word is 'borrowed'."

Charley, or Herod, stood up from his throne, believably imperious. "Dance for me, Salome. Dance, and I will give you anything you ask for."

"Anything, my king?"

"Anything. Only name it."

The mood in the auditorium changed, first subtly, then unmistakably. A wide, lascivious smile crossed Alexis's face. Even the slowest student in the audience understood what that smile meant. She meant the smile for every one of them. "Then, dread lord, I shall dance."

Alexis's Salome turned into a more-or-less frankly sexual predator. She agreed to dance for Herod/Charley, and music began for the "Dance of the Seven Veils." Diana whispered, "Richard Strauss. In case you didn't know."

"I didn't."

Strauss's music filled the air. Alexis began. Slowly, slowly, then more and more rapidly, Salome danced. Her body gyrated in the most suggestive way without ever doing anything explicit. Mrs. Bettis had directed this; Matt hadn't known she had it in her.

One by one, Salome shed her veils. She shook her breasts; her hips undulated sensuously.

And the calm, quiet atmosphere in the hall dissipated. The dance of the seven veils affected most of the male students deeply. Maybe it was just so surprising to see such a thing in school. Maybe it was something more visceral than that. But they felt themselves respond physically to what they were seeing. Some of the girls were aroused as well.

Alexis danced. Even though she undressed only down to a bikini, the hall was perfectly still, perfectly silent, except for the music she danced to. No one moved; it seemed no one even breathed. The music grew louder and more intense.

Matt felt himself responding too, and shifted uncomfortably on his feet. This was not even remotely appropriate for a school play. Why hadn't Bettis stopped it? He told Diana, "I'm going backstage."

The music climaxed and Alexis threw herself at Charley's feet. And kissed them.

Matt found Tanner in the wings, watching his sister and looking more than a bit concerned. "Mr. Larrimer. I watched rehearsal last night. She didn't dance like this. Something's wrong."

A few feet away stood the bishop, watching transfixed. Matt crossed over to him. "Didn't you read the script? How could you let a thing like this go on?"

"There is a good, Christian moral to this story. Claude's a good boy." He didn't take his eyes off Alexis.

"Well, he hasn't written a good play. At least not for a high school."

The bishop shushed him. "This is biblical, remember?"

"Maybe that's the problem."

Hinkle scowled at him. Matt looked around for Mrs. Bettis, but she was nowhere in sight.

The Strauss music ended. Onstage, Alexis and Charley were motionless for a long moment. Slowly, she stood and pulled away from him. His body language was different now, his form slightly bent; there was no doubt it was Salome in charge, not Herod. Proudly, she said, "Now I will have what you promised me, Herod."

Herod weakly replied, "Name it. Anything you desire."

"Bring me the head of the Baptist."

Herod recoiled in horror. What kind of monster had grown in his house? "No! Not that! Ask for something else." Matt had to admire, grudgingly, the conviction Charley brought to his part.

"I will have the head of this Baptist who has fouled my mother's name."

"No, Salome! Ask for something else, anything!"

"Herod, I will have the head of John the Baptist."

Herod slumped back into his throne. His voice shaking, he gave the order. A soldier in Roman armor drew his sword and walked offstage into the wings, near where Matt was standing. He caught the boy by his shoulder. "Is that the way this is supposed to play? Is that what you rehearsed?"

The boy pulled free of his grip. "Let go of me. I have to get back on. Where's my head?"

Mrs. Bettis appeared from somewhere behind a flat. "Here it is, Tony." She was carrying a silver serving tray. On it sat a papier-mâché head, covered with unnaturally red stage blood.

The soldier took the tray from her and stepped to the edge of the stage to wait for his cue.

Herod and Salome were bantering, he begging her to change her request, she refusing. At his cue, the soldier walked solemnly back onstage, carrying the tray and head.

Herod recoiled in horror. "No! No! Surely you have brought a curse upon this house!" He ran from the stage.

But Salome calmly, casually, crossed to where the soldier was standing; she circled him, smiling, and picked up the bloodied head.

The script, à la Oscar Wilde, called for her to pick up the prop head and kiss it on the lips. Everyone knew it was coming; the audience was waiting for it with obvious delight.

The moment came. Alexis put her hands on the head. It was warm. When she tried to lift it, it was much heavier than it had been at rehearsal, awkwardly so. Blood—hot, wet, sticky—flowed from the throat, a great deal of it. That had not happened at rehearsal.

She had been focused on everything but the prop, and its unexpected warmth and weight startled her. She took a good look at it; it was not the head they'd used in rehearsal. This was the head of a young man in his twenties, fair-haired and pale. It was much more realistic than the one she'd used earlier. Warm. Blood flowing from it.

Caught off guard, she looked toward the wings. Mrs. Bettis, Claude Hinkle and several others were watching her, puzzled. What was wrong? Why was she just standing there, looking at them?

The head in her hands must weigh more than ten pounds. Clumsily, she raised it high over her head. Blood poured from the throat, streams of it drenching her and soaking the stage around her. She saw Charley in the wings, watching her and laughing. *He* had done this—a sick joke. The audience was getting restless for the first time; they wanted their climax. Boys were shouting things like "Go on, suck some face!"

Alexis moved the head close to her lips. "I shall kiss thy lips, Baptist."

Slowly, deliberately, the head in her hands opened its eyes. They were blue. The lips parted. A drop of saliva drooled down the chin, followed by more blood.

"Kiss it! Kiss it!" The student body was chanting it rhythmically.

She forced herself to part her lips and kiss it. The tip of its tongue pushed slightly into her mouth. There was more bloody drool; she felt it pouring down her chin and her chest. The audience hooted and whistled.

This was a sick, sick joke. She moved the head away from her lips. Its tongue brushed her nose. It whispered something, she couldn't make out what. She screamed and dropped it, then ran off the stage. The audience jeered and booed. "More! We want more!"

Mrs. Bettis caught her as she was running by. "Alexis, what's wrong?"

"It's real." She was crying.

Bettis looked at the head lying on the stage. It was a prop. It was the same prop they'd been using for weeks. "What are you talking about? Calm down."

"It's real, it's real!"

"No, Alexis, look."

She buried her face in Mrs. Bettis's chest. Then, after a moment, she pulled self-consciously away. "I'm sorry." She ran off to her dressing room and closed the door. Mrs. Bettis looked after her, wondering what to do.

Bishop Hinkle, disconcerted by what had happened, walked onstage from the opposite side. The audience was still acting up. Not bothering with a microphone, he bellowed, "That's enough! All of you, quiet down!"

They didn't.

He roared at them again, and finally they began to settle down. "You are to return to your regularly scheduled classes. We will continue with the usual schedule for the rest of the day. Does everyone understand that? This assembly is dismissed."

There was an unhappy murmur, but gradually the students and faculty got to their feet and began to file out of the auditorium.

Tanner turned to Matt. "I have to see what's wrong with her."

"Leave her to Mrs. Bettis." Matt put a hand on his shoulder. "She'll know what to do."

"No, she won't. Lex is my sister."

"Tanner, there's nothing you can do. Give her a few minutes to calm down."

Tanner pulled free of him and ran off, following Alexis. Gradually, everyone else disappeared too, except for the stage crew, who stood looking around, wondering what to do.

"Mr. Larrimer?" It was Mike Monticelli.

"Mike. I didn't see you here."

"I'm doing stage crew. Just to keep busy, you know, till I get back on the team."

"Are you working out yet?"

"Just a light workout. They say it'll be another month or two before I'm 100 percent. So, do we leave the set up or what?"

"You'll have to ask Mrs. Bettis." A wise teacher knows when and how to pass the buck. "I'll see you in class, Mike, okay?" He started to go.

"Mr. Larrimer?"

"Hmm?"

"What happened to Alexis? I mean, is she all right?"

And a wise teacher knows how and when to put up a positive front. "She'll be fine. I think the play got to her, that's all."

"I heard about her brother, last winter." The boy seemed uncharacteristically nervous, or unsure of himself.

"Then you can see how this might have . . . upset her."

"Why did they let her do it?"

"From what I understand, she wanted to."

"They shouldn't have let her. Not if they knew about what happened."

"She wanted to try and bury the past, that's all, Mike. We all do that in our lives."

"Do we all end up the way Alexis just did?"

Glum question. Matt avoided it. "You like her, don't you?"

Mike looked away, self-conscious. "I think she's really cute, yeah."

"Just cute?"

"You know what I mean. She doesn't pay any attention to me, though. The poor kid, you know."

"Yes, Mike, I know." He was in love with Diana, and there was no denying it. "That kind of thing happens to all of us."

"Life is shit, Mr. Larrimer." Mike turned back to him, mildly concerned at the reaction he'd get. Using that language, to a teacher . . .

But Matt was in the same mood. "Life is only shit if you expect more out of it than you get, Mike. *That* kind of thing happens to all of us too. And some of us never learn."

This wasn't what Mike expected to hear, or what he wanted to. He shifted to more neutral ground, then headed off to his next class. The rest of the stage crew was cleaning up, switching off lights, readjusting scenery and props. One of them picked up the Baptist's head and threw a forward pass to his friend, and they both laughed. Matt stared out into the auditorium, vaguely hoping Diana would still be there, but it was empty.

There was something wet on the floor. Something red. He bent down and touched it: *blood*. It must be stage blood. But it looked so . . . He put a fingertip to it, then held it to his lips. Salty. It was real blood. *Real.*

He looked around the wings and found a bucket and some rags. He'd have to get water. He'd have to clean it up. No one must know. A quick trip to the nearest rest room and he was back, scrubbing furiously. Blood. Must be hidden.

From the depths of the dark, empty hall came a wail— the cry of a man in agony, mixed with laughter.

"HAVE a drink." Canning held out the bourbon bottle for Nick Brookhiser to see, as if reading the label would make him want to drink.

"Michael, that isn't going to help."

"It's bottled-in-bond."

"Even so."

It was late Friday afternoon, almost dinnertime; the light was fading and the school was nearly empty. A few cleaning people worked in the halls; there were some jocks working out in the gym and a few more doing laps outside. But Friday afternoon at Washington Academy . . . most people couldn't wait to get out. Outside, it seemed to get greyer, colder and darker each day.

The two of them sat in Canning's office. It had not been a good week.

"Michael, people are talking more and more. You're getting drunk every day during school hours. How can you expect people not to notice?"

"It's that damned bishop."

"It's not just him, and you know it."

"Peter Morgan called me yesterday. The play by kindly, wonderful, clueless Bishop Hinkle's nephew came up at the board meeting. Apparently the daughter or niece of someone important was scandalized by what she saw. She's a Christian." He said the word as if it tasted foul.

Brookhiser smiled. "We're a family values company, remember?"

"Shut up."

"It might have helped if you had been there."

"And it might not. How was I supposed to know they were going to put a mentally unstable girl on the stage, have her do a striptease and then reenact her brother's suicide?"

"Isn't it your job to know?" Brookhiser wanted to be talking about Canning's behavior, not about this. "Besides, I'm not sure that's exactly what happened."

"Well, what the devil do you think did happen, then?"

He sighed a patient, long-suffering sigh. "You haven't exactly been a hands-on administrator, Michael. I've tried talking to you about it often enough."

Canning fell silent and stared reflectively at his bottle. After a long pause he said, "Nick, there's something in this school."

"What do you mean?"

"I don't know. But I can feel it. I've always felt it. You must have too. There's something deeply wrong here."

"We have several hundred spoiled rich kids who've lived pampered, privileged lives and think they own everything, or that they're entitled to everything. Did you think that wouldn't lead to trouble?"

"It's not that. It's not just that. There's something here. These howls, these awful wails . . . I find them more and more unnerving."

Brookhiser sighed. "That again. Look, if you can't take the noise, do something about it. We've kicked around ideas often enough."

"I was here last night. Late."

"Drunk or sober?"

Canning ignored the question. "Everything was dark. I heard that horrible crying in the air. I tried to ignore it. I used to be able to just . . . shrug it off, Nick, but I can't anymore. I had to go and see where it was coming from." Without quite realizing it, he reached out and began to caress the bottle of bourbon with his fingertips. "It didn't sound like it was coming from downstairs, the way it always has. No. It was someplace else. I thought maybe the gym, but it was everywhere."

"Maybe it's the mating call of pink elephants. You ever think of that?"

"Stop it, Nick. This is serious."

He did his best to look contrite. "Sorry."

"I walked through the halls, and the cries were everywhere around me, ahead of me, behind me. . . . The halls were black. You know how dark it gets in here. Pitch-black. I tried turning on the lights in the hall, but the switch wouldn't work. There was the sound of a man being tortured, or dying. In the dark hall."

Brookhiser shifted uncomfortably. Canning was getting worse and worse; that much was clear. It was time to tell the board or simply get out. There had been other job offers. If things got much worse at Washington, there wouldn't be any more. He found himself going through them in his mind instead of listening to Canning's story.

But Canning had no clue. He went on.

"I was heading toward the gym, to see. And I passed that new lab of Bill Cullen's, the Robotics Lab. There were a dozen computers, all turned on, all linked together with cables. The monitors glowed with light. They should have been turned off. I went in. The cries were coming from the computers—from the speakers."

He stopped talking and looked at Brookhiser, who was clearly skeptical of everything he was hearing. Realizing that Canning was watching him, he looked away.

"Nick?"

"I'm listening."

"Look at me." He waited till Brookhiser did so. "It spoke to me, Nick. The computer-complex thing. It knew my name."

"It knows everyone's name, Michael. The kids who assembled it have taught it what everyone looks like. It knows all about all of us."

"It can't."

"Michael, this is foolish. You've got some computer geniuses here, and they've built this thing, and it—"

"Nick, it told me I was going to die."

This stopped him. "Don't be idiotic."

"It prophesied my death, Nick."

"Then the kids programmed it to. Their idea of a joke."

"I don't think so."

"Michael, a computer is not a living, thinking thing. It can't do such a thing. Even if it were alive . . . Prophecy? Be serious."

"Then something else has gotten into it. The spirit of that poor dead man we hid in the basement."

Brookhiser stood up. "Michael, I've heard enough.

I shouldn't tell you this, but I've decided to leave EdEntCo. My confidence in you is gone."

"Nick!"

"I mean it. Things here have gotten steadily worse, and you're not helping the situation. Have you even been sober enough to realize how much of your job your loyal faculty has been doing for you?"

"You can't leave."

"I've had offers, Michael. First thing next week, I'll be talking to the people who made them."

"Nick, no."

"Michael, yes." He moved toward the door. "I couldn't be sorrier, but, Michael, things here are out of control."

Canning got up and took a step toward him. "That's what I've been trying to tell you."

"Don't be a fool, Michael." He opened the door walked into the dark outer office. Quickly, without turning on the lights, he left.

Canning stood staring after him into the darkness. He was alone with his bottle. It would be company enough, for now. He sat down, placed a glass squarely in front of him on the desk, then decided to ignore it and drank straight out of the bottle. Soon enough, he was asleep.

And when he woke, everything around him was dark. Faint light came in from the parking lot outside his window, but most of the room was hidden in shadow. The bottle was quite empty. When he realized it, he muttered a four-letter word under his breath.

Getting to his feet, he staggered to the door and reached for the light switch. It didn't respond. The darkness was near total.

Power failure. He went to the window. Jumonville Street was empty; the strange yellow glow of the sodium streetlights at the far corners gave what illumination there was. But they were lit; the power was on. The problem must be in the building. A man cried, and his cries echoed through Washington Academy.

Mrs. Newburg kept a portable spotlight in her bottom desk drawer for emergencies like this. Canning lurched through the outer office, pulled open the drawer, groped and found it. When he switched it on, it blinded him for a moment. There were more cries, not just one man now but a great many others—men, women, children, wailing in agony.

There had to be a way to find where they were coming from. His head was spinning, but he put it down to dizziness, to his disorientation from the deafening sounds in the air.

His spotlight barely seemed to penetrate the darkness in Washington's halls. There was someone there, or some *thing*, and he was going to find it.

The Robotics Lab. There were fifteen computers now, their monitors glowing in the darkness. But tonight the wails were coming from somewhere else. Canning stood in the center of the room and looked around at the array.

"D. Michael Canning."

He didn't know which screen to look at. "They tell me your name is Cullen."

"Coulon."

"Coulon, then. Who are you?"

"You know. We have met before. And they have given me a voice, these children of yours. We shall not meet again. Not after tonight."

Cries came from the halls.

Canning's vision was not quite clear. He squinted. "You can't know the future."

"Knowing the past is enough, D. Michael Canning. The past is the future."

He swayed unsteadily; he reached out a hand and caught the edge of a table. This was foolish. He was talking to a machine. Nick Brookhiser was right; the kids had programmed it to play with his head. Without saying another word, he staggered out of the lab.

Downstairs. The cries were coming from the basement. There were more and more voices.

Leaning carefully on the handrail, Canning went down. Except for the beam from his spotlight, the darkness was complete. He followed the basement corridor past one room after another.

It was a maze, vast and complex, larger and deeper than seemed possible. The basement seemed to stretch on forever, room after dark, haunted room, one after another, endlessly.

There was someone in one of them.

Two people. Locked in an embrace. Kissing, making love. He shot his spotlight at them. Tanner Morgan. And another boy. Shocked by the intrusion, they pulled apart and gaped at him.

"Tanner. What are you doing here?"

"What does it look like?"

"This is a school, not a brothel."

"We're not whores."

Canning focused on the other boy. He was familiar, but Canning couldn't place him. "Who are you?"

Tanner answered for him. "Uncle Peter gave me the key to the building. You don't have any right to harass us."

This was not right. He was the principal; they were students. Around them were the cries of people in pain, but the boys seemed not to hear them; only he could hear them.

"Get out of here, Tanner, and take your boyfriend with

you. If you don't leave now, I'll call security and have you escorted out."

The boys looked at one another. Tanner shrugged. Holding hands, quite defiantly, they walked past Canning toward the stairs—and vanished into the darkness. Evaporated. Had they been there at all?

In the next room there were more people. He focused his light on them and, like Tanner and his friend, they pulled apart and gaped at him. Alexis Morgan. And a black man—young, handsome. It took Canning a moment to realize who he was. "You're the boy who works the parking lot."

Cal stiffened. "What did you call me?"

"Get out of here. Both of you. Now. This is my school. You have no right to be here."

Alexis spoke up. "We don't have anywhere else to go. Our families—"

"Get out!"

They, too, faded and disappeared into the darkenss at the foot of the stairs, Cal glaring at Canning as he vanished.

The cries were everywhere now, louder than he had ever heard them. And there were more people in the basement; there had to be. So many lonely, agonized voices. He went from one room to another, flashing his light. They had to be there; he would find them. They were trespassing in *his* school, on *his* property, transgressing against *his* responsibility.

In room after room he thought he saw them: women, men, children, fucking, injecting things into their veins, weeping, wailing in agony. One by one, they evaporated before he could focus.

"Where are you? Show yourselves!"

Voices cried, voices wailed in pain and loneliness.

"This is my place! Show yourselves!"

After stalking through dark eternity he reached the final room, the one where the headless corpse was buried. The cries were overpowering. It was too much for him, and he was still too drunk. He sat down, his back against a wall, and buried his face in his hands.

When, finally, the ghost appeared, Canning didn't see it. Headless, in the uniform of a soldier from the eighteenth century, it raised its sword and struck. For one startled instant, Canning felt the blade slice into this throat. Then the light, the cries, everything, stopped. Just before he lost consciousness, he found time to wonder why the blade was so dull and rough. That made it so much more painful than it had to be.

And he wondered why there was so much blood pouring down his chest from his throat.

And he wondered, finally, why that man in front of him, whose face he couldn't see very well in the darkness, kept hacking at him so ferociously.

SEVEN

MIKE MONTICELLI

CANNING'S body was not found for four days, not until Monday. And no one could quite explain why.

When he didn't come home that Friday night, and then again on Saturday, his wife called the police. They in turn called Nick Brookhiser, knowing him as the security man at Washington. The school was searched, every foot of it including the basement, not merely for Canning himself but for any hint where he might have gone. There was nothing. Not the least trace of him.

When he didn't appear for work on Monday morning, everyone simply assumed, quietly and off the record, that he was off on a drunk somewhere. His wife filed a missing persons report, but EdEntCo, in the person of Brookhiser, told the police unofficially that there was nothing to worry about.

Then finally, on a hunch, Brookhiser decided to take

another look at the place downstairs where they had buried the headless corpse.

And there was D. Michael Canning, headless too. His body lay stretched out on the rough floor. The severed head was in position relative to the body, but upside down, with the top of the head placed carefully at the neck, and face to the floor. For some reason, it all struck Brookhiser as inevitable.

Good company man that he was, he called Peter Morgan first, not the police. But he told him only that it was an emergency; he didn't give him any details.

"I don't like people being cryptic with me, Nick. What's wrong?"

"I can't talk about it on the phone."

"Does it have something to do with Michael?"

"You'll see when you get here." He hung up before Morgan had the chance to cross-examine him any more.

Then he walked the halls of the school restlessly. Everything seemed to be going on as usual. Canning's absence was causing no problems for anyone, it seemed. Mrs. Newburg was running the office with her usual unpleasant efficiency, students were worried about their own problems, teachers taught, or tried to. Brookhiser was restless, and he wanted Morgan to get there.

It was time to look actively for another job, that much was clear. With everything that had gone wrong at the school, and now this, the chief of security was bound to be under a cloud, even if no one said so. Restless, anxious, he went back downstairs. The body was still there, head on wrong. The sign Canning had posted was gone; he got some tape and cardboard from the janitor's supply room, made a No Admittance sign and posted it on the door. No one went to the basement anyway, thanks to

Canning's orders, but it didn't hurt to be sure. Then, agitated, he started walking the halls again.

Whatever—whoever?—caused the wailing in the school halls was quiet that morning, but Brookhiser didn't notice. The quiet was a negative thing, an absence, not a thing that drew attention to itself.

Morgan didn't arrive till nearly noon. Brookhiser had been pacing the halls for hours, not knowing what else to do with himself. He saw Matt and Bill Cullen having another one of their informal little meetings; they had almost become a part of the school's routine. He spent some time hovering in the main office. Mrs. Newburg, obviously a bit nonplussed, was telling everyone who asked that Dr. Canning was off on EdEntCo business.

Then Morgan's limo pulled into the faculty lot. Cal Conklin waved the driver into a VIP space, then held the door as Morgan got out.

He was all heartiness as Nick met him at the side entrance; he shook Nick's hand like a politician running for office. "Now, what's this all about?" he asked jovially.

"Come on. I'll show you."

The sign he had posted was still there. Morgan frowned at it. "Is this the best we could do?"

"Emergency. Had to make do."

"It isn't very professional."

Nick ushered him into the death chamber. Morgan stopped in his tracks and whistled. "Jesus."

"No, D. Michael Canning."

Morgan stiffened, then seemed to relax. He sighed deeply. "Who did this?"

"How the devil should I know? Maybe he did it himself, with a broken liquor bottle."

Without thinking, Morgan looked around for a bottle.

Then he caught himself. "This is no time to be funny, Nick."

"You think that was a joke? He's been on a downward spiral for months. You have to have known."

Morgan took a step toward the corpse and nudged it with the tip of his shoe. "Poor drunken bastard."

"And we closed the only bar in the neighborhood, too."

"That kind of attitude isn't going to help."

"I thought I'd get it out of my system now, before the cops and the reporters arrive."

"Shit." He turned on Nick. "Why didn't you find this until now?"

"It wasn't here. The police checked down here too. You can still see all their footprints in the dust. Read their reports: That body was not here until this morning. Someone, or something, put it here in the middle of the night."

"Don't be preposterous."

"The little cadaver that wasn't there."

"Tomorrow's Halloween, isn't it, Nick?" Morgan circled the body, bending down now and then as if he might see something that wasn't obvious.

"Trick or treat, Peter."

Abruptly, Morgan went into CEO mode. "Who else knows about this?"

"No one, so far."

"Who are the reliable people here? Who can we trust?"

Brookhiser thought for a moment. "Bill Cullen. He's been acting as a kind of surrogate principal anyway—as much as dear old Mrs. Newburg will let him. And that kid history teacher, Matt Larrimer. They've been working together a lot."

"What about Mrs. Newburg?"

"I think the phrase is 'fiercely loyal'."

"To the school or to Canning?"

Brookhiser shrugged. "I doubt if she sees a difference. And there's Diana Ketterer." He almost added, *But you know that*, but at the last second he held his tongue. "And Mrs. Bettis seems to have a good head on her shoulders."

The name didn't ring a bell. "Who's that?"

"The drama teacher."

"The one who let that damnfool John the Baptist thing go on last week? Keep her out of it."

"Bishop Hinkle's been spending a lot of time here too. Should I call him?"

"Grover? Christ, no. All he'd want to do is pray for guidance. No, leave him out. But get all the others to Canning's office for a meeting in"—he glanced at his watch—"fifteen minutes. The police commissioner's a friend of mine. I'll give him a call. This will have to be kept as quiet as possible."

"I think they all have classes."

"Have someone cover for them."

"I'll let them know now."

"The CEO of Pittsburgh Hospital's a friend of mine too, David Simkowicz. I'll see if he can't get this . . . this . . . the body taken care of quietly."

"He's dead, Peter. There's his wife to deal with. We can't just say we found him in a dumpster."

"If things go well we won't have to say anything. We might be able to get the body out of here quietly, get it autopsied and a death certificate signed. . . ."

"Peter, he's dead. Decapitated. We can't pretend nothing has happened here."

Morgan stiffened. "Damn the luck. Just what we need

is more publicity." He paced a few steps. "Don't let anyone else down here."

"Most of my staff's off today. I had them working overtime on Saturday, looking for traces of Michael."

"And they didn't find this."

"I told you, it wasn't here. The police—"

Morgan smirked. Not that he blamed Brookhiser for trying to cover his ass. "Get that kid who guards the parking lots, that black kid. Don't tell him what's up. Keep him in the dark."

"Isn't that where we all are?"

Morgan glared at him, stomped up the stairs to the office and told Mrs. Newburg to get him a private phone line.

CANNING'S office still smelled of liquor. Heavily. The meeting was switched to the small conference room just next to it, and Morgan told Mrs. Newburg to get the office aired out.

"Is there any word about Dr. Canning, Mr. Morgan?"

"No." He barked it at her.

"I'd appreciate being told what's going on, sir, if you don't mind."

"You'll be told in good time."

Things had changed, all right. Mrs. Newburg watched, unhappy and disconcerted, as Peter Morgan, Nick Brookhiser, Bill Cullen, Matt Larrimer and Diana Ketterer filed into the conference room and closed the door behind them. Her school was not the same place anymore and she, it seemed, did not have anything like the same authority.

The five of them sat around the table, sober, stone-faced; there were empty chairs between them. Morgan, of course, chaired the meeting.

"Bill, Matt, Diana . . . you know that Michael is missing."

They nodded.

Morgan turned to Brookhiser. "Tell them, Nick."

He told them. Described Canning's decapitated body and the grotesque way the head was positioned. "The police haven't arrived yet. When they get here, they will be very discreet. We thought you three should know."

"Why us?" Matt's response was reflexive.

"Because," Morgan announced importantly, "Nick tells me that you three, more than anyone else, have tried to carry on with running the school. And what we need right now is business as usual. I need people I can rely on, people with some common sense."

Matt restrained himself from making the comment that "as usual" wasn't exactly a reassuring notion, not at Washington Academy.

"We'll have to notify the media, of course. A thing like this can't be kept quiet. There's Michael's wife—widow. But Nick has been downstairs with the, uh, with Michael. He's arranged things to look like an accident."

Bill looked a bit numb. For the first time, he spoke up. "'An accident'? What kind of 'accident' could cut his head off and rearrange it for him?"

"Leave that to me." Nick was smug. "That's what corporate security is trained to do."

"But—"

Nick smiled. "Michael was working late on Friday evening. Someone entered the school, unauthorized—a crack addict or some such. He demanded money. Michael resisted, and . . ." He shrugged and smiled again, clearly pleased with himself.

Without thinking, Matt said, "Michael was working late in the basement? That doesn't make sense."

Morgan shrugged. "Michael's responsibilities took

him all over the school. Or the killer forced him to go down there. Look at the neighborhood we're in. The media will buy it without question." He said it with heavy emphasis.

Oh. Matt finally began to grasp what was going on, and what was expected of him. "Yes. Of course. There must have been a killer. I didn't think."

"Good." Peter rubbed his hands together, like a man who was enjoying a challenge. "Now, I've talked to the police commissioner, and he understands the need for absolute discretion in handling this. And the coroner understands as well."

Diana leaned close to Matt and whispered, "They're both stockholders."

Despite her whisper, Peter heard. "Yes. Precisely. The police detectives will be here shortly"—he glanced at his watch—"and they will know exactly what to do. What their report should say. With our full help and cooperation, that is."

Matt was feeling out of his depth. All this . . . spin. It wasn't something he wanted to be involved in.

Morgan went on. "There's a also medical team from Pittsburgh Hospital on its way now, to tend to the body. The CEO, David Simkowicz, has given them their instructions; they'll see that everything is done properly. Officially, Michael Canning died at the hands of an unknown assailant, most likely a drug addict. We must make certain everyone understands that."

Cullen spoke up. "And what about Canning's wife? How likely is it she'll keep quiet when the press comes snooping around?"

"Leave her to me." Again Morgan smiled. "Have you ever met her? She'll see reason. EdEntCo can be very generous."

"Why didn't the police find his body when they searched over the weekend? Why didn't they find him?"

Morgan glared at Cullen. Brookhiser quickly got between them. "Michael had always made the basement off limits, to everyone. It never occurred to anyone he might be down there."

"The police searched. How do we explain to the police that his body's down there now, when they didn't find it there Saturday?"

"We'll just have to make certain no one asks that question."

Cullen frowned. Michael used to drink in the basement when there was too much traffic in the school office. Everyone knew it, and he said so. "You can count on us, Peter, but there are a lot more faculty who know, and a few hundred students. Who's going to keep them quiet?"

Morgan didn't like hearing this. He pressed ahead quickly. "Obviously, we're going to have to think on our feet. The police will only question people who are sound."

"And the media?"

"We're getting used to dealing with the press. Unfortunately, I don't know if we can keep them from getting hold of this. But if they do, it was an unfortunate accident. An isolated incident. We all have to understand that and stay on-message."

No one said anything.

"I'll be spending a lot more time here now." Morgan looked pointedly from Matt to Bill and back again. He knew Matt was sleeping with Diana. "I haven't decided what title I'll use—acting principal, interim principal, maybe COO, something like that—but I have to think about it, and I'll have to get some input from our PR people. But I can only be here part-time. I have a company to run. So I'll be counting on all of you."

"We'll do everything we can, of course." Bill was quite pale, and there was no sign of the color coming back to his face.

"Of course." Matt seconded him weakly.

It was obvious to Diana they were both out of their depth. "Peter, you know we're all anxious to help. But if we're going to be taking on extra duties, in addition to our teaching . . ."

Morgan scowled at her. "We'll adjust your pay accordingly. Of course."

Matt noticed the tension between them. Were things cooling off, then? He didn't want to let himself hope. He decided to focus on the pay increase. "Thank you, sir."

"Good. Call me Peter." Morgan smiled. Matt thought it made him look predatory. "I'll be relying on the three of you to help me keep things running smoothly. You're to check in here as often as you can—between classes, before and after school. I'll have a talk with Mrs. Newburg and make certain she understands the new order here."

Bill was getting a bit of his color back. "You can count on us."

Matt wished he would keep quiet. He wasn't at all certain he wanted to be an administrator, not even an unofficial, part-time one. He made a vague, ambiguous gesture he hoped Morgan would interpret as promising support.

Morgan checked a page of handwritten notes. "Does anyone on the faculty besides the two of you have any administrative experience?"

"I'm not sure I have what you'd call 'experience,' Mr. Morgan." Matt had decided he wanted out.

"I told you, call me Peter. We're going to be working together."

"Peter, then." He made himself smile. "I don't. I don't

even have all that much experience as a teacher." He added weakly, "Two years."

"You're a good, solid man." Nick endorsed him without looking at him. "You've helped hold things together here."

And Morgan added, "Nick's word is good enough for me."

But Matt found himself wondering how "together" things actually were at the school. And his next thought was to wonder, who's going to hold *me* together? He looked hopefully at Diana, but her gaze was fixed firmly on the tabletop.

Morgan adjourned the meeting so they could get back to their classes. But Diana spoke up. "One more thing, Peter."

"What is it?"

"Well . . . there's been a lot of talk among the faculty. Speculation." She paused and looked around the room. "Is there even going to be a Washington Academy next year? Parents are pulling their kids out already. Lord knows, there are enough other private schools around here."

"The board is fully committed to keeping this school open." Morgan said it firmly. "We've invested too much time, talent and money to do otherwise."

"Wouldn't it make a nice tax write-off?"

"We are not going to let a series of unfortunate, isolated incidents end this school's mission. The board, all of us, believe strongly in what Washington Academy stands for. I can tell you unofficially that we've already been planning a major public relations campaign to remedy the damage that's been done by all these . . . accidents, these freak occurrences. No, none of you have to worry. Washington Academy will be here for a long time to come."

So they filed out of the conference room. No one was saying much. Morgan went first, heading for the main office to talk to Mrs. Newburg, apparently. Brookhiser lingered behind, staring out the windows, seemingly lost in thought. Just as Matt and Diana hit the hall, the tones of Beethoven's Fifth sounded, announcing the end of a class period. She glanced at her watch. "You free next period?"

"Yeah."

"Let's talk."

Bill Cullen came out of the conference room behind them, obviously rushed. "I've got a lab now. I can't tell you how I wish the science wing wasn't so far away." He swept off down the hall, avoiding students, or trying to.

Diana watched him go. "So we're the administrative team."

"You always sound like you're laughing at everything and everyone."

"You're young. Wait five years."

"I hope I never get as cynical as you."

"Is it cynicism to recognize the world for what it is?"

"It's not that bad, Diana."

She smirked. "Let's go downstairs, and you can explain that to D. Michael Canning."

"Will you stop it?"

"Matt, this place is collapsing around us, and all anyone can think of is how to spin it so it looks like the school's growing. How can I not laugh at that? Any other response would be . . ."

"Yes?"

"Well, let's just say I don't think I have much to gain from self-delusion."

Tanner Morgan stepped out of a group of students and walked toward them. Uncharacteristically, he was smiling. Matt glanced at Diana and mouthed *Drugs?*

She whispered, "Maybe he's our unknown crack addict."

"Mr. Larrimer, do you have a moment?"

"Just wait a few months, Tanner," Diana bubbled, "and he'll have all the time in the world. We all will." Without another word she walked off down the hall.

Tanner looked after her, a bit puzzled, then turned back to Matt. "I've got a great idea for a play."

Oh. This was the last thing Matt wanted to deal with. "Nothing from the bible, I hope."

Tanner's smile disappeared. "You're letting this place get to you. You shouldn't."

"I thought it had gotten to you."

"Not the same way. You used to look happy, back when school started. Now . . . Everyone in class says so."

"I've learned a lot since then." There was an unused classroom nearby. Matt gestured toward it. "Come on, let's talk about your play."

Matt leaned against the teacher's desk; Tanner sat in one of the front-row seats. "I've been reading a lot about George Washington."

"Good. I wouldn't have thought you were the history type."

"I've never been. But . . . well, there's all the stuff we learn about him, the stuff in our textbooks."

"And?"

"And then there's other stuff. I've been reading his letters—I mean, like real stuff, not just propaganda."

"I do not teach propaganda."

"Did you know all of Washington's slaves ran off? I mean, ran away from Mount Vernon during the Revolution?"

"Washington was a good slave owner. He treated them well, Tanner."

"They ran away, and they all volunteered to fight for the British."

This stopped Matt cold. "That isn't possible."

"I've found a letter. Lund Washington, George's cousin, was tending the estate for him, and he wrote to tell him all about it. Isn't that incredible? It's the kind of thing no one ever talks about. I think it could make a really good play." He got a xerox of the letter out of his backpack and handed it to Matt.

"You're doing impressive research, Tanner. But this can't be right." Matt read it as if it was an alien thing. "We'd know. It would get talked about."

"Would it? How much gets talked about around *here*? Did you know that a lot of Washington's staff officers thought he was illiterate? They said his secretaries wrote his letters and speeches for him, then he copied them out in his own handwriting so nobody'd know."

He handed the page back to Tanner. "This won't do, Tanner. We want plays that are positive. Uplifting. Patriotic. Not this. This can't be true, and even if it is, it reflects so unpleasantly on . . . on . . ."

"On all kinds of things. I know" Tanner grinned. "That's why I find it so interesting."

"Tanner, you are not to write this. I won't let it be produced and performed. This runs directly counter to the whole idea of the student play competition."

"It's the truth. You've seen it. You've read it."

"You are not to write this, not for performance here, anyway. That's final."

Tanner folded the page and put it carefully back in his bag. Not trying to hide his disappointment, he said, "I don't get it. I thought school was about learning. About wanting to learn new things."

"School is about a lot of things, Tanner, but exposing

George Washington as the illiterate owner of slaves who wanted to get away from him isn't one of them."

Without saying another word, Tanner rejoined his friends. As Matt started to walk away; he noticed the boy watching him, and called out, "How's Alexis?"

"She's okay."

"I heard she's not in school today."

"No. She isn't." Tanner turned his back on him quite pointedly.

THE police arrived first, followed just a moment later by the ambulance crew. They checked in at the office; Mrs. Newburg offered them coffee and donuts, told Morgan they were there, then went off to fetch Brookhiser.

Morgan took them all into the conference room and explained what had happened, spinning the story properly for them all. A police detective named Perkowski said he'd been there over the weekend and there'd been no sign of a body in the basement. Just then, Brookhiser came in; he was grateful to have what he'd told Morgan confirmed by one of the cops.

Morgan led them downstairs, with Nick bringing up the rear. The ambulance crew had a bit of trouble manipulating their gurney in the stairwell and through the narrow corridors in the basement.

The body was gone. There wasn't the least sign of it— not a drop of blood, no imprint on the floor where it had been lying. Morgan stammered, "But—but—"

Brookhiser took charge, assuring them all this was no joke, that they hadn't been summoned on a wild-goose chase. He could tell from the looks on their faces they weren't buying it. Sullenly, in a disagreeable mood, the medics left, struggling with their gurney again.

Detective Perkowski pointed a finger at Nick's chest. "Don't jerk us around again, you hear?"

"It was here, Bob, I saw it—we both did."

"Then where is it?" He and his partner, registering their annoyance, followed the ambulance crew up the stairs.

Morgan and Brookhiser gaped at one another across the empty space. "It was here." Morgan couldn't seem to get over his astonishment. "We saw it, Nick. It has to be here."

"I don't know what's going on, Peter, but there's no way this is possible. Somebody's playing games with us. Or giving us a warning."

"Who? How could they have done this?" He gestured at the vacant spot on the floor.

"I don't know, but what other explanation is there?"

"A warning about what?"

Brookhiser shrugged.

Puzzled, abashed that the police wouldn't believe them, they headed slowly back upstairs to the main floor. It was only when they reached the office that Morgan realized what this meant. He snapped his fingers and announced happily, "Nick, this means we're off the hook. Michael is still officially missing, not dead. For once, we're dodging the bullet, PR-wise."

Brookhiser wasn't so certain. "For now, Peter. What if his body turns up again? Someplace more public? If it's in the building at all, sooner or later it'll start smelling, and we'll—"

"Never mind." Morgan stomped into the office. "You always find a negative side to everything, don't you?"

He shrugged. "It's my job."

"Well, I wish you were a bit less efficient. The body can't be here. Where could it be hidden?"

"A hundred places."

"Be quiet. D. Michael Canning is missing, not dead. That's all anyone has to know."

Brookhiser shrugged again. "For now."

IT was long past noon when Alexis woke. The room was small, dingy, not her own. There was a faint musty smell. Voices came from the next room. Hap's voice she knew. It took her a moment to realize the other one was Sam's; he should have been at his store.

The day was bright with sunshine; she could tell even through the drawn window blinds. Going to the window, she moved one a bit, to see out. The sunlight dazzled her eyes.

The house sat at the top of Jumonville Street, facing the bottom of the hill. She could see the school clearly; it was the largest building in sight, and the ugliest. The area around it looked like a desert; so much of it had been leveled for Washington Academy. Shading her eyes, squinting, she saw that Cal wasn't at his post in the parking lot. Without thinking, she glanced at the bed, as if he might be there. But of course that was foolish. It wasn't like him to shirk. She tried to remember if this was one of the days when he had an early afternoon class, but she didn't think it was. Where could he be?

A door slammed. She saw Sam heading down the front steps to the street. He must have taken a quick break; it was plain he was heading back to the store.

Someone knocked at the bedroom door. She opened it a crack. Hap was there, smiling widely. "Good morning."

"Hap. Hello. Just a minute." She quickly pulled on one

of Cal's oversized flannel shirts, then opened the door. "What time is it?"

"Two in the afternoon. Cal said I shouldn't wake you, but I thought—"

"He should have gotten me up. I missed school."

"He said something bad happened to you there on Friday. He thought you could use a day of hooky."

She opened the door to let him in, then she yawned. "I love sleeping late. Over the summer I sleep till three or four in the afternoon. Over the Christmas holidays, too."

He laughed. "Rich, lazy white girl."

She pulled the blind back again and took another look outside. Small groups of students were leaving the school early, crossing the street to Sam's. Maybe they were cutting out on their study periods. Without looking at Hap she said, "I thought you liked me."

He pulled up a chair and sat down heavily, holding his back, which seemed to be aching. "I don't know if it's a blessing to be old, or a curse."

She turned and faced him. "Yes, you do."

Hap laughed. "Cal's in love with you. You know that?"

"Mm-hmm." She seemed pleased to hear it. "I think I'm a bit in love with him." She paused and repeated, "I think."

"You got room for doubt?"

"I've never been in love before. I don't know what it feels like."

Again he laughed. "It feels a lot like getting whacked on the head with a frying pan."

"You don't mean that."

"Just ask any of my ex-wives." He scowled. "The ones that are still alive."

"How many have there been?"

"We'd need an adding machine. The last one just left a couple of months ago."

She yawned again, eyed her clothes, then sat on the bed. "Did Cal tell you?"

"Cal doesn't tell me anything. I'm an old man."

"He loves you and you know it. Did he tell you?"

"Tell me what, exactly?"

"About the play. About how I . . . I . . ."

"There was something about a head, and blood, and I don't know what else. He was kind of vague."

"He had to be vague about it. What happened didn't make any sense."

"Very little does, to me."

"I think I'm over it now—over the worst of it anyway." She hesitated, stood up, sat down again quickly. She looked nervously around the room. "I think I'm pregnant."

Hap paused. He froze. Alexis tried to read the expression on his face, but he wasn't giving anything away. At least he wasn't registering disapproval.

She decided to go on. "I think I want to keep the baby."

"For such a young girl, you're doing an awful lot of thinking. What do your parents have to say about this?"

"My father's in Europe. My mother's in Florida." She shrugged.

"It kind of seems like they might want to know about this. I mean, their grandchild and all . . ." He reached behind him and rubbed his back.

"They've never seemed to care much about their children; why should grandchildren matter? They barely made it home for my brother's funeral last winter. 'Dear me, interrupt our vacation?' Uncle Peter made the arrangements." She pulled on her socks. "It's cold in here."

"Welcome to the inner city. So Uncle Peter raised you?"

"Nobody raised us. When we were younger, there were servants. But once we hit our teens . . . Daddy always has his eye on the bottom line. What you and Cal have here, the way you take care of each other . . . it seems so strange to me."

Hap laughed long and hard. "Cal doesn't need anyone to look after him."

"Even so, you do."

"You ought to tell your parents about this baby. They'll have something to say."

"I'll have my administrative assistant fax their administrative assistant."

Hap reached into his pants pocket and pulled something out. Alexis realized it was one of his punchboards, with fortunes. "It's a brand-new one. All the fortunes still in it. I owe you two more."

Seeing it made Alexis go a bit numb. For a fleeting instant she had a vision of Matt's head, held high in her hands, bleeding on her. "I don't want them."

Softly, almost gently, he said, "You can't escape the future, Miss Alexis."

"Lex. Please. Call me Lex."

For a long moment things fell silent between them. Alexis shifted uneasily. Hap lowered his eyes; he didn't want her to feel like he was watching her, studying her.

Finally, looking around, her voice tinged with anxiety, she said, "I seem to have done a pretty good job of escaping my past."

"Have you?" His voice was soft and reassuring, quite unlike his usual sardonic tone.

"I hope so. Do you know my brother?"

At first he thought she meant Matt. He was about to ask how he could know a dead boy when he realized it was Tanner she was referring to. "Seen him around.

Talked to him once or twice." He shrugged. "I don't think he knows what to make of me. I don't really know what to make of him."

"What do you make of me?"

"Cal loves you."

"And that's all you need to know?"

"Isn't it enough?"

"I'm fucked, Hap. Totally. I don't know who I am or what I want or where I'm going. I don't know if I want this baby because I love Cal or because I want to stick it to my parents. The look on my mother's face when I give birth to a biracial kid . . . part of me really wants to see that."

He got up slowly, obviously in some pain. "That's as good a reason as any to bring a baby into this life, I guess." He crossed the room to the window and raised one of the blinds. Brilliant sunlight poured in. "Come over here."

She did. He put an arm around her waist. "Look down there. A hundred and fifty years ago, there were slaves in hiding here, runaway slaves. Everyplace you see down there. This place has known more suffering than you can imagine."

"I didn't know. I thought—"

"But then again, so has everyplace human. We make the world such a sad place. The past never dies, Lex. And the future never quite crowds it out."

She looked him up and down; her face registered anxiety. Impulsively, she threw her arms around him. "I'm scared."

"I know, Lex." He touched her hair, quite gently. "We all are."

He let go of her and crossed to the door. "Get dressed. Go home. Find a way to talk to your parents."

"Cal wants me to have an abortion. I won't."

"Talk to your parents, Lex. Talk to your brother. Talk to people you trust."

"I thought that's what I was doing."

He walked back to her and kissed her lightly on the forehead. Then he left quickly, without saying anything else.

She started to dress. Then she realized, with a little shock, that he had left his punchboard on the chair where he'd been sitting. When she'd finished dressing, she picked it up, gingerly, as if she was afraid it might bite her. There was nothing to punch a fortune out with. She opened her purse and got a ballpoint.

Something was wrong. She could hear something, or sense it somehow, something in the air, and it was wrong . . .

She decided she wanted the fortune at the exact center of the board. But when she counted, she realized there were even numbers of rows and columns, so there were four "center" holes to punch. She chose one and slowly, carefully pushed out the fortune. It fell to the floor and rolled under the bed. She got down on all fours and groped for it. Finally she had it in her hand and unrolled it:

> *Flowers die.*
> *Parents die.*
> *Children sigh.*
> *Summer is a Lie.*

Something was wrong. There was a sound that shouldn't be. . . . She stopped moving and listened carefully. It was coming from outside. A few clouds had appeared in the sky. There were no students in the street, and still no sign of Cal. From the school came the sound of wailing—long, loud cries of pain. Even here, she could hear it. And from outside the school, it was even more disturbing; when she was inside the place, neither she nor anyone else seemed to notice it much anymore, except when it was especially loud or especially agonized.

Summer is a Lie. She reread the little fortune and slipped it into her pocket.

When she was dressed, she went out into the main room. Hap was in the process of putting on his sandwich board. It seemed heavier than she had thought; or maybe he was simply weaker.

"You're really up. I thought you'd go back to bed again. You probably should."

She got out the slip of paper and showed it to him. "Hap, where do you get these things?"

"From the future."

"I'm serious."

"From the past, then."

"Hap, please. All these fortunes and dream books and lucky numbers—who makes them?"

Getting his board on was a struggle for the old man; it must weigh a lot more than she had realized. "We make them. Ourselves."

"I'm really not up for this mystical mumbo jumbo you give your customers. I want to know." She lowered her voice a bit. "Please."

"There's nothing *to* tell, Miss Alexis." She started to correct him, but he said quickly, "Lex. I have to get out there and earn a few bucks, okay?" He reached for the front doorknob.

But she suddenly had another thought. "Hap?"

"Hmm?"

"You've been here a long time, right? I mean, you know all the local history?"

"I guess, as much as anyone does."

"Whose ghost is it, in the school?"

"That goes way back beyond my time, Lex. I'll see you later, okay, if you're still here? There's food in the icebox. Get yourself some breakfast."

Something else occurred to her. "Hap?"

He stopped halfway out the door. "Yeah?"

"Where's Jumonville?"

"What? It's right down there."

"No, I mean the place. You know, like Steubenville Pike used to run to Steubenville, back before it got all covered over by the interstates, and Steadbridge Road leads to Steadbridge. Where's the Jumonville that Jumonville Street used to lead to?"

He smiled and scratched his head. "I don't think I've ever heard anybody ask before. I'm damned if I know. People have always called it that, even back when I was a boy, before the city even bothered to put up street signs in this neighborhood."

"Maybe there's a story."

"Maybe there is. But I have to go sell fortunes, now, okay?"

He left. Alexis went to the window and watched him as he approached a group of students. By now he was a familiar part of the landscape, and they indulged him by buying things from him, nickel-and-dime stuff. The kids who had bought lottery numbers from him had actually won, though usually not a lot. Pocket money, drug money. So they had an incentive to humor him. Give the crazy old man a dollar or two and you might make back a lot more.

YOU'RE getting old." Diana stretched and yawned. "Or I am."

Peter Morgan zipped up his pants. They were in Canning's office, or, rather, Peter's now. Their quick coupling had not been successful. He wasn't happy about it. "It must be you. I'm a CEO. Strong and healthy, the spine of America."

"Well, don't look now, but I think there's a slight curvature."

They had knocked the stapler off the desk. He bent down to get it. "You have a tendency to irreverence, Ms. Ketterer."

"I'm an American."

"An irreverent sheep."

She shrugged. "Is there any of Michael's liquor left?"

He pulled open a drawer in the bottom of the desk. "Enough for a fair-size party. But the real question is, Is there any of Michael left?"

"Pour me a drink, will you? You're in a mood."

He got two glasses, wiped them with a handkerchief, filled them with two inches of bourbon and handed one to Diana. He downed his quickly, turned and poured another one. "Nick says he had a lot more, hidden somewhere down in the basement. But we shouldn't drink on school time. That's how Michael went wrong."

"Or started to. Cheers."

He scowled at his glass and put it down without drinking any more. "Yes, I'm in a mood. The board's not happy."

"Poor board."

"All this . . . all this unpleasantness." He looked at the glass and seemed to want to take a long drink from it. But he resisted. "Don't spill it, will you? This furniture cost us a fortune. We all wanted Michael to have the best."

"After all the booze that got spilled in here while he was alive, one more glassful could hardly make a difference."

She raised her glass in a toast. "Here's to Michael Canning—wherever he may be."

"All these damned accidents here. We've been having the worst luck. People are starting to pull their kids out."

Diana took a long swallow. "I'm not sure I blame them. Some of the faculty's unhappy too. People are talking about not renewing their contracts."

"Who? Why didn't you tell me this before?"

She shrugged, drank. "It never came up. Besides, you'll be able to attract more. You pay well enough."

"You'd think."

She drained her glass, got up and arranged her dress. "There's no shortage of dedicated teachers. How do I look?"

"Like a jaded wanton. EdEntCo's profit margin is pretty slim. We weren't expecting to finish in the red here for three years. Now, with all this . . . unpleasantness . . . it might take even longer. If enough people pull their kids out . . ."

She put her glass down on the desk. "I shouldn't. Last period, then the Poetry Club."

He leaned back in his chair, then seemed to think better of it and got up. "Who's talking about quitting?"

"You've never asked me to be a snitch before. I'm not sure I like it."

"You've never been on the administrative payroll before. We expect loyalty from our managers."

"Loyalty? Is that the word you mean?" On impulse she picked up her glass again and sipped.

The office door opened. Charley walked in. He was wearing a suit and tie—overdressed for a Washington student. But the style seemed to suit him. Surprised to find Diana there, he looked from her to his father. "Dad, we need to get more money."

He ignored this. "You are to knock before you come in here, understand?"

"Why? You're my dad."

"Do I have to have Mrs. Newburg police you?"

"She's afraid of me. I outrank her. Really, Dad, the Robotics Club needs more money, okay?" He paid Diana no notice.

"We'll talk about it later."

"Now, Dad. This is important."

Peter picked up the bottle, screwed on the top and put it pointedly back into the desk. "Surely there are procedures for requesting funds. Requisition forms. Something."

"Our project is too important to wait for all that. Besides, they've been denying everybody's requests lately. Cullen's too important."

"Cullen . . . Bill Cullen?"

"We named our robot head after him."

Diana kept arranging her dress. "He's a science teacher. It fits."

Peter ignored her. "You're losing me, Charley."

Charley suddenly decided to notice Diana. He smiled at her. "Do you mind if I have some of that?" Without waiting for a response, he took the glass out of her hand and drank, then handed it back to her.

Diana made a nonchalant show of handing her empty glass back to Peter. "Sorry, Charley, but your father's right. There's not a lot of money for any school group at this point."

Diana was nobody but a mistress. He turned back to his father. "We might even be able to patent what we're doing. It could make money for the school. The guys in the club are all kind of excited, really."

She made her voice into a little kewpie-doll sound. "There's nobody here but just us little women."

Charley knew she was making fun of him but he didn't quite understand what she meant. He glared for a moment, then realized he was blushing a bit. To Peter he said, "You should come and take a look, at least. Once you see Cullen, I'm sure you'll find the money for us."

Peter was watching Diana, for some reason.

"Dad?" The fact that he wasn't his father's focus was annoying Charley, quite visibly.

Still watching Diana, Peter told him, "Go. I'll come and see your robot sometime soon."

"I'd prefer you to come now."

"And I'd prefer not to." He said it forcefully. Diana tried to decide whether it was parental authority he was exercising or executive privilege.

"I'd rather stay here with the two of you. If you don't mind, that is. . . ." He looked hopefully at Diana.

She decided she'd had enough of him. "Don't you have a last period class to get to?"

"I'm cutting."

"Bonnie Prince Charley."

Charley expected his father to come to his defense; it showed in his expression. But Peter told him nonchalantly to get out. Glumly, the boy left. Peter smiled an ironic smile. "My son and heir."

"Flesh of your flesh. As near as I can tell, though, he gets more action than you do."

"He has more time for it."

"Then you should probably encourage his little robotics project."

Peter walked over to Diana and bent down to kiss her, but she turned her face away from him.

"What's wrong?"

"Nothing. It's just that . . . having you here . . . having

Charley know about us and having you here . . . it places me in an odd position."

"He'll keep his mouth shut."

"It's not that. It's just . . . I don't know, having him *know*. It makes me feel . . . hell, I don't know what it makes me feel"

He went back to his chair and sat down heavily. "I know it's not the thing you're supposed to say, but I've never much liked my son."

"An honest parent."

"Don't be snide. I mean it. I think my brother and sister-in-law have the right idea about child rearing. Be elsewhere."

"It takes a heap o' lovin' to make a home like that."

He sighed loudly, for effect. "My next girlfriend is going to be dumb."

"They don't come dumb enough for what you want."

"Just once, Diana, stop it, will you?"

"Sorry."

He swiveled his chair and looked out the window at the parking lot. "Are you free next period?"

She shook her head. "American lit. Then—I told you—the Poetry Club after school."

"I guess I'll go and see Charley's robot or whatever it is,"

"Be careful. You don't watch enough science-fiction movies to know."

"Know what?"

"They bite."

To the restless strains of Beethoven's Fifth, she headed back to her classroom. Peter stood outside the office for a few moments, watching the students go from one classroom to the next. Michael's death had not been made public yet. EdEntCo's PR team was working on it, mulling over the best way to handle it. To watch the kids, he'd have thought there was nothing wrong in the world.

He glanced at his watch. A half hour till he had to be on his way; his company needed him, or so he liked to tell himself. What to do . . . ? Hell, the robot thingy. Why not?

Mrs. Newburg was in the outer office, as usual. When he approached her, she put on a professional smile.

"I've been asked to take a look at this little device they're building in the Robotics Lab. But . . . I'm afraid I don't know where it is." He grinned a bit self-consciously. "I should have paid more attention during orientation."

"The Robotics Lab didn't exist then, Mr. Morgan. It was converted from a storeroom a few weeks ago."

"Oh. And I can find it . . . where?"

She gave directions.

"Thanks. I'll be leaving directly after I check it out. If there are any problems, check with Dr. Cullen, Mr. Larrimer or Ms. Ketterer, okay?"

"Yes, sir. Dr. Canning always liked his coffee black, and he wanted it ready first thing in the morning, early. How shall I prepare yours?"

"First thing in the morning? I'm afraid I won't be here that early, Mrs. Newburg. I don't expect to be here more than ten or fifteen hours a week."

"Really, sir?" She let her disapproval show. "Excuse me for saying so, but that is hardly enough time for all the responsibilities you'll be assuming. Dr. Canning—"

"Dr. Canning is"—he almost told her, but he caught himself—"Dr. Canning won't be back, Mrs. Newburg. There will be an announcement shortly."

She frowned. A half-dozen emotions crossed her face, none of them pleasant.

"We'll be doing a search for a new principal as soon as we can get organized. Until then, I'll be here as often as I can manage. Bill Cullen, Diana Ketterer and Matt Larrimer will be sharing the administrative duties until we can find someone to replace Michael. You're to work with them as actively as you always did with him."

"Yes, sir." She clearly didn't like it.

"Call me Peter, at least when there are no students around."

"Yes, sir."

It was no use. He forced a smile. "Have a nice afternoon, Mrs. Newburg."

He left quickly, not wanting to deal with her any more. Poor thing; how could she know who to butter up?

He hadn't gone more than a few steps down the hall when his cell phone rang. He flipped it open. "Morgan."

There was a minor crisis at the plant. He had to go. Just as well. Robots. Really.

As he was heading for the parking lot door, he ran into Matt. "I'm taking off for the day. Trouble at the mill."

"Will we be seeing you every day?"

"For the most part, I imagine."

"Well, I hope it's nothing serious. Have a good one." Matt smiled at his romantic rival.

"Oh—I'm glad I ran into you. Listen, Matt, I know you're a history teacher and it isn't really your area, but have you . . . have you ever seen this robot head some of the kids are building?"

Matt laughed. "You mean 'Cullen' or whatever they're calling it?"

Peter laughed too. These crazy kids.

"Bill's actually flattered they named the thing after him."

"Better him than me, Matt. But . . . you know my son, Charley, is one of the group?"

Matt nodded.

"He's been after me to increase their funding." Matt scowled. Peter went on. "He thinks EdEntCo may be able to patent the damned thing and make a few bucks. If they get some development money for it, that is. Could I ask you to stop by their lab and see what you think?"

"I wouldn't know a patentable invention if someone threw it at me, Peter."

"Even so. If they can convince you they're onto something, then maybe . . ." He let the thought hang between them.

"But, Peter, even if they've got something that might turn out to be profitable, surely the inventors would hold the patent, not EdEntCo."

Peter's smile got wider yet. "Read the student agreement we had all their parents sign. We own all the work they do."

"But—"

"We didn't round up the best and brightest young minds in the region solely out of a selfless devotion to education, Matt."

"But—"

"Anything they invent, anything they write, any new ideas they come up with that might have market potential . . ."

"That's why Michael asked me to vet all the plays they're writing."

Peter shrugged. "I imagine."

It was sinking in. "So these kids are paying us for the privilege of being our employees. Who would sign an agreement like that?"

"It was in a whole sheaf of forms that they—" Peter's smile disappeared. He had said enough. "I really have to be off. See you tomorrow." Without another word to his ersatz administrator, he turned and headed off to the parking lot.

Matt watched him go. This school was less and less the place he had expected—wanted—it to be. And then he found himself wondering about his own employment contract. Was there a similar clause? Not that he, or anyone else on the faculty, would likely do any work that could generate profits, but . . . He looked at the time. Talking with Peter had made him five minutes late for his last-period class.

He was expecting the class to be unruly, but they were all sitting in their seats, fairly quiet and well behaved. The topic for that day's class was "Causes of the American Revolution." The irony wasn't lost on him.

When the final Beethoven sounded and the kids headed off, he found himself trying to think up ways of avoiding the robot. Nothing he could come up with would be likely to sound plausible to Morgan. Damn. He dragged his feet, spending half an hour straightening out his room, rechecking his attendance records, doing any busywork he could think of. But he finally ran out of pretexts for staying still.

When he got to the Robotics Lab, there was no one else around. The gadget had changed. Someone had fashioned an actual head out of metal; he thought it might be bronze or brass. The robotic "brain" was now encased in it. As he stepped into the room, the head rotated; its eyes followed him.

"Matthew Larrimer."

Matt looked around self-consciously. Talking to a machine—absurd.

"How are you, Matthew Larrimer?"

"Uh, I'm fine."

"I am as well." Odd. Matt thought he could hear the

faintest trace of an accent, French or some other variety of Mediterranean.

"Good, Cullen."

"My name is not Cullen."

"I thought they—"

"Coulon. My name is Coulon."

"Oh." Again he felt foolish. "Is that . . . is that French for 'Cullen'?"

"Do not be impertinent, Matthew Larrimer."

Matt walked a few steps toward a chair. The head followed him. He could hear gears whirring, and what he thought must be relays opening and closing. The eyes glowed, very faintly; obviously there was some kind of light inside. It was too much to hope there was a short circuit that would cause the damned thing to catch fire.

Charley came in, carrying a backpack and a notebook. "Mr. Larrimer."

"Hi, Charley."

"You're making friends with Cullen."

"Uh, yes. It insists that's not its name, though."

"Don't be silly. That's what we named him. Did you happen to see my European history textbook sitting around here?" He scanned the room.

Matt looked too. But it was the computerized head that spotted it. "It is on the windowsill, third window from the rear of the room, Charlton Morgan."

And it was. Charley picked it up and tucked it into his pack. "Thank you, Cullen." Then he turned to Matt. "We've made a lot of improvements since you first met him—temperature sensors, electronic sensors, all kinds of things. He can even sense changes in the electrical conductivity of your skin. Like a lie detector."

"I wish you'd call it 'it,' Charley. Thinking of it as 'he' is a bit unnerving."

Charley laughed. "You probably don't like cell phones either."

"As a matter of fact, I—what do cell phones have to do with it?"

"You're a technophobe. Most older people are."

The word "older" stung. "I am not a—"

"Listen, I have to get moving. Lex is waiting for me in the lot. See you tomorrow."

Before Matt could say anything more, Charley rushed out the door. The robot's eyes followed him, then spun back to Matt. Slowly, carefully, the robot said, "The young. They think they know so much. And they know so very little."

It was unexpected. Could it have been programmed to say things like that? More to the point, could it have had attitude programmed into it?

"There are times when I think none of us know very much." Matt said it quite deliberately. The computer-robot-thingy could hardly have a canned response to that.

It whirred. It *laughed*. The sound caught Matt off guard. Then it said, "None of you do. Least of all these young men who tend me. They can't even remember my name correctly."

"Cullen." Matt said it reflexively.

"Coulon. My name is Coulon."

"You correct me, but not Charley. This is a game."

"You are the adult. You are supposed to be in charge. You are supposed to know history. But in fact you know very little."

This was feeling odder and odder. Matt took a step toward the machine.

"You are becoming nervous, Matthew Larrimer."

"No."

"Your eyes are moving erratically and your pupils have closed slightly. Am I making you afraid?"

"I know Charley's sense of humor too well for that."

"There have been a great many deaths in this school."

Matt felt himself getting more and more off balance. "Isolated incidents."

"Isolated?"

"Yes."

"What exactly do you think they are isolated from?"

This was absurd. Completely preposterous. Matt turned to go.

"Do not leave. You are the one who might understand me and my situation."

"I'm not a computer wonk."

"No. You are a historian."

Matt froze. This was so . . . so . . .

"I can sense your mood. You are quite nervous. I died here. On this spot."

Matt said nothing.

"More will die. More will come to be with me, as D. Michael Canning has. What was done to me will be done to them."

This was out of control. Sick. This was nothing the kids should be joking about, not even by proxy through a computerized head. It did not occur to him to wonder how they could know anything about Canning's disappearance. Without thinking, he asked, "What was done to you?"

"Washington."

"Yes. What was done to you here?"

"Death. You would hardly expect death to be a beginning, but so it was. And death—violent death, bloody death, horrible death—shall not stop. Someone is suffering death at this moment, as we speak."

From the corner of his eye Matt saw Bill Cullen passing in the hall outside the lab. "Bill!"

Bill looked in the door, smiling. "Matt. Making friends with our little pet?"

Coulon whirred. "Good afternoon, William Cullen."

Matt ignored it. "I think you need to have a good talk with the kids in the Robotics Club. They've programmed this thing with some awfully morbid language."

Coulon bellowed, "They have not told me what to say! They could not!" The sound of its/his voice was almost deafening; Bill and Matt covered their ears.

When the sound died down, Matt had a sudden impulse. "Coulon, where is Michael Canning's body?"

The robot said nothing.

"You know, don't you?"

The machine hummed.

"What are you talking about, Matt?" Bill stepped between him and the computer.

Suddenly Ron Lindsey, the black student from the Drama Club, appeared at the door. "Mr. Larrimer! Mr. Cullen! Come quick!"

"What's wrong, Ron?" Matt's ears were still ringing from the computer's voice.

"The office. Mrs. Newburg's . . . Somebody's done something to her."

They ran. Cullen/Coulon watched them go. Gears spun.

The office was a complete mess, paper strewn everywhere, furniture overturned. In the middle of it lay Mrs. Newburg, facedown, surrounded by blood. Bill entered first, saw her and told Ron to stay out in the hall.

A moment later, Matt caught up with him. Bill got down on one knee beside her. "She's still breathing. Call 911."

Matt looked around. "The phones have all been smashed."

"Find a kid with a cell."

Ron was just outside the door, looking in. "I'll do it."
He flipped open his phone and called.

"No, wait!" Bill stopped him. To Matt he whispered,
"We have to think of the school. What did Peter say is the
name of his friend at Pittsburgh Hospital? Was it David
Simkowicz?"

"Good thinking. I'll see if I can't get hold of him."
Matt stepped into the hall beside Ron and borrowed his
phone.

Slowly, carefully, Bill turned Mrs. Newburg over. Her
face was covered in blood. Bill took out his handkerchief
and daubed a bit of it away, but the cloth was saturated in
a few seconds.

Under the blood were staples. Dozens of them, covering her face. Her lips were stapled shut. Her eyes were
punctured with them; fluid flowed down her face from the
sockets. Her ears were fastened to her head. Scores of
staples. She gasped for breath; blind, she groped empty
air. Bill took her hand to try and comfort her.

"Who's there?" she asked weakly. "Who is it?"

"It's Bill Cullen, Mrs. Newburg." He whispered.

She whispered it. "Canning's sword."

In the hall, Matt was on the phone. "I have to talk to
David Simkowicz. This is an emergency. Tell him I work
with Peter Morgan."

He was put on hold.

A moment later, Simkowicz came on the line. In
hushed tones Matt explained what had happened.

Simkowicz was skeptical. "And is this one really
there? My ambulance crew called in and—"

"Yes, it's really here. We need someone right away."

Simkowicz made a comment about Washington Academy as a charnel house, but he promised to send an
ambulance, with strict instructions to be discreet and to

talk to no one but Matt or Bill. "They'll know what to do. This is getting to be a regular thing around there."

Mrs. Newburg was sobbing, gasping. With one hand she grasped Bill's shirt. He wished she hadn't; it was a good shirt, and the blood stains would be so—

"They're on their way." Matt gave Ron back his phone and rejoined Bill.

"Good."

"So much for the kickoff of the new administration. How is she?"

"For God's sake, Matt, just look at her."

Her body shuddered in a slight seizure, stiffened, relaxed. She was dead. She had not released her hold on Bill's shirt.

In the hall, Ron Lindsey watched it all, saying nothing. The blood was like nothing he'd ever seen. Shaken, he walked a few steps away from the door. There was no one else in the hall. It was late enough in the afternoon that nearly everyone had gone for the day. Almost without thinking, he dialed his father's work number. A voice on the other end answered, "Pittsburgh Sun-Telegraph."

"Randall Lindsey, please. It's his son."

A moment later, they were talking. "Dad, the school secretary's been killed." He described what he'd seen. And within minutes, a news crew was on its way.

Then Ron heard someone running up the hall toward him. It was Mandy Pinello, the girls' gym coach. Her throat and face were slashed and she was bleeding as heavily as Mrs. Newburg had.

"Miss Pinello!"

She pushed her way past him, smearing him with blood, and stumbled into the office. When she saw what had happened there, it was too much for her. She collapsed in a faint.

Matt rushed to her side. Her throat was cut; even unconscious, she was trying to hold it, to stop the bleeding. There were cuts on her face and arms. He looked at Ron. "Are you all right?"

"I don't know."

"Get some water for her, will you?"

Ron looked around the office. There was an empty mug on a desk. He got it, carried it to the water fountain in the hall and filled it. Matt held it to her lips. Sipping, she came to. Then she remembered where she was and what had happened there. "Matt, the gym."

"What happened, Mandy? Who did this?"

"He's still there."

"Who?"

"The boys' wrestling team . . . He went wild. It happened before we realized it. There was no way to stop him." She passed out again.

Bill was still on his knees beside Mrs. Newburg's corpse. He seemed a bit numb. Matt put a hand on his shoulder and told him, "I'm going to the gym. Keep an eye on Mandy." He turned to go.

Bill looked up at him. "We're all dead, Matt. This school is hell."

"Hell with a Banana Republic wardrobe." He left.

The halls were nearly empty. Ron followed him, not saying anything. They moved quickly.

Outside the gym was a boy in a unitard and sneakers, lying facedown in a great deal of blood. Matt felt for a pulse; there was none. It was Peter Dominic. Matt and Ron looked at one another for a long moment without saying anything. Then, simultaneously, they got up pulled open the gym doors and looked in.

Inside, blood was everywhere. More athletes were down, strewn about the basketball court, slashed, bleeding.

Some were moving, some were not; all but one were in sports gear. Coach Mort Mortkowski, in a black-and-white-striped referee's shirt, was cut into pieces, his head three yards away from his body. One boy's head seemed to have been smashed in with a twenty-pound dumbbell. Another had been strangled with a climbing rope.

At the center of the court, soaked deep-red with his victims' blood and wielding Canning's antique sword, stood Mike Monticelli. His eyes were open wide; he was breathing quickly and heavily. And he was smiling—almost laughing, it seemed. In his belt was a second weapon, a huge hunting knife.

Matt froze. Ron started to walk past him, but Matt held out an arm to stop him.

"Mike." He made his voice as forceful as he could manage.

Mike didn't answer, he just looked around the gym, grinning.

"Mike!"

Finally, he recognized Matt. "Mr. Larrimer."

"Mike, what have you done?"

He laughed. "Can't you see?"

"Why, Mike? For God's sake, why?"

"God? Don't be dumb."

Matt took a step toward him. Mike stiffened and held out the sword, then drew his knife, threatening.

"I thought we were friends, Mike."

"I told you, don't be funny."

"I helped you. You said you appreciated it."

"You helped me stay here, in this bloody school. I thought I wanted that. I thought it would be good. Or at least better. Can you call home and make sure you tell my parents about this?"

"Please, Mike, put down the knife and sword."

Again he laughed, louder than before. "Dr. Canning's sword. He gave us a big lecture on how valuable it is." He looked around at his dead and dying teammates, a huge smile on his lips. "Worth more than any of them. They'll sue my family for the price of the sword, if I hurt it."

"Mike, please. Put it down."

"No."

"At least explain to me why you did this. You owe me that, at least. Don't you think?"

"You're the only one here who was ever good to me."

"That can't be true."

He slashed the air violently. "There's nothing!"

"Mike."

He became quite still. Matt thought he was thinking, trying to decide what to do. To say anything might spoil whatever he was thinking.

Then it became quite apparent what he had in mind. He walked to the nearest body. It appeared the boy was injured but not dead; Matt could see his chest rising and falling slowly. Mike raised his sword and began hacking at the boy. Blood splattered; pieces of flesh fell away, some of them flying a few feet. The boy on the floor moaned and stopped moving. Stopped breathing. Stopped.

Matt did not move. Ron, beside him, took his hand without realizing he was doing it.

Mike laughed loud and hard. Then, with a startlingly quick movement, he turned the sword on himself, held it to his chest and fell on it. His body twitched and convulsed for a few seconds, then it became as still as all the others.

Ron tightened his grip on Matt's hand.

Matt knew he should do something, but he was too shocked, too numb, to think what. He stood there, gaping at the shed blood and mutilated bodies. Ron leaned against him and put an arm around his waist, needing support, but Matt hardly seemed to feel it.

When, a few minutes later, Bill Cullen entered the gym, they were still standing there, one holding the other, neither of them feeling a thing.

The scene was so awful it didn't even occur to him to call Peter Morgan. God. How many ambulances would this need?

And the air was filled with wild, demonic, anguished laughter—ghostly laughter. The laughter of the dead.

EIGHT

ALEXIS

MIKE lived. Barely.

Matt wanted to visit him at the hospital, as he had done before. Permission was denied, at least for the present. Security reasons. The boy was under a suicide watch.

The school was closed for a week after the killings. When it reopened, extra security people were hired; students were searched every morning. Cal Conklin was hired full-time; his discretion the day Canning's body had disappeared was exactly what Washington and EdEntCo needed. A team of EdEntCo counselors was brought in to help students who had lost friends in the massacre.

The new administrative group at Washington Academy went into what Peter and Nick called "crisis mode." They met daily, even during the week the school was closed, and Nick hurriedly interviewed applicants for security jobs. There were to be metal detectors at every entrance, even the ones people didn't normally use. Everyone would be searched both entering the building and leaving it. It would result in long lines in the morning and afternoon, but it couldn't be helped. Students were advised to arrive early for homeroom and to expect delays leaving at the end of the school day.

Some of this struck Matt as excessive. At one of the group's meetings he pointed out that none of the weapons in the various killings had been brought into the school; the killers had used what was there. "We can't possibly lock away everything that might be used to hurt someone."

Peter was annoyed by this. "We can try."

Nick spoke up. "We have to be as careful as we can, Matt. Things keep happening that we can't seem to control. I mean, you know that sword Monticelli used, that antique of Michael's? We can't find it. It's five feet long. It can't have just . . . slipped into a crack or something. But we can't find it. That kind of thing is why we're searching people as they leave, not just when they come in. It'll minimize theft. It's security."

"Has theft been that much of a problem?"

"Not really, no."

"Then . . . ?"

Peter got between them. "It's security, Matt."

Matt wanted to remind them that the sword had come from inside the school, which was exactly the point he had been trying to make in the first place. But the mood in the group wasn't encouraging. And security did need to be improved, he guessed.

As for Mike Monticelli, EdEntCo's PR department had hit on the idea that he had been using steroids and that what happened was the result of a 'roid rage. They prepared a statement to the effect that Washington Academy's administration and sports faculty were shocked and dismayed that any of their athletes would ever used illegal substances. Sports builds character, and Washington was proud to be part of that tradition.

Peter was the talking head for the school now. He read the statement to a crowd of approving media people. And he couldn't resist, ad libbing how personally proud he was that the school's gymnastics team was undefeated. Returning to his prepared text, he emphasised that what had happened was an isolated incident, and that steps were being taken to ensure it would never happen again.

The flow of reporters had been constant. And there had been, inevitably, sensational news stories. It was the worst kind of luck that Monticelli's killing spree had happened during ratings sweeps month. New crews swarmed around Washington, as Nick put it, like flies on shit. In the media, Washington Academy was now known as the "School of Death." It was imperative that there be no more of these incidents.

"At least," Peter told Diana and the rest, "more security staff means fewer of these damned news reporters sneaking in."

There had been some brief talk of reprimanding Ron Lindsey for calling his father on the day of the massacre, and possibly even expelling him; but that wouldn't have done anything but make matters worse.

Funerals were held for the eleven murdered members of the wrestling team. EdEntCo representatives attended all of them. The company had even offered to have Bishop Hinkle officiate; most of the families refused. No one was quite certain why; one parent even admitted it was irrational, but he couldn't have an EdEntCo representative officiate at his son's funeral services. No one had filed a lawsuit yet, but it was only a matter of time. EdEntCo's insurance company had given notice that they would not pay any claims resulting from the attacks, citing the school's lack of due diligence; so there would be a legal fight to try and force them to.

This added another reason for increasing security: "due diligence" cost a great deal less than settling any more wrongful death suits.

There was still no trace of Canning's body.

And through all of this, the school remained quiet—no echoing howls, no wails of someone in torment. The silence struck Matt as more ominous than the cries they had all become so used to.

Two weeks or so after the massacre, things were finally calming down, or at least becoming less obviously on edge. Some parents had pulled their students, and the best efforts of EdEntCo's salespeople could not persuade them to change their minds. Everyone left at the school was tense, but at least something like a normal routine was resuming.

Inevitably, the tension began to dissipate. Peter, forced to spend more time away from his own company than he would have liked, monitored the school's mood anxiously, hoping for the day when he could cut back his active involvement. The opening for a principal had been posted. The few applicants were far below the standard he would have wished.

On the first Wednesday after classes resumed, Ron Lindsey approached Matt. "Mr. Larrimer."

"Ron. How are you?" They hadn't seen one another since the day of the killings.

"Okay, I guess. What about you?"

Matt shrugged. "That was all so horrible. Seeing it the way we did, I mean."

"It could have been worse. We could have been killed ourselves." He paused. "I've been having nightmares."

"Haven't you seen one of the counselors? You should."

Ron laughed. "Why kid myself? All they can do is spout a lot of feel-good platitudes."

Oh. "Well, listen, I have to get to a department meeting. I hope you feel better."

"Can I ask a favor?"

Matt glanced at his watch. The department could wait another minute or two. "Sure."

"We need a faculty advisor for our student group. It was Ms. Pinello, but she . . . they're saying she won't be back for a couple of months."

"Which club is it?"

"The Gay-Straight Alliance."

It gave Matt a start. "But I'm not . . . I'm not . . ."

"You're not either gay or straight?" Ron smiled, then laughed out loud. "What does that leave?"

"Ms. Pinello was your advisor? I didn't know."

"The whole school's like that—everybody in their own little compartment. Will you do it?"

Matt paused. The Gay-Straight Alliance. People might think he was . . . But he couldn't let that stop him, or at least he shouldn't. And it would only be for a month or two.

Ron was watching him, trying to gauge his reaction. To be seen to be afraid of a thing like this . . . And the school *was* in crisis mode. Leadership was needed. Firmly, decisively, he said, "Sure, Ron. When are your meetings?"

"Thursday afternoons. In the library."

"I'll be there."

Ron smiled. "Thanks. We really need somebody. A lot of other teachers wouldn't . . ." He realized he shouldn't be saying it, and he let the thought trail off, unfinished.

But Matt understood. He wasn't their first choice.

Should he be pleased or offended? He promised again to be at the meeting. Ron thanked him and left, and Matt was left wondering how he could handle this on top of all the other duties he had in the school.

The Gay-Straight Alliance. Oh well, how hard could it be? They couldn't be much more than a social group; all he'd have to do is supervise their meetings. No physical demonstrations of affection would be permitted, no making dates, no . . . What else could they get into?

A minute later, he ran into Diana. "I'm the new advisor for the Gay-Straight Alliance."

"You sound like you don't know whether to be happy about it."

"I can't figure out why they asked me, of all people."

"Maybe they think you have something to give them." She was wry.

"Like what?"

"A discreet colleague would hardly say, Matt."

He wasn't much in the mood for her; sarcasm was the last thing he needed. He told her he was late for his department meeting.

"You're an administrator now. What can they do to you?"

"Even so, I ought to be there."

"I told them to ask you."

"What? Who?"

"Ron and the kids in the GSA—I told them you'd make a good advisor. I'd have done it myself, but I'm swamped. Peter has me helping him with the principal search."

"You have an extremely unbecoming sense of humor, Ms. Ketterer."

"They're good kids. You already know some of them, so I thought . . ." She shrugged and grinned.

"Who do I know?"

"Ron. Tanner. And Charley."

"They're—?" He couldn't quite bring himself to say the word.

"Is there anything on this planet slower than a heterosexual male? Go on, get to your meeting. I'll see you later."

Smiling much more widely than seemed quite appropriate, Diana walked off down the hall and into the main office. Matt decided to skip his meeting.

THE following week—three weeks after the killings—Matt finally got permission to visit Mike Monticelli. But this time it was a prison hospital. For the criminally insane.

Matt cleared himself through hospital security and found his way to Mike's room. When he got there, the boy was asleep.

There were four beds in the room, but three were empty. Even though Mike was weak and bloodless and would take months to recover from what he had done to himself, he was strapped to the bed. There was an IV plugged into his arm; the fluid in it was reddish-yellow. It bubbled now and then. Otherwise, the room was quite still.

Matt sat for a few moments and watched him, deep asleep. Seeing him wasn't pleasant. What happened had made so little sense. He was going to leave, had just begun heading for the door, when he saw Mike's eyelids flutter.

"Mr. Larrimer." It was a hoarse whisper.

"Mike." Matt made himself smile. "Hello, Mike."

"You came to see me."

Matt took a step toward him. Suddenly, he had no idea what he wanted to say.

"I didn't think anyone would." The kid had lost weight, blood, strength. He looked like hell.

"I could lie to you and say I wanted to, Mike. But something made me. I don't know what."

"You want to know why I did it, right? Everyone keeps asking."

"No. I don't want that." He moved to the bedside. "Anything but that. Tell me how you are."

"I'm tied to my bed, that's how I am. Still, it's better than being at Washington Academy."

"They said . . . I mean, they were afraid you would . . ." He had no idea how to say it.

"Kill myself? No, I never wanted to do that. I think this just makes it look like they know what to do with me or something."

Having come, Matt found he had no clue why he was there, what he wanted to say or what neutral conversation he might make. He looked around the room. "Can I . . . can I stay awhile?"

"Sure. You're the only visitor I've had. And I can't very well chase you away."

Matt looked around again, saw a chair and pulled it over to the bed. "What are they saying? About your recovery, I mean."

"My lawyer's trying to get everyone to believe I'm crazy. Do you think I'm crazy?"

"I don't know what to think, Mike. When I saw you that day, in the gym . . ."

"I'm not—crazy, I mean. The only crazy thing I did was not kill enough of them."

"You should never have done all those steroids. They can do bad things to you." He was belaboring the obvious, and he felt a bit foolish.

"I've never done them."

"They said—"

He repeated, loudly, "I've never done them."

Matt shifted uneasily. He needed the talk to be less charged. "Have your parents been coming?"

"No."

Oh. He looked at the floor and groped for something to say.

"That bitch in the office, she started it. She told me I didn't belong there."

Matt looked at him, then turned quickly away. He did not want to know.

"I went to ask to see my file, my student file. She said I didn't have a right to see it." He raised his shoulder a bit. Matt had the impression he was trying to shrug. "I knew I did."

What to say, or do? "Mike, I'll keep coming to see you, if you want."

"I don't. I don't want anything to remind me of that place. Not even you. I used to be numb every day when I went in the door. I should have killed more of them."

"Mike."

"I mean it. I think everyone there must want to slit throats. Look at the faces in the hall: You can see it. I'm the one who actually did it, that's all."

"I don't see anything like that, there."

"You're a liar."

"No, Mike." He wished he hadn't come. "Look at you. Is this what you wanted?"

"I wanted it to stop. That's all. That office bitch—she told me to keep my place, I was only the wrestler boy on scholarship."

Matt waited for him to go on, but he didn't seem to

want to add anything more. "So that's why you did it? That's what started it?"

"No. I didn't kill enough of them."

Coming here had been a mistake. Pointless. Matt got to his feet. "I should go."

"I don't care if you do. It was nice of you to come, but . . ."

"You want to be alone."

"I've always been alone. When I was in school I was alone. At least here, nobody rubs my nose in it."

This wasn't right. This was not the way things were supposed to happen. Matt suddenly felt as if he might cry. Letting the boy see that wouldn't help anything. "I . . . I'll come again, Mike."

"No. Go back to Washington Academy and fuck yourself."

"Mike, I—"

"Better yet, go back and kill more of them for me."

For the first time, Matt looked squarely at Mike, eye to eye. The boy was crying. Matt felt tears coming too, and he felt foolish for it. What did *he* have to cry about? "I'm . . . I'm so very sorry you feel that way."

"Look around that place. It's hell. You can see it in everyone's eyes. You think I'll be the last to do this kind of thing?" He started coughing.

"I hope you will be. I'm sorry you did. I wish you'd believe that, Mike."

"Do you know how much you're one of them? Do you know you've let yourself become that?"

"I don't know what 'that' is."

"Then get the fuck out of here and don't come back. But when worse things happen than what I did, remember I told you so." He coughed again, slightly. "Get out."

That was that. They had been friends, as close as a teacher and student could become. Or so Matt had thought. Had he been deluding himself? Had Mike been hiding something from him, his true nature?

"No, Mr. Larrimer, I'm not the one who's hiding something awful. Get out of here."

The boy had read his mind. It was not possible. "Mike?"

The boy turned his head away from him, and said nothing.

"Mike."

Nothing.

His visit was over, He had no idea why it had gone the way it had. Mike's IV bubbled. Matt slid his chair back and left.

LATE afternoon. School almost empty. Jocks working out, clubs meeting, though not many.

Alexis was at a table in the library, poring through a stack of history books. Tanner came in and sneaked up behind her. He wrapped his arms around her. "Boo!"

She jumped. "Jesus Christ, Tanner. Grow up!"

"Sorry." He reached into his pocket and offered her a Snickers. "Peace offering?"

She eyed it. "No, thanks."

"Take it." He smiled sweetly. "You're eating for two now."

She looked him up and down. "Scaring people. A fine uncle you'll make."

"I couldn't make a better one."

"You're not exactly a poster boy for good behavior."

"Look who's talking." He laughed and patted her on the stomach.

Slightly alarmed, she looked around. "Be quiet. I don't want people to know."

"When you start wearing maternity smocks, they might guess."

She scowled at him. "What do you want, Tanner?"

"I was just wondering how you're doing. Since you started spending nights at Cal's . . ."

She shrugged. "I'm okay. How's everything at home?"

"Mom's actually home for a week." His tone made it clear he wasn't happy about it.

"Have you come out to her yet?"

"Nope."

"You should."

He pulled out a chair and sat down beside her. "You should tell her she's going to be a granny."

"That's different."

"How, exactly? She's not happy about you not coming home."

"Let her call the cops, then." Her tone was offhand; no Morgan would ever involve the police in a family matter. Their mother had been scandalized that their brother's suicide had become public knowledge.

She turned away from him and reached for one of her books. He caught it out of her hand and read the spine. "*An Informal History of Northwestern Virginia, 1750–1760.* What's wrong? Isn't the latest Brad Pitt biography out yet?"

"I'm doing some research."

"No kidding. Why don't you just do it during your study period?"

"Too many people, too much noise. I've never tried doing this kind of serious stuff before, and it's harder than I thought."

He grinned at her but didn't say anything.

"I mean, it takes more concentration than I thought."

"Where no single mother has gone before."

"Go away, Tanner."

She hadn't touched her candy bar. He picked it up, tore it open and bit into it. "What do you care about 'Northwestern Virginia, 1750 to 1760'?"

"I don't. This is local—Pittsburgh."

He read the spine again. "Am I missing something?"

"You usually are. Here." She tossed another book at him. It was *Notes on the State of Virginia* by Thomas Jefferson.

He looked from the book to her and back again. "You said 'Pittsburgh'."

She took the book out of his hand and opened it to a page she'd marked. "See? This area was part of Virginia back then. He describes it all—the three rivers converging at the Point, all of it."

"Son of a gun." He didn't bother to read the passage she'd indicated.

"George Washington passed through here more than once in the 1750s. I haven't figured out what he was doing yet."

"Chasing some runaway slaves?"

She took what was left of the Snickers out of his hand and ate it. "That's as good a guess as any, I guess."

"So what's this for?" Before she could answer, he snapped his fingers. "You're after the prize for best student play."

"I'm trying to figure out why Jumonville Street is called that. I can't find any indication that any place in the region was ever named Jumonville. Even Hap doesn't know, and he's like a living history book."

"Barely living."

"He's a sweet old man, Tanner. He's nice to me. I think he actually cares about me."

"That must be a real novelty. Maybe I should come around."

"Maybe you should."

"How would he feel if I bring my boyfriend?"

This was the first thing he'd said that surprised her. She put her book down. "You're actually seeing someone? Really seeing someone?" He blushed. She was pleased to see it.

"His name's Tyler."

"Tanner and Tyler." Her voice dripped with sarcasm. "It's better than something like Tom and Tim, I guess."

"Or Cal and Lex?"

She elbowed him and he pulled back, laughing.

"I don't think I know any Tylers. What's his last name?"

"Nothing."

"Tanner, who is this guy?"

"Schuyler. His name's Tyler Schuyler, okay?"

She laughed long and hard. "You're kidding. The things our parents do to us."

"He's a great guy." He rearranged her books on the desktop. "Well, he's a bit of a nerd. But he looks cute in his glasses. And at least he treats me better than Charley ever did."

"That wouldn't be hard." She took her books away from him and stacked them up.

"Are you coming home for Thanksgiving dinner, Lex?"

"I don't know."

"Dad's going to be back." He frowned, "Well, till Saturday, anyway. He's taking us to some posh, new restaurant."

"I can't think about it now." She looked at the stack of books in front of her and sighed. "I don't know why I want to do this. But I have to find out where Jumonville was, and what happened there. Once I started wondering about it, I couldn't get it out of my mind."

"What makes you think anything happened there?"

"The fact that it's hidden so well. Why go to all the trouble to pretend it never existed? I'm going down to the main Carnegie Library later. They have all these old maps of the region. I might find something on one of them."

"And you might not. Why don't you just Google it?" He was still hungry. "Who cares? Do you have any more candy?"

"Nope."

"Damn."

"I tried a Google search. Jumonville, Pennsylvania; Jumonville, Ohio; Jumonville, West Virginia. Nothing. I even tried Jumonville, Maryland."

"And I thought the Internet knew everything. Did you ask Mr. Larrimer?"

"Why? He's shot down everything everyone wanted to do a play about. Except safe stuff. Valley Forge. John Hancock signing in big handwriting. Stuff everyone already knows."

He stood up, stretched and straightened his clothes. "Well, I've got to meet Tyler now."

"Now?" She glanced at her watch.

"After practice. He's on the racquetball team."

"Well, don't go following him into the shower or anything."

"Yes, mother."

She swatted at him but he ducked. "See you later, Lex." Laughing, he ran out of the library.

She turned back to her books. Jefferson's writing wasn't exactly easy to follow. Eighteenth-century spelling, grammar, syntax . . . But, despite herself, she found it interesting. Pittsburgh a part of Virginia—who knew?

It occurred to her that even that might make an interesting topic. She crossed to the library's bank of computers, opened the search engine and typed in "Pittsburgh" and "Virginia." The cursor turned to an hourglass.

"Alexis." A voice came from the speakers. "Alexis."

It startled her. She stared at the monitor, trying to guess what was happening.

"You are trying to find me."

The library computer was talking to her. She looked around. The school librarian was off working in the stacks, or simply gone somewhere else. She was quite alone.

She typed "Who are you?" on the keyboard and hit enter.

"I am Coulon."

Oh. It was the damned robot Charley and his friends were building. The computers that ran it had somehow connected to the school network. She wasn't enough of a computer wonk to know how that could have happened, but . . .

She typed in another question: "Coulon who?"

"The one you are trying to find."

"The only one I'm trying to find is a good obstetrician." Let it process a bit of sarcasm.

But Coulon ignored it. "I have been hidden too long. You will be the one to find the truth."

Sarcasm didn't throw it. With Charley programming the thing, that made sense. How about abstract thought? "What is truth?"

"Truth is the last thing people want to know. Until it hurts them."

The computerized voice had a trace of an accent. "Are you French?"

"Not anymore." So it could be wry, too.

This was foolish. She had research she wanted to do, and Charley's damned robot had hijacked the school's computers. She was about to get up and go back to her books when another voice spoke. "Alexis Morgan, don't let them stop you from uncovering the truth. I tried to hide the truth. And it killed me."

She recognized the voice. It was D. Michael Canning.

"**ELECTIONS.** Why haven't there been elections?"

Peter Morgan was at the head of the conference table, brainstorming with his administrative group.

Diana was doodling on a scratch pad. "That was Michael's idea. He thought the elections might mean a bit more if we held them off till January." She looked up at Peter. "New school, kids didn't know each other. It made sense."

"I think we should move them up, then. Have them as soon as possible."

Bill Cullen seemed nonplussed by this. "You think not having a student government is one of the bigger problems we're facing?"

"I think," Peter said heavily, "it might help stabilize the atmosphere around here. Having some responsible students help us in that effort, natural leaders the others know and trust. . . ." He smiled and fell silent, as if the thought could finish itself.

"And who would these 'natural leaders' be?"

Peter shrugged. "The best and brightest students will want to run."

Diana almost said, "Yes, the ones who are still alive.

And who want to come back here next year." But she held her tongue.

"It could be good PR, too." Peter was warming to his idea. "The best of the best, the finest students in the finest school in the region, all committed to helping Washington Academy over its troubled start. We get smart, photogenic kids, see? And we—"

Matt interrupted. "Suppose they elect not-so-smart, unphotogenic kids?"

"That isn't possible, Matt. The cream always rises to the top."

On her pad Diana wrote, "So does the scum." She pushed it toward Matt, who read it and had to hold in a laugh.

She couldn't resist goading Peter, just a bit. "And do you expect Charley to run?"

"Uh . . . er . . . well, yes."

"A Morgan dynasty."

"There will be other candidates."

"And will they win?"

He wasn't in a mood for this. "Diana, student elections will help things around here. They'll give the student body something to focus on besides death."

There was a loud knock at the door. It opened and Bishop Hinkle stuck his head in. "I hope I'm not interrupting?"

Everyone was surprised to see him. It showed in their faces; the last thing they wanted was members of EdEntCo's board prowling around.

Peter turned hearty. "No, of course, Grover. Come in. We were just talking about moving the student elections up from January. We want to hold them as soon as possible."

The bishop sat down, beaming. "That's wonderful. Claude will run, of course." He was in his full clerical getup, complete with collar. Matt noticed a smudge on it.

Diana made her face carefully blank. "Of course he will. He's a natural leader."

"But I wanted to discuss something with you all." Hinkle crossed himself for some reason, then went on. "I talked about this with Michael, back before he—back before the unpleasantness. Since you're the people in charge now, I thought . . ." Again he smiled, quite broadly.

Peter had been standing. He sat. "What is it?"

"Well . . ." Hinkle smiled a sly, timid smile and took a deep breath. "An exorcism." His tone suggested it as the sliest suggestion ever.

The administrators had to force themselves not to react visibly. Diana shifted in her chair; Bill reached back and scratched an imaginary itch on the nape of his neck.

Hinkle looked around the room, his smile radiant. "Surely you must see how much it could accomplish. It would give the students and their parents a clear demonstration that we know there's something wrong here, and that we're doing something about it. And it would be wonderful for our image. You've all seen these stories in the news about 'the Washington Academy Ghost.' A show of piety can cover up a great many problems."

The silence in the room was quite leaden.

Hinkle was apparently oblivious to the reaction he was getting.

Finally, Peter spoke up. "Well, we'll certainly have to give that some thought, Grover. Now, if that's all you wanted, perhaps you can leave and skip the more tedious business we have to deal with."

It finally began to dawn on the bishop that his suggestion wasn't going over. "Er . . . has any of you come up with a better idea?"

Weakly, Bill said, "No, but—"

"Then, there you are. It will have enormous psychological effect—raise the student body's spirits. The media will see that we're doing something. And the public, including all those troubled parents out there, will see that there are sound Christians at the helm. That always helps any institution."

Everyone but Peter seemed at a loss for what to say. "But—but Grover, an exorcism? I mean . . . do people even *do* exorcisms anymore?"

"We can. They're infrequent, but we can. We have to exorcise whatever's wrong with Washington Academy."

"But—but—"

"Look, Peter, take the word of someone who does this for a living. We all know these horrible occurrences were flukes." Hinkle relaxed; for the first time, he was talking like a person not a bishop. "So they're bound to stop, right? Sooner or later? In the meantime, we get a PR boost, we help repair the school's public image. And if the freak happenings do stop after the exorcism, so much the better."

Diana leaned close to Matt and whispered, "What he means is, it would help his church's market share."

Hinkle heard her. Smugly, he added, "Yes. Exactly. Isn't that what we're all here for? Isn't that what drives the American system? We all have to have faith."

"Faith in the free market and the bottom line. I'm not sure that'll help around here."

The bishop was benignly silent.

Peter announced, without asking anyone, that they'd be happy to think about Hinkle's suggestion. The bishop, only mildly annoyed at not being asked to stay, put on his ecclesiastical manner again and left, smiling beatifically.

Once he was out of the room, Diana told them all,

"He's good. I'll give him that. Now, let's get back to business."

"He *is* on EdEntCo's board." Peter was relieved he had left, and it showed. "We ought to give him the courtesy of at least discussing it."

"There's nothing to discuss, Peter. Can you imagine what the media would do with that? Hinkle in his satin robes, prowling through the school halls, chanting Latin, spraying holy water, ringing a bell to scare away ghosts? No parent in his right mind would keep his kid in a school like that."

"They're pulling their kids out anyway."

Bill Cullen had been largely silent since Hinkle first showed up. "I think the idea may have some merit, Diana. After all, he *is* a bishop."

She smirked at him but didn't say anything.

"This is a Christian nation, Diana. He has a point. If we do it right, this could help the school's image enormously."

Peter asked Matt what he thought. Matt had been hoping to pass on the issue. Pressed, he said, "I grew up in a religious household. We were praying all the time. I can't remember that it ever did much good."

"Listen to you all." Peter decided it was time to act like a CEO. "You're supposed to be leaders. We should do what will play with the public." He looked around, waiting for someone to respond, but nobody did. "I'll run it by our PR team and see what they think."

They got back to business: expenditures, attendance figures, requisitions, discipline . . .

"LEX."

It was early Monday morning. Alexis hadn't slept well

all weekend; she looked like hell. Tanner approached her in the crowded school hall as she was heading for homeroom.

"Tanner." She yawned and didn't bother to cover her mouth.

"You need more sleep."

"If you tell me I'm 'sleeping for two now,' I'll slap you."

"No, here, I've found something." He rummaged in his backpack and pulled out a thin stack of papers.

Alexis looked them over quickly and yawned again. "What is this?"

"Can't you read? I found your stuff on Jumonville. And it's dynamite."

She focused and tried again to read them. "Shit. Life at Hap's is one big party. There are always people there, drinking, dancing. . . . What is this?"

"I hope you're not drinking in your condition. You have to take care of my nephew."

"Niece."

"Whatever. Is it morning sickness?"

She scowled at him. "Do you even know what morning sickness is, Tanner? Do you know a thing about pregnancy?"

"No more than I want to." He paused. "Lex, Jumonville wasn't a place, it was a man. Joseph Coulon-de-Villiers de Jumonville."

She stared at him and blinked a few times. This was beginning to wake her up. "Who?"

He repeated it. "You were doing the wrong Web search. He was a man, a young French officer. Back when the French occupied this region."

"You're losing me. Why would they name a street after a Frenchman no one's ever heard of?"

Beethoven's Fifth sounded; time for homeroom. Tanner took the papers back from her and put them in his pack. "I'll tell you later. See you at lunch?" Smiling widely, he headed off to his room. Alexis was left holding out an empty hand, wondering what this was all about.

Midmorning, Tanner approached Matt Larrimer with what he'd found and suggested that he and his sister write the play about it. Matt scanned the printouts from Tanner's Web search and told him, emphatically, no. Not under any circumstances. Period, end of discussion.

The cafeteria was thronged at lunch, as usual. When Alexis finally found Tanner in the crowd, she was still waking up, and his mood had changed.

"What's wrong?"

He looked around for an empty spot where they could talk. He gestured for her to follow him and headed for an empty table in the far corner. Over his shoulder, as they were walking, he said, "I talked to Mr. Larrimer about what I found. I thought you and I might write this play together. But he said absolutely not."

"Why not? Are you going to tell me what you found?"

"He was murdered. Slaughtered."

"Who was?"

Patience, Tanner. "Joseph Coulon-de-Villiers de Jumonville. The French officer."

"You're going to have to back up a few spaces."

"Lex, this was French land. They had a fort down at the Point, remember? Fort Duquesne?"

She sat down and poked at her food. "I don't get it."

"The Virginians wanted it too. Washington came here time after time, leading armed squads, scouting, looking for an opening."

"This is Pittsburgh. Who would want it?"

"It wasn't Pittsburgh then. It was rich, fertile, unspoiled

territory. With three good rivers for transport. Valuable real estate. And the Native Americans were friendly, not hostile. They got along with the French and helped them get the most out of the land."

"Tanner, I'm really not up for this. Can you get to the point?"

"Washington wanted this region. I think he was in business, some kind of land developer or speculator or something. He kept leading scouting parties here. Then he finally decided to make his move."

Alexis ate her lunch and listened. Tanner obviously wasn't about to be hurried.

"So Washington came here with a band of men—1759, see? And they encountered a little band of French soldiers."

"This is starting to sound like a Mel Gibson movie."

"Shut up. They met this French detachment. Joseph Coulon-de-Villiers de Jumonville and his men. And the French were accompanied by some Indians. There are different versions of where it happened. Some say it was someplace east of here. But I think it must have happened here.

"There had been tension before, and the French wanted to ease it. Joseph Coulon de Jumonville, as the leader of the French unit, approached Washington to talk. He was under a flag of truce."

"Hmm?" She had a mouthful of food.

"And Washington blew his head off."

"What?!"

"Washington ordered his men to point a cannon directly at him, and blasted his head off."

For a moment Alexis didn't seem to know what to say. "George Washington would never have done anything like that."

"You sound like Mr. Larrimer."

"Don't be rude." She looked directly at him for the first time. "That really happened?"

He handed her the printouts from his search. "It's all there, with footnotes. It happened."

"So you think—?"

"Coulon de Jumonville is still here. That's what I think. The Indians buried him. But the place was cursed. He's the one we hear, Lex, howling through the halls. He's even been talking to us through that damned robot head. He's here."

She looked at the sheaf of papers in her hand, than back at Tanner. "It can't be true. We'd know. Mr. Larrimer's a history teacher. He'd—"

"He'd tell us the ugly truth about the father of our country? Right. Do you know how many ideas for plays he's shot down because they weren't 'sound'?"

"But . . . but *George Washington*, Tanner."

"Killing Jumonville pretty much triggered the French and Indian War, Lex. Three years later, the French were gone and Virginia owned this territory. And Washington and his partners got rich."

This was too much for Alexis to digest. She put Tanner's search results on the table and reached for her juice. And spilled it on the report. "Sorry."

"It's okay." He smiled. "I bookmarked the pages. Lex, Coulon de Jumonville is here. We hear him. This must be where he was killed, and where the Indians buried him."

Alexis found herself listening, as if the wailing might begin on cue. But there was nothing other than the sound of the busy cafeteria, kids shouting, laughing, talking loudly to be heard over it all. "Tanner, this just doesn't sound like George Washington."

"He was a land developer, Lex. Do you know why the District of Columbia is our capital? That particular piece of land, I mean? Washington and his business partners had bought it, hoping to make a profit. But it was a swamp. People who went there kept getting malaria and dying. So he and his partners worked a deal to fob it off on the Congress and the new country."

"Tanner, this can't be true."

"It is. He wanted land. He killed to get it." He lowered his voice and looked around. "And we're paying. I'm telling you, Lex, the Washington Academy Ghost is Joseph Coulon de Jumonville."

"But . . . but . . . where's his grave, then? Why didn't they find it when they built the school?"

Tanner shrugged. "I don't know. But he's here, Lex. I know it."

Suddenly, out of nowhere, Matt Larrimer appeared at their table. Smiling, he picked up Tanner's search results. "I told you, Tanner, this isn't right. It can't be. You will not write a play demeaning a great American like Washington." He tore the pages in half and handed them to Tanner. "He's the father of our country, and the man this school is named for. Do you understand that? We will not have him slandered. We can't permit it." Just as quickly as he had come, he left.

Tanner glanced at Alexis, then watched Matt walk away. "That's why they didn't find his grave, Lex. They didn't want to. Everyone keeps things hidden. We mustn't upset any apple carts. Even if they found it, we'd never know about it. But it must be here. Someplace."

Alexis took the torn pages out of Tanner's hand. Then she, too, looked after Matt. "There can't be anything to this. Mr. Larrimer—"

"Works for the establishment."

"I have to think about this, Tanner. And I have a chem-lab exam this afternoon."

"Don't get too close to anyone handling the acid, okay?"

She looked at her watch. "I should go see Hap. He knows everything about this neighborhood. Maybe he'll know about this if I jog his memory."

"All he'll do is sell you a fortune and tell you it's real." He glanced at his watch. "I'm supposed to meet Tyler at 12:30. I'll talk to you later."

Alexis finished her lunch alone, more than slightly upset by her conversation with Tanner. She loved him, he was a good brother, mostly, but she knew he tended to go off the deep end sometimes.

Yet she couldn't get it all out of her mind. If it was true . . . it would explain a great deal.

Her chem-lab test went well. The rest of the afternoon dragged. When it was finally time for her study period, she decided to check out the Robotics Lab. Tanner couldn't have told the guys in the Robotics Club about Jumonville, and even if he had, they wouldn't have had time to program any of it into their little creation.

Alex Marston was the only one in the lab when she got there. He had some hardware spread out on a table.

"Hi, Alex."

"Alexis, hi. Charley's off in class. I think he has physics now."

"I'm not looking for him. I've been hearing a lot about your robot, Coulon, and I thought I'd check it out."

"Cullen. It's called Cullen."

"I heard 'Coulon'." She decided to bait him and see if he knew anything. "Coulon de Jumonville."

"I don't know anything about Jumonville, but it keeps calling itself Coulon. We can't figure out why. At first I thought it must be a problem with the voice synthesizer, but I'm damned if I can find anything. It must be a bug in the programming, somehow."

"Can I talk to it?"

He gestured to the gadgets on the table. "This is its voice. I won't have it connected again for an hour or so."

"Oh. Well, I'll stop back sometime, then."

She still had nearly a half hour before her next class. And she was feeling restless. She decided she needed to be alone. The auditorium was not far away, just at the end of the next hall. It should be empty; she went and sat in the first aisle seat she came to.

The place was dark; the only light came from the hall doorway and a work light hanging over the stage. The darkness unsettled her. She was hardly over the trauma of what had happened when she played Salome for Claude Hinkle.

Voices came from out in the hallway. She didn't want to be hearing them. She got up, closed the auditorium doors, then found the bank of dimmer switches that controlled the lights and switched a few of them on, just enough to see by.

Idly, she walked up and down the aisles, turning it all over in her head. Tanner had to be wrong. It didn't make sense.

"Alexis." The voice was a whisper.

She stopped and looked around. There was no one. God help her, now she was hearing things.

"Alexis Morgan."

It was coming from the stage. From the place where she had—she couldn't think about it.

"Alexis."

She walked to the front of the hall and stood at the foot of the steps that led up to the stage. "Tanner? Charley?" There was no response. "Who's there?"

There was more whispering, faint, indistinct: more than one voice. Against her better judgment, she climbed up to the stage. She had to see who was playing with her head.

"Alexis Morgan, there is evil here."

"Charley, is that you? For God's sake, stop it!"

"Alexis!" This time it was a shout, not a whisper.

She froze. It wasn't Charley's voice, or Tanner's. But she thought she recognized it.

"There is evil here. Hidden here. It is only by knowing the evil, understanding it, confronting it, that you can live."

She looked around. Why was the voice familiar? "Please tell me what this is about. Who are you?"

"Confront the evil, Alexis. Embrace the evil. I know. I did the reverse."

She knew the voice. It was D. Michael Canning's. Exactly the same voice she had heard in the library. She ran to the light switches, threw them all and flooded the hall with light. "Dr. Canning? Are you here? Nobody knows what happened to you."

The voice dropped to a whisper again. "Some know. And will not say. They will not embrace what happened, and grow. You must."

She ran back to the stage and began looking behind curtains and pieces of scenery, trying to find him. "Dr. Canning? Dr. Canning?"

But she was quite alone, and in time she understood it.

Beethoven's Fifth sounded, the knock of fate. She headed to her last class.

IT was Thursday afternoon, the day of Matt's third weekly gig advising the Gay-Straight Alliance. After some initial nervousness, he had decided they were good kids. And there wasn't much for him to do, really.

They had been talking about a schoolwide Gay Pride day for the end of the school year. He only had to explain which suggestions were doable and which weren't. No parade. No drag. No . . . By the time he was finished, there wasn't much left for them to do, but there was enough to make them feel like they were standing up for themselves.

He was, as usual, late for the meeting. He walked quickly through the halls. Suddenly, he found Ron Lindsey walking beside him.

"Hi, Mr. Larrimer."

"Ron. How's it going?"

"Okay, I guess." Ron was smiling and apparently happy. He had gotten over the gym massacre more quickly than Matt, it seemed.

"Did you have a chance to run our 'Pride Day' idea past Mr. Morgan?"

"Yes. I think he'll okay it."

"That's great!"

They were just outside the door of the meeting room. Ron stopped walking and caught Matt by the arm. "My dad collects handguns." Then he went into the room, leaving Matt to wonder about the comment.

Inside, the kids were just taking their seats. Charley Morgan was chair of the group. He made a point of mentioning, at each meeting, that he wasn't gay, he was bisexual. He had a little gavel. Just as Matt walked into the room, Charley rapped it on the desk.

Everyone kept talking. Charley rapped louder.

Ron pulled a .44 Magnum from under his shirt and began shooting. A bullet struck Charley squarely in the forehead. Another one winged Tanner. Ron turned it on Matt, but Matt was too quick for him. He ducked to one side, then rushed Ron and tackled him.

The pistol went off again. The right side of Ron's head exploded. Blood covered Matt and sprayed nearly everyone else in the room.

And there were howls, agonized wails, mixed with demonic laughter.

NINE

JUMONVILLE

Two weeks later. Sunset.

"HAP, do you believe in ghosts?

"What?!" He laughed at her.

"Ghosts. Are they real? Do you believe in them?"

"I believe the dead are still with us, Lex. Whether we want them or not. Whether we believe in them or not. You want to call them ghosts, that's all right with me."

"So you do, then?"

He didn't seem to want to talk about this. "Well . . . I guess in a roundabout way you could say I do. Anyone who thinks the past is dead and safely buried is a fool."

They were in his living room. Dinner was simmering on the stove; Cal was late. Alexis was feeling restless.

Pointedly, in a tone that said she didn't want any equivocation, she asked, "What do you know about why

Jumonville Street is called that? I've asked you three times, now, and three times you've avoided answering."

He peered at her. "That's because you already know, I think."

"Tell me."

"Get me some whiskey."

She went to the cabinet where he kept his liquor, got a bottle and poured him a glassful. Taking it, he said, "I sure do miss Sam's bar. Seagram's always tasted just a bit better there." He took a long sip. "There, you see what I mean?"

She didn't, and she said so.

"Just a little neighborhood bar, shut down for the sake of 'progress.' And no one around here has forgotten a thing about it." He frowned. "Not that there are all that many of us left."

"So you remember about Jumonville, then?"

He laughed. "Not even I am that old."

"You know what I mean, Hap. People remember. The legend or whatever it is, that's still alive." She paused. "Among people who have reason to remember, at least."

He started to sip his drink again, thought better of it and took a long swallow instead. "I was still a boy first time the city put up official-looking street signs around here. Till then, it was just a matter of knowing. We all knew where the church was, where the social hall was, where the volunteer fire department was, where our friends lived. . . ." He shrugged. "All gone now."

"You're the oldest man in the neighborhood."

"Don't rub it in, Lex. All the places where runaway slaves were hidden, we all still knew that, too, when I was a boy. The Underground Railroad ran right through this neighborhood."

She made the connection. "The school. You're telling me there were hiding places there."

"I didn't say that."

"Yes, you did. Hap, where? Where are they?"

"All forgotten, Lex."

"Not by *you*." She said it forcefully. "Tell me."

"Sometimes it's better to find out for yourself, don't you think?"

She realized he had evaded her question yet again. "Not when someone can tell me and save me the trouble."

Cal came in, looking tired. "Sorry I'm late. Rehearsal ran long."

"It's okay." Alexis got up and kissed him, and he kissed back in a way that told her, yes, he was happy to be home.

She quickly set the dinner table and served up the food. There was table talk—Cal's day, Lex's, Hap's.

Finally she turned to Hap and pressed him to tell her everything he remembered about Jumonville from when he was a boy. Cal wanted to know why she'd care about that, of all the trivial topics, and she explained it to him.

And so Hap turned thoughtful. "We all knew the name, Lex." Hap ate a lot for a frail old man; she was always surprised at how he tucked it away. "We all knew it was connected to something horrible General Washington had done here. At least that's what everyone always said." He shrugged.

"And that's all?"

"We always knew there was a ghost. Sam and I tried to warn your Dr. Canning way back when. But why would he listen to the likes of us?"

"Why wouldn't he? You live here."

"Why haven't you told your mother about your baby?"

"Oh."

"I guess I'm being a bit arch with you. Are there any more potatoes?"

She got up, went to the kitchen and brought back the pot.

He went on. "A bit arch. No, we don't remember everything. Nobody does. But that poor French boy . . . he wouldn't let us forget. Before they put up that school, there was a little foundry there—used to make metal hinges and such. Used to employ a lot of the women in the neighborhood; didn't have to pay them as much as men. But it only lasted a dozen years or so. The building was full of howls and cries. People went mad. And I think there were a few deaths. I barely remember it.

"Before that, there was a church there, a Roman Catholic church. That was back before even I was born, ancient history. They used to say the howls drove the priest insane.

"And before that, there was a row of little shops there. Two of them were taverns. Sam's grandfather owned one of them. Or was it his great-grandfather?"

Alexis was fascinated. "So all those cries we hear—it's not just the school. It's not just the building settling or anything, like Dr. Canning used to say."

Like her, Cal found it all very interesting. "Why haven't you told me this before?"

"You never asked." Hap was offhand.

"I've been thinking of writing a play. A neighborhood with a haunted place in it . . ." He turned the idea over in his mind and seemed to like it.

Hap helped himself to still more potatoes. "You should work at being a good actor, first. Write plays later, Cal."

"I can do both."

"Funny thing about that old church, though. Or so they used to say."

"What, Hap?"

"Well, you know, the Catholics, they always have what they call relics in their churches, little snippets of dead saints. In what they call an altar stone. Well, when they shut down the church, the bishop should have taken the altar stone back." He eyed the potatoes another time but decided to pass. "But they couldn't find it. Someone had taken it, or hidden it."

"The ghost." Alexis made the connection.

"That's what my aunt used to say. He wouldn't be quite so alone."

There was a loud, insistent knock on the door. Cal got up and went to answer it.

It was Tanner. Without saying hello, he looked past Cal into the room. "Lex."

She stood. "Tanner. What are you doing here?"

"I—I wanted to—" He looked from one of them to another uncertainly. "Mom's coming."

"Oh God."

"She says she's let you 'get away with this' long enough and she wants you home."

She froze. "I won't go."

"She says if you don't, she'll have these men arrested. We're still underage, Lex."

Alexis went pale. No one said a word.

Tanner put his head inside and looked around the room. "Can I come in?"

Hap put on his biggest smile. "By all means, come in, young man. Your sister's cooked us an excellent dinner. Why don't you have some?"

He looked at Alexis. "You can cook?"

"Tanner, you have to talk Mom out of it."

"How? You know her."

"What's she doing here, anyway? Shouldn't she be wintering in the Bahamas or something?"

Tanner shrugged. "Believe me, I'm no happier to have her around than you are." He lowered his eyes. "She caught Tyler and me."

"Oh."

"Lex, I think she means it."

"No, dragging me home is just her latest fixation. As soon as she's invited to a Christmas party in Monaco or a New Year's fête in the Virgin Islands, she'll be gone again." She scowled and added, "As long as Dad's not going to be there too."

All of this was news to Cal; Alexis had never talked much about her home life before. "She can't have anyone arrested. The age of consent in this state is sixteen."

"But," Tanner said importantly, "we're still legally minors till we're eighteen. The law can have it both ways."

Cal asked Tanner, "How's your arm?" Tanner looked down at it, as if he'd forgotten about getting shot.

"It's okay. Like a character in a bad cowboy movie, I only got a flesh wound."

Alexis was growing more and more obviously agitated. "God, hasn't our family been through enough? Matt last winter, then Charley . . . Why can't she leave me alone?"

Tanner walked to her and put a hand on her shoulder.

But suddenly, she brightened up. "Wait a minute, she can't do anything. If she does, I'll talk."

"About what?" Cal and Hap asked it almost simultaneously.

"About everything. The way she neglects us. Her affairs. And Dad's. Dad's illegal business stuff. Her drinking, her pills, and Dad's. All of it. If she makes trouble for me, I'll make sure every last thing I know is read into the public record."

Tanner laughed out loud. "Lex, that's great! We've

been letting her buffalo us for years." He did a biting impersonation of a middle-aged matron. " 'Family business should stay in the family'."

"Like the mafia." Cal was suddenly enjoying himself.

"It's not good to keep things hidden." Alexis was positively beaming. "When I threaten to air it all, she'll be mortified into silence."

"You're forgetting, though." Despite his warning, Tanner was still smiling.

"What?"

"She'll cut you off. You won't inherit a nickel."

"So what? I've got a family now. That's something she was never willing to give me."

"She's already cutting me off, or says she is." He turned shy. "Because of Tyler. She says all I'll get is a little trust fund."

"What would you rather have, Tyler or a bigger trust fund?"

"Well, both, actually." They both laughed.

From outside, from the school, came more howls.

PETER Morgan sat at his desk—or, as he still thought of it, Michael Canning's desk—every morning and tried to convince himself things at Washington Academy were better now that he was in charge. He and his team (this was an afterthought).

Today was his first back at the school. The murder of his son had shaken him in a way nothing else had. His son and heir. Charley had been his only child.

The funeral had been well attended; Peter was important and influential enough to ensure that. He hoped that Charley, wherever he was now, appreciated it. Even the local news media had covered it respectfully, dropping the "School of Death" angle. He and his fellow board members, among them, owned more than enough stock in their parent corporations.

At the graveside service, Peter had fought back tears. There was no Morgan empire now; the line stopped with him. On the opposite side of the open grave had stood his brother and sister-in-law, and their two surviving children. Lucky bastards.

But now he was back at Washington, back at the place where his boy, his problematic boy, had lost his life. It seemed more than even a CEO should have to do. Bill, Diana and Matt had kept things running well enough, but they were not executives; they didn't have the training or the temperament for it. Dealing with the media had pushed them to the limit. Peter had sent a PR man to work at the school full-time, but only for a week.

Fortunately, there had been no more emergencies, at least not major ones. One boy, a racquetball player and chess champion, had overdosed in the men's room. Minor things like that.

In the time since Mrs. Newburg was killed, they had brought in six different school secretaries, all on a temp-to-hire basis, and not one of them had lasted more than two days. Sometimes it was the howls and cries that unnerved them. Sometimes the school was quiet, but they found it unbearable anyway for some reason. One said she could feel evil in the air there, hidden evil. Another quoted the press line about "the School of Death."

EdEntCo's PR man decided he didn't much like Bishop Hinkle's idea of conducting a public exorcism, but he hadn't been able to come up with anything that might be more effective in reconstructing the school's image.

And anything was better than nothing. So, after talking with his colleagues at corporate, he signed off on it. With reluctance.

It was to be done on a weekend, without any prior notice to the students. Too many awkward things could happen if word spread among them, and their parents, in advance. It was scheduled for the Saturday after the Christmas/New Year's break. Hinkle was excited. No one else was certain what to expect from it.

But Tanner heard his uncle talking about it with Diana, the first day Peter came back.

"Uncle Peter, you can't do that."

He laughed. "We can do anything we want, Tanner. We're EdEntCo."

"That's not what I mean."

"We have all the authority we need—city council, the mayor's executive assistant, county government, even the state. We're EdEntCo."

Tanner tried not to sound too urgent; that would only make them dismiss him as a hysterical kid. "It's not a matter of authority. It's a matter of the ghost."

Diana smirked at him. "You believe this stuff about a ghost, Tanner?"

"The ghost of Coulon de Jumonville." He said it emphatically. "That's why this street's named what it is. Some old memory of what happened here."

Peter looked around. There were too many people who could overhear this. He ushered Tanner and Diana into his office. "Now, what the devil are you talking about?"

He told them, in as much detail as he could. "Lex and I want to write a play about it all. We're going to be talking to Mr. Larrimer this week. He said no once, but . . ."

Peter shifted uncomfortably. If this story got out . . . Not that anyone would believe it. Not about George

Washington. But it would be one more PR hit for the school and the company. "You don't have to bother talking to Mr. Larrimer. You are not to write that play. Nothing like that will ever be performed in this school."

"But Uncle Peter—"

"I said no, Tanner. That's that. Now get to class."

Glumly, he left.

Peter looked at Diana; she saw the concern and tried to reassure him. "No one would believe it, Peter. This isn't Millard Fillmore or Zachary Taylor we're talking about, it's George Washington. Everyone knows what he was like. He was a good man, the father of our country. You might as well try and convince people Jesus didn't really walk on water."

He looked at her, obviously unhappy, but didn't say anything.

"Oh." She realized what she'd said. "I see the problem."

"Fewer and fewer people believe in anything anymore, Diana. Least of all our shared myths. How's society supposed to function without anything to believe in?"

"I don't suppose you have any of Michael's bourbon left under there, do you?"

He did. He poured them drinks. "Even if it *was* Millard Fillmore or Zachary Taylor . . ." He held his glass up. "All of our presidents were good men, and most of them grew in office. Everyone knows it."

Diana looked around, expecting a howl to come. There was nothing. She raised her glass. "Here's to the things we all believe in."

They drank without saying much more. After two drinks each, they had sex. Peter had had a sofa moved into the office.

* * *

"COULON? Joseph Coulon de Jumonville?"

Alexis stood in the center of the Robotics Lab, quite alone. There was a pep rally on for the jai alai team. The team her brother Matt had wanted to captain, she remembered. But she pushed the thought out of her head. There were more important things for her to do.

"Coulon de Jumonville?"

The computers, thirteen of them, whirred and hummed; thirteen CRTs blinked and flickered. The bronze head rotated to look at her. Illogical as it seemed, she had the impression it had been sleeping. From the speakers came a voice. "Yes, Miss Alexis Morgan."

"You are Joseph Coulon de Jumonville, then, aren't you?"

"Yes."

She hesitated. "If you were, you wouldn't say 'yes,' you'd say 'oui'."

"This is America. And I died an American, for better or worse. And it is in America that I have my vengeance, on the children of the man who killed me."

"It is you who howls and cries so terribly all the time." She paused. "Isn't it?"

"Of course." As if to prove it, a low howl came from the speakers, not loud, only for Alexis's ears.

"You are in pain, then?"

There was a brief silence. "Everyone is in pain. Everyone who understands how to think and how to feel."

She didn't like the sound of this. This was not the conversation she had wanted to have. "I'm not."

Whir. "You are. When you say you are not, you are lying. There are many kinds of pain. The pain of loss, the pain of abandonment, the pain of rootlessness. You life is as empty as all the others."

"No."

"Lying to yourself, perhaps?"

"No."

"I can tell, Miss Alexis Morgan. I can hear your pulse, I can see your pupils dilate, I can sense the conductivity of your skin. As your late cousin always said"—there was undisguised amusement in his voice as he said those words—"I am a lie detector."

She shifted, ill at ease. "I want to know what you want."

"My head."

"No one has it."

"I want my head, so I can rest in peace. Not that that will leave all of you in peace. There are too many others like me, in too many places, for that to be possible."

"Don't say that."

"It is true."

"We do not have your head, Coulon. It must have been—it must have been—"

"Shattered by Washington's cannonball. Yes."

"You know that? But you said—"

"Illogical, is it not?" He let out another cry, this one almost a laugh. "I have watched as the man who slaughtered me has been made all but a saint. I saw the bloody, awful truth then, and I have heard the lies. And there are too many others like me. We will have our vengeance, soon or late."

From the auditorium came the sound of the student body cheering. Alexis turned her head in that direction. "Listen to them. Everyone's happy today. No one here is hurting anyone. Why do you want that to change?"

"Everyone? Hardly."

"Everyone here, in the school."

"There are children beaten by drunken parents. There are children raped by them. There are children so sad they can only find relief in morphine and heroin. In the last row of your auditorium sits a young woman in a pink dress whose mother sells her to her friends. She eats drugs every few hours to kill the pain."

"Please, Coulon, stop terrorizing us. Stop making us mad and murderous."

"Give me my head, then. This bronze one hardly suits me."

She backed a step toward the door. "You know we can't."

"This is better than nothing. I have a voice now, I can speak, but no one wants to know who I am."

"Except me and my brother." Another step toward the door.

"Do not go."

"I should be at the rally."

"I shall have my vengeance, Alexis Morgan."

She stopped at the door. There had to be something she could say. . . . "Why take vengeance on the innocent? Why us?"

"Does not the Christian church teach us that no one is innocent?" Coulon paused. "Besides, you are here."

"Haven't you killed enough of us?"

"Not one of you, not ten, not a hundred will satisfy my vengeance. It is not merely your deaths I want, it is the truth. I will not be kept hidden. The ones who have died, they are not my victims. They are victims of the lies, all the many lies."

There were more loud cheers from the rally. Alexis looked around the room uncertainly, as if she might see something that could help her.

"Do you know anything about the Knights Templar, Alexis Morgan?"

The shift of topic startled her. "Uh, no, I don't."

"They worshipped, it is said, a bronze head. They called it Baphomet. And it prophesied for them. It foretold their futures. They worshipped it even though it prophesied their deaths. Their defection from the worship of the Christian god was the principal charge against them. Blasphemy. But Baphomet, as they called it, saw their true future. As I see yours."

"What is my future?"

Coulon laughed, a tinny, hollow laugh.

"When I realized that your cousin and his friends were constructing a metal head . . . How could I resist the opportunity to inhabit it? They gave me a voice. But vengeance, I take myself."

"We have not hurt you."

"You have hurt the truth, all of you. You breathe an atmosphere of deceit."

Suddenly, Tanner rushed into the room. "Lex. They've noticed you're gone. They're looking for you."

"Who is?"

"Diana, Mr. Larrimer, Uncle Peter."

"Why? I can't be the only student skipping their damned rally."

"They say you know too much to be safe on your own. They're afraid you're in the basement. I don't know what they mean."

"Yes," Coulon announced loudly, "you do. If you do not understand me now, you are the fool your brother Matthew always thought you."

Tanner gaped at the computer bank. "Did you hear what that thing said?"

"Yes." Alexis took him by the arm. "Let's slip into the auditorium and pretend we were there all the time."

"We can't fool them."

"It's easy enough to let them fool themselves. We'll

just sit someplace other than with our classes, and they'll think what's easiest to think. Come on."

"But Lex—"

"Go!" Coulon roared.

Tanner froze for a moment. He looked around the room, from the head to the array of computers, one of them after another. Then he walked quietly to the wall where a bank of surge protectors held a bank of plugs. One by one, he unplugged them.

From the air around them came Coulon's laughter. "You cannot possibly think that stopping me could be that simple. I am here. I am a fact. I do not need that artificial voice when my own resonates so clearly."

Alexis, not knowing where to look, stared at the floor. "If your voice is so clear, why doesn't anyone know you're here?"

"I told you to go!" The room shook with the sound.

Tanner put an arm around Alexis and they left quickly. On the way to the rally he told her how he had overheard the plan for Bishop Hinkle's exorcism. "Do exorcisms work, Lex?"

"How should I know? A church used to stand here. They must have tried that too." She wasn't certain whether this was ironic or frightening. "So I guess not."

Everyone in the auditorium was in a cheerful mood. They slipped quietly into a pair of seats at the rear. Alexis whispered, "I wonder what happens to people who try to exorcize ghosts that don't want to leave . . . ?"

"I guess we'll find out soon enough."

"Why do I feel more and more scared every time I come into this building?"

"What else would anyone feel?"

The team on the stage was lit brilliantly, almost blindingly. They were all in white—white slacks, white sneakers, white sweatshirts with crimson Ws on the front. The coach told a joke impugning the masculinity of their rivals, and everyone laughed. Alexis took Tanner's hand and held it tightly.

NICK Brookhiser, like Michael Canning before him, was drinking heavily. Drunk, he reeled into Sam's store one afternoon. "What kind of candy bars do you have?"

Sam gestured at the racks. He was hanging a few Christmas decorations, as many as he could afford. Which wasn't many.

Brookhiser started stuffing bars into his pockets.

"Hey, take it easy. I have to ring those up."

"Fuck it." Brookhiser put a fifty-dollar bill on the counter. "This cover it?"

"I guess. But don't you want change?"

"Fuck it."

"Whole lotta fucking going on today." He arranged a string of twinkle lights around his cash register. "Are you all right?"

Brookhiser laughed at him and pointed out the window. "Look at that place. Ugly old building."

"They don't come any uglier."

"You'd think that would have told us, wouldn't you?"

Sam put the bill in the register. "I wish you'd let me scan that candy. It'll screw up my accounting."

"You were right to have a saloon here. This place needs one." Without another word, he lurched out into the street and crossed to the school.

The place had to be watched. Watched very carefully. Down in the basement . . . only he knew about that. No one else must know. He had to watch.

The air was cold. The feel of it sobered him up a bit.

There were flurries. He circled the school, checking the basement windows. All shut, all secure.

Cal was on duty at the front door. He had become a key man on Brookhiser's security team. "Afternoon, Nick. You okay?" It was obvious he wasn't; he hadn't been for days.

"Fine, Cal, just perfectly fine. Anyone been in the basement?"

"Nope. Your orders."

"Good." He looked up at the school's façade. It seemed more unattractive every day. "Cal? You're a good man."

"Uh, thanks." How much did that count for, coming from a drunk?

"The best I have."

"Thanks. What's on your mind, Nick?"

"I need you for my assistant. I want you to quit school and work for me all the time. Long hours, fifty, sixty hours a week. Good pay."

"Oh." It was hard for Cal to know how to respond. Saying "no" to your boss is hard enough under normal circumstances. With a boss who'd been drinking . . . "I'm not sure I can do that. School's important to me."

Brookhiser narrowed his eyes, as if he was having trouble focusing. "Didn't you tell me you're training to be an actor?"

"An actor and playwright, yes."

"Take my advice. Quit."

Careful what you say, Cal. "I'll have to think about it. Thanks for the offer."

"Take it. Don't be a fool."

"I'm not a fool." He said it emphatically enough for Brookhiser, even in his condition, to get the message.

Brookhiser pointed down toward the basement. "I've

been thinking we need to close it off altogether. Keep anyone from ever going down there."

"Ever? I'm not sure that's possible, Nick. How do we do maintenance? How do we fire the boilers? Safety inspectors, fire inspectors, who knows who else—they all have to have access."

"We need to close it off." He said it too loudly, then quickly hushed his voice and looked around. "Safety inspectors. That's a laugh."

Cal wanted to tell him he knew about the ghost and even had a good idea whose ghost it was. But it hardly seemed like something Brookhiser might want to hear. "I'll give it some thought, then, Nick. Maybe we can find a way."

"We have to, Cal." Nick patted him on the back. "We have to, if we're going to live."

"Uh, right."

"Come be my assistant."

"I told you I'd think about it. See you later, Nick."

Brookhiser went inside. The place depressed him. Everything, *everything* was too old and too ugly. When he was drunk enough, he even thought he could see blood staining the walls, the floors, the windows, the entire school.

If he wasn't head of security, he could buy drugs from one of the students. They must be better than booze. Some of the teachers were taking pills. He knew it; he'd seen them. Why shouldn't *he*? Maybe he could ask Cal; Cal knew the neighborhood, he must have connections. He started to head back to the entrance, then decided it wasn't worth the effort.

Down the stairs. Through the maze of rooms. He didn't bother to turn on any lights. Finally, he reached the blank wall at the rear; behind it, he and Canning had buried the headless skeleton. In what faint light there was, he inspected the wall they had put up. Plaster intact, no scratches, no sign anyone had ever touched it. Good.

Next to it was where Canning had stored his cases of bourbon. Reaching into the top one, he pulled out a bottle and twisted the cap off. Then he got a Baby Ruth out of his pocket, tore off the wrapper and sat, back to the wall, and alternately ate and drank. Before too long, he drank himself to sleep.

Half an hour later, he woke drowsily. He'd heard something. No, not something: someone. Approaching.

It had to be the ghost. Blind panic set in. To the air around him he cried, "It was Canning's idea. I only did what he told me."

More footsteps.

"Please, leave me alone. You got Canning. Leave me alone."

Slowly, uncertainly, Diana Ketterer and Matt Larrimer came into the room. Diana reached for the light switch. She smiled at Brookhiser, but it was a tight, professional smile, not a warm one. "Nick. What are you doing down here?"

"Just checking the place out."

Matt went over to him. "We've been looking everywhere for you."

"I'm head of security. I have to watch."

Diana laughed. "Keeping an eye on all the pink elephants? Nick, you can't do this."

"I have to watch, dammit!"

"Watch what?"

He looked around, apparently frightened. "I can't say."

Matt put a hand on his shoulder. "There were some kids dealing drugs in one of the bathrooms. We needed you for the bust."

"Let the little shits get high. I don't blame them."

"Nick!" Diana was more and more concerned. "You need to get some coffee, then go home and sleep this off. We won't tell Peter." She added, pointedly, "This time."

"But we need to rely on you." Matt was trying to be more conciliatory. "You can't do this."

"Michael did it."

"Yes, and look where it got him."

"Where?" Brookhiser raised his voice. "Tell me. Where?"

They each put a hand under one of his arms and tried to lift him to his feet. He fought them. "Leave me alone! You don't understand. You don't know."

"Then why don't you tell us?" Diana was losing patience.

He looked blearily from one of them to the other. "Tell you what?"

"Come on." Diana gave an exasperated sigh and pulled him up. "We're getting you sober and out of here."

He was too drunk to resist much more. They half carried him upstairs to the office. A few students saw them. Neither Diana nor Matt offered any excuses or explanations. The latest temp secretary got a cup of strong black coffee for him.

Diana held it to his lips. "Here. Drink."

He looked up at her. "We have to let it out."

"Drink, now, Nick. Let it out later. Whatever it is. Okay?"

"No, I mean it."

Matt and Diana left him and moved to the far corner. She seemed more concerned than Matt. "What do we do?"

"Fire him?" He seemed to think the situation was funny.

"We need security. You know why."

He looked back at Brookhiser. "So he's a bit drunk. He'll sober up."

"Remember Ron Lindsey? If something else like that happens, would you want to have to rely on him?"

"Diana." His tone made it clear he didn't want to deal with this. "There are other security people. Let's talk to Peter and start a search."

"We can't even find a secretary who wants to work here full-time, Matt. Or a principal, God help us. What makes you think anyone will want Nick's job?"

He sighed. "You're probably right. You usually are."

"Good. We'll talk to Peter, and—"

Suddenly and rather violently, Brookhiser threw up. All over the temp secretary. She screamed, then announced that she'd had enough of the place. She had Diana sign her time card, got her coat and left.

CHRISTMAS came and went.

Alexis and Tanner's parents decided it would be inappropriate to celebrate. They sent out plain, black-bordered cards commemorating the anniversary of their son Matt's death. Then they flew to Europe. Christmas was always extra special in St. Petersburg, and there would be no gossips to see them getting festive.

Alexis and Tanner refused to go with them. They spent the holiday at Hap's. Their mother had made no more trouble about it, once Alexis had threatened to spill the family beans. Tanner's boyfriend, Tyler, whose family didn't approve of him, went there too.

Then a wave of snow-and-ice storms hit, one after another. It was more than the region could handle. Streets went unplowed, even major roads; there wasn't nearly enough rock salt to keep the city open. Businesses shuttered. Churches canceled holiday services, a major blow to their bottom lines. The mayor and county executive were in Florida, apparently for some sort of conference; minor functionaries did their best to deal with the crisis. And Bishop Hinkle's exorcism was postponed.

New Year's Eve was somber. There was still another heavy snowstorm, more than two feet, and the city was immobilized. People were trapped in their homes. Celebrations, when there were any at all, were small and low-key. Tanner, Tyler and Alexis were trapped at Hap's, and that suited them just fine.

Once the holiday was past, things began, quite gradually, to return to something like normal. Washington Academy reopened, but only the students who lived in the city were able to get there, and not all of them bothered. The ones who had to commute from the suburbs simply stayed home.

It was a bit of a relief to both Diana and Matt. Fewer students meant fewer problems and less potential for any more crises.

Most of the school's maintenance crew were local, and that was fortunate. There were nearly four feet of snow and ice on the roof, and it was creaking ominously. The crew worked overtime trying to clear it. The roofs of other buildings around the city had collapsed under the weight, and Washington Academy was a nearly hundred years old. The groans from the roof were almost as unsettling as the ones that came from the basement, from the PA system's speakers, from the Robotics Lab . . .

Matt found himself hoping the roof *would* collapse. "It would put an end to all this."

He and Diana sat in the principal's office. Like Brookhiser, they had taken to drinking Canning's bourbon, though neither of them got as drunk as Brookhiser always seemed to. "What a cheerful administrator you make."

"I want out, Diana. I can't take this place anymore." He drank. "I wake up in the middle of the night, hearing those awful sounds."

"Maybe you should move to a better apartment."

"Will you stop that? I'm trying to be serious."

She put her glass down, stood up and stretched. "Face it, Matt, we're stuck here. Even if EdEntCo were to close the school next week, what would we do? Do you have enough in the bank to go without work till next school year?"

"There's unemployment."

"And that's assuming anyone would hire a refugee from this place. You know the kind of press we've gotten."

"That's the school and the company, not us personally."

"Some parents are demanding the state Department of Education investigate us."

"Good. Maybe that'll put an end to this. Diana, I want out."

She walked to the window and looked out. The parking lots had only been partially plowed; there was, quite simply, no place to put all the snow. And there were patches of ice that no one had been able to break up; they were too thick and too hard. Rock salt barely did a thing. Students were parking in the faculty lot, such of it as had been cleared. "It's just as well most of our students are staying home. Where would they park? The streets are worse than the parking lots. But we need to do something to get that cleared." She turned back to Matt. "The natural order must be restored."

"What, exactly, *is* the natural order, here?"

"Don't be glum, Matt. Bishop Hinkle's finally doing his damned silly exorcism tomorrow. Who knows, maybe it'll work."

"Or maybe he'll end up dead." He got up and stared out at the mounds of snow. "Maybe we all will."

NEXT day. Saturday. Bishop Hinkle was to exorcise . . . whatever it was that had haunted the school. Of course, the real object was to exorcise the school's bad image, but that was hardly anything to say openly.

Peter Morgan and his administrators had agreed to the exorcism strictly on condition that it be done simply, in the lowest possible key, on a weekend, and only for a small audience of invited journalists. Hinkle was unhappy about this, but agreed.

Peter showed up at seven-thirty that morning, hung over and in a foul mood. He had flown the red-eye from Manhattan, where he'd been on his own company's business. Just as he was pulling into the faculty lot, he saw Diana getting out of her car. He honked and waved at her, and she waited for him.

The sky was dark, still nearly black; there would almost certainly be more snow. She looked around, made sure no one was watching and kissed Peter good morning. "I'm glad you're back. Nights are too long to spend them alone this time of year."

"Aren't you still seeing Larrimer?" He looked up at the sky and frowned.

"No, that's pretty much fizzled. Just as well. He kept talking about love and such."

"He's a kid."

She grinned. "With a kid's energy."

"Shut up."

As they were going inside, Matt and Bill Cullen both pulled into the lot. A moment later, they were all together at the entrance.

No one seemed to be in a pleasant mood. Diana said it was the weather. "I can feel the snow in my bones."

But it was the day's big event that had them on edge, and they all knew it. How would it play in the press? What would it accomplish? What *could* it? They vented to each other for a moment or so, but there wasn't much need for conversation. They all had the same thing on their minds.

Matt seemed especially edgy. "I wish we weren't doing this."

"Well, we are." Bill seemed not to want to talk about it at all.

"At least I'm glad the bishop agreed to do everything quietly, no excess, no bells and whistles."

"He's a bishop." Diana reverted to her usual wry manner. "His idea of 'low-key' and ours may not be the same."

Matt grunted and walked on ahead of them.

The latest temp secretary was already in the office. She was short and plump and her name was Alice. She smiled and said good morning to them. Peter became the hearty executive. "It's good to see such dedication."

"Are you kidding? I'm just happy for an extra day's pay. With overtime." Alice fussed over the coffee maker.

Some students pulled into the lot. Jocks. Peter watched them, concerned. "I thought the idea was to have as few people as possible here."

"The coaches insisted it would be a mistake for them to miss a day's practice." Bill dropped heavily into a conference chair. "There shouldn't be too many of them—the track team, jai alai. I think that's it."

"Judo." Diana looked out the conference room door into the office. "Don't forget judo."

"They shouldn't be here at all."

"Sports builds character, Peter."

"I wish the damned coffee would hurry up."

The bishop was due at nine. The group spent the time till then talking among themselves. Matt, more and more on edge, left them and walked the halls. He spent some time in the athletic wing, watching the various teams go through their paces. All boys. The way it should be, of course. But for some reason, this morning it looked odd to him.

A reporter showed up at eight-thirty, with a cameraman. From the TV station that had been most relentless in its stories about "the School of Death." Peter had had Alice prepare coffee and pastries in a classroom; he escorted them there.

The guy put down his notebook and bit into a doughnut. "So, you're really serious about this?"

"Bishop Hinkle is one of the most respected religious leaders in the country."

"I know that. Now will you answer the question?"

This was wrong. Media people were supposed to play softball with CEOs, not ask pointed questions.

Another reporter showed up, this one from the local all-news radio station. Peter left them to each other and headed back to the office.

At quarter to nine the bishop arrived, and Alice showed him into the conference room where the others were waiting. He had four altar boys with him, all in bright red cassocks and spanking white surplices. One of them carried Hinkle's vestments—satin, bright purple— on a clothes hanger; a second one carried a tray with a bell, a book and a candle; another carried salt and oil. And Hinkle had brought the boys choir from the cathedral, similarly dressed. He smiled cheerfully. "The others will be here shortly. Their bus is parking now."

"Others?" Bill took a big swallow of coffee.

"Bell ringers. We have a group of Swiss-style handbell ringers at the church. They play the loveliest hymns. I thought they would—"

"Grover!" Peter barked at him. "You promised us you'd keep this simple, remember? We don't want this looking like a sideshow in front of the media."

The bishop was clearly offended. "I've kept it as simple as I could, Peter. But these things must be done with a certain pomp and ceremony."

"And Swiss bell ringers." Diana laughed at him.

His dignity was affronted. "Miss Ketterer, may I ask where you worship?"

"At the bar around the corner from my apartment."

"Then might I suggest that you leave this matter to the professionals?"

Peter got between them. "I'm afraid Miss Ketterer is out of line, Grover. We're all a bit tense this morning." He called Alice and asked her to find another empty room for the bishop's various attendants.

"Good heavens." He seemed genuinely surprised. "Why?"

"Because having them in here will only add to the tension, Grover." Bell ringers, for Christ's sake.

A minibus pulled into the lot and skidded into a snowbank. Diana couldn't resist. "And who's this? A troupe of acrobats?"

"No." Hinkle decided to meet her sarcasm head-on. "Yodelers."

"All right, now, look." Peter decided it was time for him to assert himself. "We're all nervous about this. A lot's at stake. Snapping at one another won't help."

"It's only a few more choirboys," Hinkle said half-apologetically.

"Snapping at someone always helps." Diana stalked out of the conference room and into Peter's office, pulled open a drawer, got out a bottle and took a long drink.

Peter followed her. "Diana! Not now! For god's sake."

"No, for my sake."

The building groaned, cried, wailed. Loudly, much more so than usual. Agonized screams came through the loudspeakers and echoed throughout the building. Then everything went silent again.

Diana took another drink, recapped the bottle and put it away.

Alice looked in the door. "That was a loud one, wasn't it?" She seemed to find it funny.

Diana gaped at her. "This is just a guess, but you've been out of town for the last few months, haven't you?"

"How did you know?" She giggled.

"A stab in the dark, that's all."

One of the reporters appeared. "What the hell was that?"

"Just feedback in the PA system." Peter took him by the arm and escorted him back to his colleagues in the classroom. There were eight of them now.

Bishop Hinkle, fully enrobed, walked grandly into the office, opened the desk drawer and took a drink, right from the bottle. Diana watched, startled. He was beaming, clearly pleased with himself. "Are we all ready?"

Diana shrugged. "Why not?"

She and Hinkle went back to the conference room to get Bill; Peter rejoined them all a moment later. Diana looked around. "Where's Matt?"

Bill grunted. "Off someplace. He couldn't take it, I guess."

The bishop's procession formed in the hall outside the office. He led; the altar boys followed; the bell ringers came next; then the administrators and the press. The bell ringers began the first hymn, and the choir joined in: "Holy, holy, holy, Lord God Almighty." They sang in hushed, almost muted tones as if it were a requiem, which in a way it was.

They moved slowly, almost regally, along the hall. The altar boy with the candle had trouble keeping it lit; breezes kept extinguishing it, and he had to fumble under his robes for a lighter. Hinkle stopped at one classroom after another, scattering salt, spraying consecrated oil, chanting and praying the appropriate prayers to expel the spirits of the dead. The altar boy with the bell rang it solemnly three times at each room. With the handbell crew ringing out hymns, it struck Diana as redundant.

Peter, Diana and Bill followed, not talking, not betraying any emotion at all. The reporters were less circumspect; it was clear they were finding it all very entertaining. Diana whispered to Peter, "They're not buying it."

"Do you?"

"Point taken."

But the bishop was stone-cold serious. He blessed, he prayed. There were no cries or howls. Diana found herself wondering if this might actually be working.

At the end of the first hallway he came to the men's room. He looked over his shoulder to Peter as if to ask, Should I? Peter shrugged. Why not?

An altar boy pulled the door open for him. Inside were six student athletes smoking weed. They fumbled quickly, trying to hide the joints, but what they were doing was only too apparent. The looks on their faces as they were unexpectedly confronted by a religious procession made Diana laugh without wanting to. Bill shushed her.

Everyone stood still, unsure how to react. The bell ringers and the choir fell silent. Just at that moment Matt rejoined the group.

"What's wrong?"

Diana gestured into the room and at the boys, who were busily flushing evidence.

"Where's Nick?"

Everyone looked around. Brookhiser was supposed to be there. And they certainly needed him for the bust. Peter stepped into the men's room and confronted the boys. Matt pulled Diana aside. "Where the hell's Nick? He promised he'd be here for this, if only to help us spin it with the press."

"I haven't seen him all morning, Matt."

Hinkle joined them. "Nick Brookhiser? Our security man? Why would we need him for this exorcism?"

"The press is here."

"Oh. I see." He arranged his robes. "Do we have any idea where he might be?"

"I saw his car in the lot." Matt was suddenly tense again, more than before. "But I haven't seen him all morning. He should have checked in at the office."

And then there was another howl, achingly, deafeningly loud. The building shook. Everyone covered their ears. The lights flickered off, then on again. Screams poured out of every speaker in the building. Dust and plaster fell from the walls and ceilings. Hinkle's altar boys dropped the things they were carrying and pressed their hands to their heads, crying out in pain. The six jocks rushed out of the men's room, arms wrapped around their heads, and dashed off down the hall. Peter was too shaken to follow them.

Abruptly, it stopped, and the school was silent again.

For a long moment, no one moved or spoke.

Matt whispered to Diana, "He must be in the basement again."

Peter overheard. "Who? Nick?"

"He's been spending a lot of time there."

"Why?"

Matt shrugged; so did Diana.

"I'll go get him." Peter was grateful for the chance. It was something concrete he could do instead of just following along behind the bishop. He told Hinkle he'd be right back and rushed off down the hall. Hinkle and his boys slowly recovered their dignity, the hymns began again, and the procession moved on.

Before long, they came to the Robotics Lab. Thirteen computers blinked and whirred. Hinkle walked into the room, glanced down at his prayer book and began the chant. The choir followed. This was the first room they'd come to that was large enough, and empty enough, to hold them all.

A voice commanded, with shattering loudness, "Stop! Now!"

Hinkle raised his own voice and went on.

"Stop!" The voice was like thunder. The room shook. Plaster cracked. Dust fell from the ceiling.

And thirteen monitors exploded. Glass sprayed everyone in the room, slicing faces and hands, piercing eyes, cutting robes to shreds. Hinkle raised his hands to his face and cried out. The boys shrieked hysterically. Fire erupted from the monitors. People ran, frantic, into the hall.

All except Hinkle, who was blind. He stood in the center of the lab, hands covering his face, calling, "Help me! Someone help me!"

No one did. They had their own lives to worry about, their own pain to confront. A few of the boys stopped, or slowed, to help friends. Others simply ran. Before long, those who could make it were outside in the parking lot, staring at the building.

It seemed to tremble before them.

* * *

FROM Hap's front window, Alexis and Tanner watched the school. They had seen the various parties arrive for the exorcism.

"A choir." Alexis could hardly believe what she was seeing. "They actually have a choir."

"At least there are no clowns, right?"

She looked at him. "Aren't there?"

The sound of Coulon de Jumonville bellowing "Stop!" reached their ears; it was that loud. They thought they saw the building shudder in the wake of it.

"We have to go and warn them, Tanner."

"Warn who?"

"They have to stop this."

"You think they'd listen to us? Have you ever tried talking to Larrimer about something he didn't want to hear? Or Uncle Peter?" He mimicked him. "I'm a CEO. Don't bother me with this."

"We have to try, now. Come on."

Reluctantly, he followed her down the steps and across the street to the school.

They found the administrators and a few remaining boys in the hall, dazed and shaken. Some of them had bloody faces. Just as they reached Matt and Diana, another ear-splitting howl went up. No one seemed to know what to do; everyone tried to cover their heads.

Alexis rushed to them. Shouting, she told them, "You have to stop this."

"He won't let it happen," Tanner screamed.

Diana and Matt could barely hear them over the howling. "He?" Diana kept looking around, as if she might see something that made sense of what was happening. "Who is 'he'?"

The wails grew even louder. The building was rumbling; light fixtures shook off the walls and crashed to the floor. A boy crawled past them, groping ahead of himself with one hand. His face was shredded flesh, nothing more. To the extent it was possible to make out his expression, he seemed to be quite numb.

"Coulon de Jumonville," Tanner cried at the top of his voice.

Matt interrupted. "You both have to get out of here—now!"

But Alexis went on. "He won't let himself be hidden anymore, and he won't let himself be exorcised."

"Alexis, this is crazy."

"What do you think is happening here?"

And again the howls and the trembling stopped. The silence seemed almost thunderous in itself.

Everyone in the hall stared at one another.

Loudly Alexis announced, "You all need to go—now! This is only the beginning of what he'll do."

Only Matt and Diana understood what she meant. Everyone else responded with a chorus of questions: "Who?" "What's she talking about?"

There came another howl, a long, low one this time. Then, from the basement, came the sound of screaming. It was Peter Morgan's voice.

Tanner caught Alexis by the hand and pulled her toward the front entrance. "Come on, Lex, they won't listen. We have to save ourselves."

"But—"

"Come on, dammit!"

He kept pulling her, and after a few steps she stopped resisting. Tanner put an arm around one of the injured boys. Alexis helped the one who was crawling blindly; she got him to his feet, and took him by the hand.

"Who are you?" he asked.

"No one. Never mind. Come on."

They led the boys to the lot and left them with their friends.

Then, in a matter of minutes, they were back at Hap's, watching the catastrophe unfold. The building howled again. They saw it quake. The walls shook as if they were made of thick gelatin, not stone.

"Why won't they listen?" Lex turned to her brother. "Why?"

"We're the ones who know, Lex."

"They should listen to us."

"They won't. They never have."

She put an arm around him and they stood at the window and watched. There was nothing else they could do.

IN the blood-soaked hallway, Matt and Diana helped the boys, a few at a time, to the entrance. In the confusion they somehow forgot about Bishop Hinkle, who lay on the floor of the Robotics Lab, sobbing. Oddly, he wasn't praying, simply venting his grief and pain. The air was full of dust, and he began to cough uncontrollably.

When they had shepherded the last of them out of the building, Diana turned to Matt and said, "Peter's in the basement. Maybe Nick, too. We have to get them."

"We don't know what's down there."

"What difference does it make? We have to help them. Then we can get out of here."

"But—"

"Come *on,* Matt."

She took him by the arm and led him down the stairs to the basement.

There was light. For once the place was not dark; a strange green light covered everything. The strangeness of it didn't register with either of them. The building was still, perfectly quiet. Diana led Matt through the rooms, one after another, to the rear. The light was coming from there.

"Diana, something's wrong here."

She shot him an exasperated look. "No wonder they made you a teacher."

"But—" He tried to pull free of her, but her grip on his arm was too strong.

"Come on, Matt. They're down here."

The light grew brighter and brighter.

Then they reached the last room and saw at last the horror at the heart of Washington Academy.

The green illumination was glaring, almost blinding. As horrible as the sounds had been earlier, the light was that painful now.

Part of the rear wall had been broken down. Beyond it was a small, low-ceilinged, hidden room. Two men were there, one on the floor, the other kneeling over him.

Matt and Diana stopped, and she finally let go of him. "Matt, where's all this light coming from?"

"What difference does it make?"

"It's hurting my eyes."

On the floor in the little room lay Nick Brookhiser. His body was sliced and torn. Blood soaked him. What seemed to be pieces of his flesh were everywhere, spread across the floor, sticking to the walls . . .

Beside him knelt Peter Morgan, looking down at him numbly. There was no blood on him.

"Peter." Diana took a step toward them.

Slowly, Peter looked up. "He's dead."

"We can see that."

Matt assumed Peter had killed him. But there was no sign of a weapon. What could he have done it with, to have lacerated him so completely?

"He's dead," Peter said again.

Matt stepped forward. "He's not the only one. How did it happen?"

"I don't know." He had barely moved. "He was like this when I found him. Nearly dead when I got there, dying, then gone."

"Peter, come on." Diana took another step toward him.

"He said the corpse did it to him. What can he have meant?"

The building began to howl and rumble again. They heard a low cry from someplace deeper, even, than where they were.

The sound grew, becoming louder and coarser and more terrible. Again the walls shook. Again plaster and debris fell from the ceilings and walls.

Diana ran to Peter and took him by the hand. "Come on. We've got to get out of here *now*."

Matt stepped back, closer to the door. He noticed the stockpile of liquor and was tempted to stop and drink, but his survival instincts overrode that. Being drunk now, in this place, with all that was happening . . . no.

Unsteadily, Peter began to climb to his feet with Diana's help. The building groaned. The sound of walls crashing down came to them. The upper floors must be collapsing.

From the ground beneath Peter and Diana's feet came a hand, a skeletal hand. It thrust up through the earthen floor and caught hold of his ankle.

Diana screamed and backed away. "Peter!"

The fingers tore into his flesh, stripping it away. He cried out and fell to the floor.

"Oh, my God. Peter!"

From the earth emerged more and more of the skeleton of Joseph Coulon de Jumonville, headless but alive. Its fingers tore at Peter relentlessly, ripping strips of flesh from his body. He cried for help but the skeleton wrapped itself around him and kept clawing, scratching, tearing. It ripped his eyes from their sockets, it scratched his heart out of his chest, it clawed a handful of veins and arteries from his throat and held them up like an athlete in triumph.

Matt was frozen with terror. Diana again took him by the arm. "Come on, we've got to run!"

They turned and headed for the door.

But there in front of them stood the animated, half-decayed corpse of D. Michael Canning, wielding his antique sword. Swiftly, the blade descended and took off her head first, then his. Canning hacked their bodies into pieces.

And the wailing cry that engulfed the building turned from one of agony to one of joy, of triumph.

It grew louder and louder, and the walls shook like no earthquake could ever have shaken them.

In the parking lot, the boys who had escaped watched as an enormous crack opened in the rear wall of Washington Academy. Then the wall collapsed, crushing some of them to death; the others ran to the far end of the lot, quivering in the cold. A few of them huddled together.

Sam watched from his storefront as part of the front wall crumbled and fell into Jumonville Street.

From the front window of Hap's apartment, Alexis

and Tanner saw most of what remained of the building shudder and collapse inward, onto its own ruins. A cloud of thick dust rose slowly above it, almost as if it was alive.

And finally the wailing stopped.

Tanner took Alexis's hand, then moved closer and put his arm around her shoulder. She leaned against him.

Softly, he said, "We should call someone."

"Who?"

"Nine-one-one? I don't know. Anybody. We can't just . . . leave it there."

"They won't understand what happened. They can't."

He let go of her and walked over to the telephone. "You're probably right. But they don't have to, Lex. There are people hurt there. Someone has to help them."

From her spot at the window she asked, "Should we go back?"

Tanner nodded at her as he dialed. "We're the only ones here."

The 911 operator came on the line. "What's your emergency?"

"Washington Academy." He almost whispered it. "The building fell down. People are hurt. People are dead. Come." He hung up.

In the parking lot, boys were moving, trying to help one another and to warm themselves, not knowing what to do. Their vans had been crushed in the collapse; they couldn't see anyplace they might shelter.

Sam stepped out into the street and stared fixedly across the street, not quite certain the destruction had stopped.

The first emergency vehicles pulled up red lights spinning.

Alexis and Tanner watched them all.

"How can we tell them what we know, Lex?"

She leaned against him again. "I don't know. They'll think what they want to, anyway. I don't know, Tanner. I just don't know."

EPILOGUE

FAMILY

Mid-July. Early on a Monday afternoon.
Demolition.

THE authorities had condemned what was left of the
building. Not wanting to probe too deeply or inquire too
carefully, they simply used eminent domain and shut the
place down. There were too many prominent people on
EdEntCo's board; it wouldn't do to ask a lot of inconvenient questions.

The state Department of Education had stepped in to re-
locate Washington's students to other schools, and made
certain that none of them lost any academic credit. A cousin
of the governor, another member of the board, arranged it.

Most of the building had collapsed, and construction
crews had hauled away the debris, being careful to sort
out the human remains. Two dozen people died when
the building collapsed—administrators, coaches, athletes,

choir members, altar boys. . . . The only one to receive posthumous public recognition was Bishop Grover Hinkle, whose remains were buried with pomp, ceremony and eulogies from all sorts of notables.

The skeleton of Coulon de Jumonville was recovered from the rubble. Minus the head, of course. It was taken away and quietly buried in consecrated ground. The official story, as contained in an EdEntCo press release and reported by the media, was that the headless corpse of an unknown person, apparently from the eighteenth century, had been found beneath the school and removed for burial. No one asked any more about it; no one seemed to want to. None of the reporters even asked what had happened to the head. The demolition of the remains of the huge old building was a better story—with that kind of great video, it would lead the evening newscasts.

Tanner and Alexis's father had been persuaded to become the new CEO of EdEntCo, and he plunged busily into making plans for the corporation's future. The first job he took on was making certain that the collapse of the school—which was to say, the loss of property and the insurance liabilities it caused—would become a valid tax write-off. And he initiated lawsuits against the city, for selling them what had clearly been a substandard building, and the contractors, who had clearly done substandard renovation work on it. The lawsuits from the families of the dead wouldn't come to much—not as much as the company stood to gain.

So things were looking bright. EdEntCo would end the year in the black. The first bulldozers and wrecking cranes had been maneuvered into place that morning.

Cal and Alexis watched from Hap's front window. There was to be a little ceremony before the first swing of the wrecking ball. The media were there, cheerfully prepared to give the story of Washington Academy what they called "closure." Lex's father was there too, overdressed and looking fairly ridiculous in a bright yellow hard hat. She tried not to think too much about what a fool he was.

She and Tanner had been accepted back into their old school, and she had graduated with honors. Alexis and Cal were to be married soon, and they'd be getting their own place nearby. Neither of them wanted to leave the neighborhood.

In a corner of the room, Tanner and his boyfriend hugged and kissed.

Hap sat in his old easy chair, smiling and watching over them all. His health had been failing more and more. Getting about had become quite difficult. It had been months since he'd been able to get out and sell his fortunes—not that there was anyone left to sell them to. But there were always people at his place to help take care of him.

A ham was baking; the aroma filled the apartment.

Outside, the speeches ended. A wrecking ball swung violently and knocked down the parts of Washington's walls that were still standing. But they fell in an unexpected direction. Bricks, mortar and window glass sprayed across the street; the whole block trembled unnervingly. Mr. Morgan and his associates scrambled out of the way. One was hit by a brick and knocked unconscious. Fortunately, there were medics on hand.

"That's the end, then." Alexis leaned her head on Cal's shoulder.

Tanner smiled and took his eyes off Tyler for the first time. "At least the beginning of the end."

"Nothing ever ends, Tanner." Hap spoke softly, patiently. "The whole concept of history, as something distinct from the present, is an illusion. I thought you'd understand that by now."

"I'm not sure I want to."

Tanner and Tyler joined Lex and Cal at the window. Tanner's face showed half a dozen conflicting emotions. "I can't tell you how I hated that place."

"And it hated you." Cal pulled free of Alexis and went to the kitchen to check on the ham. A moment later, he was back, smiling. "We can eat any time now."

Tyler offered to set the table and headed for the kitchen. Cal helped Hap to his feet, and they led everyone in.

The ham was juicy, succulent, wonderfully flavorful. There were baked potatoes, greens; a sweet-potato pie waited on the sideboard. Everyone smiled as they ate; they were too busy to talk. From the street, every few minutes, came more sounds of demolition.

When they were finished with the main meal and Alexis was serving dessert, Hap took hold of her hand. "I still owe you something."

"You don't owe me a thing, Hap. I owe you. More than I can say."

"No, this is business."

She was lost. "Don't be silly." She dished out big slices of the pie for her brother and Tyler.

"Last fall you paid me for five fortunes." His demeanor abruptly turned serious, and the mood in the room changed. "You only took four."

Lex froze. "I don't want the last one."

"I owe it to you. You have to take it."

"No, Hap. I don't want it."

She was quite visibly upset. Cal spoke up. "If she doesn't want it, Hap, she doesn't want it."

"This is a matter of honor, Cal. She paid me. I have to deliver."

No one seemed to know what to say. Hap struggled to his feet, refusing any help, and crossed the room to the corner where his sandwich sign had stood for months, untouched. He got one of the fortune punchboards and carried it back to the table. "Here."

"No, Hap." She was pale. She did not want this.

"Take it. I don't care if you read it, and I know you probably won't believe whatever it says, no more than you did before. But I owe you."

Slowly, unhappily, Alexis took a fork and poked the little paper out with a tine. The fortune dropped onto the table and rolled a few inches. No one touched it. "There. I took it."

"Are you going to see what it says?"

"No. I don't want to know."

But Tanner reached out and picked it up. He unrolled it and read it. Tyler turned to Cal. "Cal?"

"Yes, Tyler?"

"What's the city going to do with that property? Do you know?"

"They're selling it to some developer. He wants to put an urban mall there. Says it'll revitalize the inner city or some foolishness. Can you imagine anything revitalizing this neighborhood now?"

Tanner folded the fortune in half and tore it into small pieces. Then he shoved them into his pocket. "Let's have dessert, okay?"

Lex couldn't contain herself. "What did it say?"

"I thought you didn't want to know."

"Why did you tear it up, Tanner?"

"No reason. Let's eat."

From outside came the sound of howling, as of someone in pain.

They all looked at one another. There was nothing to be done.

The pie was delicious.

New York Times Bestselling Author

PETER STRAUB

THE BLUE ROSE BOOKS

Houses Without Doors
0-451-17082-2

This spectacular collection of thirteen dark,
haunting tales exposes the terrors that hide beneath
the surface of the ordinary world, behind the
walls of houses without doors.

"STRAUB AT HIS SPELLBINDING BEST."
—*PUBLISHERS WEEKLY*

Koko
0-451-16214-5

The haunting, dark tale of a returned Vietnam
veteran and a series of mysterious deaths.
A *New York Times* bestseller, this is considered by
many to be Straub's scariest novel.

"BRILLIANTLY WRITTEN...AN INSPIRED THRILLER."
—*WASHINGTON POST*

The Blue Rose series continues with
Mystery *and* The Throat

Available wherever books are sold or at
penguin.com

S411/Straub